The Best of John Bellairs:
The Johnny Dixon Mysteries

The Curse of the Blue Figurine

The Mummy, the Will and the Crypt

The Spell of the Sorcerer's Skull

DIAL BOOKS
NEW YORK

The Curse of the Blue Figurine

JOHN BELLAIRS

*Frontispiece
by Edward Gorey*

For Gerry, who knows about ushabtis

The Curse of the Blue Figurine

CHAPTER ONE

It was a cold winter evening in January. The year was 1951. A short, pale, bespectacled boy named Johnny Dixon was sitting in a big comfy easy chair in the parlor of his grandparents' house. Outside, it was snowing. Through the bay window you could see the flakes falling. The room was dark except for the faint yellow light that shone from the fan-shaped dial on the front of the big walnut Atwater Kent table-model radio that was next to the easy chair. Johnny's eyes were wide open. He was staring into the darkness and listening intently to the program. On his lap was a plate of Ritz crackers spread with pink pimiento-flavored cream cheese—Johnny always munched while he listened to the radio. This evening he was listening to one of his favorite programs,

The House of Mystery. In this episode Sir Philip Stapleton, the renowned archeologist, had entered the forbidden temple of Kali in the jungles of India. With him was Inspector Marcus Quaterly of Scotland Yard, who had traveled all the way from London to help Professor Stapleton unravel the mystery of the savage killings that had plagued Delhi recently. The temple was dark. Each footstep that the two men took raised endless sinister echoes. Suddenly at the far end of the pillared hall something began to glow eerily. It was a huge golden statue of the four-armed goddess Kali. Now, as the two men stood frozen in their tracks, the statue began to move its arms slowly back and forth. And a hideous croaking voice chanted:

Yaa-maaa
Yaa-maaa

Professor Stapleton's voice was an incredulous gasp. "What is it? What can it mean?"

Inspector Quaterly answered grimly, "*Yama* means death—it means death!" And then . . .

"Johnny! Johnny! Didn't you hear me? I've called you three times! Your grampa 'n' I are waitin', and your dinner's gettin' cold!"

Johnny looked up, startled. He really hadn't heard his grandmother calling. With a sad sigh he turned off the radio. He got up and brushed away some cracker crumbs. Then, meekly, with the plate in his hand, he followed his grandmother out to the dining room.

A few minutes later Johnny was sitting at the big mahogany dining room table with his grandfather and grandmother. As usual Grampa sat at the end by the window, in the chair with the arms. Grampa was a tall, slightly stooped old man who always wore gray work shirts and gray wash pants. He had a high, freckled forehead, and on his big sunburnt nose was perched a pair of gold-rimmed glasses. A few strands of white hair were strung carefully across the top of his head. Loose wrinkled flesh hung down in wattles from his cheeks, and his large hands were covered with brown freckles. Grampa was seventy-four years old. He was old, but he was cheerful—most of the time. He sang songs like "Oh, Susanna!" and "Peter Gray," and went on long walks all over the town with Johnny. He listened to baseball games with Johnny and helped him with his homework and played checkers and cribbage with him. Grampa was a good egg. He was almost like a father to Johnny, which was a good thing because (these days) he was just about the only father that Johnny had. And Gramma—for that matter—was the only mother he did have.

Up until about six months before, Johnny had lived in New York State, in the town of Riverhead on Long Island. But then his mother got sick and died of cancer. At first it seemed to Johnny as if the world had come to an end. Then, as the shock and grief wore off, he began to think that he was getting used to the idea of living alone with his dad. But the Korean War changed things. Johnny's father had been a bomber pilot during World

War II. So the Air Force asked Mr. Dixon to come back and serve again, this time as a jet pilot. Mr. Dixon could have refused. He was the sole surviving parent of a child under the age of eighteen. But Mr. Dixon was itching to get into the cockpit of a fighter plane. And when he found out that Gramma and Grampa Dixon would be glad to take care of Johnny, his mind was made up. So Johnny went north, to the town of Duston Heights, Massachusetts, to live with his grandparents. It had been hard for Johnny to adjust to his new surroundings. He felt lonely a lot of the time, and he was also a little scared. But Gramma and Grampa had been as nice as they could be to him, and that helped a lot.

Johnny smiled happily as Gramma spooned mashed potatoes onto his plate. It was snowing outside, but it was warm and comfy in the big old house. A coal fire was roaring in the furnace in the basement, and the register in the floor breathed warm air into the room. The black Sessions clock on the sideboard ticked quietly and re-assuringly. The dining room table was covered with a white linen cloth, and on it were good things to eat: roast beef, cabbage salad, mashed potatoes, and plenty of thick dark-brown gravy. And for dessert there would be either chocolate pudding or lemon meringue pie. The food that Gramma Dixon made tended to be the same, day after day, but it was always good.

As they ate, Gramma and Grampa talked quietly. Sometimes they talked about things that Johnny liked to talk about, but this evening they were chewing over some local gossip, about what so-and-so down the street was doing. Johnny thought all this was very dull, so he just munched and drank and went back to living in his own little dream world. He thought about how great it would be to be an archeologist. That was what he wanted to be, right now, more than anything in the world. He imagined himself with a pith helmet on his head and a pickax in his hand, wading through sand while the hot sun sizzled in the sky. Or exploring by moonlight, which was much more dramatic. Johnny saw himself wandering among the columned halls of the temple of Dendur or Karnak at night, when a pale, silvery sheen fell upon the mysterious hieroglyphs and the carved shapes of pharaohs and beast-headed gods. Was there danger here? Who could tell? What if a shape wrapped in tattered bandages stepped from the shadows and confronted him? What would Professor John Wellesley Dixon, Ph.D., do? Of course there was the large British Army service revolver in the holster that hung from his belt. But it would not be of much use against . . .

The doorbell rang.

Once again Johnny was jolted out of his daydream. He glanced quickly toward the front hall. Gramma heaved a deep, discontented sigh. "Lord, I wonder who *that* is?" She hated to be interrupted during meals.

"I'll go see," said Grampa. He shoved his chair back and got up.

"Me too," said Johnny. He got up and followed his grandfather out to the front door. He really had no reason to go along, but he went anyway, out of sheer uncontrollable curiosity.

Grampa pulled at the front door, and it opened with a rattle. There on the snowy porch stood Professor Childermass. Professor Roderick Childermass, Ph.D., to be precise. Professor Childermass was a short, elderly, red-faced man. A wild nest of white hair covered the top of his head, and mutton-chop whiskers sprouted from the sides of his face. His nose was red and pitted and reminded Johnny of a strawberry. Perched slightly askew on the professor's head was an old shapeless gray fedora, and thrown over his shoulders—sort of like a cape—was an unbelievably dirty and threadbare tweed overcoat. In his left hand the professor clutched a shovel—or what had once been a shovel. It had been one of those little collapsible shovels that the Army calls "an entrenching tool." But the red-colored blade had been battered into a shapeless mass of metal, and the hinged wooden handle was splintered and almost broken in two.

"I am so angry that I can't see straight!" the professor announced through clenched teeth. "I'm so angry that I'd like to *murr-der* someone!"

Grampa couldn't help grinning. He and the professor were old friends. They had had many heated arguments about politics and life and things in general and had always managed to stay friends. Grampa knew that the professor was basically a very kindly man, although he had a rotten temper. Johnny did not know the professor quite as well. He had seen him a few times on the street, and he was—to tell the truth—a bit scared of him. But when he saw his Grampa smiling in such a friendly way, he figured the professor must be an okay person.

"So you wanta murder somebody?" said Grampa, still grinning. "Are you gonna start with the two of us and then work your way down the block? From the way things look," he added, pointing to the shovel, "you've already got started. Who was it? Mrs. Kovacs? Or didja get a cop?"

"Oh, shut up," muttered the professor. He scowled at the broken shovel. "Just you shut up. I destroyed this thing by beating it against the fire hydrant outside my house. I am mad because my car is stuck in the snow and I can't get it out. I've tried everything. I've dug, I've rocked the car, I've . . . oh, drat! Just drat! Can I come in and get warm?"

"Sure," said Grampa, chuckling. "Anything to keep you from standin' there in the doorway and lettin' the cold air in. Come on out to the dinin' room and I'll getcha a cuppa coffee. Then, when you're all thawed out, we'll go get your dad-blasted car outa the dad-blasted snow-bank. Okay?"

"Thanks," said the professor stiffly. He stalked through the hall and into the house without taking off his hat, his coat, or his galoshes. As he went he left big gobs of melting snow behind him. *Uh oh*, thought Johnny, *Gramma is gonna have a fit*. Gramma was one of those fussy types who vacuum the house twice a day. She was always dusting and picking up and emptying wastebaskets and ashtrays. Johnny watched with amusement and horror as Professor Childermass stomped to the dining room table and sat down.

"Evening, ma'am," he said, nodding curtly to Gramma. "Just go on with your dinner. Don't mind me." He leaned forward, put his elbows on the table, stared off into space, and began to hum tunelessly. Humming was what he always did when he was trying to cheer himself up after losing his temper.

"Professor Childermass," Gramma said in a biting tone, "do you think you could manage to go out to the front hall and take off your galoshes?"

The professor looked startled, and then he looked sheepish. He glanced hurriedly at his feet and got up. "Excuse me, madam," he said hastily, and he tramped back out to the front hall, leaving a pool of water at every step. Gramma went to the cupboard and got out a small plate. She cut a piece of pie for the professor, and then she went to get a mop. When the professor came back, he apologized for tracking up the floor, and Gramma said, "Ummm," which was her way of accepting an apology. Then everybody ate lemon meringue pie and listened to the professor as he complained about his car and life in general.

Later Grampa and Johnny got their coats and boots and hats on and went out to help the professor get his car unstuck. It was still snowing on Fillmore Street. Flakes came whirling down out of the dark sky. They looked black as they swept through the light of the streetlamp. Across the street was the professor's car. Its rear end was buried in a heap of snow. The situation looked hopeless, but Grampa reassured everybody. He said that he had once driven a Model T on muddy dirt roads in the springtime. And, said Grampa, if he could do that, he could get a car out of a miserable little bitty snowbank.

They set to work. The professor got into the car and started it. Grampa told him to rock it, and he and Johnny would push. The car rocked, and the wheels spun and whined. Spurts of snow flew up into the air. The professor had his car window open so he could give and get directions. Johnny could hear him cursing under his breath as the car lurched back and forth. At first nothing happened. The car just seemed to be digging itself deeper and deeper into a snowy rut. "Cramp the wheel over!" Grampa called. "Cramp it way over!" The professor cramped it over, and suddenly, with a jolt, the car shot forward, spraying wet snow all over Johnny and Grampa. The professor—who was not a very good driver, even under the best of conditions—pulled the car out into the middle of the street and did a U-turn, fish-tailing madly. The engine died, and he started it again. Finally he managed to nose the car over to the curb in front of Grampa's house. It was not a very good parking job. The rear end of the car was sticking out into the street. But the professor didn't care: he was disgusted and tired. He got out of the car, slammed the door, and stood there with his hands on his hips, glowering.

"Cars!" he snorted. "I *hate* them! Hate them, hate them, hate them! If I didn't have to have one to drive to work, I'd push this thing into the Merrimack River! So help me, I would!"

Grampa ambled slowly across the street, brushing snow off himself. "You know, Rod," he said slowly, "it would kinda help if you would put chains on your tires."

The professor looked startled, and then he waved his hand in an irritated way. "Oh, chains! Yes . . . hmm, yes, I suppose I *should* have thought of them! But I have so many things on my mind these days . . . hmmm . . . chains . . . yes. By the way, Henry, don't call me Rod. I hate to be called Rod. You know that."

"Sorry," said Grampa, shrugging apologetically. "I keep forgettin'."

"Think nothing of it," said the professor brusquely. "Can I come into your house and get something strong to drink? Some booze, I mean. It would make me feel better."

Johnny gasped. He had always had it drummed into his head when he was little that you never, never invited yourself into other people's houses. It was terribly impolite. But here was the professor—a college teacher and a respected member of the community—doing just that. And to top it all off, he was asking for liquor! Asking for it first, instead of waiting to be served. And Grampa didn't seem to mind at all. It seemed unfair, somehow.

Laughing and talking, the professor and Grampa

stomped through the snow and up the stairs to the porch. Johnny trailed along behind. When they got to the front door, they found Gramma blocking the doorway. She had a mop in her hand, and she looked grimly determined. She was not going to let the professor track up her rugs and floors a second time. He took the hint. Meekly, with downcast eyes, he shuffled over to the coat-tree, sat down on the boot box, and began peeling off his galoshes.

A few minutes later Johnny, Grampa, and the professor were all sitting around in the parlor, talking. Johnny had gotten a Coke from the refrigerator, and Grampa was drinking coffee. The professor had a water glass half full of whiskey in his hand. Gramma disapproved of liquor, so she was not present. She was upstairs in her bedroom, listening to the radio after saying her rosary.

"So, y'see, it wasn't such a big job after all," said Grampa amiably as he sipped from the steaming mug. "It only took us, oh, I'd say about twenty minutes, at the outside."

"Is that all?" grumbled the professor. He was trying hard to be grumpy, in spite of the cheerful company. "It seemed like *hours*. You know," he went on, wagging his finger at Grampa, "you know, Henry, in a hundred years people will think we were out of our ever-loving minds to spend so much of our valuable time taking care of automobiles. Think of it! Everybody on this block owns a two-ton hunk of metal that he has to feed gas and oil into, wash, and get fixed when it goes flooey. We spend half our lives thinking about cars! It's ridiculous, I tell you! Ree-*dick*-u-lous! Why . . ."

Suddenly the professor stopped talking. He had noticed something. On the floor next to the armchair that Johnny was sitting in was a pile of books. They were books on archeology that Johnny had taken out of the library recently: there were *Gods, Graves, and Scholars*, by C. W. Ceram, and *The Mountains of Pharaoh*, by Leonard Cottrell, and James Henry Breasted's *History of Egypt.* Egypt was Johnny's latest craze: he read everything he could about Egypt, and he was always combing the library for Egypt books that he hadn't read.

The professor looked at Johnny questioningly. "Are . . . are those books yours?" he asked. He said this as if he could scarcely believe that the answer might be yes.

Johnny did not see what was so unusual about reading books on Egypt. He was always reading books about something. "Yeah, they're mine," he said casually. "I mean . . . well, they're not really mine, they belong to the library. But I took 'em out to read, if that's what you mean."

"You took them out to read," the professor repeated in a wondering tone. "Do you have an assignment in school about Egypt? Is somebody *making* you read those books?"

Johnny grinned and shook his head. "Nope. I like to read."

The professor was astounded. He acted as if Johnny

had just told him that he was the pope, or the sultan of Zanzibar. "Good heavens!" he exclaimed. "You can read, and you *like* to read! Please excuse my amazement, but I have just come from visiting my sister's daughter, who lives up in New Hampshire. She has two children about your age, but they couldn't read their way through a book of cigarette papers. Which is scarcely odd, because their parents don't read anything except the phone book and the directions on spaghetti boxes. You like to *read*! Lord have mercy! Will wonders never cease!"

Johnny found that he was beginning to like the professor. He smiled happily and felt proud. Usually grown-ups were not in the least interested in Johnny's reading ability. If they noticed it at all, they said, "Oh, that's nice," in a polite sort of way. But what they really thought—as Johnny well knew—was that boys who liked reading as much as he did must be weird.

Johnny asked the professor some questions about mummies, and the professor answered them as well as he could. From mummies the conversation turned to ghosts, and the professor told about the haunting of the Borley Rectory in England and other spooky happenings that he had heard about. Johnny loved ghost stories. That was one of the reasons he listened to *The House of Mystery* and *The Hermit's Cave*. But, as he told the professor, he didn't actually believe in ghosts, not really. As far as Johnny was concerned, believing in ghosts was . . . well, it was like believing in Santa Claus, or the Easter Bunny. It was for little kids, not for him.

"Oh, is that so?" said the professor, eyeing Johnny curiously. A faint half-smile curled the corners of his mouth. "Is that really so? It's kid stuff, is it? Well, my friend, you might be surprised someday. Do you know about the ghost of Father Baart that haunts the church you go to every Sunday? Do you? Hmmm?"

Johnny was really taken aback. He went to St. Michael's Catholic Church all the time, with his grandmother and grandfather. But he had never heard about any ghost.

The professor grinned. He could see that he had Johnny's attention. And then, without any further ado, he launched into his tale.

"Now then," he said, rubbing his hands, "it all began when . . . oh, by the way, Henry, I feel like some sort of cheap guzzler drinking this whiskey all by itself. Do you have anything to go with it? How about some of your wife's fudge? I think she makes wonderful fudge! Could I have some?"

Once again Johnny was amazed by the professor's crust. And, as before, Grampa didn't seem to mind. He went out to the kitchen and came back with a blue Willoware plate that held several thick squares of dark chocolaty fudge. Everybody took one, and as he munched the professor went on with his story.

"Father Remigius Baart," he began, "was the rector of St. Michael's Church way back in the 1880s. He was the one who had the church built—the church that's there now. And he hired a wandering artist—a mysterious character who showed up in Duston Heights one day—he hired him, as I say, to do the altarpiece in the church." The professor paused and stared thoughtfully out the window. "I often wonder about that man—the artist, I mean. He claimed that his name was Nemo, but *nemo* is Latin for 'no one.' Well, whatever his name really was, he was a talented wood-carver. All those saints and angels and prophets on the altar screen! I've never seen anything quite like it. But it seems that the wood-carver was more than just a wood-carver. The story is that he had dealings with the devil, that he diddled around with the black arts. The truth, I suppose, will never be known. After he finished the altar screen and got paid, this Nemo character left town and was never seen again. But people claim that before he left, he gave Father Baart something."

Johnny by this time was totally fascinated. He was sitting way forward on the edge of his seat. "What was it?" he asked. "What did this Nemo guy give to the priest?"

The professor stared at Johnny strangely. "Nobody knows. He may not have given him anything, but a lot of the older people in this town—your grandmother, for instance—will swear up and down that the artist gave Father Baart a talisman, or a book, or some sort of evil object that allowed him to do all kinds of nasty things, and may—in the end—have caused his own destruction."

The professor paused and grabbed another piece of fudge. He stuffed it in his mouth and chewed it slowly, savoring every chocolaty smidgin of it. The professor loved dramatic pauses. He felt that they added to his stories. Johnny squirmed impatiently in his seat. He wanted to hear more.

"Mmmm! Dee-*li*-cious fudge!" said the professor, smacking his lips. "Absolutely scrumptious! By the way, where was I? Ah, yes. Now, at this point you have to know what sort of man Father Baart was. He was not popular. He had a sharp tongue, and he used it often, and he had made quite a few enemies in the town of Duston Heights. If the people in the church had had their way, they would have got rid of him. They would have found a new rector. But only the bishop could fire him, and he didn't feel like it, so Father Baart stayed and made enemies. Well! A little while after the mysterious artist left town, funny things started to happen. Mr. Herman—he was a rich farmer in the area, and there was no love lost between him and Father Baart—Mr. Herman, I say, was standing looking up at the tower of the church one day—they were still building it at the time—and a carved stone, a big, heavy pinnacle that had just been put in place on top of the tower, fell off and hit Mr. Herman—killed him outright!"

Johnny wanted to say something, but the look on the professor's face told him he wasn't finished talking. So he waited.

The professor took another little sip of whiskey and another little nibble of fudge, and then he went on. "So Mr. Herman was dead. There were no workmen on the tower at the time, so nobody could be blamed. The coroner's verdict was 'accidental death.' Nothing to argue about—the stone was probably loose for some reason. But a few days later somebody else got eliminated. This time it was Mrs. Mumaw. She was another one of Father Baart's enemies. She had disagreed with him publicly, at parish meetings, and she had told him his qualities in no uncertain terms. And what happened to her? She got run down by a horse pulling a wagonload of barrels. One minute the horse was standing quietly in front of a store on Main Street; the next minute it was charging wild-eyed at Mrs. Mumaw, dragging the wagon, hell-bent for election, behind. Well, that was the end of *her*!" The professor paused and peered at Johnny over the tops of his glasses. "Now, then, my fine feathered friend," he said, "does anything occur to you? Hmmm? Does it?"

Johnny looked thoughtful. He saw what the professor was getting at. "It sounds kinda like . . . like Father Baart made those accidents happen. Like maybe he murdered those two people some way."

"You catch on fast," said the professor dryly. "Many of the people who were living in this town back then thought that Father Baart had murdered Mr. Herman and Mrs. Mumaw. But there was no way they could prove it. No way at all." The professor paused and sipped at his drink. "However," he went on, "however, and be that as it may, Father Baart got his comeuppance. He got it in spades!"

Johnny's eyes were wide. "What happened to him? Did the ghosts of the people he killed come back and get him?" Johnny had read some stories where things like that had happened.

The professor smiled mysteriously. "Nobody knows what happened to Father Baart," he said somberly. "One morning he didn't show up to say Mass in the church, and people got worried. His housekeeper and some other people went to the rectory and searched all the rooms, but he was gone. His clothes were still in the bedroom closet, and everything else was in its usual apple-pie order. But Baart was gone. The only clue left behind—if you want to call it a clue—was a note, found under a paperweight on his desk. The note was not written in Baart's handwriting—nobody knows who wrote it. To tell the truth, the note was not terribly helpful. It was simply a quotation from *Urne-Buriall*, which is an essay that was written long, long ago by an Englishman named Sir Thomas Browne. I like the essay—I like it a lot. And I've memorized parts of it. Let me see . . . I think I can quote for you the passage that was in the note."

The professor paused and closed his eyes. Then he smiled and nodded and opened his eyes again. "Ah. Ah, yes. I have it. This is the way it goes: 'The man of God lives longer without a Tomb than any by one, invisibly interred by Angels; and adjudged to obscurity, though not without some marks directing human discovery.' "

The professor paused again. He looked at Johnny. "There! Did you understand any of that?"

Johnny shook his head.

The professor sighed. "Well, it's a bit obscure, I must admit. The passage refers to Moses. According to the Bible, when Moses died, his body was carried away by angels and was buried secretly somewhere. Now, what that has to do with Father Baart's disappearance I don't know. But that was the message that was found on his desk after he vanished. He was never seen again . . . not *alive*, anyway."

Johnny looked puzzled. "Do you mean . . . did they find his body somewhere?"

The professor shook his head and smiled tantalizingly. "No. I didn't mean that. They never found his body. But he has been seen in St. Michael's Church, several times. Every now and then late on a winter night somebody will be sitting in the back of the church saying the rosary or praying. And then this person will feel a sudden chill and hear a funny noise. And they'll turn around, and there he'll be, big as life!"

Johnny's mouth dropped open. "Father Baart?"

The professor nodded. "The same. He was quite a striking-looking person—you'd never mistake him for anybody else. He was short and wore a black cloak, and he had a big head and a jutting chin and lots of grayish hair that he wore long. And an overhanging forehead, and a hawkish nose, and deep-set, burning eyes. So if you're ever in the church late at night, well . . ."

"Oh, for pity's sake!" said Grampa, cutting in. "Don't scare the poor kid to death! I'll never get him to go to church with his gramma on Wednesday nights if you carry on like that! By the way, I think it's a shame that a man like that, a priest and all, should have gone over to the devil. Servin' the powers of evil and darkness. Can you imagine?"

The professor twisted his mouth into a wry smile. "It's happened before," he said. "If you read your history, you'll find that some of the great medieval sorcerers were priests. Like Roger Bacon and Albertus Magnus. Of course, they stayed on the white magic side . . . most of the time. But if you fool around with magic, there must be a terrible temptation to call upon the powers of hell. After all, white magic can only do so much. It can't get revenge for you. It can't help you to wipe out an enemy. Only the bad guys can help you with that."

Silence fell. The story was over, and neither Johnny nor Grampa felt like asking any more questions. The professor gobbled the last piece of fudge, and then he announced that he had to go. It was getting late, and he had papers to correct before he went to bed. Johnny had homework to do, so he went out to the dining room table, turned on the light, and sat down to struggle with the square-root problems he had been given. The front door opened and closed. The professor was gone. Grampa went back to the parlor to get the plates and glasses. On his way to the kitchen he stopped by the table where Johnny was working.

"Some story, eh?" he said, chuckling. "That old so-and-so sure knows how to scare you, don't he?"

Johnny looked up. "You mean you don't think it's the truth, Grampa?"

Grampa looked thoughtful. "Well, I wouldn't go so far as to say that the old boy was feedin' you a line of bull, but . . . like I say, he loves good stories, and he sure knows how to tell 'em!"

Johnny felt disappointed. He was not nearly as skeptical as he thought he was. When he heard a good story, he always wanted to believe that it was true. "It . . . it *might* be true," he said weakly.

"Oh, sure," said Grampa with a humorous shrug of his shoulders. "It *might* be!" He chuckled and went on out to the kitchen with the dishes.

Johnny struggled a bit with his homework, but he found that his eyes kept closing. Oh, well. He could get up early tomorrow and do it before breakfast. Johnny closed his book and turned off the light. He went to the front door and rattled it, as he always did, and then he started up the steps. Halfway up he paused. There was a tiny square window there, and he liked to peer out of it. He watched the snow fall for a while. He imagined it falling on the cemetery, far away, where his mother lay buried. Sadness welled up in Johnny's heart. Tears sprang to his eyes. He wiped the tears away with his sleeve. Then he turned and climbed on up the stairs to bed.

CHAPTER TWO

Days passed. Weeks passed. Nothing very exciting happened to Johnny. He had the usual things to do, like snow shoveling, dish drying, and homework. Johnny went to St. Michael's School, a Catholic grade school in the town of Duston Heights. It was a two-story brick building with a slate roof and a pointed stone arch on the front. At St. Michael's, Johnny was taught by the Sisters of the Immaculate Heart of Mary. They wore navy-blue robes with black scapulars and black veils. The seventh-grade teacher was Sister Electa. She was nice, most of the time, but she really piled the homework on. Not that Johnny had a lot of trouble with homework. He was a real brain, and everybody at St. Michael's School knew it. Most of the other kids didn't mind that

Johnny was smart. They thought it was odd, but they didn't hold it against him. But there was one kid who was really jealous of Johnny. The kid was named Eddie Tompke.

Eddie was a seventh grader, like Johnny. He lived on a farm outside of town, and as everyone knows, farm work builds up your muscles. Eddie was strong, and he was good-looking. He thought that he owned the world, and he was ready to fight any kid who got in his way. Eddie had problems, though: He was not doing very well in school. His last report card had been all C's and D's, and as a result he had gotten a royal chewing-out from his father. So Eddie was mad a lot of the time now. He was mad at the world in general, but he was particularly mad at Johnny Dixon. Lately Johnny had begun to notice the way Eddie felt about him. Standing in line during lunch hour one day, he had happened to turn around, and he saw Eddie scowling at him. And later Johnny had been standing around on the playground, talking to another kid, and Eddie had walked by and kicked him in the shins for no reason at all. And now, whenever Johnny passed Eddie, Eddie would glower and say things like "I wish *I* was a brain!" or "It must be great to be a brown nose. Is that how you get those good grades, kid? Because you're the biggest brown nose in the school? Is that how you do it?"

All this had Johnny worried. He was short and he wore glasses and he was not very strong. Also he was in a new school, and he had not yet made any close friends.

And he had a very great fear of getting beat up. It was one of his really big fears, like his fear that someday he would step on a nail, get an infected puncture wound, and die of lockjaw. Johnny was always reading things in the paper about people who had gotten "beaten to a pulp" or "beaten beyond recognition," which meant that they had gotten smashed up so badly that no one could tell who they were. Stories like this hit Johnny right in the pit of his stomach. And he wondered, often, whether someday Eddie Tompke might get it into his head to beat him up.

One cold dark February day Johnny was standing under the big stone arch out in front of St. Michael's School. The school day was over. Everyone else had gone. As usual he was the last kid out of the building. He fiddled with his scarf and adjusted his stocking cap on his head. Johnny was a fussy kid—everything always had to be just so, or it was no good. Finally he was ready to go. Johnny peered out to his right. Oh, no. There was Eddie! He was standing on the corner, talking to some other kid. His back was to Johnny—he hadn't seen him yet. But he would when Johnny came that way, and he had to go that way to get home. Johnny peered quickly around the corner. A narrow alley ran between St. Michael's Church (which stood on the corner) and the school. If he moved fast, Johnny could zip down the alley and get out onto the street in any of three different ways. But for some reason Johnny decided that he would duck into the church. He could say a prayer for his mother and hang around till Eddie went away.

St. Michael's Church was a tall brick building with a brick steeple on the northeast corner. There were three big, pointed wooden doors at the front of the church. A flight of worn stone steps led up to each one. Johnny headed for the nearest door. It was a short dash, and he made it easily. Now he was tugging at the heavy iron ring. The door swung open. Johnny slipped inside, and the door closed behind him, *Clump!* Johnny heaved a sigh of relief. He had made it.

Johnny was standing in the vestibule, which is what the front hall of a church is called. He dipped his fingers in the holy water font, made the sign of the cross, and shoved open one of the inner doors. He was in the main body of the church now. Rows of wooden pews stretched away before him. Overhead arched the high vaulted ceiling. It was painted midnight blue and was powdered with little gold stars. At the far end of the nave was the Communion rail, and beyond it was the altar and the massive carved altarpiece. Johnny liked the old church. It was vast and gloomy and smelled of incense and candle wax. He loved the flickering red sanctuary lamp and the strange pictures on the stained-glass windows. The church was a place where he often went just to sit and get away from the world.

Johnny walked down the main aisle. His footsteps, though soft, seemed to echo from the high ceiling. When he got to the broad polished steps that led up to the Communion rail, Johnny stopped. With his arms folded over his chest he gazed up admiringly at the altarpiece that the mysterious Mr. Nemo had carved. It was quite a production. Over the altar table rose a three-decker wooden screen with lots of pointed niches in it. Each niche had an elaborately carved hood, and in the niches were wooden statues. The statues were painted all different colors, and gold paint had been used lavishly. The statues in the lower two levels were of saints. There were Saint Peter and Saint Paul and Saint Catherine and Saint Ursula and some nameless saints with swords and palms in their hands. At the top of the screen there were only three statues. These three were angels. One held a trumpet; one held a sword and shield; and one held a golden censer on a chain.

Johnny went on staring at the altar screen for a while. Then he went over to the iron vigil-light rack that stood near the confessional. He lit a candle for his mother, and then he walked down the side aisle and out into the vestibule again. Cautiously Johnny pushed the main door of the church open. He didn't open it far, just a crack. Darn! Eddie was still there!

Johnny let the door fall softly shut. Now what was he going to do? Gramma would be expecting him—he couldn't stay here forever. There was a back way out, but you had to go up into the sanctuary and out through the sacristy to get to it. And only Father Higgins and the altar boys and the sisters were allowed to go out that way. If Father Higgins caught him going through the sacristy, he would have a fit. Johnny stood, pondering, in the dark vestibule. He felt frustrated; he felt trapped. Then suddenly he had a very strange and interesting idea. He would go have a quick look in the basement.

Johnny grinned. He was a well-behaved kid most of the time, but he wasn't all *that* well behaved. Like most kids he enjoyed poking around in places that were forbidden. And he knew he was alone—there wasn't anybody in the church but him. Now was the time!

Quickly Johnny walked down to the far end of the vestibule. Now he was standing under the belfry. Overhead was a wooden ceiling with holes in it: the bell ropes hung through the holes. There was the dark, varnished wooden staircase that led up to the choir loft. And under the staircase, set in a paneled wall, was a narrow door with a black china knob. It led down to the basement. Johnny paused. He was thinking about the ghost of Father Baart. What if he appeared now? Or what if he suddenly materialized in the dark basement? Johnny shrugged and forced himself to smile. Hadn't Grampa told him that the professor's story was really a lot of hooey? Sure. There was nothing to worry about.

Johnny put his hand on the knob. He twisted, and the door opened easily. Mr. Famagusta, the janitor, was supposed to keep this door locked. But, as Johnny well knew, Mr. Famagusta was a rather careless man. Johnny put his foot on the first step, and then he pulled it back. He needed something . . . ah! There it was! The flashlight! Johnny had heard Mr. Famagusta say that there was no electric light in the church basement. And, sure enough, on a little dusty ledge near the door was a small and rather battered flashlight. Johnny picked it up, snapped it on, and started down.

The flight of creaky steps turned once at a wooden landing and went on down to a hard-packed dirt floor. Johnny played the flashlight beam around. Some rickety shelves had been built into the wall underneath the steps. He saw a silver censer that was so tarnished that it looked black. A grimy, cobwebbed box that said AD ALTARE DEI INCENSE. A headless plaster statue of some saint. A glass tumbler full of cassock buttons. A pipe wrench and a section of brass pipe, left—no doubt—by the careless Mr. Famagusta.

Johnny played the beam back into the darkness of the basement. He saw the brick pillars that held up the floor of the church. Beyond the first row of pillars was a stack of tabletops. Leaning against the stack was a raffle wheel, the kind they used for the turkey raffles at Thanksgiving time. And in the shadowy distance he could see the big sooty iron furnace that heated the church in the wintertime. Johnny sighed. The whole place was a lot less interesting than he had hoped it would be. He pointed the beam of the flashlight here and there. Without much interest he noticed a bookcase with warped, sagging shelves. The top shelf was empty, but the second shelf held a row of thick, black volumes. Johnny reached for one of the books, but he jerked his hand away with a disgusted cry. The book was crawling with little gray spiders.

Johnny closed his eyes and shuddered. He couldn't help it. He hated spiders, and the small gray ones were, to him, the most disgusting of all. A bad taste rose into Johnny's mouth, but he swallowed, and it went away. Johnny opened his eyes. He shone the flashlight at the book again. The spiders were gone! Well, now, that was odd—where had they gone to? Johnny looked at the floor. Nothing there. Then he pointed the flashlight at the wall behind the bookcase. It was a brick wall, and it was in pretty bad shape. The mortar looked powdery and loose, and the bricks were crumbling. In one place the mortar between two bricks had fallen out, and there was a hole. Maybe that was where the spiders had gone. Johnny went back to looking at the row of books. For some reason he was interested in the book that had had the spiders on it. He wanted to take it out and look at it. Three times he reached out his hand to touch it, and three times he jerked his hand back at the last minute. Finally, on the fourth try, his hand closed over the end of the grimy book. He pulled it out quickly and stepped back. Now he carried the book over to the stairs and laid it down on one of the lower steps.

Johnny played the flashlight over the cover of the book. The faint gold letters said ROMAN MISSAL. Now Johnny reached out in a gingerly way and took hold of the dog-eared cover. With a quick motion he flipped it back.

And then he gasped.

The inside of the book had been hollowed out. Only the outer part of each page was left. And in the hole that had been made were two things: a small rolled-up piece of yellowish paper tied with a faded red ribbon, and a strange little blue ceramic statue. The statue was shaped like an Egyptian mummy case. It had staring eyes and a tiny beaked nose and a smiling mouth and a scrolled goatee. The figure's arms were crossed over its breast in the Egyptian style. Apparently the mummy was supposed to be the mummy of a pharaoh, because it held in its hands the crook and the flail, the symbols of kingly power in ancient Egypt.

Johnny was utterly amazed. With the flashlight held steady in his left hand he reached into the hollow book with his right hand. He did this very cautiously, as if he expected something to bite him. But nothing did. He pulled out the little paper scroll and yanked at the rotting ribbon, which was tied in a bow knot. The ribbon came off, and Johnny held the paper up to the light. It had been rolled up for so long that it was permanently curled. Nevertheless Johnny could read the shaded, heavy, masculine script:

> Whoever removes these things from the church
> does so at his own peril. I abjure you by the living
> God not to endanger your immortal soul.
> *Vengeance is mine; I will repay, saith the Lord.*
> Remigius Baart

CHAPTER THREE

Johnny's eyes grew wide. He felt cold all over. Care-fully, with a trembling hand, he put the scroll back in the hollowed book. He was about to close the lid when he heard a noise behind him, a rustling noise, like something moving about.

Johnny panicked. He didn't have time for making decisions; what he did was sudden and automatic. He lunged at the book, gathered it up in his arms, and stumbled madly up the steps. He never looked back to see what had made the noise. And when he got to the top of the stairs, Johnny slammed the door and leaned his body against it. He was panting and breathless, and when he looked at his hands, he saw that they were black with dust. The front of his parka was dirty too. And here was the book in his arms, and inside were the things that Father Baart had put into the book. It was all true, then, about Father Baart and the magical something that the mysterious wood-carver had given him. Or was it? Johnny felt that his brain was whirling. Nothing made any sense. He thought about what it said on the scroll. Should he put the book back? No. He was not going down into that basement again, not right away. Then should he drop the book and run? Slowly he walked toward the middle door of the church. He pushed it open and peeked out. Eddie had gone at last. There was no one around, no one at all. With the book clutched tight in his arms Johnny edged out through the half-open door. He paused for a second more, and then he hurried down the steps.

As he tramped along through the snowy streets with the book in his arms Johnny found that his mind was beginning to clear. He was thinking again. He thought about what Gramma would say if he came waltzing in the front door with this enormous black book. She would be upset about his dirty hands and his dirty parka, and she would certainly get nosy about the book. At the end of his own street Johnny stopped. He cut across a vacant lot and walked on down Marshland Avenue, which was the next street over. Then he stopped again in front of a big gray house that had a For Sale sign on it. This house was directly behind his own house. Johnny had used this sneaky shortcut before: down the driveway, over the bent wire fence, and into his own backyard. From there Johnny headed straight for the cellar door. It was an old-fashioned cellar entrance: two slanted wooden doors set up against the foundation of the house. These doors were never locked. Grampa was always going in and out this way, carrying papers to the incinerator or garbage to the garbage cans. Johnny glanced quickly up at the back windows of the house to see if anyone was looking out, and then he opened the doors. Quickly he raced down the steps and dumped the book in a dark corner. Then he raced back up the steps and closed the doors. Whistling softly, Johnny tramped up the snowy driveway and mounted the front steps. He took off his boots and stepped in the front door. He felt very pleased with himself—he had made it.

That night, after Gramma and Grampa had gone to bed, Johnny went down to the cellar and brought up his prize. He carried it to his bedroom, closed the door, and threw the bolt. After putting the book down carefully on the floor Johnny went to the closet and dug a soiled undershirt out of his laundry bag. He used the undershirt to wipe some of the soot and grime off the old book. Then he opened the cover and knelt there, admiring. He looked like a worshiper, and in fact that was how he felt. This was—Johnny felt sure—a sacred object, a magic object. He had no doubt that this was the very thing that the mysterious wood-carver had given to Father Baart. Johnny felt awestruck and also a little afraid. Should he even touch the statue? Well, he had already touched it, and nothing had happened to him. He had done something else too. He had disobeyed the grim command that Father Baart had written out: He had taken the statue out of the church. Johnny gazed at the little figure that smiled up at him, and he wondered if maybe he had done something foolish. He wanted to talk to somebody about the statue. But who could he talk to? Not Gramma—that was for sure. She would go through the roof if she knew that he had this thing. Grampa would be more understanding, but he would definitely not approve of stealing things from a church. So who could he talk to?

The professor! Of course!

Johnny grinned. Why hadn't he thought of the professor before? The professor was smart, and he knew about a lot of things. He probably knew about magic. And he was the one who had told Johnny the story of Father Baart in the first place. He would be very interested in Johnny's discovery. Furthermore Johnny did not think that the professor would tell on him. The professor was kind of a nut, and nutty people don't rat on you. Nice, friendly, ordinary next-door-neighbor types —they would rat on you and think nothing of it. But a nutty person never would.

Johnny closed the book up again and carried it to his closet. He put it down in the bottom and heaped old sweatshirts and bare blankets and copies of *Boys' Life* on top of it. Gramma wasn't nosy. She never poked into Johnny's private things. He figured his treasure would be safe there, for the time being.

Days passed. Johnny bided his time, waiting for a chance to go see the professor. The time came on a Saturday afternoon. Gramma and Grampa went down to the A&P to shop, and Johnny was left alone in the house. From the bay window in the front parlor he could see the professor's big gloomy gray stucco house. The professor's car was sitting in the driveway, so Johnny figured that he had to be home. He ran upstairs to his room and dug the black book out of his closet. In no time at all he was on the professor's doorstep with the book in his arms. Johnny set the book down on the doormat and pushed the doorbell button. He waited—no answer. Again he pushed the button, and again. Still nothing. Johnny shifted nervously from one foot to the other. What was the professor doing? Johnny fussed and fretted. He really wanted to talk to the professor, and he wanted to talk to him now. Finally he got so impatient that he took hold of the knob and turned it. The door was not locked —it flew right open.

Johnny stood and watched as the door swung back. Should he go in? It would certainly not be polite. But what if the professor had had a heart attack? Shouldn't he rush in and try to help him? Johnny decided that the professor needed him. He picked the book up, took a deep breath, and stepped over the threshold.

Straight down the long front hall he walked, and into the dining room. Nobody there. He peered into the kitchen. There was nobody there, either, but on the drainboard next to the sink lay a large hinged metal gadget. Johnny knew what it was—it was a jar wrench. You used them to get the lids off bottles and jars. Curious, Johnny moved closer. He peered into the sink and saw smashed pieces of glass, a jar lid, a lot of olives, and a pool of green brine. Johnny stared at this mess for a few minutes. Then—still holding the book carefully in his arms before him—he moved into the dining room. Now he began to hear muffled thudding and bumping noises. They seemed to be coming from upstairs. Johnny was becoming alarmed. He set the book down on the dining room table and galloped up the stairs. "Professor! Professor!" he called. No answer. Johnny ran down the hall and paused by the door of the room that the noises seemed to be coming from.

"Professor! Are you all right?"

A muffled answer came. "Yes, blast it, I'm *all right*! Half a minute and I'll be with you!"

Johnny waited, and presently the door of the room opened. There stood the professor, and he was quite a sight: He was wearing a baggy gray sweat shirt and gray sweat pants. His feet were bare, his hair was a mess, and he was not wearing his glasses. He blinked peevishly at Johnny.

"Yes? Yes? Who is it? I can't see a blasted thing without my glasses. And what are you doing here, anyway, whoever you are? This is a private home, you know. And if you're selling something, I'm not interested."

Johnny was bewildered by this crabby speech. "It's

. . . it's me, Professor. Johnny Dixon. I heard these noises, and I thought maybe you were being strangled or having a heart attack or something, so I came on up."

The professor's manner changed. He blinked some more, and then he smiled. His cheeks turned red, and Johnny saw that he was really quite embarrassed. "I'll . . . I'll be with you in a moment," the professor muttered. He turned and groped his way over to his desk. More groping, and he found his glasses. He put them on.

"Ah! Ah, yes, it *is* you, isn't it? And I'll bet you're wondering what I'm doing all dressed up like this, aren't you?"

"I . . . I was, kinda," said Johnny shyly.

The professor took Johnny by the arm and led him over to an open closet door. Johnny looked in. He saw that the walls and the floor of the closet were covered with padded gymnasium mats. Taped to the inside of the closet door was a hand-lettered sign that said:

TO FUSS IS HUMAN;
TO RANT, DIVINE!

"This is my fuss closet," the professor said casually. "As you know, I have a rotten temper. And I lost it, just a few minutes before you came in, because I could *not* get the lid off that bloody jar downstairs! So, I came up here—as I always do in such cases—and I put on these clothes and took off my glasses and went into my fuss closet, and I *fussed*! I cursed and yelled and pounded the walls and floor. And you know, I feel *much* better now.

Sweatier and tireder, perhaps, but better!" The professor heaved a deep, self-satisfied sigh and folded his arms. He smiled kindly at Johnny. "Now, then, what can I do for you? Hmmm?"

Johnny was so flabbergasted by the tale of the fuss closet that it took some effort to drag his mind back to what he wanted to talk about. "I . . . I found something, Professor," he began slowly. "I was . . . kind of pokin' around in the basement of the church, and I think I found the . . . the stuff that that wood-carver guy gave to Father Baart."

Now it was the professor's turn to be amazed. "Good God!" he exclaimed. "Are you *serious*? Do you really mean what you just said?"

Johnny nodded emphatically. "Uh-huh. It was all inside of a fake book. Do you wanta see it? It's downstairs. I brought it over so you could have a look at it."

The professor sighed and looked down at the clothes he was wearing. "Well," he said, chuckling, "I hardly feel professorial in this getup, but I would like to have a look at what you've found. Sure. Go get the stuff and bring it up, and meanwhile I'll get some shoes on. These floorboards are like ice."

A few minutes later the professor was sitting at his desk with the fake book open before him. Johnny stood behind the desk, next to the professor's chair. The expression on his face was anxious. The room they were in —the room with the fuss closet—was the professor's study. Along one wall was a bookcase made out of bricks and boards. It was full of paperback books. Stacked here and there on the floor were blue exam books with grades and comments scrawled in red ink on their covers. Framed diplomas with gold seals hung crookedly over the bookcase. And next to the desk, piled against it like a rampart, was a wild, disorderly heap of papers and notebooks. In the corner behind the desk stood a stuffed owl on a tall fluted wooden pillar. And on the owl's head, perched a little to one side, was a small Boston Red Sox baseball cap.

The Professor harrumphed and jiggled around in his chair. Johnny wanted him to get down to business, to start examining the figurine. But the professor liked to take his own time about things. He brushed eraser dust off the faded green blotter that lay on the desk. Then he reached into a drawer and took out an ashtray and a small, flat cardboard box. The box was black and on its lid was a splendid golden two-headed eagle. The lettering on the box said BALKAN SOBRANIE. The professor opened the box and peeled back two whispery layers of gold-leaf paper. Johnny saw in the box a row of black cigarettes with gold tips. As he watched in exasperation the professor searched in the drawers of his desk for matches. At last he found some. He lit a cigarette and took a deep drag. Then, finally, he reached out toward the cavity in the hollowed-out book.

First he took out the scroll. He unrolled it and read it. His face was absolutely expressionless—he might have been reading the want ads in the daily paper. The professor put the scroll back in the box. Carefully, using both hands, he lifted out the blue figurine.

Johnny was on pins and needles. He watched as the professor examined the thing, puffed on his cigarette, said "hmmm" several times, and pulled the floor lamp closer to his desk. Now the professor tilted the figurine up so he could look at its base. Johnny noticed—for the first time—that there was a small, faded brown-paper label on the base. The professor adjusted his glasses and peered closer. Then he let out a loud whoop of laughter. He set the figurine down, threw back his head, and roared.

"Hah! That's a good one!" exclaimed the professor, pounding his hand on the desk.

Johnny was startled and utterly bewildered. "What... what is?"

The professor giggled some more. Then he picked up the figurine and held it so Johnny could see the label. "Here, have a look! This is funny, it really is! See—right there. There it is!"

Johnny looked. There was printing on the faded brown label, old-fashioned Victorian ornamental printing. It said:

SOUVENIR
OF
CAIRO, ILLINOIS

CHAPTER FOUR

❧❧❧

Johnny felt crushed. He felt cheated and humiliated and angry. He had been so sure, so absolutely sure, that he had found a genuine bona fide Egyptian magic amulet. And now, to find out that the thing was a souvenir! A crummy, cheap, stupid souvenir! Johnny had souvenirs in his room. One was a small birchbark canoe that he had gotten when he visited Glen Ellis Falls in New Hampshire with his parents. And there was the old crusty bronze hand bell with a handle shaped like Father Junipero Serra, a priest who explored California in the eighteenth century. Johnny's uncle had gotten that in California, and he had given it to Johnny. And now . . .

Johnny gazed forlornly at the professor. "Are you

sure it's a souvenir?" he said weakly. "I mean, couldn't the label be a fake or something?"

The professor had stopped laughing. He saw now that Johnny was very disappointed, and he felt sympathetic. "I'm sorry, John," he said, shaking his head sadly. "But I'm afraid this is a real genuine souvenir and nothing more. I'm not an Egyptologist—my field is the Middle Ages. But this is just the kind of thing that a town like Cairo, Illinois, would peddle as a souvenir. They pronounce it *Kay*-ro, by the way. It's a town way down in the southern part of Illinois, and it happens to have the same name as the capital of modern-day Egypt. So somebody probably thought it was clever to make a souvenir that looked like an Egyptian ushabti."

"A what?" Johnny had never heard this strange word before.

The professor was astonished. He knew that Johnny read a lot, and so—unreasonably—he thought that Johnny ought to know all sorts of obscure things. "You don't—well, I never! All righty then—this is what a ushabti is." The professor paused and laid the figurine down on the desk. He stubbed out his cigarette, shoved his chair away from the desk, folded his hands in his lap, and stared dreamily up at the ceiling. "First," he said, "you ought to know that the ancient Egyptians thought the next world—the place you go when you die—would be a lot like this world. And so in the next world people would have work to do. Plowing and sowing, carrying water up from the river, making bricks out of clay—

stuff like that. Well, to the Egyptians it didn't seem right that the pharaoh would have to do work in the next world. It would be . . . well, it would sort of be like making the President of the United States polish his own car. So the Egyptians made these little dolls called *ushabti*, and they were supposed to do the work *for* the pharaoh in the next world. Sometimes they put whole armies of these ushabtis in the tombs with the pharaohs. They come in all shapes and sizes: sometimes they look like dolls, and sometimes they're just miniature mummies, like this one here. The guy who designed this souvenir must have seen a ushabti in a museum, and he must have copied it. But this is a souvenir and nothing else. I'm sorry to disappoint you, but I'm afraid that's the case."

As Johnny listened to what the professor was saying he found that he was struggling to find some way of proving that the figurine was really magic after all. Johnny was a stubborn kid about the things he believed. He did not give up easily. "But, Professor," he said plaintively, "what about Father Baart and the wood-carver and all that stuff? People always said that the wood-carver gave Father Baart something magic, didn't they? And there's that piece of paper there, with Father Baart's handwriting on it, isn't there? What about that?"

The professor turned to Johnny. There was a sheepish, sad look on his face. "I'm afraid, my boy," he said, "that I started all this business by telling you that ghost story. I'm terribly sorry—I deserve to be punched! The trouble with me is, I love to tell stories, and I like to make them seem as realistic as possible. Now, it is true that several people have claimed that they saw Father Baart's ghost in the church. And for all I know they may really think that they *did* see him. Personally I don't believe in ghosts, except when I'm telling ghost stories. As for this scroll here"—he tapped the paper with his finger—"it *is* Father Baart's handwriting—that much I can tell you. I used to be the official historian of St. Michael's Church, and so I know about things like that. But what does this prove? Not much. The whole business with the book, the figurine, and the warning note may have been Baart's idea of a joke. Or he may have been serious. He may have thought this silly statue was really enchanted. Who knows?"

Johnny hung his head. "Is it all a fake, then? The whole darned story? Did you make it all up?"

The professor shook his head vigorously. "Oh, goodness, no! Most of the details in the story I told were true. Mr. Herman and Mrs. Mumaw really did get killed, and Father Baart really did disappear. But the two deaths were just a coincidence, and I don't think there was anything supernatural about Baart's disappearance. Baart was insane, and he probably had some insane reason for wanting to disappear. As for the note that was found on his desk, he probably wrote it himself. It's easy enough to disguise your handwriting if you want to do that sort of thing."

The professor paused and flicked the ash off his cigarette. He gave Johnny a hangdog, guilty look. "I'm sorry to pull the rug out from under you this way, John," he said in a low voice. "Next time I'll think twice before I tell a ghost story. But *please* don't think that this blue doojigger is magic—it isn't!"

Johnny sighed. He wanted to be mad at the professor, but he just couldn't manage it. In spite of his lousy temper, in spite of his love of making up things, the professor was really a nice guy. Johnny could tell that, and he felt that he could forgive the old man for having told a few white lies.

At this point the professor glanced at his watch. He said that he had papers to grade and that he was going to have to chase Johnny out of the house.

"However," the professor added, grinning slyly, "I would like to issue an invitation: This evening, after dinner, how would you like to come over for a game of chess and a piece of chocolate cake? I play a superlative game of chess, and the cakes I make are also excellent. How about it? Are you interested?"

Johnny nodded and grinned. He loved to play chess, but right now he didn't have a partner. Grampa's game was checkers, and sometimes Johnny got very bored with it. And he was nuts about chocolate cake with chocolate frosting. So it was decided: Johnny would come back after dinner and have dessert. But before he went, he had one more question.

"What should I do about this stuff?" he said, pointing to the book and the two objects that lay inside it. "Do you think I should try and take it all back?"

The professor thought a bit. He drummed his fingers on the desk top, and he puffed at his black and gold cigarette. "I definitely think," he said at last, "that you should *not* take these things back. In the first place, if Father Higgins or Mr. Famagusta caught you in the basement of the church, there'd be hell to pay. And in the second place, it occurs to me that the blue figurine may be valuable. People collect things, you know. They collect salt shakers and medicine bottles and old flatirons and buttonhooks. The figurine is only a souvenir, but it's an *old* souvenir—sixty years old, or more. I think you should write to *Hobbies* magazine and find out if your doohickey is worth something. In the meantime, however, if I were you, I'd keep the thing hidden. If your Gramma sees it, she'll ask where it came from, and then where would you be? Just take it back and put it in your closet. First, though, you'd better make sure the coast is clear. Come on. I'll go down with you and check."

Johnny took the book in his arms and followed the professor downstairs. At the front door they stopped, and the professor peered cautiously out.

"Good!" he said, nodding. "They're not back yet. You'd better get while the getting is good. Bon voyage! And don't forget about our chocolate cake date tonight!"

"I won't," said Johnny, grinning. "G'bye!"

While the professor held the door for him Johnny raced across the street. Into the house he went, and up the stairs to his room. Once again he put the old black book in the bottom of his closet. Again he piled stuff on top of it. Then he closed the closet door and went across the hall to wash his hands, which were dirty from handling the book.

That evening at dinner, just as Gramma was about to serve dessert, Johnny announced that he had been invited over to the professor's house for cake and a chess game. He announced this shyly and hesitantly, because he didn't know what Gramma's reaction would be. Grampa was a pretty easygoing sort—he usually let Johnny do what he wanted to do. But Gramma was more strict, and she didn't like the professor much. Furthermore she was proud of her desserts—Johnny didn't want to hurt her feelings or make her angry.

But all Gramma said was "Humph! I guess it's all right." And she added, in a disparaging tone, "I didn't know he baked cakes." Gramma had lived across the street from Professor Childermass for twenty years, but there were a lot of things she didn't know about him.

Johnny excused himself and went across the street. He had a great time that evening. The professor was a crafty and merciless chess player. He was every bit as good as Johnny was, and maybe even a bit better. As for the cake . . . well, Johnny had theories about chocolate cake. He felt that the cake part of the cake was just an interruption between the layers of frosting. As it turned out, the professor's opinions about cake were similar to Johnny's. The cakes he served had three or four thin layers, and the rest was a huge amount of good, dark, thick fudgy frosting. And he served second helpings too.

Around ten o'clock that night Johnny said good-bye to the professor and started across the street toward his house. He paused on the curb for a minute or two to look around. It was a beautiful cold winter night. Icicles hung from all the houses, and they glimmered gray in the moonlight. Snowdrifts lay everywhere. In the street were ridges of ice, knotted and iron-hard. Johnny blew out his cloudy breath and felt contented. He had made a new friend, he was stuffed with chocolate cake, and he had won one of the three chess games they had played. Once more he looked around, and then he stepped forward into the street. As he stepped he happened to glance to his left, and he stopped dead.

There was somebody standing across the street, watching him.

Johnny stared. Who was it? He couldn't tell. All he could see was a short, stocky figure standing in front of Mrs. Kovacs's house.

"Hi!" called Johnny, waving.

No answer. The figure did not move.

Oh, well, thought Johnny, *it's probably Mr. Swartout*. Mr. Swartout was a creepy little man who lived at the end of the street. He never said anything to anybody —wouldn't give you the time if you asked him for it.

Shrugging, Johnny walked straight on across the street and into his house. Later, upstairs, when he was in his pajamas and getting ready to climb into bed, Johnny looked out the window. His bedroom was at the front of the house. From it you could get a good view of the whole length of Fillmore Street. He looked toward the place where the figure had been standing, but there was no one there. For some reason Johnny felt relieved. Then he peeked at the moon, which was silvering the shingles of the professor's house. Johnny yawned and climbed into bed, and very soon he was asleep.

CHAPTER FIVE

In the weeks that followed, Johnny and the professor became friends. It was an odd kind of friendship, the old man and the twelve-year-old boy. But the friendship worked. Johnny was a shy kid. He did not feel at home with very many people. But he felt comfortable talking with the professor. At chess they were pretty evenly matched: Johnny won about half the games they played. As for the professor's famous temper . . . well, he didn't use it around Johnny. He crabbed now and then, but he crabbed in a humorous and kidding way, so that Johnny always knew he was not being serious. Gramma —as you might guess—did not know what to make of the friendship that had developed between these two. She herself did not care much for the professor's company, but she didn't have anything serious against him, so she just sighed and shook her head and said many times that it takes all kinds to make a world.

The blue figurine stayed in its box in Johnny's closet. One afternoon when he was on his way home from school, Johnny took a detour and stopped in at the library. He went to the reading room and picked up a copy of *Hobbies* magazine. As the professor had said, it was a magazine for antique collectors. It was full of information about mechanical banks and oil lamps and bisque figurines and Toby jugs and Simon Willard clocks. And on one page there was a question and answer column. Johnny sat down and copied the address of the magazine into a notebook he was carrying. Later, when he was back at home, he went up to his room and got out his Royal portable typewriter. He set it up on his bed, and kneeling in front of it, he pecked out a note:

Dear Sirs:

I own a blue statue shaped like an Egyptian mummy. It is old and the label on the bottom says SOUVENIR OF CAIRO, ILLINOIS. I wonder if this statue is valuable.

> Sincerely,
> John Dixon
> 23 Fillmore St.
> Duston Heights, Mass.

P.S.: Do not send a reply to my home. I will go to the library in the coming months to read your magazine and see if you have answered my query.

Johnny folded this note up neatly, put it in an envelope, and printed the *Hobbies* magazine address on the outside. He slapped on a stamp and put the letter in his briefcase, and the next day, on his way to school, he dropped the letter into a mailbox. And he thought about how nice it would be if the blue gizmo turned out to be worth fifty thousand dollars or something like that.

March was a wintry month in Massachusetts that year. Sea gales battered the town, and the snow stayed on the ground. Life went on in its usual routine for Johnny, for a while. But in the middle of March some rather odd things started to happen.

First there was the problem of the spiders. One day Johnny came home from school and found Gramma down on her knees on the parlor floor. She had a spray gun in her hands, and she was squirting insect spray along the baseboard. She looked upset.

"Hi, Gramma!" said Johnny. He threw his books onto the couch and walked over to get a closer look at what his grandmother was doing. "Whatcha doin', huh?"

Gramma glowered. She hated stupid questions. "What does it *look* like I'm doin', huh? I'm sprayin' away like crazy with this Black Flag insect stuff, on account of the house is full of spiders! *Spiders!* Can you imagine it, in the middle of winter?"

Johnny wanted to point out that it was not exactly the middle of winter but more like the end of it. But Gramma didn't like being corrected, so he said nothing.

He watched for a few minutes as she shuffled along on her knees, spraying as she went.

"I haven't seen any spiders," said Johnny after a while. "What kind are they?"

"Those rotten little gray ones," Gramma grumbled. "And if you haven't seen 'em, you must be goin' blind! Go out in the kitchen and have yourself a look. You'll be lucky if they don't carry you away with 'em. Spiders in winter! Lord! Where do you suppose they can be living?"

Johnny went out to the kitchen and looked. Sure enough, scooting here and there over the floor were small gray spiders. They were like the spiders he had seen crawling over the black book. Johnny felt an odd, queasy stirring of fear in his stomach. Quickly he told himself that he should not let his imagination run wild. These were just spiders and nothing more. And to prove this to himself he put out his foot and crushed one.

The spider invasion lasted several days. Then, mysteriously, they disappeared. Gramma was convinced the Black Flag spray had done its work. Johnny was not so sure.

One windy night toward the end of March Johnny went to the movies by himself. He went to see a spooky show called *The Ghost Returns*. By the time he got out of the theater, he was in a pretty nervous state. And as he made his way along the dark deserted streets toward home he began to get the feeling that someone was following him.

This is a maddening and frightening feeling, as everyone knows. Johnny kept telling himself that it was all in his mind, but still, as he walked from streetlight to streetlight, he found his fear growing. Once or twice he stopped suddenly and spun quickly around, but there was never anyone there.

When he got home, Johnny was somewhat taken aback to find that the house was dark. A note was taped to the window of the front door:

> *Gone next door to visit.*
> *Home later. Key under mat.*
> *Gramma and Grampa*

Johnny got out the key and let himself in. He was determined to shake off the nervous, frightened feeling that had come over him. First he turned on some lights. Then he marched straight out to the kitchen and got the pimiento-flavored cream cheese and the crackers. Then he went to the parlor, planted himself in the bristly brown chair, turned on the radio, and sat back to listen and munch. It wasn't a spooky show. It was *Camel Caravan*, a musical program that did the hit tunes of the week. Vaughn Monroe was on it, and some other singers that Johnny liked. Nevertheless, as he listened Johnny found his nervousness returning. He kept glancing toward the dark doorway of the room, but the doorway was always empty.

At ten o'clock Gramma and Grampa came home, and Johnny was very glad to see them. Gramma went straight up to bed. Grampa hung around downstairs to talk with Johnny for a while. But he was pretty pooped, so he did not stay very long. After a few minutes he too went to bed, and Johnny decided that it was pretty lonely sitting around downstairs. Wearily he climbed the steps. He washed up and brushed his teeth and put on his pajamas. Then he jumped into bed and pulled up the covers. Almost immediately he went to sleep. And he had a very odd dream.

He dreamed that he was back in Riverhead, walking down Main Street late at night. He was headed for the United Cigar Store. In real life Johnny had gone to the United Cigar Store many, many times. He had bought his first deck of Bicycle playing cards there, and he had picked up other things too. Odd trinkets like a ball-and-cup magic trick, a Chinese puzzle, a dribble glass, a joy buzzer. Now, in the dream, he was going to the United Cigar Store again, though he really didn't know why. He passed the Sunoco station, and then he was there. But what had happened to the store? Over the big red-and-white United Cigar sign a weathered wooden slab had been hung. The letters on the slab said:

R. BAART · ANTIQUES AND CURIOS
In the midst of life, we are in death.

Johnny looked up at the sign. It wasn't the sort of sign you usually saw, even on antique stores. But there was a light on inside, and for some reason Johnny wanted very much to go in. As he started up the steps he glanced at one of the display windows and noticed that the pipes and fishing reels and Kodak cameras were gone. Instead the bottom part of the window was full of grayish sand, and from the sand little blue mummy figurines stuck out. Each one had a grinning skull for a face.

Johnny opened the door and went in. The shop was dusty and disorderly. Gray spiders scurried across the floor. There was a heap of broken furniture in the back, and the only light came from a bare bulb that hung from a frayed black cord. There was a counter, with a display case below, but the windows of the display case were so flyspecked and dirty that Johnny couldn't see what was inside. Behind the counter stood the proprietor of the shop. She was an old lady, in a shapeless gray sack of a dress. She wore a large green eyeshade that covered the top half of her face.

"Can I help you, young man?" The voice was horrible and croaking.

Johnny knew that the old woman was really Father Baart, but for some reason he was not afraid. He said calmly, "I have come here to search for the answer to the mysteries of life."

The old woman grinned—Johnny could see her wrinkled mouth and strong, jutting chin below the shade. "Come around behind the counter, then," she barked. "Step this way, step right this way. . . ."

Johnny moved around behind the counter, and he saw

—to his horror—that the old woman was standing in an open grave. Behind her was a gravestone, and all around was long, matted grass. Johnny tried to turn and run, but his legs were like lead. The old woman had hold of his hand now, and she was pulling him down. He struggled. He planted his feet and tried to resist, but the old woman's grip was like an iron vise. The harder Johnny pulled, the closer he got to the grave. His feet were sliding, inch by inch, to the brink. And now he saw that the woman's face was a skull, a horrible grinning skull covered with black crisscrossed strands of spider web. Johnny was screaming, but he couldn't hear any sound. And now he was plunging down, down . . .

With a sudden jolt Johnny woke up. He was trembling all over. Was there anyone in the room? No, no one that he could see. The room was dark and quiet. From far away came the steady rattling roar of a freight train that was passing through the town. Johnny lay down and pulled the covers up over himself. But it was a long time before he could get to sleep again.

The next morning at breakfast Johnny was unusually thoughtful. Also his appetite was gone. He only ate a few spoonfuls of Gramma's delicious oatmeal (served with brown sugar, maple syrup, and raisins). Gramma asked him if he had something on his mind, and, lying, he said no. He just couldn't tell her, because he was thinking about the blue figurine. How would she feel if she knew he had swiped that gizmo from the church? Johnny had a pretty good idea of how she would feel. So he said nothing.

The school day passed in its usual way, except that Johnny was in a fog. He was usually quite alert and raised his hand a lot, but not today. In fact he got bawled out a couple of times by Sister Electa because he was not paying attention. Johnny was thinking about the spooky things that had happened to him lately. He was wondering if there was any connection between them and the blue figurine. He could not get Father Baart's grim warning out of his mind: *Whoever removes these things from the church does so at his own peril. I abjure you by the living God not to endanger your immortal soul. Vengeance is mine; I will repay, saith the Lord.* Was this warning just craziness, or was there something more to it? By the time school was over for the day, Johnny had made up his mind: He would have to see the professor about all this.

That evening, after dinner, Johnny went across the street to see his friend. He had called the professor up, and the professor had said sure, come ahead, he would be up in the bathroom sailing boats in the tub! Johnny did not know what to think of this, but he had learned to expect the unexpected from Professor Childermass. When he arrived at the door of the professor's bathroom, he found the old man kneeling beside the tub. He was wearing a rubber waterproof apron, and the sleeves of his shirt were rolled up. The tub was half full of water, and in it floated a fleet of little wooden boats. They were galleys, with matchstick oars and little triangular sails. Little paper flags fluttered from the sterns of the ships. Half of the flags were red and gold and had coats of arms on them. The other half were green and had gold crescents. The professor explained that he was re-enacting the Battle of Lepanto, which had taken place in 1571. In it the Christian ships led by Don John of Austria had defeated the ships of the Turks. With a little book open in his left hand and a stick held in his right the professor moved the ships around. When a ship got taken or sunk, the professor would reach in and lift it out of the water and put it on a shelf over the tub. Next to the tub was a blackboard where the professor kept score. The scoreboard looked like this:

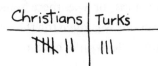

"Now then," said the professor as he pushed two boats together, "what did you want to see me about?"

Johnny told him. He explained about the spiders and the feeling of being followed that he had had the other night, and about the dream. The professor listened thoughtfully while Johnny talked, but he did not seem particularly worried.

"Is that all?" said the professor when Johnny was through. "I mean, is that all that's got you worried?"

Johnny felt offended. Here he was trying to tell the

professor his troubles, and what he was getting in response was *Ho, hum, is that all?* "I . . . I thought you'd tell me what to do," said Johnny in an offended voice.

Immediately the professor saw that he had hurt Johnny's feelings. He hadn't meant to. Now he heaved a deep, dispirited sigh. He stood up and started untying the strings of his apron. "Look, John," he said slowly, "I am not trying to make light of your worries. But I do think this whole business is in your mind. Spiders can find places to live and hatch their eggs in an old house even in wintertime. As for your dream and your feeling that you were followed . . . well, the power of suggestion is pretty strong. You heard my ghost story—which, by the way, I wish I had never, *ever* told you—and then you found that dratted hunk of blue crockery. You've got Father Baart and ghosts on the brain, my boy, and that's why you've got the heebie-jeebies these days. And do you know what I suggest as a cure? Hmmm?"

Johnny shook his head. "I dunno, Professor. What?"

The professor paused dramatically. He folded up his apron and put it away in the bathroom closet. Then he turned back to Johnny, rubbing his hands and grinning hugely. "I would suggest," he said, "that you let me beat the holy bejesus out of you in a chess game or two, and that you then eat a huge, glutty, calorie-filled hunk of my delectable prune cake, with creamy smooth chocolate frosting, and whipped cream on top. How's that for a prescription? Eh?"

Johnny liked the idea. His little visit to the professor turned into a long and enjoyable—and filling—stay. When he went home that evening, he felt that maybe the professor was right after all. The whole business was just his imagination working overtime.

A month passed. Windy March turned into sloppy wet April, and—much to Gramma's annoyance—the spiders came back to 23 Fillmore Street. On the other hand the spooky feelings and dreams that had been bothering Johnny went away. And one evening, when he was down at the library, Johnny picked up the new April issue of *Hobbies* and saw that his question had been answered. This was the answer:

> We have consulted antique dealers in the city of Cairo, Illinois, and we have discovered that mummy-shaped souvenir figures were sold in that city late in the nineteenth century. They were made in three colors, gold, blue, and red, and they were manufactured by Mound City Novelties of St. Louis, Missouri. We are informed that such an object, in good condition, would be worth about $25 today.

Johnny closed the magazine and shook his head. Twenty-five dollars! Phooey. So much for his wonderful dream of getting rich in a hurry. But at least now he knew that the figurine was not some mysterious talisman from ancient Egypt. It was what the professor had said it was. Johnny felt very relieved, and once again he scolded himself for letting his imagination work overtime.

Toward the end of April St. Michael's School had its yearly paper drive. At St. Michael's it was turned into a big contest, the east side of the school against the west side. Sister Electa made up a song set to the music of "The Sidewalks of New York," and all the kids sang it in class:

> East Side, West Side,
> Which is going to win?
> We're looking for the paper
> In cellar, barn, and bin,
> Boys and girls together
> Working one and all,
> Bringing loads of paper
> From the sidewalks of our town!

Every day for three days the students of St. Michael's School were let out of class in the afternoon so they could go hunt for wastepaper. They went everywhere looking for it. Some kids went from house to house. Others—the cleverer ones—had aunts and uncles who had been saving newspapers for them all year. Now they gleefully lugged the bales in, tied up nice and neat. For the kids it was like a holiday. And it was a contest too— each side was fighting hard to win.

On the last day of the paper drive Johnny and a lot of other kids were over at the Parish Hall, working hard. The Parish Hall was a long red brick building that stood just to the west of the school. This was where the Friday-night bingo games were held. At paper drive time all the folding chairs and tables were stacked over on one side of the hall, and the bundles of tied newspapers lay in big heaps. Kids swarmed everywhere, and everybody was supposed to have something to do: Some kids tied loose paper into bundles, others counted the bundles, and still others helped unload paper from the flatbed trucks that backed up to the open freight door. Everybody worked, and everybody seemed to enjoy working. It was such a treat to be doing something besides school-work for a change!

On into the late afternoon Johnny toiled. He got paper cuts and twine burns on his fingers, and his shirt was soaked with sweat, but it didn't matter. He was working to help the east side of St. Michael's School win. Johnny was weary but happy. At last he felt like he belonged at St. Michael's School.

Around three thirty the Parish Hall began to empty out. Kids started to go home in ones and twos and threes. Johnny was still busy tying bundles. Then he heard somebody cough over his head. He looked up and saw that it was Sister Correda. Sister Correda was the first- and second-grade teacher. She was nice, but she was kind of scatterbrained. She was always forgetting where she left things.

"Uh . . . John?" she said in her hesitant way. Sister Correda always acted apologetic when she was about to ask a favor of somebody.

"Yes, Sister?"

"Would you please go over to the school and get my watch for me? I must have left it on the desk in my classroom."

"Sure, Sister. I'll be right back."

Johnny went out the door into the afternoon sunlight. He crossed a corner of the playground and climbed the concrete steps that led to the back door of the school. Now he was inside again, in the cool gloom of the building, which always smelled of varnish and chalk dust and library paste. Johnny went straight to the first-grade room. He opened the door and peered inside. There on the teacher's desk lay Sister Correda's watch. It was a silver-plated pocket watch, with a long braided piece of leather attached to it. And standing next to the desk with his hand reaching out toward the watch was Eddie Tompke.

As soon as Eddie saw Johnny, he jerked his hand back. Then he grinned nastily.

"Hello, Brown Nose," he said. "You're just in time. I was gonna take this watch over to Sister What's Her Name. Now you can save me a trip."

Johnny stood dead still, staring at Eddie. *I bet you were gonna take the watch over to Sister*, thought Johnny. *I just bet you were.*

Eddie glared right back at Johnny. His eyes were mean and hard. " 'Smatter, Brown Nose? Doncha believe me? Think I'm lyin' to ya? Huh?"

Johnny didn't know what to say. He was scared of Eddie, but he stood his ground. He wasn't going to run away. "You're not s'posed to be in here," he said in a strained, nervous voice. "If the sisters find out—"

"Well, the sisters won't find out unless you tell 'em, will they, Brown Nose? C'mon and get the watch. You scared to come and get it?"

Johnny felt the muscles in his stomach tighten. He wanted to turn and run. But he forced himself to walk forward to the desk. Now he was standing face-to-face with Eddie. For a second Johnny thought that he would have to fight Eddie to get the watch. But Eddie pulled his hand back as Johnny approached.

"Brown noses always run errands for the sisters, don't they?" said Eddie in a hateful, crooning voice. "That's how they get their good grades. Everybody ought to know that."

At this something inside Johnny snapped. Eddie was bigger and stronger than he was, but he just had to say something. Johnny looked at Eddie, and their eyes met. "I'm not a brown nose," he said evenly. "I just do my work."

For some reason this remark really seemed to make Eddie angry. Quick as a flash he reached out and grabbed Johnny's hand. With his other hand Eddie picked up something that lay on the desk. It was a kid's pair of scissors. Eddie reached out and clamped the scissors around the index finger of Johhny's hand. The finger was caught in the part of the scissors just above the rivet that held the two blades together. Eddie squeezed. It felt awful— it was like being tortured. Johnny bit his lip to keep from yelling. He didn't want to give Eddie the satisfaction of hearing him scream.

Eddie kept squeezing. Tears were in Johnny's eyes. Weakly he tried to shove Eddie away. At last Eddie let go. He dropped the scissors on the desk and said, "See you 'round, Brown Nose." Then he turned on his heel and left.

Johnny stood at the desk. He was crying and clutching his injured finger. It burned, it stung. Slowly the hurt began to go away. Johnny took off his glasses and wiped his eyes with his handkerchief. Then he put the glasses back on again and picked up the watch. Sister Correda would be wondering why it had taken him so long. He wanted to tell her what had happened, but he knew he wouldn't tell on Eddie. That was for tattletaling babies, not for him.

Johnny went back to the Parish Hall and gave Sister Correda her watch. As soon as she saw him she knew something had happened. His face was red and streaked with tears, and he was sniffling.

Sister Correda was the flustery type, and she immediately got upset. "Good grief, John!" she exclaimed. "What . . . what happened to you?"

Johnny had a powerful urge to tell on Eddie, but he resisted. "I . . . I caught my hand in the door to your room," he said. And as proof he held up his sore and reddened finger.

Sister Correda was properly sympathetic. She took Johnny over to the sisters' house and put Unguentine on his finger. She gave him a glass of milk and a couple of Oreo cookies, and then she told him that he probably ought to quit working and go home. He wouldn't be able to tie up any bundles with his sore finger, and anyway it was about time to call it quits for the day.

"Besides, it looks as if your side has won," said Sister Correda, smiling. "That ought to make you feel good. And thank you for all the work you did. You're a real trouper—you never give up!"

Compliments alway made Johnny feel shy. "It was a lotta fun," he said, staring at the tablecloth.

Johnny talked a bit more with Sister Correda, and then he set out for home. At first as he walked along he felt good. His finger wasn't hurting much anymore. And he was very, very proud that his side had won the paper drive. But slowly the good feeling began to die away, and black anger took its place. Who did Eddie think he was, anyway? And what had he, Johnny, ever done to him? Nothing. Nothing except get good grades in school. And for this Eddie hated him. Well, right now Johnny was hating him back. He wanted to strangle Eddie, he wanted to murder him. In his mind's eye he saw himself pushing Eddie in front of cars, or beating him bloody in a boxing match. By the time Johnny got home, he was fairly tingling with hatred of Eddie.

Straight in the front door Johnny marched. Straight in the door and up the stairs to his room. He slammed the door of his room and threw the bolt. And then he did a very strange thing. He went to the closet, opened the door, and knelt down. Carefully he removed the sweat shirts and blankets and copies of *Boys' Life* that were piled on top of the black book. He opened the cover and took out the blue figurine. Then he clenched the thing tight in his hands and yelled at the top of his voice, "*I hope he breaks his goddam neck!*"

Johnny was silent. His face felt flushed, and he was breathing hard, and his heart was going like a trip-hammer. He felt scared. Scared of himself, scared of his anger, scared of what he had just said. And why was he holding the figurine? He had no idea why—no idea in the world.

With trembling hands Johnny put the figurine back in the book. He closed the worn, dog-eared cover, and he was about to start piling blankets on when he heard a knock at the door. Hastily Johnny threw stuff on top of the book. He got up and closed the closet door. Then he went to the door of his room and opened it. There stood Gramma. Her arms were folded, and she looked mad.

"John Dixon," she said severely, "I would like to know who gave you the right to come tearin' in here the way you did just now. When I heard your door slam, I thought the house was comin' down on top o' me! What's the matter with you, anyway?"

Johnny looked remorseful and stared at the floor. "Aw, I got in a fight with Eddie Tompke," he muttered. "He hurt my finger, and I got real mad. That's all."

Gramma looked a little less grim when she heard about Johnny's finger. "I know those Tompkes," she said, nodding meaningfully. "They're a mean bunch, all of 'em. Old Jack Tompke, he belonged to the Ku Klux Klan. Did you know that?"

Johnny said no, he didn't know that.

"Well, he did. Could I have a look at your finger?"

Johnny held out his hand. Gramma winced and made a *tsk-tsk* sound. "How'd he do *that* to you?" she asked.

"He caught it in a pair of scissors."

Gramma made more clucking sounds and shook her head. "Well, like I said, they're a mean bunch. Come on downstairs, and I'll put some witch hazel on that. It'll make it feel better."

So Johnny went downstairs with Gramma, and for the second time that afternoon he got his finger doctored. As Gramma fussed over him she went on about the Tompkes and their relations, the Tadmans and the Sweets and the Schemanskes. Gramma was like that. She had lived in Duston Heights all her life, and she knew everything about everybody. Usually this kind of thing bored Johnny, but right now he was happy that Gramma had the Tompkes to think about. It would make her forget about this door-slamming.

Later Johnny did some KP work in the kitchen for Gramma. He set the table for dinner, and he washed the celery, and he peeled some potatoes. But as he worked shapeless dark fears came crowding into his mind. Had he done something awful by grabbing the figurine and saying what he had said? If the professor knew about his fears, he would laugh and say that Johnny was letting his imagination run hog-wild. And it was certainly true that the figurine was just a souvenir and nothing more. The stories about Father Baart were just stories—that was also true, beyond doubt.

All the same Johnny was worried.

CHAPTER SIX

The next morning after breakfast Johnny went off to school as usual. At St. Michael's the school day always started with Mass in the church at eight. On this particular morning, as Johnny saw the great gloomy brick church looming up before him he felt a tightening in his gut. There was something he wanted to know—or rather there was something he was afraid of finding out. Up the worn steps and into the church he went. He paused in the vestibule to dip his fingers in the holy water font and make the sign of the cross. Then he pushed open the inner doors and walked down the aisle. The seventh graders always sat in the third and fourth pews back from the front, on the left side of the main aisle. When

Johnny reached the end of his pew, he genuflected and then started in.

Then he stopped. He stared, and his blood ran cold.

At the far end of the pew sat Eddie Tompke. His right arm was in a cast, and the cast was in a sling. Eddie had broken his arm.

Johnny stood dead still. His mouth hung slightly open, and he went on staring. Finally Eddie noticed him. He turned and scowled. He looked as if he wanted to say something nasty, but you weren't allowed to talk in church, and Sister Electa was sitting in the row behind.

"Hey, Dixon," somebody whispered. "Move it!"

Johnny came to himself with a jolt. He realized that he was blocking the entrance to the pew. He muttered " 'Scuse me" and sidled on down the pew till he was sitting next to Eddie. Johnny had barely gotten seated when the sanctuary bell tingled, and the priest and the altar boys came out of the little door to the right of the altar. The morning Mass had begun. Throughout the service Johnny stood and knelt and said prayers along with everyone else. But his mind was not on his prayers. He was thinking of something else. Yesterday he had held the blue figurine in his hands, and he had wished that Eddie would break his neck. He hadn't broken his neck, but he had broken his arm. Was it a coincidence? Johnny didn't think so. He felt scared, and he felt terribly guilty. He felt like he was sitting next to the body of somebody he had murdered. He wanted to turn to Eddie and say "I'm sorry," but Eddie would not have understood what he was talking about. And Johnny would have gotten bawled out for talking in church.

Mass was over, and the kids filed out of the church two by two. Soon Johnny was seated at his desk in the second-floor classroom. Sister Electa announced that the east side had won the paper drive. Everybody whooped and cheered. Johnny tried to cheer, but what came out was kind of weak. Yesterday he would have been thrilled. But now a dark fear filled his mind, and he could not get rid of it.

Johnny went through the rest of the day mechanically, like a robot. He did his arithmetic and religion and history lessons, but his mind was in a fog. Out of the fog thoughts came floating: he told himself that he was getting upset over nothing. It was all just a coincidence. Eddie's broken arm had nothing to do with him. He hadn't caused the arm to break. How could he? By saying words over an old souvenir? But what if it wasn't a souvenir? What if the stories about Father Baart were true?

By the time the school day was over, Johnny was a wreck. He was eaten up with guilt and fear and worry. What could he do? He couldn't tell Gramma or Grampa. They wouldn't understand. But he could tell the professor. The professor was a smart man and a wise man. When he had heard the whole story, he would know what to do.

Johnny was strangely silent during dinner that evening. Gramma and Grampa were used to his daydreaming during meals, but this was something different. He seemed to be worried, and his face was pale. Twice Grampa asked Johnny if anything was wrong, and twice Johnny said no, everything was fine. Finally, after dessert, Johnny cleared his throat and announced that he had a chess date with the professor this evening. This was a lie, of course. The professor didn't even know that he was coming.

"Don't stay out too late," said Gramma as Johnny got up to go. Gramma was a real bug about sleep. She was convinced that nine tenths of the things that were wrong with people were caused by lack of sleep.

"I won't," said Johnny.

"And please put on your sweater," Gramma added. "It's cold out there tonight. Remember, it's not summer yet."

"Uh-huh," said Johnny.

He walked out to the coat-tree in the front hall and took his sweater off the hook. As he put it on he found that strange images were floating around in his head. In his mind's eye he saw himself standing before the altar in the church, staring up at the gilded figures. Then he saw himself standing across the street from the church in the wintertime. Snow was blowing past, and somebody was standing on the steps of the church, waiting for him, but he couldn't tell who it was. Johnny shook his head. The images were gone. With a thoughtful look on his face he went to the door, opened it, and stepped outside.

It was a chilly April night. It had rained earlier, and the sidewalks glistened. Johnny walked across the porch and clumped down the steps. He stood for a moment, looking across at the professor's house. The lights were on in the study upstairs. But now that he was out here, Johnny realized that he did not have the faintest desire to go talk to his friend. He wanted to go someplace else instead. Suddenly he swung into motion. He trotted down the sidewalk, turned right, and kept on going.

A few minutes later Johnny was standing across the street from St. Michael's Church. He stared up at its massive dark shadow, and he realized that he was actually in the picture that he had seen in his mind a few minutes earlier. Only it wasn't wintertime, and there was no dark figure waiting for him on the steps. Still, Johnny couldn't shake the feeling that he had stepped into a dream. He felt strange, weirdly calm. Quickly he crossed the street. He mounted the steps and tugged at the iron ring. The door swung open, and he was inside, in the dimly lit vestibule. Johnny pushed the inner door open and stepped into the church.

At first he just stood there in the back, in the darkness under the choir loft. He drank in the musty, incensy, waxy smell. Two of the overhead lights were on. They cast a dim yellowish light in the cavernous interior of the church. Up in the sanctuary Johnny could see the gesturing, staring figures on the altarpiece. In its bracket on the sanctuary wall the red lamp flickered. Rows of empty pews stretched away before Johnny. Empty? Well, no . . . not quite. Somebody was sitting up in the front pew. Just sitting quietly and staring up at the altarpiece. The light was bad, but the person seemed to be a short, gray-haired man in a black overcoat. Johnny felt a sudden chill. He thought about the ghost of Father Baart. Then, in the next instant, Johnny realized that his imagination was running away with him again. He had been thinking all day about Eddie's broken arm and the figurine, and it had made him edgy. Lots of old people came to the church to pray, especially in the evening. It was nothing to get all worked up about.

Johnny slipped into a pew, knelt down, and made the sign of the cross. He stared up at the golden door of the tabernacle. Johnny wanted to get rid of his guilty feelings. He wanted to get rid of the feeling that he was the one who had broken Eddie's arm. He knew it was silly to think that a souvenir of Cairo, Illinois, was magic. But his guilt wouldn't go away. Now he wanted to say a prayer that would make him feel peaceful and happy again. Silently, his lips just barely moving, Johnny said the Act of Contrition:

> Oh my God, I am heartily sorry for having offended thee, and I detest all my sins because of thy just punishments. But most of all because I have offended thee, my God, who art all good and deserving of all my love. I firmly resolve, with the help of thy grace, to sin no more and to avoid the near occasion of sin. Amen.

After he had said this prayer, Johnny knelt, silent, his chin resting on his folded hands. He would have liked to hear the voice of God telling him that everything was okay. But all he heard was the rushing of blood in his ears and the swish of traffic passing outside. He felt better—a little better, anyway. And he decided, on the spur of the moment, that he would like to light a candle for his mother. He got up, sidled out of the pew, and walked down the aisle to the vigil-light rack near the confessional. He lit a candle and then knelt and said a brief prayer for his mother. He got up, and as he was turning around he got his first good look at the man who was sitting in the front pew. In a way it was a relief. This little man did not look in any way like the evil Father Baart. He had a bland freckled face and a little snub nose. His hair was iron-gray and was swept back in wings along the sides of his head. His eyebrows were black and arched, so that he had a permanently surprised look. The man was wearing a pin-striped gray suit, a gray vest, a black overcoat, and a gray tie with a pearl stickpin. His shoes were polished, and everything about him looked spotless and neat and prosperous.

As soon as the man saw that Johnny was looking at him, he smiled shyly.

"Good evening, young man," he said. "What brings you to the church so late at night, eh?"

Johnny moved closer. When he answered, he whispered. He always whispered in church. "I was saying a prayer for my mom," he said. "She died a little while ago."

"Ah!" said the man, and he nodded knowingly. "That is sad. I am sorry to hear it." Then, quite unexpectedly, he went on. "You know, young man," he said, fixing Johnny with his large surprised eyes, "I am a pretty good judge of character. And I think that you are a young man with a problem. Isn't that so?"

Johnny was startled. He didn't know what to say.

The man smiled. "Ah, it's true, isn't it? I can see it in your face." He patted the seat of the pew. "Would you care to sit down here and tell me all about it?"

To his own great surprise Johnny found himself sitting down next to the little man. And then he told him everything. It all came tumbling out, about Eddie's broken arm and the blue figurine and all. To Johnny, talking to the little man seemed as easy . . . well, as easy as walking across a room. The man was so warm and sympathetic. He shook his head and frowned when Johnny told him about the nasty things Eddie had done to him. And those large dark eyes seemed so wise, so knowing.

When Johnny had finished his tale, he sat silent, hands folded in his lap. He wondered what the man would say. At first the man said nothing. He stared thoughtfully at the floor. Then, at last, he spoke.

"Well, young fellow," said the man slowly, "it seems that you have a problem. Your problem is that you imagine things, and you worry too much. The figurine isn't magical—that much seems clear. But," he added oddly, "wouldn't it be fun to pretend that it was?"

Johnny was puzzled. "I don't get what you mean."

"Just this: you are afraid of this big bully Eddie. Maybe if you were to *pretend* to yourself that the blue figurine was magic, you would be able to stand up to him. It might give you . . . some unexpected strength. What do you think of that idea, eh?"

Johnny was still confused. "Would . . . would you explain that to me again, sir?"

The man smiled patiently. "What I'm suggesting is very simple. I'm merely saying that you should *pretend*. Use the powers of your imagination. Every morning before you go to school, rub the figurine and say some silly prayer. Make one up. Call upon the gods of Egypt if you want to—you'll find their names in any dictionary. You see, if you imagine that you're strong, you really *will* be strong! I think it'll help you—I really do."

Johnny frowned and bit his lip. He didn't like this plan—he didn't like it at all. "Look," he said slowly, "you . . . you have to understand. I wouldn't want to hurt anybody. I mean, what if the little blue statue really *is* magic? What if I used it to make somebody have an accident, or to kill them? I wouldn't—"

The little man burst into laughter. High-pitched, silvery laughter. "My, you *do* have an imagination!" he exclaimed, still laughing. "A real, grade-A imagination, that is for certain!" He laughed a bit more, and then suddenly he grew serious. He fixed Johnny with those uncanny large eyes. "Listen, young fellow," he said in a low, sincere voice, "I would not for the world have anything bad happen to you. Not for the *world*! I'm merely suggesting something that you can do to help yourself. People are funny creatures. If they think they're ugly, then they really are ugly. If they think they're weak, then they really are weak. Whatever you think you are, that's what you are. If you use that little blue figurine to convince yourself that you're strong, then maybe you really will become more confident, stronger. At least I think it's worth a try. Give it a try, and if you don't like the way this little game makes you feel, you can quit. How about it, eh? Will you try?"

As Johnny listened he found that he was agreeing with the man. The man's voice was low and purring and very persuasive. And his eyes . . . well, they were hypnotic. They were like great black pools. *Maybe it's a good idea*, thought Johnny. *Maybe it would work.*

"I . . . I guess I'd like to try it," said Johnny hesitantly.

The man smiled broadly. "Good!" he exclaimed enthusiastically. "Try it, and let me know if it works. I come in here often, just to sit and think or to pray. Stop in . . . oh, let's say in a week's time, and let me know how you're getting on. Good luck, by the way."

Johnny shook hands with the man and thanked him for listening to his problems. He started to get up, but the man reached out and laid his hand on his knee to stop him.

"Just a second," he said, smiling. "I have something for you." He reached into his vest pocket and took out a ring. "It's just a silly trinket, but it might help you with the little game that you're going to play. Here. Hold out your hand."

Johnny held out his hand, and the man laid the ring in it. Curious, Johnny looked down at what he was holding. It was a rather odd ring. It looked as if it was made from a bent nail. At the place where the two ends of the nail met, they held a small transparent stone that was tinted yellow. There was something under the stone. It looked like tiny slivers of wood, arranged to form the letter B.

"It's a monogram ring," said the man, tapping the stone with his forefinger. "My name is Beard. Robert Beard. The ring has been passed down through several generations of my family. It's worthless, except for its sentimental value. I thought you might like to have it."

Johnny gazed at the man wonderingly. He couldn't figure out why this total stranger was giving him an old family ring. But it felt good in his hand somehow. He liked it. "Thanks," he said, and he slipped it on to the third finger of his left hand. Johnny did not have a ring of his own at present. He had worn a silver Boy Scout ring for several years, but it had irritated the skin of his finger, and he had had to take it off. Now it felt good to have a ring again.

Johnny got up. Again he thanked the strange little man. Smiling blandly, the man waved good-bye and wished Johnny luck with the little game. Down the aisle Johnny walked, and through the two sets of doors. At the bottom of the stone steps he paused. There was a streetlamp nearby, and by its light he could see the ring. Way down in its depths the yellow stone was doing odd things. Johnny saw little flashes of iridescent blue and bloody red. He turned the ring back and forth and watched the way the light played over it. It was funny. He had come to the church feeling terribly guilty about Eddie's broken arm. Now he did not feel guilty at all. And he had made a new friend. Smiling in a satisfied way, Johnny walked away into the night.

CHAPTER SEVEN

The next day after school Johnny went to the Public Library and consulted the unabridged dictionary. The unabridged was fun to use. It was a very thick and floppy book, and it stood on a swiveling wooden stand in a corner of the reference room. A lot of its definitions were strange and interesting, and the book was full of pictures of weird objects, like arbalests and brassards and undershot waterwheels. Johnny flipped straight to the *T*'s, because he had seen a picture of an Egyptian god there—at least he thought that he had. Ah. He was right. Here it was, a picture of the god Thoth. Thoth was a funny-looking thing. He had the body of a man and the head of an ibis, which is a hook-beaked bird that looks sort of like a heron. Thoth held in his hands a bunch of

Egyptian hieroglyphs. The dictionary said that Thoth was the god of magic and mathematics. He would be a good one to use in the game Johnny was going to play with the blue figurine. Johnny copied the name of Thoth down on a note pad he had brought with him. Then, idly, he flipped a couple of pages and found himself staring at the picture of another Egyptian god. This one was even more weird-looking. Her name was Touëris, and she had the body of a pregnant woman. Her head was the head of a hippopotamus. Touëris—according to the dictionary—was the goddess of childbirth, and of revenge. The revenge part was what interested Johnny. He copied Touëris's name down, closed the book, and went home.

That evening at dinner Grampa asked Johnny about his ring. He had noticed it the first time Johnny had showed up with it on, but he had not said anything then.

"That's really some ring, Johnny," said Grampa amiably as he sprinkled salt on his mashed potatoes. "Where'd you get it?"

Johnny's hand had been resting on the table. Now for some reason he jerked it away and hid it under the tablecloth. He felt shy about the ring. In school kids had noticed it, and at first they had made fun of it, claiming that it looked like a woman's engagement ring. To stop the kidding, Johnny had come up with a pretty snappy explanation. He had claimed that the ring was a Captain Midnight death ray ring. He said he had gotten it by sending in Ovaltine labels. But he did not think that an explanation like this would work on Grampa.

"I, uh, the professor . . . he gave it to me," said Johnny, glancing away evasively.

Grampa stared wonderingly at Johnny for a minute. He could not understand why Johnny was so nervous about the ring. Could Johnny have stolen it? No, Grampa told himself, that didn't seem very likely. Johnny was not the thieving kind. Grampa was curious, but he was not the sort of person who would give you the third degree. So he just dropped the subject and started talking about baseball.

That night Johnny dreamed a lot. At first he dreamed that he was a moth, fluttering about on a summer night. He kept hovering outside a lighted window, and through the window he could see Mr. Beard, the little man he had met in the church. The man was sitting at a table, reading. But no matter how much Johnny the moth beat at the window with his wings, the man never looked up. Then the dream shifted, and Johnny was outside R. Baart's antique store again. He went in as before, and there was the horrible old lady in the green eyeshade. But this time, instead of trying to drag him down into the grave behind the counter, she chased him around and around the shop, up steep rickety staircases, down long dark hallways lined with dusty bureaus and bookcases and looming dark bedsteads.

Johnny awoke around three in the morning, and he

felt exhausted. Exhausted, and strangely nervous. He got up, put on his slippers and bathrobe, and padded down the stairs. He tried the front door, but it was locked tight, as always. Then Johnny stood in the front hall listening. It was a still night. The apple tree outside the hall window hung perfectly motionless. But for some reason the house was making noise. All old houses make noises at night, creaks and cracks and pops. But this was different. It was a rustling noise, a strange ghostly whispering. As Johnny listened the noise died away, and the house was silent again. Eyes wide with wonder and fear, Johnny turned toward the stairs and slowly began to climb.

Johnny did not get much sleep that night. He kept waking up and glancing anxiously around, straining to hear strange sounds. The next morning he stood at his bureau in his rumpled pajamas. The face that stared back at him from the bureau mirror was red-eyed and woozy. On the clean white runner lay the ring Mr. Beard had given him. Johnny picked the ring up and turned it over in his hands. After the dreams he had had and the sounds he had heard in the night, he was beginning to wonder about the little game that Mr. Beard wanted him to play. Mr. Beard was a nice man—that was certainly true—and he was only trying to help Johnny. But what if the figurine really *was* magic? What if Eddie's broken arm hadn't been just a coincidence? Johnny fussed and fumed and thought some more, and as he thought he slipped the ring on his finger.

He looked at himself in the mirror and blinked. Things were suddenly clearer. How silly all his doubts and fears were! He ought to go ahead with the "magic" game. If he played the game, it would make him feel stronger and braver, and then he would *be* stronger and braver, just like Mr. Beard had said.

Johnny went to the closet and opened the door. He knelt down and took the blankets and magazines and sweat shirts off the black book. He opened the lid and took the figurine out. Holding it in his hands, he said the "prayer" that he had made up:

> Thoth attend me! Touëris be my avenger! Let those who oppose me beware, for I will make them rue the day when they raised their hands against me! By the name of Amon-Ra I swear it!

Johnny paused. If he was expecting magical fireworks, he was disappointed. The blue figurine smiled up at him as always, but it looked and felt exactly the way it always had. No voices spoke to him out of the air. No thunder rolled. No dark clouds came rushing in to hide the morning sun.

Johnny felt slightly silly. He was glad there wasn't anyone in the room watching him. "This is a dumb idea," he muttered to himself. "It isn't gonna make me any braver or anything." He got up and started peeling off his pajama top. It would be time to go to school soon.

When Johnny walked into the church that morning, he suddenly remembered that it was the first day of May.

On the altar were fresh flowers, and the six tall candles were lit. May meant processions, with kids marching solemnly around the church, and hymns and incense and organ music. That was all right with Johnny. He loved parades and processions. Later, after Mass, Johnny was up in the seventh-grade classroom, sitting at his desk. Sister Electa had not called the class to order yet. In fact she was not even in the room. So everybody was just talking and goofing off. With his finger Johnny idly drew circles in the layer of polish on the top of his desk. For no reason at all his prayer book popped into his head. Johnny was very proud of his prayer book. His dad had given it to him as a going-away present, before he had sent Johnny off to live with Gramma and Grampa in Duston Heights. Johnny used the prayer book every day. It had a black cover of genuine leather, with a gold cross stamped on the spine. The pages were made of onionskin paper, thin and whispery, and the top edge of each page was gilded, so when the book was closed, a glimmering gold bar shone out at you. There were illustrations all through the book, and fancy capital letters, and there were two bookmark ribbons, one purple, the other red. The prayer book was one of Johnny's prized possessions. It felt good just to hold the book in his hand.

Smiling he reached down to the briefcase that stood on the floor next to his desk. The prayer book was in there with his other books. But Johnny's smile faded when he saw that the clasp on his briefcase was undone.

Johnny was very fussy about the clasp. He always did it up after he had taken something out of the briefcase. So it seemed pretty likely that somebody had been fooling around with his stuff. Alarmed, Johnny reached down and lifted the briefcase up into his lap. He opened the flap and peered inside. He could hardly believe it. His prayer book was gone!

Angry tears sprang to Johnny's eyes. Who could have done such a dirty, rotten thing? His mind began to race. Had the briefcase been out of his sight this morning? Johnny thought hard. He had had it with him in the pew this morning, and then he had brought it over to the school, and since then he had been sitting here at his desk, except for one brief trip to the pencil sharpener. So who . . .

And then it came to him. Phil. Phil Absen, the kid behind him.

Phil Absen was a weird kid. There was something wrong with his head, and so he did strange things and said strange things. Gramma had often said (grumblingly) that Phil was proof of the fact that Catholic schools would take *anybody*. Johnny didn't like Phil much, but he didn't dislike him much either. And up until now he hadn't figured that Phil was a thief.

Johnny turned and looked at Phil. He was pretending to be very busy, leafing madly through his geometry book. When Phil saw Johnny giving him the fisheye, he got even busier. It seemed pretty plain to Johnny that Phil was the guilty one. Who else could it be?

Johnny felt his face getting flushed. Anger was building up inside him. He wanted to grab Phil by the collar and shake the truth out of him.

"Hey, Phil!" he began loudly. "Did you—"

But then Sister Electa's voice cut in. She was summoning them all to attention. She was asking them all to stand and recite the Pledge of Allegiance. Johnny bit his lip. He turned and got up. He would settle with Phil later.

All through the first two morning classes Johnny steamed about his missing prayer book. He kept hoping that Sister Electa would leave the room so he could turn around and give Phil holy hell. Johnny was scared of kids like Eddie Tompke, but he was not scared of Phil. Phil was a real wimp, and even Johnny could terrorize him if he set his mind to it. And if Sister Electa ever left the room, Johnny *would* terrorize him. He would turn around and grab Phil's arm and squeeze it and make him give the prayer book back. It would be as simple as that— at least Johnny hoped it would be.

But the first two class periods passed, and Sister Electa never left the room. Then eleven o'clock came. It was time for religion class—but Sister had a surprise for everyone. Instead of holding the regular class, she announced, they and all the other students were going to go over to the church and start rehearsing for the May procession. Some kids groaned, and Sister Electa glared sternly at them. Then she walked quickly to her desk and dinged the little hand bell. Everybody stood up, and then, beginning with the row nearest the door, they began to file out of the room, just the way they did during a fire drill.

A little later Johnny was with the other kids, marching slowly around, two by two, inside the vast, dark, echoing church. Nuns were rushing here and there, making sure that the lines were straight and bawling out kids who were fooling around. Mrs. Hoxter was playing the electric organ up in the choir loft, and the kids were singing:

Bring flowers of the fairest
Bring flowers of the rarest
From garden and woodland and hillside and vale . . .

As Johnny shuffled moodily along he began to wonder why he had thought that processions were fun. This one was about as interesting as watching grass grow. Of course it was only a rehearsal. They hadn't even chosen the girl who would crown the Blessed Virgin's statue yet. Johnny wondered who they would choose. Probably Mary Jo Potter. The sisters were the ones who got to choose the girl, and Mary Jo was so holy and pious and religious and sweet that it was sickening. . . .

The procession came to a sudden, lurching, bumping stop. Something had gone wrong up in front, though Johnny couldn't tell what. Now that the marching had stopped, he turned and began looking around in a vague, aimless way. Suddenly he stopped. He had seen something that made him boiling mad. Halfway back along the line stood Phil Absen. And he was holding Johnny's prayer book in his hands.

Johnny had trouble controlling himself. He was a pretty mild-mannered kid most of the time, but when he lost his temper, he lost it. He knew that Phil was a little weak in the head, but all the same, this was too much. Just a little teeny bit *too much*! Johnny clenched his fists and gritted his teeth. He wanted to jump out of line and tear back there and snatch the book out of Phil's hands. But, as angry as he was, he knew better than to do that. Sister Electa—or some other nun—would climb all over him if he started a fight in the church. So Johnny controlled his anger. There would be time to settle with good old Phil later.

The rehearsal for the May procession only lasted an hour, but to Johnny it seemed like it went on forever. Finally, though, around noon the nuns decided to call it quits. Streams of talking and laughing kids poured out through the three doors in the front of the church. Johnny went running out with the rest. He paused on the sidewalk, and he squinted and winced. After an hour in the dusky gloom of the church the light made his nearsighted eyes hurt. But when the pain passed, Johnny found that—once again—he was staring at Phil Absen. There he was, out by the bicycle rack, with the prayer book under his arm. He had a very pious, prissy look on his face, and he was talking to Sister Electa. Well, this was just too much. Johnny took off on the run, and he didn't stop till he came to where the two of them were standing.

"Hey, Sister!" Johnny exclaimed breathlessly. "Phil stole my prayer book! That's my prayer book! Make him give it back!"

Phil stared at Johnny with wide, scared eyes. He clutched the prayer book to his chest. "It's *not* his, Sister! He's lyin'! This's *my* prayer book. My . . . my mom gave it to me."

"I'm not a liar, but *he* is!" Johnny yelled, pointing a trembling finger at Phil. "He's a dirty, rotten liar! Sister, make him give it back! It's mine, I swear to God it is!"

The kids who had been standing and talking outside the church now crowded around Phil and Johnny. They knew that something was up. Somebody was going to get in trouble, and they wanted to watch.

Sister Electa looked from Johnny to Phil and back to Johnny again. She seemed perplexed, but she was determined to stay in control of the situation. "John," she said with a pained look on her face, "I know you're upset, but please try to lower your voice. And it is not a good idea, at any time, to use God's name in a loose way. Now then!" Sister Electa folded her arms under the scapular of her gown. She turned to Phil. "Phillip," she said in a mild but firm voice, "John here has accused you of taking his prayer book. I know John, and I know that he doesn't usually run around making wild accusations. However, it is possible that he has made a mistake in this case. Now, are you *sure* that that prayer book is yours?"

Phil's eyes grew wider and gogglier. It was clear that he was scared out of his mind. Still, though, he clung to the book. "It is *too* mine!" he said in a loud, childish voice. "He's a liar, Sister! He's a real liar!"

Sister Electa stared pityingly at Phil. She knew him pretty well, and she knew he had problems. She was well aware that there was something wrong with Phil's mind. Most of the time she tried to treat him just like any other twelve-year-old. But right now he was acting like a kid of six, and she felt she had to handle him differently.

Sister Electa unfolded her arms. She held out a well-washed hand. "Phillip," she said gently, "could I see the prayer book?"

Reluctantly Phil offered her the prayer book. Sister Electa took it, and then she turned to Johnny. "Now, John!" she said in a brisk, businesslike way. "Are there any identifying marks in this book? Is your name written in it anywhere?"

"It sure is, Sister. My dad wrote my name on the blank page in the front. Look and see if it's there."

Sister Electa opened the book. The flyleaf was gone. It had been torn out, torn out roughly. A ragged strip of white paper still protruded from the binding.

Sister Electa was silent for a moment. Then she looked searchingly, accusingly at Phil and once again held out her hand.

"Phillip," she said in a commanding voice, "I'd like to see *everything* that's in your pockets!"

Several of the kids in the crowd snickered and laughed.

Phil went white, but he did as he was told. First he pulled out a very dirty handkerchief and gave it to the nun. The crowd roared, but Sister Electa remained stern and unamused.

"Very good, Phillip. Now the other pocket, if you please."

Phil dug his hand into the other pocket and gave Sister Electa a handful of change. Still, however, she was not satisfied.

"Turn both your pockets all the way out," she said.

Phil did this, and a small wad of paper dropped from his left-hand pants pocket. The nun stooped and picked it up. Without a word she handed it to Johnny. With difficulty he uncrumpled the tight little wad of paper. But even before he had done this, he knew what he had: It was the missing flyleaf.

Suddenly Phil Absen started to cry. His childish face got all red and twisted up. He raised a trembling finger and pointed into the crowd. "Eddie Tompke made me do it!" he wailed. "It's his fault! He told me to do it!"

Johnny whirled and looked where Phil was pointing. Sure enough, there on the edge of the crowd stood Eddie, broken arm and all. There was a cynical, crooked grin on his face.

Sister Electa glowered skeptically at Phil. "Young man," she said severely, "don't try to blame things on other people when they're your own fault! Now, I'm going to give this prayer book back to John Dixon, and I'm also going to ask you to tell him that you're sorry you took it. And I'm afraid that you're going to have to stay after school today and have a little talk with me. Stealing is a somewhat more serious matter than you seem to think it is. Now, tell John that you're sorry you took his prayer book."

Still sniffling, Phil turned to Johnny. He stared at Johnny's shoes and blew his nose before he spoke. "I'm sorry I took it," he said in a dull, defeated monotone, "but like I said, Eddie—"

"*Please!*" exclaimed Sister Electa, cutting Phil off. "Please stop trying to blame others for what you did! Now, Phillip, go into the school and wash your face and pull yourself together. As for the rest of you," she added, turning to the crowd of kids who were still eagerly watching, "please find something else to do with your time. Go eat your lunches. You've only got half an hour till classes begin again. Go on, all of you! Make yourselves scarce!" Sister Electa made shooing motions with her hands.

The crowd broke up. Johnny thanked Sister Electa hurriedly and turned away. He should have felt triumphant, but he didn't. Something was bothering him. Phil had said that Eddie made him steal the prayer book. Sister Electa did not believe Phil, but Johnny did. Eddie liked to boss around weak, helpless kids, and Phil was about as weak and helpless as they come. Even with a broken arm Eddie could be pretty terrifying. He had probably threatened to do all sorts of nasty things to Phil unless he followed orders.

As Johnny was still standing there, thinking, he suddenly felt somebody's hand patting him on the back. He turned. It was Eddie.

"Boy, old Absen-minded can really tell 'em, can't he?" Eddie chortled. "Glad you got your prayer book back. They oughta toss that kid in the booby hatch! What a liar!"

Still chortling, Eddie walked away. Johnny watched him go. That settled it. Eddie would never have done what he had just done unless he was the guilty one. Johnny felt angry, but he also felt helpless and depressed. How long was he going to have to put up with Eddie? Would Eddie follow him around all through eighth grade, playing dirty tricks on him and making his life miserable?

Johnny did not have any answers to these questions. So he went back to the school building, clumped down the stairs to the basement lunchroom, and ate the sandwich and banana that he had brought with him. The rest of the school day passed in its usual way. Social studies and arithmetic for the last two hours of the day, the final prayer and the ringing of the bell for dismissal. And then all the kids swarmed down the worn, creaky stairs and out the front door into the sunlight. As usual Johnny was one of the last to leave. And when he finally did walk out the door, briefcase in hand, he didn't feel like going home. Not right away, anyway. So he decided to go down and walk by the river.

The Merrimack River, one of the widest and longest

rivers in New England, flowed through the middle of Duston Heights. Along its banks stood abandoned factories, long red brick buildings with tall brick smokestacks rising above them. Many years ago these factories had made cloth, but now they were closed, and their narrow windows were broken. Johnny liked the old factories. They were almost like haunted houses. As he walked along the grass-grown sidewalks of Water Street he peered up at the buildings that towered over him. High up, set in the brick walls, were little red terra-cotta decorations, leering monster faces or the solemn bearded masks of—Johnny imagined—Greek gods. Or you might see a stone plaque that said LEVERETT BROTHERS EST 1882. And here and there in the empty spaces between the buildings you might see an old rusted piece of machinery or a wooden clock face that had once been in a cupola somewhere.

After he had walked for two or three blocks, Johnny came to a place where a weedy courtyard opened out between two buildings. At the far end of the courtyard was a low half-ruined brick wall. Set neatly in a row on top of the wall were some old glass bottles. And standing there, slinging rocks at the bottles with his good arm, was Eddie Tompke.

Johnny froze. For a moment he just stood there watching. Eddie hadn't seen him yet. He was busy slinging away, throwing sidearm and then overhand, imitating the motions of a big-league baseball pitcher. His aim was pretty good. Pieces of broken glass lay at the base of the wall. Johnny wondered what he ought to do. Should he just slink on past, go about his business? Normally that was what he would have done. But Johnny was feeling strange. A force was rising up inside him, something irresistible. It was this force that made him do what he did next.

"Hey, Eddie!" he yelled suddenly. "You made Phil steal my prayer book, didn't you? You rotten flatheaded creep, I hope you fall down a manhole and break your other arm! You hear what I said, you rotten creep? You hear me?" Johnny gasped and turned pale. He hadn't meant to yell like that. It had all just come pouring out of him, almost as if somebody else was using his body and his vocal chords. Now what was going to happen?

Eddie turned around slowly. His mouth was set in a tense scowl, and his eyes were like two gray stones. When he spoke, his voice was dangerously calm.

"Come over here and say that, John baby."

Johnny was terrified. He wanted to run, but his feet wouldn't move. Even with a broken arm Eddie could make mincemeat out of him. The muscles in both his arms were like ropes, and his chest was like a cement wall. He would break his glasses and give him two black eyes and a split lip. He would beat Johnny to a pulp.

"I . . . I . . ." Johnny began, but he couldn't get the words out. Rooted to the spot with fear, he watched as Eddie began walking slowly toward him. And then something strange and totally unexpected happened. Johnny felt a sharp pain in his ring finger, and it seemed to him that the yellow stone flashed. And then a strong wind began to blow. It sprang up out of nowhere and blew past Johnny. The bushes that grew in the courtyard flailed madly to and fro. Bits of paper sailed up into the air, and a cloud of yellowish dust flew at Eddie. Coughing and sputtering, Eddie staggered backward. The wind blew harder and threw him, stumbling and reeling, against the brick wall. Bottles flew this way and that, and when Eddie stuck out a hand to steady himself, it came down on a piece of broken glass.

Eddie howled and jerked his hand toward his mouth. He sucked at the bleeding cut. Then silence fell. The wind died as suddenly as it had sprung up, and the yellow dust settled. Eddie looked at Johnny, and Johnny looked at Eddie. And which of them was more frightened it would have been hard to say.

CHAPTER EIGHT

❧

It was a bright, sunshiny Saturday in May, and the professor was up on the square Italian cupola that jutted above the roof of his house. He was wearing overalls, his mouth was full of nails, and he had a hammer in his hand. The cupola had windows all around and a tiled roof with a silly wooden finial sprouting from it. All around the cupola rickety scaffolding had been built, and attached to the cupola roof was a fantastic framework of wooden slats, braces, joists, and whatnot. Someday, when it was finished, this framework would support an elaborate radio aerial. The professor was a wild Red Sox fan. He loved to listen to the Sox on the radio while he corrected his students' papers. The problem was this: WITS in Boston was the only station that carried the baseball games, and its signal was pretty faint by the time it reached Duston Heights. But the professor was confident that his superduper whizbang aerial would solve the problem. He had been reading up on aerials in *Mechanix Illustrated* and other handyman magazines, and in his study was a blueprint that he had drawn up, all by himself. Now if he could only get the job done, everything would be fine.

But as he worked the professor frowned and muttered to himself. He was worried. Not about his work but about Johnny. It was May 10, ten days after Johnny's run-in with Eddie Tompke. And in all that time the professor had not seen Johnny to talk with, not once. Normally Johnny came over three or four times a week for chess and conversation and chocolate cake. But not now. At first the professor had felt hurt. Then he had told himself that he was an old fool, that Johnny had—no doubt—found some young friend who was fun to be with. But then he began to watch for Johnny out of the front windows of his house. And what he saw alarmed him. Johnny was never with anyone. He always walked alone, head down, briefcase in hand. And he looked awful. His face was very pale, and there were dark circles under his eyes. He looked as if he had not slept for a week.

And so the professor was concerned. He wanted to know what was wrong. So far he had resisted the urge to butt in on the Dixons' family affairs. He couldn't imagine that Gramma and Grampa were mistreating

Johnny. That did not seem possible. But then, what *was* going on?

The professor drove in another nail. The framework creaked and shuddered, and the professor growled at it. He ordered it to hold together. From somewhere below a door slammed. The professor glanced over and saw Johnny plodding down the front steps of his house. Now he was moving along the sidewalk, head forward, hands folded behind his back. *Oh, this is just unbearable!* grumped the professor to himself. *I have got to go see the Dixons, or I will go out of my ever-loving mind!* And slowly he began to clamber down the scaffold.

A few minutes later the professor was knocking at the front door of the Dixon home. Presently the door rattled open. There stood Grampa. He was wearing a blue denim apron, and his sleeves were rolled up. In one hand he held a hypodermic syringe. The professor was not surprised at this. He knew that Gramma Dixon had diabetes and that Grampa had to give her an insulin shot once every day. Normally in this kind of situation the professor would have made some sort of wisecrack. He would have called Grampa Young Dr. Malone or some such thing. But he was not in a wisecracking mood. And he could see from Grampa's long face that he was not feeling very jokey either.

"Hi, Henry," said the professor, smiling faintly. "All right if I come in?"

"Sure. Come on out to the kitchen. It's shot time, as you can see. It'll be over in a minute."

The professor followed Grampa out to the kitchen. There he found Gramma, sitting at the white enameled table. The sleeve of her dress was rolled up, and on the table was a bottle of rubbing alcohol. Nearby lay some wads of cotton. The professor sat down, and he politely turned away his face as Grampa shoved the needle into Gramma's arm. Then, when it was over and Grampa was rinsing the hypodermic in the sink, the professor cleared his throat harrumphily.

"I came over to talk to you two about Johnny," he began. "I . . . well, I'm a bit worried about him."

"So 're we," said Gramma, frowning. "He don't sleep good at night, an' he has bad dreams. Woke up screamin' an' yellin' to beat the band the other night. Scared the dickens outa me, but he wouldn't tell us what the heck was wrong."

"He don't eat good, either," added Grampa as he dried the glass hypodermic tube with a linen towel. "Just picks at his food like a little bird. I asked him the other day if somethin' was wrong, but he said no, everything was fine. Can you beat that? I don't know what to make of it. Do *you* know what's eatin' him, Rod? I mean, you're his friend an' all, so I thought maybe . . ."

"Well, you thought wrong," said the professor gloomily. "I haven't seen him to talk to in about two weeks. I came over here hoping that you two might enlighten me." The professor gazed disconsolately around the room. He looked at the hexagonal red electric clock that hung over the stove and at the rack of test tubes that stood on the windowsill. "I saw him going somewhere the other night. Do you know where he goes?"

Grampa shrugged. "Far as I know, he goes down to the church. He says he wants to light a candle for his mom an' pray. I don't see anything wrong with that, do you?"

The professor shook his head. "No. Not if that's what he's really doing. But you know—with your permission—I think I'm going to follow him one of these nights to see where he goes. I'm good at tailing people. I was an intelligence officer during World War I. My code name was the Crab."

Gramma laughed loudly, and the professor glared at her. "What's so funny about that?" he snapped. "I don't see anything to laugh at, do you, Henry?"

Grampa bit his lip and shook his head solemnly. And then, to cover up the giggling fit that had come over him, he rushed over to the stove and poured the professor a nice hot cup of coffee. Gramma, Grampa, and the professor talked for a while longer, and they cooked up a scheme: Grampa would call up the professor the next time he knew that Johnny was going on one of his nighttime visits to the church. Then the professor would shadow Johnny, and . . . well, they all three hoped that this would help them get to the bottom of the mystery. They cared for Johnny a lot, and they did not want anything bad to happen to him.

As it turned out, the three conspirators got a chance

to put their plan into action sooner than they might have expected. That evening at dinner Johnny announced that he was going down to the church to pray. When? Oh, around eight o'clock. Gramma looked at Grampa, and Grampa stared at the saltcellar. Both of them tried hard to act unconcerned.

Gramma smiled weakly and said in a falsely cheerful voice, "Well, that's fine! I sure think it's good when a boy your age goes to church without bein' dragged there by the heels." Then she looked hard at Johnny and added in a more serious tone, "Johnny?"

Johnny laid down his fork and stared back at Gramma. He felt defensive. His guard was up. What did she want to know? "Yeah, Gramma? What is it?"

The tone of Johnny's voice was so unfriendly that Gramma was startled. She glanced quickly down and began to toy with a piece of celery on her plate. "Well . . . your grampa and me were wonderin' if . . . if you felt okay these days. I mean, if there's anythin' on your mind, we could . . . well, kinda help you with it."

Johnny's eyes were stony. "I don't know what you're talkin' about, Gramma. I'm all right. I just wanta go down to the church to pray tonight, that's all. Is that okay with you?"

Gramma nodded helplessly. And that was the end of the conversation. The meal went on in silence. After dessert Johnny went upstairs to his room, closed the door, and bolted it. He sat down on his bed and stared around at the old-fashioned furniture. The tall gloomy clothespress with the scrolled decorations on the front. The marble-topped bureau with the mirror. The bristly brown armchair, the old pictures in heavy black frames, and the Motorola radio on the scarred black end table by the window.

And then the hard, tense look on Johnny's face melted. He burst into tears.

Ever since the first of May, Johnny had been living inside a nightmare. He was hearing and seeing strange things, and he was doing things without knowing why he did them. He felt that he was in danger—terrible danger—but he was scared to death to tell anybody about it.

First there was the figurine. It was magic, it was enchanted—he knew that now. Every morning, as regular as clockwork, Johnny would get out of bed, take the figurine from its hiding place, stroke it, and say the prayer to Thoth and Touëris. He had to—he wasn't sure why he did this, but he knew he had to. And at night sometimes, as he was lying in bed trying to sleep, Johnny would hear whispering coming from the closet where the figurine was hidden. Sometimes he almost thought he could figure out what the whispering voice was saying. And there was the ring. It was magic too. It was connected with the figurine in some way that Johnny didn't understand. He wanted to take the ring off, but he was scared to. It hurt his finger sometimes, made the bone of his finger ache and throb, so that he wanted to cry out with the pain. But something in his mind, an insistent voice, told him that he couldn't take the ring off, not even for a minute. If he did, awful things would happen to him.

And then there were the dreams. Over and over, every night, Johnny had the dream about R. Baart's antique shop. Over and over the old lady in the green eyeshade chased him through endless rooms, up endless cobwebbed staircases, or dragged him down into dark, earth-smelling, wormy graves. And he would wake up many times during the night, and he would look around wildly, convinced that there was somebody in his room. But when he turned on the lights, there was never anyone there.

Johnny blew his nose and wiped his eyes. He smiled wanly. One good thing had been accomplished: Eddie Tompke was scared to death of him. After that afternoon down by the factories Eddie had avoided Johnny like the plague. Whenever he passed Eddie on the stairs or in the lunchroom or wherever, Eddie would give him this goggle-eyed, frightened stare and hurry past. Johnny had always daydreamed about having power, the power to scare off bullies. But now that he had the power, he didn't want it—not if it was going to make him feel like this. Johnny was miserable, utterly miserable. He wanted to tell Gramma and Grampa that he was frightened, but something—the ring, or some other awful and evil force —forced him to keep his mouth shut. Johnny felt like somebody inside a glass-walled soundproof prison. He pounded on the walls, but nobody heard. He screamed, but no sound came out.

Nervously Johnny glanced at the Big Ben alarm clock that ticked loudly on his bureau. It was a quarter to eight. He'd better get a move on. He didn't want to stay out too late. And where was he going? He was going to St. Michael's Church, to see if he could find Mr. Beard, the little man who had given him the ring. Mr. Beard had said he would see Johnny in about a week's time. But had he meant a week exactly, or what? Johnny didn't know, but he did know one thing: He desperately needed to talk to the man. Night after night he had gone down to the church hoping that Mr. Beard would show up. But he was never there. Did Mr. Beard know that the ring was magic? That was another large question in Johnny's mind. If he did know, that meant that he was evil, that he had conned Johnny into taking the ring. For his own peace of mind Johnny wanted to think that Mr. Beard was a nice guy, that he hadn't known anything about the awful powers that lay hidden in the ring. Somewhere Johnny had read a story about a magic amulet that hadn't seemed magic until somebody said a secret prayer over it. Maybe this was what had happened. Maybe the ring had passed down through Mr. Beard's family for generations, and nobody had known that it was enchanted. And then Johnny had aroused the sleeping magic with his prayer to Thoth and Touëris. And what about the figurine? That was another deep, dark, frightening mystery that

Johnny couldn't fathom. But he felt that he could deal with the blue figurine if he could ever get the ring off his finger. He was hoping, hoping frantically, that Mr. Beard would turn out to be an okay guy, that he would be willing to help. If he knew something about the ring, something that would allow Johnny to get rid of it, then, later, he would take a hammer and smash the smiling blue idol into a million million tiny blue pieces.

Johnny got up and glanced nervously around the room. He stared at the closet door, and for a second he had the horrible unreasoning fear that the door would open and the blue figurine would come waddling out, like a windup toy soldier. Johnny shuddered and left the room, turning out the light as he went.

Outside, in front of the house, Johnny paused. It was a chilly May evening. He was glad he had his suede jacket on. He glanced up and down the street. Lights were on in most of the houses, but the professor's house was a dark mass of shadow. He was probably out at the movies or visiting one of his friends. Johnny felt alone and frightened. He listened to the wind that was rustling the new May leaves on the trees. Suddenly he had a great urge to rush across the street into the professor's house and turn on the living room lights and sit there until the professor came home. Johnny could do this if he wanted to. The professor had given him a door key—it was on the key ring in the pocket of his jacket. Johnny pondered. Then he felt a sharp twinge of pain in his ring finger, and that made up his mind for him. The professor couldn't help him with the ring. He had to find Mr. Beard. Johnny clenched his teeth. He turned suddenly to the right, like a soldier making a turn on a drill field. Swinging his arms, he began to march down Fillmore Street.

The sound of Johnny's footsteps grew fainter and then died away. He had disappeared into the darkness at the end of the street. Now, out of the shadows that shrouded the professor's house, a figure stepped. It was Professor Childermass himself. He was wearing his ratty tweed coat and a wide-brimmed felt fedora. On his feet were tennis shoes. With quick, springy, soundless steps he began to move down the sidewalk, and soon he too had disappeared.

When Johnny got to the church, he was—once again —disappointed. There was nobody there but Mrs. McGinnis. Mrs. McGinnis was a tall, big-boned, and rather silly old lady who wore floppy wide-brimmed hats and held her head to one side, as if she lived in an attic room with a sloping ceiling. She was kneeling in the front pew and thumbing her rosary beads. Johnny was more than disappointed—he felt almost desperate. What had happened to Mr. Beard? Why didn't he come here anymore? But as Johnny was turning away to go something caught his eye. Something small and white lying on the seat of the last pew. It was a piece of note-paper with writing on it. Probably it was somebody's grocery list. Why was he wasting time gaping at it? But it was oddly fascinating all the same. Johnny bent over and picked the note up. He saw spindly, scrawly handwriting. The note said:

Meet me in Duston Park.
Yours very truly,
Robt. Beard

Johnny was startled and a bit amused. What an odd duck Mr. Beard was! And why had he left the note here in the back pew, in the darkness? How could he be so sure that Johnny would find it? Nevertheless, he *had* found it. And he knew where Duston Park was. It was over on the other side of the river, about a fifteen minute walk from the church. Should he go? Johnny felt that he had to. He set his mouth in a determined frown. Abruptly he turned and walked out of the church. The swinging doors queaked and quacked behind him as he went.

Duston Park was over in Cranbrook, which was the snooty part of Duston Heights. The park was a long grassy triangle with a rail fence around it. It was surrounded by houses and one tall white colonial church. Inside the park were benches and a few young maple trees, and in the center of the park was a bronze statue of Hannah Duston. She stood there, tense and defiant, on her high granite pedestal. In one hand she held a tomahawk, and in the other, ten Indian scalps. Hannah was a famous woman. She had scalped ten Indians long ago on an island in the Merrimack River, to get even with them for having murdered her baby right before her eyes. On the base of the statue was a list of the people who had paid for the statue and an inscription in Latin. But her name was not on the statue, and unless you knew the story of Hannah Duston, you might have wondered who the lady with the hatchet was and what she had done.

When Johnny got to the park, it was deserted. There was an old-fashioned streetlamp in the middle of the park, and a bench under it, but there was no one sitting on the bench. Once again Johnny's heart sank. He had walked as fast as he could. Now what was he going to do? With a dejected sigh he slumped on into the park and sat down on the bench by the lamp. He glanced at his watch. It was getting on toward nine. He didn't dare stay too long—Gramma would be worried about him. He decided that he would wait for exactly ten minutes and then get up and leave.

Minutes passed. Johnny hummed to himself and looked aimlessly this way and that. He looked at the greenish bronze statue that held a tomahawk poised over his head. He peered across the street at the Unitarian church, with its six white Corinthian pillars and its tall graceful colonial spire. Now as he watched he saw somebody step out of the darkness next to the church. The figure moved forward quickly into the light. It was Mr. Beard. Pausing briefly at the curb, he started to cross the street. Mr. Beard was wearing his black coat and a kind of black hat called a homburg. When he saw Johnny, he glanced impatiently at him. Mr. Beard did not seem to be in a good mood.

"Well," he said snappishly as he sat down on the bench, "you certainly took your time about getting here." He glared at Johnny, and his large black eyes seemed mean and hard.

Johnny was utterly confused by this remark. What was Mr. Beard talking about? He sounded as if he and Johnny had made a date to meet at some certain time. Johnny felt hurt, and there was also something in Mr. Beard's manner that frightened him. He wanted to get up and leave. But Mr. Beard's great dark eyes fascinated him. He stayed where he was.

Mr. Beard smiled, but it was a crooked, lopsided smile. "And what is on your mind, pray tell?"

Johnny held out his hand. "The . . . the ring . . ." he stammered. "It . . . it's . . ."

"Magical?" said Mr. Beard in a cold, mocking voice. "Magical? Of course it is. Does that bother you? Eh? Eh?"

Johnny was stunned. So Mr. Beard had known all along that the ring was magic! A vague, shapeless fear began to form in Johnny's mind. What else did Mr. Beard know? And why, why on earth, had he given him this ring?

Mr. Beard took off his hat and laid it on the bench. His well-combed grayish-white hair seemed to glimmer and sparkle in the lamplight. It made Johnny think of snow.

And now Johnny noticed something else. Although he looked neat and well cared for, there was a faint musty odor about Mr. Beard. As if, perhaps, his overcoat had been kept in a damp, dark closet too long. Again Johnny had an overwhelming urge to jump up and run for home. But Mr. Beard's enormous eyes held him riveted to his seat.

"So the ring bothers you. Well, that's too bad," crooned Mr. Beard. His smile was cold and pitiless. "Yes, that is very, very sad. Perhaps this will help."

Mr. Beard raised his left hand. And suddenly Johnny felt as if his whole left arm was on fire. Pain shot up toward his shoulder, and the ring pinched, pinched horribly, far more painfully than Eddie's scissors had pinched. It felt as if red-hot pincers were squeezing his finger to the bone. Johnny's breath was taken away by the suddenness of this attack. He writhed to and fro and gasped, *"Stop! Stop! Please stop!"*

Mr. Beard lowered his hand, and the pain stopped.

"There now," he said, grinning evilly, "isn't that better? Of course it is. But I'm afraid you can't take the ring off. That is not part of my little plan. This should teach you to be careful about accepting gifts from strangers. You can never tell what the gift may turn out to be. But you accepted my ring, my little friend, and you will have to accept the consequences."

Mr. Beard chuckled. It was a low, weird chuckle that raised the hairs on the back of Johnny's neck. Johnny's face was pale and haggard. Sweat was streaming down his cheeks and stood in beads on his forehead. He felt like some small frightened animal caught in a trap.

Mr. Beard went on grinning. It was a goblinish grin, a grin that seemed to change the features of his face. "Haven't you guessed yet who I am?" he asked suddenly. *"Haven't you guessed?"*

Mr. Beard's voice sounded strange and wavery now. It was like the sound you get when a radio is not tuned in quite right. *Haven't you guessed? Haven't you guessed?* The question seemed to echo endlessly in Johnny's brain. And now the air around him was shimmering, wavering like water. And Mr. Beard's face changed, changed slowly, to the face of an old man with an overhanging forehead, a jutting chin, a hawkish nose, and deep-set, burning eyes. Instead of an overcoat he wore a heavy black woolen cape, and around his neck was a stiff white collar, the collar of a Catholic priest.

Johnny stared. He felt as if his eyes were going to pop out of their sockets. His forehead throbbed, and he was afraid that he might faint. Meanwhile across the street a shadowy figure was watching. It was the professor. He was crouched behind a large evergreen bush in somebody's front yard. What he saw was Johnny sitting on a bench that was bathed in the pale light of the street lamp. Johnny was staring hard at something, but the professor could not figure out what that something was. As far as he could tell, the bench—except for Johnny—was empty and bare.

CHAPTER NINE

The Sessions clock on the Dixons' sideboard was striking ten as Johnny opened the front door and stumbled in. Johnny felt numb and unbelievably tired. Every bone in his body ached. He felt as if he had stayed up three nights in a row without sleep. Was he awake or asleep now? It was hard to tell. He had seen the ghost of Father Baart. And the ghost had given him orders that in seven days he must return to Duston Park. He had to return at midnight next Friday, and he had to bring the blue figurine with him. He did not know why he had to do this, but he had been given very strict orders. He had to do this or he would die. The ring could kill him—this he had been told. He had also been told that the ring would be taken from him that night. He would be set free then, and nothing bad would happen to him. His life would be his own to live. But if he told anyone about the midnight meeting, or if he failed to show up, then he would die—he would die in horrible torment.

Dully, mechanically, Johnny unzipped his suede jacket and hung it on the coat-tree. He gazed blearily around at the friendly hall furniture. At the china umbrella stand, and the old pictures, and the deer head that was missing a glass eye. These things failed to comfort him. Was Grampa still up? The door of the living room was open, and a narrow bar of light shone out into the dark hall. Johnny heard a chair creak, and then he heard Grampa's voice.

"Johnny? That you?"

"Yeah, Grampa," Johnny answered wearily. He shuffled to the open doorway and stopped. "I'm sorry I was out so late."

Grampa shrugged. "It's okay. Your gramma's the worrier in this family, but she's gone to bed. I'm headed that way too, the way I feel." Grampa paused and looked at Johnny in a guarded way. "Do a lot o' prayin', did you?"

"Uh-huh. Well, g'night, Grampa."

"G'night, Johnny. Sleep tight."

Johnny stood in the doorway a moment longer, staring in at Grampa. He had an overwhelming urge to rush in and fall down on his knees at the old man's feet and tell him everything that had happened. But he was scared. He was scared, and he felt cut off from the rest of the world, like a prisoner in a dark, windowless dungeon. Still, he had to pretend that everything was all right. So he merely smiled wanly, turned, and began climbing the creaky oak staircase toward his bedroom.

Grampa Dixon rocked back and forth in his rocking chair. He looked thoughtful, and also tense. Suddenly he got up and walked across the room to the doorway that opened into the hall. He stood there a few minutes, peering up at the dark staircase. From the bathroom came the sound of running water. Grampa stepped back into the living room and pulled the sliding door shut. Then he walked over to his smoking stand and picked up the chipped green glass ashtray. He turned it this way and that in the lamplight and examined it as if it were a rare museum object. Then he set the ashtray down and began to pace back and forth on the rug, limping slightly because of his arthritis.

Tap, tap. What was that? Grampa turned toward the bay window and looked. There in the lower part of the window, his nose pressed to the glass, was the professor. He looked like a crabby sort of ghost, peering in. Grampa grinned. He had been expecting the professor to make an appearance. Quickly Grampa limped across the room and pulled back the door. Once more he glanced up at the dark staircase. No sound. Johnny must be in bed now and—probably—sound asleep. Grampa went to the front door and opened it. There stood the professor. He looked as if he had been wading through deep, wet underbrush. The knees of his pants were soiled, and there were sprigs of juniper decorating his coat here and there. His tennis shoes were soaked and caked with mud.

"Come on outside," whispered the professor hoarsely. He pointed back over his left shoulder toward the front yard. "I can't talk in the house. I'd be afraid Johnny would be listening down the hot-air vent or something."

Grampa followed the professor out across the front porch and down the steps. Halfway down the sidewalk the professor turned.

"Okay, this is fine," he hissed. He dug his hand into one of his coat pockets and pulled out a box of Balkan Sobranie cigarettes. Opening it, he took one out and lit it.

"Something is very wrong, Henry," he began as he puffed at his cigarette. "Very wrong indeed. I followed John down to the church, and then from there over across the river to Duston Park."

Grampa's mouth dropped open. "Holy God! What the heck'd he want to go over *there* for?"

The professor grimaced. "Your guess is as good as mine, Henry. But the most disturbing part is yet to come. When he got there, he sat down on a bench. Well, for a while then he just sat there. But all of a sudden he looked up, as if he saw somebody coming. And then, I swear to God, he sat there and had a conversation with somebody who *was not there*!" The professor paused and stared grimly at the ground. "Make something of *that*, if you can!"

Grampa was at a loss for words. He glanced up at the

dark window of Johnny's bedroom, and he shook his head. "My Lord!" he said in a low, somber voice. "What the devil do you think is wrong with him?"

The professor puffed some more at his cigarette, and he made little *hem! hem!* noises in his throat. This meant that he was thinking. "Henry," he said at last, "how long ago was it that his mother died?"

Grampa thought a bit. "It was . . . well, in July of last year. Almost a year ago now."

The professor nodded. "Mm-hmm. And then, right after that, his dad got hauled back into the Air Force, and Johnny got shipped up here to a strange new place, to new surroundings and new . . . new everything."

Grampa looked puzzled. He put his hands on his hips and peered down at the professor over the tops of his glasses. "Rod, what the heck are you tryin' to say?"

The professor gave Grampa a dirty look. "Don't call me Rod. But to answer your question, what I'm trying to say is just this: I think Johnny may be suffering— suffering mentally—because too many bad and upsetting things happened to him in too short a space of time."

Grampa wrinkled up his forehead. He looked very concerned. "You mean . . . you mean you think Johnny's gone *crazy?*"

"No, no, *no!*" snapped the professor, waving his hand impatiently. "I didn't say that! I didn't say that at *all!*" He heaved a deep sigh and, with an effort, controlled his temper. "What I am *trying* to say," he went on through clenched teeth, "is merely that people—even reasonable, sane people like you and me—can go off our trolleys temporarily if bad things happen to us. I don't mean that Johnny is ready for a straitjacket. But he *is* acting a mite peculiar, and he seems to be pretty unhappy. And so I think we'd better get him some help, and get it quick."

"Help?" said Grampa, still mystified. "What kind of help?"

The professor looked exasperated. "Mental help. Henry, you are living in the twentieth century, whether you like it or not. I know that psychiatrists aren't terribly popular yet in America, but I will venture to predict that in ten or twenty years there'll be hordes of them all over the country, making money hand over fist by solving people's problems. But all this is beside the point. We need to do something for Johnny right now. What's the name of your family doctor?"

"Doc Schermerhorn. You know him, don't you?"

The professor frowned. "Hmm. Yes, I know him. He's the one who diagnosed my cousin Bea's brain tumor as bad teeth, shortly after which she died. But I suppose he'll do. Any port in a storm, as they say. All right then: Why don't you get Johnny an appointment with good old Doc Schermerhorn? Explain the problem to the doctor, but don't tell Johnny why you're making him see the doctor. Tell him . . . well, why don't you tell him that you think he needs a checkup. Yes. That's it—a checkup. Meanwhile I'll see if I can figure out something else that might be done. All right?"

Grampa nodded. "All right. And thanks a lot for your help, Rod. You're a real good friend to Johnny."

"Don't mention it. Eventually John may need to see a real psychiatrist. I wish I could recommend one, but I know only one personally, and I wouldn't use him as a shield in a mud-ball fight. See you tomorrow. By the way, if you keep calling me Rod, I'll start calling you Hank. How about that, huh?"

Grampa shrugged helplessly. "But what the heck else can I call you? It's your name, isn't it?"

The professor grinned mischievously. "Call me Randy. My middle name is Random. I was named for Roderick Random, a character in a novel by Tobias Smollett. Good night." He turned abruptly and marched back across the street to his house, humming as he went.

Johnny did not get much sleep that night. He tossed and turned and kept waking up to listen for noises that weren't there. When he arrived in the kitchen for breakfast the next morning, he looked like the walking dead. His eyes were red, and his hair was mussed, and he felt prickly all over. He kept glancing nervously this way and that, as if he expected things to come springing at him out of the corners of the room.

Grampa was sitting at the kitchen table. He was sipping coffee and munching on a piece of toast. He glanced quickly at Johnny and then looked down at his plate. Gramma was over at the stove, stirring the oatmeal she always made for Johnny's breakfast.

"Hi," said Johnny sluggishly, and he slumped into his seat.

"Hi, there," said Gramma without turning around. "Nice morning, eh?"

"Uh-huh," said Johnny tonelessly. Bright sunshine was streaming in through the kitchen window, but it might have been raining or blizzarding for all he cared.

Silence. You could hear the electric clock over the stove buzzing.

"Johnny," said Gramma at last, turning and smiling kindly at him, "we want you to go see our doctor, Doc Schermerhorn."

"Yeah," Grampa added. He coughed to hide his nervousness. "We . . . we think you look kinda under the weather these days, an' so . . . well, we think you oughta have a checkup. We got you an appointment for this mornin', an' we called up the school an' told the sister you was gonna be home t'day, on account of you felt sick. The appointment is at nine o'clock. After you have your breakfast, we can get in the car an' go."

Johnny looked warily at Grampa, and then at Gramma. How much did they know? Had they found the figurine? Did they know about Mr. Beard? He swallowed hard and tried to look healthy and bright-eyed, which under the circumstances was rather difficult.

"Gee," he said, trying to be jaunty, "I don't see what

you guys are all worked up about. I mean, I feel great, I really do!"

This was more than Gramma could stand. She turned around with the bowl of steaming oatmeal in her hands, and she glared at Johnny. "John Dixon!" she exclaimed, indignantly. "That is the *worst* lie I have ever heard in my life! You look like the wreck of the *Hesperus*! I wouldn't be surprised if you was runnin' a fever! So don't sit there with your face hangin' out an' say that you feel all tippy-tip-top an' fine! Lord above!"

Johnny hung his head. Tears came to his eyes, and he bit his lip. Once again he had a strong urge to confess everything, but, as before, his fear held him back. The ring on his finger was like a dynamite bomb strapped to his body. If he told everything, it would go off.

"I . . . I'm sorry," he said in a low, sniffly voice. "I guess I don't feel too good today. I . . . I'd like to go see the doctor."

And so later that morning Johnny went downtown with his grandparents to see Dr. Schermerhorn. Dr. Schermerhorn had an office on the third floor of the First National Bank building on Merrimack Street. Dr. Schermerhorn was a fat, shambly man who chuckled a lot and told very bad jokes. He examined Johnny and announced that there was nothing wrong with him. He suggested that Johnny stay home and rest for a day or two. Gramma and Grampa were not satisfied with this, however. They insisted on talking to the doctor in private, and they told him about the strange things that

Johnny had been doing lately. Dr. Schermerhorn thought a bit, and he hemmed and hawed a bit, and finally he took a pad and a piece of paper and wrote a name and address on it:

> *Highgaz Melkonian, M.D.*
> *Zero Brattle St.*
> *Cambridge, Mass.*

"This guy is a psychiatrist," said Dr. Schermerhorn as he handed the slip of paper to Grampa Dixon. "Now, speaking personally, I don't care very much for headshrinkers. But it might be worth a try. This guy is as smart as a whip, an' he speaks about sixteen languages. Hypnotizes people too—that's one o' his big techniques. Watch out he don't hypnotize you outa too much money." Dr. Schermerhorn laughed a great deal at his little joke, and he was still chuckling as Gramma and Grampa left his office.

Gramma and Grampa went home and told the professor about their meeting with Dr. Schermerhorn. He listened with great interest and said that in his opinion Dr. Melkonian might be able to help. He added that he himself would pay for any fees that Dr. Melkonian charged. And he would also take care of getting Johnny an appointment with the doctor as soon as he could possibly manage it.

Johnny stayed home for the day. He did picture puzzles and read and listened to the radio. That evening he took some pills that Dr. Schermerhorn had given him, and he slept soundly all night. The next morning he felt much better and was ready to go back to school. But when he got downstairs, he found that he had another doctor's appointment. That morning he was going to go down to Cambridge with the professor. The professor did not tell Johnny that Dr. Melkonian was a psychiatrist. He was afraid that this might scare Johnny off. So he told him that the doctor was a hypnotist. He would help Johnny to relax and sleep soundly at night. Johnny had heard of hypnotists, of course. He had always kind of wanted to be hypnotized, just to see what it was like. So when he got in the car to drive down with the professor, he was a little afraid, but mainly he was eager and curious. In the back of his mind, though, like a dark cloud on the horizon, was the other appointment that he had: at midnight, on the seventeenth of May, in Duston Park. It would be scary, he told himself, but it was something he had to do. At least afterward he would be rid of the ring and the blue figurine. And maybe someday, far in the future, he would sit around and tell his grandchildren about the run-in he had had with a real live ghost.

Later that morning Johnny found himself sitting in a rather luxurious waiting room. There was a red Oriental rug on the floor, and the two big couches had puffy, hissy cushions of chocolate-colored leather. Near the door was a bookcase full of books in green and red morocco leather bindings. The books were about spiritualism and the occult, for the most part. While they waited the professor leafed through the books, and now and then he would say things like "Rubbish—utter rubbish!" or "My God, and people actually *believe* stuff like this!" Eventually the door of the inner office opened, and Dr. Melkonian stepped out. He was about as tall as the professor, and he had jet-black, greasy hair that ran in ripples across his head. His beard was also black, and well trimmed, and his lips were rosy red. He wore a light-gray cutaway and dark-gray pinstriped trousers and a double-breasted waistcoat and an ascot with a pearl stickpin. He looked like somebody who was getting ready to go to a wedding.

"Ah!" he said, nodding politely and smiling. "You're here—good! Please come in."

The professor and Johnny followed Dr. Melkonian into his book-lined inner office. They sat down in two easy chairs, and the doctor sat down behind his desk.

"Now then," said the doctor as he picked up his dagger-shaped letter opener and began to play with it, "what seems to be the trouble?"

The professor explained. He said that Johnny was very nervous and had had trouble sleeping. Dr. Schermerhorn had examined him and had found nothing wrong—nothing physical, that is—and so they had come here, hoping that Dr. Melkonian would be able to give help of a somewhat different sort.

Dr. Melkonian smiled suavely and turned to Johnny. He folded his hands on his desk, sat back, and asked

Johnny a couple of questions. Then he took a pair of collapsible pince-nez glasses out of his desk drawer, opened them up, and peered hard at Johnny through them. Then he got up and walked around to the other side of the desk and stood over Johnny, stroking his beard and sizing Johnny up through the glasses, as if he were going to paint his picture. Finally Dr. Melkonian paced back and forth a bit, and then, halting abruptly, he picked up the beater of a small bronze gong that stood on top of a glazed bookcase. He hit the gong and stood listening as the deep vibrating tones died away. Then he asked the professor to go out into the waiting room and wait.

Time passed. The professor smoked half a pack of Balkan Sobranie cigarettes, and he read quickly through several of the books in the bookcase. Finally the door of the inner office opened, and Dr. Melkonian appeared. He motioned for the professor to come in.

"Please sit down," said the doctor. "Would you care for a cigarette?" He held out a flat gray tin box of Balkan Sobranie cigarettes.

The professor grinned, and he took one. "So you smoke these filthy things too! It's my favorite brand!"

The doctor seemed pleased. "Ah! You are a man of distinction and culture. Of course I could tell that the moment you walked in. You are a professor—an intellectual. I like intellectuals. By the way, in case you are wondering where young John is, he is asleep on a bed in my examining room. I gave him a dose of sodium pentothal to ease him into hypnosis, and he's sleeping off the effects." Dr. Melkonian looked thoughtful and shook his head. "My, my! His case *is* a strange one! I've never handled one quite like it." He paused and looked hard at the professor. "You're a friend of his, aren't you? I mean, you're his special friend, I gather. Isn't that so?"

The professor nodded.

"And," the doctor went on, "you know him pretty well. Eh?"

Again the professor nodded.

"Well, then, tell me: Does he lie much?"

The question was so unexpected that the professor laughed. Then he shook his head. "No," he said firmly. "No. He doesn't lie much. Why do you ask?"

"Because his story's a real doozer, that's why. Actually I would agree with your impression of him. He seems like a pretty truthful kid. And he seems to really believe what he told me when I put him under hypnosis." Dr. Melkonian puffed at his cigarette. He stared at the green desk blotter and drew circles on it with his finger. Then he looked up suddenly. "He thinks he's met the ghost of a priest who used to live in your city."

The professor's mouth dropped open. Then he slapped his forehead with the palm of his hand. "Oh, *no!* Good gravy, I should have *known!* This is all my fault! I told him that stupid, idiotic tale about Father Baart, and he *believed* it!"

Dr. Melkonian gave the professor an irritated glance. "My dear sir, this is more than believing a story. Johnny has been having delusions—hallucinations. He actually thinks he's met with this ghost. And the ghost gave him a magic ring, and there's a blue statue mixed in with the whole mess somehow. What he told me just sort of came tumbling out, and it was all a bit confused. Anyway, he thinks he has to show up in this park next . . . next Friday, I think it is. If he doesn't, then bad things will happen to him. The ghost will kill him."

The professor looked worried. An odd thought had come into his mind. He examined the burning end of his cigarette and wrinkled up his nose. "You don't think . . ." he said hesitantly, "you don't think there might possibly *be* a ghost, do you?"

Dr. Melkonian looked at the professor incredulously for an instant. Then he burst into loud, uproarious laughter. "Oh, that's a *good* one!" he exclaimed, still laughing. "A *ghost*? Good night, man, what century are you living in? Ghosts went out when the electric light was invented! Ha-*haaa*! Ghosts! My, how you do run on!"

Dr. Melkonian went on chortling. Meanwhile the professor folded his arms across his chest and glowered crabbily. The psychiatrist's laughter died away when he saw the way the professor was looking at him. He picked up his letter opener and began nervously fiddling with it. It was almost as if he were going to use it to defend himself in case the professor sprang at him.

"Now, listen," said the professor, still glaring fiercely, "I am a cranky old man, and I don't enjoy being made fun of. If you think ghosts are such a great big fat joke, then what are all those ghost books doing out in your waiting room? Eh?"

Dr. Melkonian smiled and waved his hand airily. "Oh, they are there to amuse my patients. If you're a psychiatrist, you get a lot of nuts as patients, and nutty people often believe in ghosts. But you don't seem nutty to me. That's why I was surprised at what you said."

"I'm not nutty," said the professor through his teeth. "I'm as sane as you are, and possibly even saner."

"All right, all right, you're sane!" muttered the doctor irritably. "Let's change the subject! I believe you told me over the phone that Johnny lost his mother recently. Is that correct?"

"Yes. And, in a way, he also lost his father when he was hauled back into the Air Force to be a jet pilot. And these two things, to my way of thinking, may have—"

"Yes, yes!" cut in Dr. Melkonian with an impatient gesture. "I was about to say something like that myself. It seems to me likely that Johnny's delusions may be caused by the losses and dislocations that have occurred in his life recently." The doctor coughed self-importantly and picked up a pen. He began to doodle on the green blotter. "Now, what I would recommend," he went on, "is this: First I think we should explain to him, as best we can, that his mind has been playing tricks on him. Then I think you should go with him to that park—what was its name? Dusty Park? Is that right?"

"Duston Park," said the professor. "It's named for— but never mind. Go on."

"Ah, yes. Duston Park. Well, I think you should go there with him. He should keep his 'appointment' with this idiotic nonexistent ghost. Then, when no ghost shows up, and nothing hideous or nasty happens to him, he'll feel better. After that, as soon as school is out, I think he ought to be gotten out of town. Can his grandparents afford to take him on a vacation?"

The professor frowned and shook his head sadly. "No. They're as poor as church mice—poorer even. They—" He stopped because a thought had struck him. He snapped his fingers. "By God!" he exclaimed. "But *I* can take him on a trip! I'd *love* to! How about that? Eh? Eh?"

Dr. Melkonian grinned and nodded approvingly. "I think that would be just peachy-dandy. After the experience he's had—or thinks he's had—he needs to get away. Good. Excellent. I'm glad you'll be able to take him. Oh, by the way, I have something that belongs to him. A ring. It was on his finger, and he told me—under hypnosis—that the ghost of Father Baart had given him the ring. There's a letter B under the stone, and I suppose you could imagine that that stood for *Baart*. At any rate, according to Johnny the ghost had told him that he couldn't take the ring off. He would die if he did. Well, I took it off while he was asleep, and needless to say, he didn't die." Dr. Melkonian paused and dug his hand into his coat pocket. He fished out the ring and handed it to the professor. "Here. Do you know anything about it?"

The professor took the ring and turned it back and

forth, examining it. The small yellow stone sparkled fitfully in the lamplight. "No," he said slowly. "No, I don't know a blessed thing about it. I saw it on Johnny's finger one day, and I asked him where he had gotten it, and he said that his grandfather had given it to him. Then I asked his grandfather about it, and he said that Johnny had told him that *I* gave it to him. And from all this I concluded that Johnny had gotten the ring in some weird way and didn't want to tell anyone how." The professor flipped the ring up in the air and caught it. "I can't imagine that he stole it. I mean, he's not the thieving kind, and anyway, it doesn't look like it'd be worth stealing. The stone looks like a piece of bottle glass, and the body of the ring seems to have been made out of a rusty—"

At this point the door of the examining room opened, and Johnny came stumbling out. His hair was mussed, and his glasses were stuck on crooked, and his eyes were heavy with sleep.

"Hi," he said shyly. "Can I come out now?"

Dr. Melkonian asked Johnny to sit down in one of the easy chairs. And then he and the professor had a long talk with him. They explained to Johnny that Mr. Beard —otherwise known as Father Baart—was just a figment of his imagination. When Johnny heard this, he was shocked and bewildered. And then he got angry.

"Whaddaya mean, I didn't see him!" Johnny burst

out. "He was right there in front of me, just like you are!"

Dr. Melkonian smiled blandly and folded his hands on the desk. "Yes, yes, young man," he said smoothly. "You saw him, all right—only he wasn't there. He existed only in your mind. You've heard of mirages, haven't you? Well, Mr. Beard was like a mirage. You've been through a great deal of sorrow lately, young man. And sorrow can make us do strange things and . . . and *see* strange things. Please try to understand. I'm not saying that you're crazy or that you are lying. I'm merely trying to help you understand what happened to you."

Johnny was stunned. He didn't know what to say. "But . . . but . . ." he stammered, "he . . . he gave me a ring. . . ." Johnny looked down at his left hand. The ring was gone! Immediately he felt panic. What would happen to him now?

The professor held up the ring. "Dr. Melkonian took this off your finger while you were asleep," he said gently. "And don't worry—you're not going to die. There's no ghost, and no curse on you, or on that stupid blue hunk of crockery. So relax. Everything's going to be all right."

Johnny was not so sure about that. Dr. Melkonian and the professor talked very seriously with him for a long time. They argued and wheedled and were terribly logical as they tried to prove to Johnny that the ghost was just imaginary. Johnny resisted. Like most people, he resented it when somebody told him that he had not seen something that he really thought he had seen.

"But what about the ring?" he said insistently. "I mean, I didn't make it up. It's right there on the desk!"

"I know," said Dr. Melkonian patiently. "But you may have found the ring somewhere. Maybe you found it in the church that night when you thought you ran into Mr. Beard for the first time. Don't get me wrong. I'm not accusing you of lying. Mr. Beard must have seemed very, very real to you, as real as the professor here, or as me. But hallucinations are that way. You can't tell them from the real thing—you really, truly can't!"

Johnny was beginning to feel desperate. "But he talked to me! I *heard* him!"

Dr. Melkonian was not impressed. "Auditory illusions are common," he said. "Haven't you ever imagined that you heard somebody calling your name?"

"Okay, okay! But what about the time I told you about, when the ring flashed and this big wind knocked Eddie Tompke for a loop? How about that, huh?"

"Ring stones flash in the sunlight sometimes," said the doctor smoothly. "And as for the sudden wind . . . well, when you live in New England, you learn to expect things like that. The sea causes violent and unexpected changes in the weather."

"But Eddie was scared! He really was!"

Dr. Melkonian smiled faintly. "I'm sure he was. Something startling like that, a wind strong enough to knock you off your pins . . . well, it would have scared me too.

But it's a *natural* occurrence, not a supernatural one! Can't you see that?"

And so it went. After an hour of this sort of thing Johnny was beginning to have doubts about what he had seen and heard. He was still not entirely convinced, but he did have doubts. To tell the truth, he *wanted* to have doubts. If Father Baart was imaginary, that meant that he was not being threatened with death and destruction. On the other hand, the whole experience had been so real, so very real. Johnny's mind began to whirl. Nothing made sense anymore. Was Dr. Melkonian real? Was the professor real? Was *anything* real?

After the session in Dr. Melkonian's office Johnny rode home to Duston Heights in the professor's car. On the way the professor asked Johnny if he would like to go on a little trip with him after school was over. He explained that they would be going up into the White Mountains to sight-see and hike around, and maybe even do a little mountain climbing. Johnny was delighted by this idea. He had seen pictures of the White Mountains of New Hampshire, but he had never actually been up there on a visit. The trip sounded great. But now his mind shifted to a totally different subject: What was he going to do about the meeting that he was supposed to have—or wasn't supposed to have—with Mr. Beard in Duston Park next Friday night? The professor, glancing sideways, saw the look on Johnny's face, and he read his thoughts.

"Are you worried about your midnight rendezvous?" he asked with a slight smile.

Johnny nodded glumly. "Yeah. What . . . whaddaya think I oughta do?"

The professor's smile got broader and more confident. "Dr. Melkonian and I discussed this," he said briskly, "and we think that you should keep this so-called appointment. I'll go with you, and if a ghost shows up . . . well, I've always kind of had a hankering to see one. Are you game? Are you still willing to go?"

Johnny nodded. And so that was settled.

When they got back to Fillmore Street, the professor had a little talk with the Dixons. He explained to them as well as he could what Dr. Melkonian had said about Johnny and his problems. They were suspicious because they didn't like psychiatrists. They thought psychiatrists were like witch doctors, and they also thought that only crazy people believed in the things that psychiatrists said. But they were glad to hear that Johnny was not seriously ill, or ready for the insane asylum. And they thought that the trip to the White Mountains was really a very wonderful idea.

Several days passed. One afternoon when the Dixons were out shopping, the professor sneaked over and took away the blue figurine and the hollow book that held it. He had told Johnny that he was going to do this, and Johnny agreed that it was probably a good idea. Meanwhile Johnny went about his usual routine. He felt much, much better than he had felt in a long time. He slept soundly at night, and he did not hear any strange noises. He felt as if a great weight had been lifted from his shoulders. Naturally he was still a bit worried about Friday night. He did not know what was going to happen—not really. But, he reminded himself, the ring was gone from his finger, and he was still among the living. That was an encouraging thought, to say the least.

Friday night came, and it was pouring rain outside. The professor, umbrella in hand, met Johnny at the front door of his house at a quarter to twelve. Off they went, through the wind and wet, and finally they arrived in Duston Park. They stood around by Hannah Duston's statue and waited. The streetlight burned placidly, and the bronze Hannah hovered as menacingly as ever. The rain pelted down and made a racket on the stiff cloth of the professor's umbrella. Across the street the columned church loomed ghostly and white, thrusting its tall spire up into the night sky. Time passed. Fifteen minutes, half an hour. Nobody came.

The professor unbuttoned his raincoat, reached into his jacket pocket, and pulled out his watch. He glanced at it, sniffed, and looked around.

"Well," he said dryly, "Shakespeare would say that this was a night when the sheeted dead might squeak and gibber in the streets. But they ain't out, and on a night like this I don't blame them. No, sir, I don't blame them at all." He put his watch back in his pocket and peered owlishly around. Then he folded his arms, leered jauntily, and began to whistle. It was an old tune, "The Ghost of John." After he had whistled it through once, he sang softly:

> Have you seen the ghost of John?
> Long white bones and the flesh all gone?
> Oh, ooooh-ohhhhh!
> Wouldn't it be chilly with no skin on?

Johnny was not in such a jolly mood. He would have liked to be, but he couldn't manage it. He was staring intently at the great mass of shadow on the right side of the Unitarian church. Mr. Beard had walked out of that darkness last Saturday night. Try as he might, Johnny just couldn't persuade himself that Mr. Beard was imaginary. Yet the professor had told him that Mr. Beard didn't exist. Dr. Melkonian had told him this too. And now, here in the park, the professor was singing silly songs and making fun of ghostly fears. Johnny asked himself why he couldn't let go of his lingering fear and be cheerful too.

The rain kept pouring down. Now the wind began to blow, and Johnny felt rain slashing across his legs. A hard gust hit them, and the professor staggered sideways.

"Drat!" growled the professor as he pulled the umbrella back over their heads. He turned and looked at Johnny, who was still peering anxiously this way and that. "Look, John," he said in a more gentle tone, "we ought to be getting on home. Nothing is going to happen here, believe me. Nothing except that we might go to sleep on our feet. I'm an old geezer, and these late hours are not for the likes of me." He yawned hugely and flapped his hand against his mouth. "Let's head for home. How about it? Eh? Are you with me?"

Johnny nodded. They trotted off down the long sidewalk that ran diagonally across the little park. They paused at the curb, and a car whooshed past. Its taillights stained the pavement red. As they started across the street Johnny glanced back, one more time, over his shoulder. Nobody there. Why couldn't he be calm? Why couldn't he heave a deep sigh of relief? Well, he couldn't. Johnny felt nothing but foreboding, the fear of someone who is waiting for something to happen.

CHAPTER TEN

On a bright but chilly day in June, Johnny was sitting in the front seat of the professor's mud-spattered maroon Pontiac. They were zooming along on U.S. 3, which winds north into the White Mountains. Johnny felt happy. He was eating Planters peanuts out of a can, and he was gaping this way and that. They were in the mountains, in the mountains at last. For some time they had driven through rather blah, ordinary, slightly hilly country. Then in the distance Johnny began to see rumpled blue shapes. Now they were among those shapes. Great humped masses rose above the road. Trees marched up the sides of the mountains or bristled on their ridges—pines and maples for the most part, with here and there the startling white fork of a birch tree.

Crags and horns of stone topped some of the mountains or jutted from their sides. Here and there the masses of trees would part, and dizzyingly high on the side of a mountain, Johnny would see a slanting green pasture and wonder if animals or people could ever get to such a place.

Johnny was entranced. Growing up on Long Island, he had never seen mountains, except in pictures and in movies. Now here he was.

The professor darted a quick glance at his companion. "Well, are you enjoying yourself?" he asked.

Johnny nodded. He was sublimely happy. The sense of foreboding that had hung over him for days had finally passed away.

He had had three more sessions with Dr. Melkonian, and finally, after a lot of thought, he had become convinced—well, more or less convinced—that Mr. Beard was a product of his imagination. "Insufficient grievement" was the phrase Dr. Melkonian had used when he was explaining Johnny's problem. It was a pretty highfalutin term, but what it meant in plain English was that Johnny had not cried enough over the death of his mother. This, together with the other changes that had taken place in his life, had caused Johnny to see and hear things that weren't there. All these horrors and hallucinations were behind him now. The "magic" ring was in his desk drawer. The blue figurine was over at the professor's house. And right now the only question in Johnny's mind was, when do we eat?

He asked it aloud: "Hey, Professor! When are we gonna eat?"

The professor smiled secretively. "When we get there. And if you want to know where 'there' is, I won't tell you. So shut up and look at the scenery and munch your peanuts."

Johnny sighed. They had been driving since eight in the morning, and now it was one thirty. Even with the peanuts his stomach was rumbling. But he knew the professor well enough to know that pestering wouldn't help. He would just have to wait.

They drove on, through Franconia Notch, a gap in the mountains, and into the little village of Franconia. Then they came to the Gale River, a cheerful, sparkly little stream that ran noisily over a bed of smooth white stones. They crossed a green iron bridge that had flower boxes hanging on it, and they crawled up and down some steep hills. At last they came to a place high up in the mountains where a sprawly white farmhouse stood. Next to it was a building that looked like a large shed. It was covered with shaggy bark, and tacked to the front of the building were crooked letters that spelled POLLY's PANCAKE PARLOR. Johnny and the professor went in, and they gorged themselves. They ordered the All You Can Eat Waffle Special, which meant that the waitress kept bringing you buckwheat or corn-meal waffles until you couldn't stuff in one more single delicious syrup-soaked crumb. Then they stumbled outside to stare at the Presidential Range, Mount Washington, Mount Jefferson, and the others. They sat on a green bench for a while and talked while an enormous elm tree rustled overhead. And then they climbed back into the car and drove on to do more sight-seeing.

At the end of the day, tired and sunburned and happy, the two travelers found themselves standing outside a motel called Hag View Cottages. It was really a rather nice motel, in spite of its sinister name. Each cottage was a miniature house, with a steep green shingled roof and a little brick fireplace and a teeny-tiny screened porch. The name of the place came from the big tourist attraction in the area: the Hag. The Hag was a curious rock formation high up on the side of Hellbent Mountain. If you looked at the mass of shelving rock from the correct angle, you saw the face of an old witch. People came from all over the country to gape at the Hag and take pictures of it and buy souvenirs in the various gift shops in the area. Everything for miles around was named for the Hag: there were the Hag Kumfy Kabins, there was the Haggis Baggis Bar and Grill, there was Hag Lake, and there was Hagtooth Harry's Bear Ranch, featuring trained bears that did all sorts of fascinating tricks. Johnny and the professor had visited all the attractions and had seen the bears and had prowled through gift shops. They had slogged along wilderness trails and had sipped water from mountain streams. Now they were tired, just incredibly tired, and all they wanted to do— for the time being—was *rest*.

"Nice evening, eh?" said the professor. He gazed

placidly off across the road at Hellbent Mountain, which towered above them, a massive, dark presence. The late sunlight touched the horn of rock at the top with reddish fire. Birds rustled in a nearby tree, settling themselves for the night. In the deep blue of the evening sky a black bar of cloud hung.

Johnny was about to say something by way of response when the professor let out a loud exclamation.

"Drat! Double drat with cream and sugar! I'm out of cigarettes!" He held up the black Balkan Sobranie box and flapped the lid. "Now, where am I going to get cigarettes at this time of night? Hmmm? Tell me that!"

"How about the gift shop across the road?" Johnny suggested. "I thought I saw some cigarettes in there. Up in front, behind the cash register."

The professor was amused. He had almost gotten thrown out of the gift shop across the road. He had been criticizing the souvenirs, laughing at them and calling them "trash" and "rubbish." And he had done his criticizing in a rather loud voice. The lady who ran the shop, a persnickety sort of woman with chains on her glasses and a permanent frown on her face, had glowered at him a lot; finally she had told him that if he didn't like her stuff, he could keep his opinions to himself.

"Hmh!" snorted the professor. He squinted across the road. "My eyes are not good for distance, John. Tell me, does it look like the place is still open?"

Johnny nodded. "I think so. I mean, the light in the window is still on."

The professor heaved a deep pull-yourself-together-and-prepare-for-the-worst sigh. "Very well," he said resignedly. "If I must, I must. If you hear a loud crash, that will be the lady breaking one of her cheap souvenir lamps over my noggin. I'll be back in a minute." And he set out for the road with quick, purposeful strides.

Johnny watched him go. He felt a sudden pang of fear, fear of being left alone. Then he laughed. Imaginary ghosts, Father Baart, hallucinations—all that was in the past. He was okay now. Nothing could hurt him. He turned and started walking back toward the cottage, whistling softly to himself. As he went his footsteps crunched on the gravel path. Some of the cottages were lit; others were not. Out in front of one a car was parked, and a man was lifting luggage out of the trunk. Johnny walked on. Even though all the cottages looked alike, the one he and the professor were staying in was not hard to find. It was the one on the very end. Ah. Here he was. The yellow insect light burned over the door. And the professor had left one of the lamps burning, so the place had a homey look. Johnny looked up at the darkening sky, took a deep breath, and went inside.

But he had barely stepped through the door when he had the sudden, creepy, alarming feeling that something was wrong. What was it? He looked nervously this way and that. His suitcase lay open on his bed, just as he had left it. The professor's shirts were draped over the back of the armchair, but there was nothing frightening about that. *What could it be?* What had upset him?

And then he noticed. There was a small black book lying open on the bureau.

Johnny stared. He knew what the book was: It was a Gideon Bible. There is a society called the Gideons, and they put Bibles in hotel and motel rooms all over America. The professor had explained all this to Johnny when they found the Bible in the top drawer of the bureau. But then the professor had put the Bible back in the drawer. Johnny remembered seeing him do this. So what was the book doing out where it was?

Johnny drew closer to the bureau. The book was propped open with one of the professor's silver-backed hairbrushes. Johnny saw that the Bible was open to the twelfth chapter of Saint Paul's Epistle to the Romans. And he saw that part of the nineteenth verse had been underlined in red ink:

Vengeance is mine; I will repay, saith the Lord.

Johnny stared. The words seemed to squirm and writhe before his eyes. He felt cold all over. Those words were well known to him: They were part of the warning note that Father Baart had put into the black book. Johnny felt creepy, cold panic growing in his mind. Everything had been so peaceful, so happy all day. He had been having so much fun, and now . . . well, these words were like a lump of ice that had been placed suddenly in his hand. He was frightened and startled. And he felt very alone.

When the professor got back to the cottage, he was smoking a Murad, which was like a Balkan Sobranie only smellier. Slam went the screen door. The professor looked vaguely around, and he was brought up short by the sight of Johnny. Johnny was sitting, rigid and deathly silent, on the edge of his bed. It didn't take too many smarts to tell that Johnny was scared out of his wits.

"My God!" exclaimed the professor, taking the cigarette out of his mouth. "What on *earth* is the matter with you?"

Johnny didn't answer. He raised a trembling hand and pointed toward the bureau. The professor gaped at Johnny uncomprehendingly. Then he stepped quickly to the bureau and examined the book. Still, the professor was mystified.

"I don't get it," he said, turning to Johnny again. "I mean, is this some kind of game, or what? Did you underline these words?"

With an effort Johnny managed to speak. "I . . . I didn't do . . . it. The . . . the ghost must've."

"Oh, ghost my *foot*!" exclaimed the professor angrily. "I thought we were through with ghosts!" Immediately the professor was sorry that he had exploded at Johnny. He saw the hangdog, miserable look on Johnny's face, and he cursed himself for having such a rotten temper.

"I'm sorry, John," he said gently. "I shouldn't have snapped at you like that. I can see that you're upset—very upset. But all I see here are some words underlined in red. Now, they're certainly threatening words, but . . ."

The professor's voice trailed away. Suddenly he had remembered. "Oh, *I* see! And you think . . . no, no, it's just not true! These words here, about vengeance, they're really rather famous words. And people are always underlining passages in Bibles. Especially Gideon Bibles. They're kind of . . . well, they're common property, like the soap and the towels in the bathroom. This is nothing to get upset about, really it isn't!"

Again Johnny tried to speak. He was so upset that it was hard for him, but he managed it. "But . . . Professor! The . . . the book was propped open there when I came in. It wasn't like that before!"

The professor frowned. He bit his lip and thought. "Hmm. Well then, if what you say is true, this is a serious matter. But it doesn't have anything to do with spooks and specters. No. There's some fruitcake on the loose, some nut who runs into motel rooms and leaves threatening notes. Don't you see? That's what's happened."

Johnny tried hard to convince himself that the professor's explanation was the right one. While he was struggling with his thoughts the professor went over to the door and peered out into the night.

"I should've locked this door when we went out," he muttered. "But I didn't think there'd be anything to worry about way up here. Well, I'll lock the door tonight, and put the chain on too. Will that make you feel better?"

Johnny nodded. He was calmer now. The panic he had felt before was draining away. "Are you sure it's just some nutty guy?" he said at last.

The professor chuckled. "No. No, I'm not sure. It might be some nutty woman. But whoever it is, it's a flesh-and-blood kook, and not a ghostly one. Get Father Baart out of your mind, *please,* and let's settle down to a game of chess before we hit the sack. How about it? Eh?"

Johnny smiled and nodded. The professor went to his suitcase and got out his peg chess set. He set the game up on a little low table and moved the lamp on the bureau over so they could see to play. Johnny got a stool to sit on, and the professor perched on the edge of his bed. The professor lit another Murad, and Johnny ate some of the maple-flavored chocolate creams that he had bought earlier in the day. They started moving pieces, and the game got under way.

The first game went to the professor. He used the Nimzo-Indian Defense, which Johnny had not yet learned to overcome. But Johnny came roaring back in the second game, and halfway through he was up by two pawns, a bishop, and a knight. Then fatigue set in. It had been a long, tiring day, and now Johnny was feeling the effects. His eyelids kept closing, and his head began to sag forward. The professor was sleepy too. He started to yawn, and he yawned and he yawned. Finally he burst out laughing.

Johnny blinked. "What's so funny?" he asked sluggishly.

"Us!" said the professor, grinning. "We're both so socked that we can hardly stay awake, and yet we keep hacking away at each other in this game as if we were Nimzovich and Alekhine. Let's call it a day, eh? I'll put the set up on the bureau, and we can finish the slaughter tomorrow. What d'you say? Hmm?"

Johnny thought this was a great idea. He went into the bathroom and brushed his teeth and got into his pajamas. The sheets felt icy cold on his feet when he climbed into bed, but they soon felt warmer. He stretched his weary legs out, and the feeling of relaxation was delicious. Johnny sighed happily. The little window over his head was open, and through it he could hear the pines hissing in the wind. Across the room he could see a tiny red dot of fire as the professor smoked his last cigarette of the day. Soon he too would be in bed asleep. Johnny felt himself sinking down, down, down into warm furry darkness. His eyes closed, and he was asleep.

Night lay over the little cluster of green-roofed cottages. Now dark clouds came rushing in to cover the stars, and it rained. Wet drops pattered on the slanted roofs and on the gravel path. It rained for half an hour, a heavy pelting downpour. Then the clouds, driven by a strong wind, blew on past over the ragged top of Hellbent Mountain, and the stars shone down once more. Inside the cabin Johnny and the professor slept on. The chain lock and the sliding steel bolt held the door fast. But what was this? A tiny tinkling sound, and the chain fell from its groove. Now the bolt moved slowly, silently back. And the door of the cabin opened. A dark hunched shape stepped inside. Its body was a mass of shadows, but its face was lit by a pale, trembling light. The face was that of an old man with a heavy, over-hanging forehead, a jutting chin, a hawkish nose, and deep-set, burning eyes. Long sheaves of whitish hair hung down from the balding dome of the head. And the smile on the man's curled lips was evil and unearthly.

The shape paused just inside the door. It turned this way and that, as if doubtful about what to do next. Then it raised a shadowy hand, and suddenly, on Johnny's pillow, there appeared a yellow dot of light. It was the ring, the ring made from the bent nail. It had been locked up, safe and sound, in Johnny's bureau. But it was here now. Johnny slept on, but his hand crawled up onto the pillow, inching slowly forward, till the third finger of his left hand was thrust through the hollow circle of the ring. And now Johnny sat up. His face was lit by a pale light, and though his eyes were open, he did not seem to be awake. Slowly, moving stiffly and mechanically like a robot, he stood up, and began walking across the floor toward the door. The dark hunched form moved away, out through the open doorway, and Johnny followed.

CHAPTER ELEVEN

~~~

The professor slept on, but his sleep was uneasy. He was tossing and turning and moaning, and muttering words aloud from time to time. The professor was dreaming, and in his dream he was a boy again, and he was back in the little white schoolhouse where he had learned his lessons long, long ago. Up in the front of the room was his old teacher, Miss Vary. She was wearing her usual floor-length dress and stiff starched blouse with ruffles at the cuffs. On her head was a bun of gray hair, and on her face was a frown. She was frowning because young Roddy Childermass could not answer the question she had asked him. To make things easier, she had even written the answer on the blackboard. But he couldn't read the answer. It was all blurry and out of focus. Now

Miss Vary, her lips barely moving, asked the question again: *How could . . . Johnny . . . Dixon . . .*

"Yes, yes!" muttered the professor in his sleep. "How could Johnny Dixon *what?*"

But Miss Vary wouldn't tell him. She wouldn't repeat the rest of the question. Young Roddy asked her again; he pleaded tearfully, but she still refused. The professor thrashed back and forth in his bed, muttering and cursing. *How could . . . how could . . . how could Johnny . . .*

Suddenly the professor sat up. He was groggy but awake. And now, to his astonishment, he found himself thinking about something that he had never thought about before. He thought about the name Beard. Mr. Beard. That was the name of the man Johnny claimed he had met in the church. This was the man who had —supposedly—turned into the ghost of Father Baart. The professor was a learned man, and he knew several languages. He asked himself what the German word for beard was. *Bart*, that was what it was. There was a similar word in Dutch, *baard*. But Johnny didn't know German or Dutch. How on earth, then, how on earth had he hit upon a name that meant the same as . . .

The professor was wide awake now. Wide awake, and frightened. He fumbled for the lamp and turned it on. He found his glasses and shoved them onto his face. When he looked across the room he saw that Johnny was gone.

In an instant the professor was on his feet. He was pulling on his pants, pulling them on over his pajama bottoms. Now he was putting on his tennis shoes and lacing them up. He rushed to his suitcase, unsnapped it, and took out his flashlight. Cursing and growling to himself, he hurried to the door and yanked it open. Outside, the wind had died down, but the sky was overcast. Thunder rumbled in the distance—a storm was brewing in the mountains. The professor snapped on his flashlight and played the beam this way and that. Beyond the gravel path was long grass. A matted track had been beaten down through the middle of the grass. That had to be the route that Johnny had taken. The professor moved forward cautiously, eyes to the ground. The grass, slick with rain, squished under his feet. Now he was at the edge of the highway. Quickly he looked to the right and to the left. No cars. He raced across.

On the other side he stopped to pick up the trail again. As it turned out, there was no problem about that. The shoulder of the road was muddy from the rain, and there were tracks in the mud. They were the tracks of a boy's bare feet, and they were the only tracks around. *Good!* said the Professor to himself. *Stay on the muddy ground, for God's sake!* Setting his jaw grimly, he plodded on behind the footprints.

Before long the professor was swinging along on one of the trails that ran up the side of Hellbent Mountain. Luckily the White Mountains were low, humped mountains, and they could be climbed by anyone who could set one foot in front of the other. The White Cross was one of Hellbent Mountain's easier trails. Not that this mattered much to the professor. He was a tough, wiry little man who walked several miles each day and exercised with dumbbells. And in the mood he was in right now, he could have tramped up the side of the Empire State Building. He had—as the saying goes—the bit between his teeth.

Onward and upward. As he climbed the professor kept checking for footprints. When the trail ran over muddy ground, he had no problem. But for long stretches the trail was rocky. Nevertheless the professor did not falter. He marched grimly on, hoping that he would pick up the muddy tracks again. And he always did. But as he went he kept thinking: *Where is he going?* and *Is there anyone with him?* There was only one set of tracks—Johnny's tracks—but if the professor's suspicions were correct, Johnny might have company, company that left no tracks on the ground. He plodded on.

Up and up and up. Higher and higher, over rocks and roots and logs. The thunder was rumbling louder, and now and then lightning would flash off to the right or to the left. Drops of rain pattered among the leaves. *If there is a ghost, and he has dragged me out on a night like this, I'll brain him!* The professor said this to himself, grumbling as he climbed. He said this and things like it to keep up his courage. For to tell the truth, there was a cold pool of fear in his heart. He didn't know what he would find when he reached the end of the trail.

Finally the professor came to a place where the White Cross Trail met another trail, a rocky trail that ran off to the right, and to the left. Heaving a weary sigh, the professor stopped. He was beginning to get tired. He had been climbing for an hour, and his legs felt rubbery. His feet felt like they were going to fall off, and his shirt was wringing wet with sweat. "Ohhhh . . . *Gawwwwwd!*" said the professor, and he took off his glasses. He cleaned them with his handkerchief and put them back on again. Before him were two signs. One pointed off to the right. It said:

TO THE WHIMBY SCENIC OVERLOOK

The other pointed off to the left. It said:

TO THE ANGEL SCENIC VIEW

Tacked to the bottom part of this sign was a rain-spotted piece of cardboard. A message had been scrawled on it in ink. The ink was runny, but the message could still be read: Danger. *Rockslide.*

"Oh, great!" muttered the professor. "Rockslide! But have the rocks slid, or are they getting ready to slide? It would be nice to know which." Still grumbling, he played the beam of the flashlight back and forth over the trail. Lots of rocks, and some tough, knotty roots, but not much dirt to leave tracks in. The professor's heart sank. How would he know which way to go?

And then he saw something. Off to the left a root stuck up out of a clump of stones. And caught on the end of the root was a ragged patch of black cloth. The professor pounced on the cloth and ripped it away from the root.

He held it up, but then his nostrils twitched, and a shudder of disgust ran through his body. The cloth smelled. It smelled of mold, and of things worse than mold. With a quick twitch of his hand the professor threw the piece of cloth to the ground. At least he knew the way to go now.

The path curved around to the left, and the professor followed it, head down, flashlight beam constantly playing back and forth. There were no more tracks, but he had decided that this had to be the way. It was very dark. He couldn't see a thing beyond the pale circle cast by the flashlight's beam. He did notice, however, that the trail was getting narrower. And for some reason—he didn't know exactly why—he had the feeling that the ground was dropping away on the left. Finally he stopped and flashed his light to the right. A beetling, shelving rock wall rose above him. He flashed the light to the left, and he gasped. He was aiming his light out into nothingness. Now everything was clear—altogether too clear. He was on a very narrow path that skirted the edge of a precipice. How far was the drop? It was impossible to say—the beam of his flashlight didn't reach that far. Then thunder rumbled, and lightning leaped from the clouds above. The professor saw, for a split second, the glimmering surface of a lake. It was so far below that it looked about as big as his hand. The professor closed his eyes and swallowed hard. He was afraid of heights. High places gave him attacks of dizziness. But he gritted his teeth and said to himself a line from

Shakespeare that had always given him courage: "Before my body I throw my warlike shield. Lay on, Macduff, and damned be he that first cries hold, enough!" Then he began to pick his way forward again.

More lightning. More thunder. By the fitful pale flashes the professor caught glimpses, now and then, of where the path was going. It seemed to be winding up the eastern face of the mountain. Most of Hellbent Mountain was covered with trees. But the eastern side was a great shattered wall of stone three thousand feet high. Far above the professor's head, in the darkness, were the rocks that formed the face of the Hag. Not that he was terribly interested in scenic rock formations—not right at this moment, thank you. He was just hoping that the trail would hold out. And while he was hoping and wishing and worrying about Johnny, he saw, ahead of him, a glimmering yellow square. It was a wooden sign on a post. The sign said:

NO TRAIL BEYOND THIS POINT

The professor stopped. He inched closer to the sign and played the flashlight beam out into the darkness beyond. Immediately he saw what had happened. A rock slide had wiped out part of the trail. There was a little, narrow, wispy trail left, a ledge about a foot wide. If you were a mountain goat, you would have no trouble bounding along it. The professor's heart sank. Was this it, then? Was this as far as he could go? He tried to imagine himself picking his way along that narrow, bumpy lip of rock. Below, the vast empty darkness gaped. The professor shuddered. As he stood there he was in an agony of indecision. What should he do? What *could* he do?

And then the lightning flashed. Far ahead he saw something.

The trail—what was left of it—straggled along the mountain face to a wide, flat patch, a little grassy lookout that hung over the precipice. And when the lightning flashed, the professor saw two figures standing in this place.

"Oh, God!" said the professor, and he clenched his teeth and closed his eyes. He opened his eyes and began to pray. And as he prayed he crept forward out past the sign to the narrow rocky ledge. He shut off his flashlight, stuck it in his hip pocket, and stepped out into blackness. Splaying his body against the rough rock wall, he began to sidle along. The right side of his head scraped against the stone, and as he went his lips moved constantly. He was saying one of the prayers he had learned as a boy:

> St. Michael the Archangel, defend us in the hour of battle. Be our safeguard against the malice and snares of the Devil. Rebuke him we humbly pray, and do Thou O Prince of the Heavenly Host, by the power of God, thrust into Hell Satan and all the other evil spirits that wander about the world seeking the ruin of souls . . .

On crept the professor, inch by inch. He was in an ecstasy of terror. He hardly knew who he was or what he was doing. Horrible thoughts came into his mind. He kept having the awful, insane urge to throw himself backward over the ledge. His temples throbbed, and his glasses steamed up. His body was soaked with sweat. A flake of rock crumbled away under the pressure of his foot. He heard it clatter down, down into the void. Now he imagined that the rock wall was expanding and contracting, like a bellows. It would heave him over no matter what he did. He said the St. Michael prayer again, and the Our Father and the Hail Mary and several Glory Be to the Fathers. Slowly . . . slowly . . . had he reached the wide place yet? In the dark how would he know? Yes, how would he know? *That's a problem we haven't worked out yet,* the professor said to himself, and he began to giggle madly. Then he began to feel like throwing up. Inch by inch . . . inch by inch. . . .

The lightning flashed. He was inching along over solid grassy ground.

He had made it. The sick taste of vomit was in his throat, and he was shuddering, shuddering uncontrollably. But he had made it. And now the professor pulled himself together. He felt his old comfortable rage returning. Where was his blasted flashlight? It was in his hip pocket, where he had put it. He pulled it out and snapped it on. There in the middle of the grassy space stood Johnny. His arms were folded over his chest, and his eyes were closed. The corners of his mouth were curved up into an awful corpselike smile, and on his finger the yellow stone of the ring gleamed. Near Johnny stood a dark, fearful shape. Its face glowed faintly, and it was a face the professor had seen in old pictures. The lips of the figure moved. It spoke in a horrid, rasping, croaking voice:

"Why have you come here, old fool? This is my time of triumph! You have come to the place where my power is greatest. Soon I will live again, and this detestable creature will die. A fair exchange, they say, is no robbery. What say you? Are you ready for death too?"

The professor was frightened, but he felt anger welling up inside him. "My mother met you once when you were alive!" he roared. "And she said you were the rottenest, meanest creature that ever crawled on the face of the earth! Go back to the dead and leave this poor child alone!"

The professor was amazed at himself. He hadn't expected to say anything like this. But the anger felt good. It cleared his head and made him feel stronger. On the other side of the grassy patch the dark shape hovered, motionless. Then it raised its hand, and the professor felt a numbing shock. And his legs started to move. He was walking forward. He didn't want to go, but he had lost control of the lower part of his body. Frightened, the professor dropped his flashlight. It hit the ground and lay there, still burning. And then—without knowing why he did this—he jammed his right hand into his pants pocket. His fingers closed around his Nimrod pipe lighter. The lighter was a tube about two inches long.

When the two ends were pulled apart, a hole opened in the middle, and flame shot out. Nimrod lighters used a lot of fuel, but they worked in a gale, or in the rain. Fortunately the professor still had control of his hands. He pulled the lighter out and jerked at the ends. A spear of yellow flame shot up into the night. At the same time the professor dug in his heels and struggled as best he could to stop himself.

It worked. He came to a shuddering halt. And the dark shape sprang backward, covering its face with its hands.

The professor looked madly this way and that. He wanted . . . Ah! Glory be to God! Over in a corner of the little lookout place, piled against a cairn of stones, was some wood. But then his heart sank. It had been raining—the wood would be soaked. Frantically, still holding the blazing lighter, he whirled around. And now, for the first time, he saw the cave, a dark hole in the beetling rocky wall. Still holding the lighter up before him, he began to back toward the cave. A few more steps . . . he was in it now. Again he peered around. Ah! Magnificent! Stupendous! Piled in a corner just inside the mouth of the little cave were brush and twigs and sticks. The professor had his firewood after all.

He had to work fast though. The lighter might run out of fuel any minute now, and then where would he be? The professor's mind raced. Tinder. He needed tinder. Some old leathery oak leaves still clung to the broken branches in the pile of firewood. The professor ripped off a handful of them and piled them on the floor of the cave. He touched the lighter to the leaves, and they blazed. Working with mad, headlong speed, the professor snapped his lighter shut and raced over into the corner of the cave. He came back with handfuls of brush and little twigs. The fire grew. The twigs crackled merrily, and now he was throwing on thicker pieces of wood. Every now and then he glanced nervously outside. His flashlight lay where it had fallen. It still cast a line of pale light out across the grass. But except for that he could see nothing.

Now the fire was burning well. The professor stuck a broken branch into it, and it blazed. Armed with the branch, he stepped out into the open. Johnny had been standing in the middle of the little grassy space. But he was not there anymore. Sick with fear, the professor rushed forward. There stood Johnny, at the very edge of the precipice. One more step and he would plunge thousands of feet to his death. With a quick dash the professor made it to where he was standing. He grabbed Johnny's arm just as he was going over the edge and hauled him back to safety.

The professor turned. One hand was clenched tight around Johnny's arm. The other hand grasped the burning branch. It was raining lightly now, and the drops hissed in the fire, but the fire did not go out. Nearby, just outside the circle of light, hovered the dark figure. Its eyes were pinpoints of red light. Johnny sagged to the ground. His body was a dead weight. Stooping, the professor grasped Johnny under the right armpit. Slowly, painfully, he dragged him back toward the cave. He still held the blazing branch up with his free hand. It seemed to take forever, but finally they made it. And just in time too, because the rain was really pelting down now, and it was putting out the fire on the branch. With a sudden thrust the professor heaved the smoldering branch at the red-eyed figure that still hovered menacingly in the darkness. "Take that, you rotten thing!" the professor growled. Immediately he was sorry he had thrown the branch. He was going to need all the wood he could find.

Inside the cave the professor squatted. A pile of sticks lay near him, and he fed them, one by one, into the crackling fire. Beyond the shimmering wall of flame lay darkness. Darkness, and something else. The professor glanced anxiously to his right. There lay Johnny, cold and still. An awful thought occurred to the professor. Was he . . . *No, no, it couldn't be, he wouldn't allow it!* And suddenly a new thought came to the professor. He felt like a fool for not thinking of it before. He shuffled over toward Johnny on his knees and raised his limp left hand. Slowly he began working the ring off of the finger. It didn't want to come off, but the professor had strong hands. Bit by bit it moved, and then it was off. Johnny groaned. He opened his eyes and blinked and looked around blearily.

"Wha . . . where . . ." he muttered thickly.

The professor was overjoyed. Tears sprang to his eyes. "Thank God, thank God . . ." he whispered. He looked at the ring that lay in his hand. The stone was as dull and dark as a chip of coal. It did not even reflect the firelight. The professor had a great urge to fling the ring into the fire, but he thought better of it, so he stuffed it into his pants pocket. Someday some expert on magic might tell him what to do with the ring—if he lived to tell his experiences to anyone.

Right now there was a problem. The fire was keeping the evil creature at bay, but what would happen when the fire went out? Maybe the creature would have to vanish at dawn, but how far away was that? The professor hadn't brought his watch with him, and he hadn't noticed the time when he dashed out of the cottage. He looked at the pitifully small pile of wood, and he felt panic rising inside him.

Meanwhile Johnny was slowly returning to the world. He was bewildered and scared. Only a moment ago, or so it seemed to him, he had fallen asleep in his nice comfortable bed in the motel. Now he was in this dank, dark place where firelight leaped on the walls. And the professor was here too. What on earth had happened?

The professor would have comforted Johnny, but he had no time to be soothing and friendly. His mind was racing as he tried—tried desperately—to think his way out of the mess they were in. The professor believed in thought. He was always telling his students that you could get to the unknown by using the known. If you just put the facts that you knew together in the proper way, you might get some truly amazing results. *All right,* he said to himself grimly as he fed another stick into the fire, *what do you know?* Well, he knew that the ghost was there, outside the cave, waiting. And the ghost had said that he was strongest in this place. *Why?* Why was he strongest here, on the side of Hellbent Mountain, Why? Why? Why?

The professor scrambled to his feet. He began to pace back and forth while Johnny watched him, bleary-eyed and astounded. The professor's thoughts had run up against a blank wall. As he well knew, there are times when logic will not do you the least little tiny bit of good. So he let his mind ramble. It began to leap from one absurd thought to the next. He found that he was humming "Angels From the Realms of Glory," an old Christmas carol. How did it go?

> Angels, from the realms of glo-ry,
> Wing your flight o'er all the earth;
> Ye who sang cre-a-tion's sto-ry,
> Rum te-e dum and diddle durf . . .

It went something like that, anyway. From there, the Professor's mind leapt to the sign he had seen on the trail:

TO THE ANGEL SCENIC VIEW

What was this angel, anyway? High above their heads was the formation known as the Hag. But hags are not angels—that was a well-known fact. So the sign probably referred to some other rock formation. Hmm. Hmmm.

Now the professor found himself thinking about the note that had been found on Father Baart's desk the day he had disappeared, the note that had been a quotation from Sir Thomas Browne's *Urne-Buriall:*

The man of God lives longer without a Tomb than any by one, invisibly interred by Angels; and adjudged to obscurity, though not without some marks directing human discovery.

Again the professor returned to the fire. He crouched down and fed more wood in. There were only a few twigs left, and the fire would use them up in no time. He looked out through the shimmering waves of heat and the orange flames, but he could see nothing. Nothing but darkness and falling rain. *Angels . . . angels . . . interred by angels. . . .* What on God's green earth did that have to do with Father Baart? The quotation referred to Moses, whose body had been carried away by angels. That was what the Bible said, anyway. Moses had been buried in some secret place. Well, now: What about Father Baart? His body had never been found. *Interred by angels . . . interred by angels . . .* What if . . .

Suddenly the professor was down on his knees, scrabbling madly at the hard dirt floor of the cave. He had no tools, only his fingers, and this made digging difficult. Johnny, watching groggily, decided that the professor must have gone completely out of his mind.

"Hey, Professor!" he called. "Whatcha doin'?"

"I'm digging!" the professor yelled over his shoulder. "And you should dig too! Dig over there? Use your hands! Use anything! But hurry! We haven't got much time!"

Johnny didn't understand why he was supposed to dig, but he did as he was told. He grabbed a broken piece of wood and began gouging at the floor of the cave. Dirt flew, and dust rose in a choking cloud. It was a strange scene, the two of them scraping away like dogs looking for bones. Gouge, gouge, scrape, scrape! Johnny wielded the stick like a trowel, and before long he had dug a pretty good-sized trough in the hard-packed dirt floor. But he had to stop because his glasses were covered with steam and powdery dirt. He laid down the stick and pulled out his handkerchief. Then he took off his glasses and wiped them and put them back on. Johnny looked down. He did a double take and looked again. At the bottom of the trough he had made, he could see stone. Rough, flat stone, part of a slab maybe. And imbedded in the stone was something that glimmered faintly in the firelight. A coin. A gold coin, it looked like.

"Hey, Professor!" Johnny yelled. "Come over here! Come over here quick!"

The professor looked up. His fingers were bleeding and sore, and his eyes were wild. "What? What? What is it?"

"I dunno, only . . . only I think you better come over here quick!"

The professor stumbled to his feet. He hurried over to

where Johnny was kneeling and dropped to his knees beside him. The professor's mouth fell open. "It's a coin," he said wonderingly. Then he looked closer. He brushed dirt away with his fingers and winced as he did this, because his fingertips were rubbed raw from the digging. Now he pulled out his Nimrod lighter again and snapped it open. He held the flame down close to the coin, and then he let out a loud, joyous whoop. The professor knew a lot about old coins, and he knew that this was an Elizabethan gold coin called an angel. On the side that was up, there was a picture of an angel. He had wings and a halo and a spear in his hand, and he was killing a dragon with the spear.

"An angel, by God!" roared the professor. He turned to Johnny and grabbed the stick from his hand. Madly he jabbed at the earth with the stick. "We've got to get this stone up!" he muttered feverishly. "We've got to, we've *got to*!!"

Meanwhile behind them the fire burned low. It had collapsed into a heap of red coals. And beyond the fire, at the mouth of the cave, a fearful shape hovered. Johnny turned and looked, and he went rigid with terror. He opened and closed his mouth and tried to speak to the professor, but nothing came out. The professor went on flailing with the stick. At last he had uncovered the ragged edges of the flat stone. He forced his sore, bleeding fingers down into the dirt and pried with them. "Oh, God, oh, God!" he breathed, and he gasped and winced because of the pain in his fingers. But he got a grip on the stone and forced it up. Underneath was a dark hollow space. The professor plunged his hands down into the hole. He came up with a small wooden box. He handed it to Johnny, and then, suddenly, he seemed to become aware of something.

There was very little light in the cave now. The fire was down to a few smoky red embers, and there was no wood left.

"Johnny! Pick up the lighter! Quick!" The professor's voice was feverish.

Johnny set the box down on the ground. He looked around frantically. "I can't see it! Where is it?"

"There! There! God's teeth, man, can't you see it? It's right down by my knee! Hurry! *Hurry!*"

Johnny scrabbled around in the dirt, and his hand closed over a small cold metal object. He had seen the professor use the lighter many times, so he knew how it worked. He tugged at the ends of the cylinder, and there was a snap and a tiny white spark, but nothing else happened. He tried again and again and again. But the lighter was out of fuel. And behind them the last red coal of the fire winked out. Now Johnny felt his flesh go goose-pimply all over. And he smelled a horrid, sickening odor, the odor of corruption. Johnny and the professor turned. At the mouth of the cave they saw a face. An ugly, cruel, grinning face. It was lit by an unearthly light, and it hovered in the thick darkness.

The professor sprang to his feet. "Go away!" he yelled. "Go away, you rotten thing, you filthy, evil—"

But the professor never finished his sentence. A shadowy hand stretched out toward him, and as Johnny watched in horror the professor *disintegrated*. His body turned to dust, and his empty clothes fell in a heap and lay there on the cavern floor.

CHAPTER TWELVE

Johnny was stunned. He was numb with horror. What had happened was so awful that he could hardly believe it. The professor was gone. There was not even a body left. Just a heap of clothes. And now the nightmarish face of Father Baart floated closer.

"It is your turn now," said the croaking voice. "You must die so that I may return to the sweet land of the living. Stand and face me! *I command you to obey!*"

Johnny hesitated. He was frightened half out of his mind, but he was angry too. Ferociously angry. Tears sprang to his eyes. He wanted to throw something—a rock or a boulder— at the horrid mask that floated before his eyes. With a sudden lunge he reached out and grabbed the small wooden box. He leaped to his feet and threw it. The wood of the box was rotten, and it disintegrated as the box flew through the air. And suddenly the air was full of dust. The grinning mask crumpled like a paper lantern thrust into a fire. And then there was a blinding flash of red light and a deep *boom* that seemed to come from far, far down in the bowels of the mountain. The floor of the cave began to shake and tremble and jump crazily about. Clots of dirt and pebbles fell from the ceiling of the cave. Johnny looked around, panic-stricken. What could he do? Suddenly the floor of the cave heaved, and Johnny was sent sprawling. He fell across something soft, something that cried out with a loud crabby voice.

"For the love of God, would you stop kicking me? What do you think I am, anyway?"

Johnny could not believe his ears. The voice was the professor's voice! He was there, alive, lying under Johnny!

With a loud triumphant yell Johnny scrambled to his feet. He was so excited and overjoyed that he hardly knew what he was doing. "Professor? Is that really you?"

The familiar raspy voice responded. "Of course it's me! Who else would it be up here in this disgusting, dank, smelly cave? I came all the way up here to rescue you, and the least you could do is—"

The professor's speech was cut off by a sickening jolt. Once again the cave floor heaved, and more rocks and pebbles came raining down. Now the professor was on his feet. "*Outside!*" he yelled, and grabbing Johnny's arm, he hauled him out through the mouth of the cave. The mountain went on shaking and shivering. It was very dark outside, and it was still raining, but from somewhere far above them Johnny and the professor heard a drumming, thundering roar that grew louder and louder by the second. In terror they clutched each other and waited. It was a rockslide, another rockslide. Down the side of the mountain, boulders came crashing, thundering, and rolling. The din was terrific. Johnny and the professor put their hands over their ears and closed their eyes. Any second now they would be killed, crushed by tons of rock—or so they thought. But then the din died away. From far below they heard splashes and more rumbling. Then came silence.

Johnny opened his eyes and took his hands away from his ears. He was soaked with rain, and it was still black as pitch outside, but he knew that the avalanche had passed them by. He turned to the professor excitedly. "Hey, Professor!" he yelled. "Hey, we're safe! We're safe! The ghost is gone! Hey, you were great, you really were! I thought you were dead, but you're alive! It's wonderful! Whee! Whee!" He waved his arms and started dancing around on the grass.

The professor stood stock still. He smiled faintly. "Oh, I assure you, it was nothing!" he said with a modest wave of his hand.

And then he fainted dead away.

When the professor woke up, he found Johnny kneeling over him. He looked very anxious. It was getting light out. The sky was blue again, and the sun was rising from a reddish haze over on the other side of a wide valley. Birds were twittering in a crooked little juniper tree that grew near the mouth of the cave.

"Are you all right, Professor?" Johnny asked.

The professor sat up. He harrumphed and looked at Johnny, and then he quickly looked away. Plainly he was embarrassed. Fainting was not the sort of thing he usually did. "I'm perfectly all right," he snapped, brushing dirt off his sleeves. "And by the way, what is all that nincompoopery about me being dead? Do I look dead to you? Eh? Do I?"

Johnny explained to the professor as well as he could what he had seen—or rather, what he *thought* he had seen—inside the cave.

"Well, well, well!" said the professor. He cocked his head to one side and looked thoughtful. "It must have been an illusion. Old Shagnasty must've known that we had him in a corner. We were within an inch of victory when we found the box that had his ashes in it. He wanted you to despair and give up. I'm so glad you didn't!"

"So'm I," said Johnny. Once again there were tears in his eyes, and he shuddered as he realized how narrow their escape had been.

The professor got to his feet. Fussily he brushed off the seat of his pants and his trouser legs. He glanced this way and that. "By the way," he said, "what was all that godawful noise? When I woke up from . . . from whatever happened to me, it seemed like the whole bloody mountain was coming down around our ears."

Johnny pointed off to the right. It was not hard to see the path that the rockslide had made. A great raw gash ran down the rugged face of the mountain. The falling stones and boulders had wiped out what was left of the trail. Johnny and the professor would have to be rescued by somebody, somehow.

"Heavenly days, McGee!" exclaimed the professor in wonder. He walked to the edge of the drop-off and looked down. The path of the rockslide continued down the steep side of the mountain. Far down, near the bottom, you could see where trees had been mowed down by the rolling boulders. The professor squinted and strained to see, but his eyes were not good for distances. "Tell me, John," he said, beckoning for Johnny to come closer, "are those boulders in the lake way down there?"

Johnny walked to the edge and looked. "Yeah . . . yeah, I guess so," he said uncertainly. He turned and pointed up. "They came from up there."

The professor looked where Johnny was pointing, and then, in a flash, it hit him. He knew what had happened. The Hag had come down. The jutting, shelving boulders that formed the face of the Hag had been dislodged by the earthquake, and now they were down in Hag Lake, thousands of feet below. The professor started to laugh. He couldn't help it—it all seemed terribly funny. He thought about all the things that had been named for the Hag. He thought about Hag View Cottages and Hag Kumfy Kabins and pieces of pine-scented soap shaped like the Hag and most of all of Hagtooth Harry's trained bears. It was just a stitch, it really was.

When the professor's laughing fit had died down, Johnny asked timidly, "Did . . . did the ghost make the earthquake happen?"

The professor was startled by this question. Now all the things that had happened last night came flooding back into his mind, and he grew serious again. "Yes," he said, nodding, "or rather, his passing caused the earth to shake. But he's gone now, gone for good. At least, I hope—" The professor paused. He had been gazing vaguely around while he talked. Now he found that he was looking at a funny-shaped outcropping of rock that rose above the entrance to the cave. The morning sun was shining on the eastern flank of the mountain, and it touched the ragged finger of rock with golden fire. The rock looked like an angel. It had wings and a head and even something that looked a bit like an outstretched hand.

"*Interred by angels* . . ." muttered the professor, nodding. "One was up there, and the other was a coin. Clever, clev-*er*! But I wonder who planted him up here? Who did the burying, I mean?"

Johnny had not understood anything that the professor

said. Not that it mattered much to him at the moment. He was just happy to be alive. He still did not understand how he managed to travel from his bed at the motel to this wild, lonely place in the mountains. But he knew it all had something to do with the ghost of Father Baart— who had turned out to be real, after all. And he also knew—or hoped—that the professor would explain everything to him in good time.

Right now, however, there were other problems. "How're we gonna get down, Professor?" Johnny asked.

The professor made a puckery face. "Oh, I suspect that we will have company shortly," he said dryly. "Earthquakes are not common up here in the White Mountains, and when the local yokels see what has happened to their chief tourist attraction, there'll be lots of people swarming all over the mountain, taking pictures and saying tsk-tsk and standing around with their mouths hanging open. So don't worry. In the meantime, however, we will have to wait. It'll be boring, I know, but it beats plunging thousands of feet to our death. Don't you agree?"

Johnny agreed. So he sat down on the dewy grass with the professor, and they talked about this and that as the sun rose higher and higher. In the middle of their conversation the professor got up and went into the cave. He came back with the slab of stone that had the gold coin embedded in it. He remarked sadly to Johnny that Elizabethan gold angels were much prized by coin collectors. Then he added that the coin had lain for years over the grave of a wicked sorcerer. And after that the professor took the slab to the edge of the precipice and heaved it over, coin and all. Then he went back and sat down next to Johnny on the grass and talked some more. Presently they began to hear a *whap-whap* sound in the air and the whirring of motors. They looked up and saw a helicopter. It was coming down over the top of Hellbent Mountain.

Johnny and the Professor sprang to their feet and began yelling and waving frantically. The helicopter hovered briefly near the top of the mountain, and then, slowly, it moved closer. It floated down onto the grassy patch while its whirling propeller stirred up a mighty wind. The engine sounds died, and the propeller spun to a halt. A door in the cabin of the copter opened, and a state trooper climbed out. He was a man about sixty years old, with a leathery, seamed, sunburnt face and a gray crew cut. He wore the green uniform of the New Hampshire State Police, and when he opened his mouth, he talked with a heavy New Hampshire accent.

"Hi, there!" he said, waving. "I bet you guys was wonderin' how you was gonna get down, wasn't you?" He turned and peered down over the edge of the chasm. Then he let out a long, low whistle and shook his head gravely. "Gonna be hard on the tourist business," he said mournfully. "What in heck you think people'll come up here to see now?"

The professor thought of the towering, rugged mountains, and how they looked in autumn, when their sides were alight with colors, yellow and orange and red. He thought of the mountain streams and steep gorges and the layers of brown needles covering the forest floor. He thought of the mountains in moonlight, and lonely night drives along the Kankamagus Highway.

"Oh, I imagine there'll be *something* to look at," he said sarcastically. "There's always Hagtooth Harry's trained bears, after all."

The policeman sighed and shook his head. "Kids'll be awful disappointed," he said. Then he added, as an after-thought, "You folks like a ride back, would you?"

The professor and Johnny climbed into the helicopter with the trooper and rode back with him to the motel. Johnny enjoyed the ride tremendously. He had only been in an airplane once before in his life, and he had never ridden in a helicopter. The professor closed his eyes and spent his time trying to remember the kings and queens of England and which one came after which. After an amazingly short ride the copter set them down on the front lawn of the Hag View Cottages. But as soon as they stepped out onto solid ground again, Johnny and the professor ran into more trouble. A State Police cruiser was pulled up in front of the cottage they were staying in. The owner, a bald, red-faced man with a big overhanging beer belly, was talking excitedly with two policemen. When he saw the two missing persons walk-ing toward him, he nearly had a conniption fit.

"*Jeezus!*" he exclaimed in a loud foghorn voice. "Where'd *you* two come from? Gawd, I thought you two was at the bottom o' Hag Lake or someplace! What happened to ya? Huh?"

On the spur of the moment the professor made up a cock-and-bull story: He explained to the owner that Johnny was nervous and excitable. He had been under a doctor's care recently because of the loss of his mother. Last night, for no reason at all, Johnny had plunged out into the night, and the professor had followed after, and then the two of them had got trapped by the earthquake and had to be rescued.

The owner accepted the story—at least he said that he did—but he glowered suspiciously at the professor. The professor didn't know it, but he had been under suspicion from the time he signed the register in the motel's office. He had signed it "Roderick Childermass, Ph.D.," and as far as the owner was concerned, all Ph.D.'s were kooks and Communists and God knows what else. As for the policemen, they were just glad that they could call off the search and go home.

After the policemen had gone and everyone had calmed down a bit, Johnny and the professor packed their bags and got ready to leave. The professor went to the motel office and paid the bill, and off they went. They drove straight back to Duston Heights, stopping only in the town of Rochester to grab lunch at a drive-in. When the professor's car pulled up in front of the Dixon house, Gramma and Grampa knew right away that something had happened. The travelers had come back from their trip two days early, and they had come back suddenly, without calling, without explanations. At first Johnny and the professor were very secretive and close-mouthed about what had happened. Finally, though, the professor admitted that something very strange and mysterious and scary had happened. And he said that he'd tell the Dixons the whole story in three days time. In the meantime he needed to make a few phone calls and confer with a friend of his. Then—after grabbing a Bible out of a bookcase and making Johnny swear to secrecy on it—the professor left.

Three days passed. During this time Johnny stayed at home. He did jigsaw puzzles and played cribbage and checkers with Grampa. Meanwhile across the street the professor was busy. First he called up Dr. Melkonian and chewed him out. Without giving the doctor a chance to get a word in edgewise, he told him that he was a pompous, posturing bearded hornswoggler, who ought to have his psychiatric license revoked. He accused him of mystagogic muckification and pointless prattle, and he said that he'd ask for his money back if he thought that there was any chance it'd be returned. He ended up by slamming the receiver down hard in the doctor's ear. This little rant did not make a whole lot of sense, but it left the professor feeling relieved and curiously satisfied. Next the professor hired a cleaning lady to whip his house into shape so he could have visitors in. Finally he made a long-distance call to an old friend of his up in Durham, New Hampshire, the town where the University of New Hampshire is.

On a Friday night at around eight o'clock Gramma, Grampa, and Johnny went across the street to the professor's house. When he met them at the door, he was wearing a red damask smoking jacket that smelled of mothballs, and he was smoking Balkan Sobranie tobacco in a pipe—he had decided that cigarettes were bad for his health. The professor ushered his guests into the living room. A bright fire burned in the fireplace, and the crystal pendants on the ormolu candlesticks on the mantel glistened and glittered. In an easy chair by the fire someone was sitting—a stranger. He was a tall, weedy man with a fluff of white hair on his head. He wore big, goggly, horn-rimmed glasses, and his long pointed nose was bent and ridged. The shoulders of his tweed jacket were covered with dandruff, and the elbows had leather patches. His pants were baggy and shapeless, and his long pointed shoes looked as if they were made out of cardboard.

"This is Professor Charles Coote," said Professor Childermass, pointing toward the man. "He is an old friend of mine, and he has written a very important book on Egyptian magic. He also knows a great deal about *ushabti*—of which we shall have more to say later."

Professor Coote stood up and made three quick nods of his head: one toward Johnny, one toward Gramma, and one toward Grampa. Then he sat down and folded his hands in his lap. Professor Childermass led Gramma and Grampa over to the sofa and asked them to sit down.

Johnny sat down on a straight chair and squirmed impatiently. He did not know what the professor was going to say or do, and he was impatient and extremely curious.

The professor took his pipe out of his mouth and harrumphed. He looked around as if he didn't know where he was, and then, with a sudden abrupt dash, he went to the sideboard and came back with a rattling tray full of bottles and glasses. He set the tray down on the coffee table with a jolt, and then he backed away into the middle of the room. Entertaining people was a chore for the professor. He didn't do it often, and whenever he did it, he acted as if he was trying to get things over with as quickly as possible.

"Well, uh . . . just help yourselves," he said, waving his hand awkwardly. "There's . . . well, there's sherry for those who drink it, and imitation nonalcoholic sherry-flavored punch for those who, uh, like that sort of, uh, thing. Just . . . uh, help yourselves." When this little speech was over, the professor retreated to the fireplace and stood there, fidgeting. Professor Coote got up and loped across the room to the coffee table. He poured himself a glass of sherry and went back to his chair. Then everyone else started to help themselves. Johnny wanted a glass of sherry, but he could tell from the look in Gramma's eye that he'd better have some of the other stuff instead.

When everybody had something to drink, the professor poured himself a glass of sherry. He downed it all in one gulp, wiped his mouth with the back of his hand, and slammed the glass down on the mantelpiece. After some harrumphing and nose blowing he turned again to face his company and began to speak. He had called them here, he said, to clear up some of the mysteries of the last few months. First he wanted Johnny to speak.

"Who, me, Professor?" Johnny asked, tapping his chest with his finger.

The professor nodded. "Yes, you, my friend. I want you to begin at the beginning and tell these folks everything you can remember about the whole crazy business that you have been mixed up in."

Johnny thought about the figurine that he had stolen from the church. He glanced nervously at Gramma and Grampa. "Do I have to tell . . . *everything?*" he asked.

"Yes," said the professor firmly. "Everything! Don't leave out a jot or a tittle or a smidgin. And don't worry. No one's going to disown you or clap you in irons. Please begin."

So Johnny told his tale. He told about how he had stolen the figurine from the church. He told about Mr. Beard and the ring and the weird and ghostly things that had happened to him after he put the ring on his finger and began saying the prayer to Thoth and Touëris. Finally he told about what had happened to him and the professor up on Hellbent Mountain at midnight, amid lightning and thunder and rain. Of course, since Johnny had been unconscious or sleepwalking during part of this last episode, the professor had to fill in details. He did this in a very dramatic way, with lots of gestures. Finally, when Johnny and the professor had both said their piece, silence fell. There was no sound in the room but the crackling of the fire. Then Gramma stirred restlessly in her seat. She gave Grampa a hard nudge in the ribs with her elbow and said to him in an accusing tone, "How about *that*, eh, Mr. Smarty-pants? Mr. Know-it-all? You're the one that said the ghost was just a lot o' foofaraw, an' I was just an old superstitious Irish lady. What d'ye say now? Eh?"

Grampa groaned. "I think I'm gonna be hearin' about this for the next six months," he said, and he gave Johnny a humorous look, as if to say "What're you gonna do?"

Gramma turned to the professor next. She gave him her best glower, as if she felt everything that had happened was his fault. "Them spiders," she began, wrinkling up her nose in disgust, "was . . . was they somethin' that came with the blue doojigger in the black box?"

The professor turned to Professor Coote and grinned. "You're on, Charley," he said. "Help the lady."

Professor Coote spoke up. He sounded very scholarly and precise. "In a manner of speaking, yes. They were a manifestation of the forces—the evil forces— that dwelt inside the blue figurine. Insects have often been associated with evil spirits. Beelzebub was one of the Seven Devils, and his name means 'Lord of the Flies.'"

"What was that blue thing, anyway?" Grampa asked. "Did old Baart make it, or was it a souvenir?"

Once again Professor Coote responded. "No, in spite of that label he put on to confuse people, it was a genuine *ushabti*. A tomb figurine. But it was not Egyptian. It came from Kush, which is an ancient kingdom far up the Nile, beyond Egypt. The kings of Kush conquered Egypt in the eighth century B.C., and they ruled there for a while. When they were driven out, they carried Egyptian customs back to Kush with them. Then, when they were back in their own little kingdom, the Kushites pretended that they were Egyptians. They followed Egyptian religious practices, wrote Egyptian hieroglyphics, and they made *ushabti*. Of course, the workmanship of these *ushabti* was rather crude." He turned to the professor and smiled patronizingly. "No doubt, Roderick," he added, "that is why you failed to see that the *ushabti* was genuine. A genuine ancient object, I mean."

The professor scowled. "Oh, don't be silly, Charley," he snapped. "I wouldn't have known a genuine Egyptian *ushabti* if it bit me on the rear. But like most scholars, I like to pretend that I know more than I really know. So I screwed up. Shut your trap and have more sherry."

There was an awkward silence. Professor Coote blew his nose, and then he made a dash for the coffee table. He refilled his glass and hurried back to his seat.

Grampa still had some questions to ask. "Look, Rod," he said, pointing a long freckled finger at the professor, "if that blue doohickey was really ancient, where'd old Baart get his hands on it? D'ye think that guy, that wood-carver, gave it to him?"

The professor stuck his hands in his pockets and shrugged. "I think that the wood-carver must have given the figurine to Father Baart. By the way, would you care to see it—or rather, what's left of it?"

Gramma, Grampa, and Johnny all said "Yeah!" or "Sure!" or "You're darn tootin'!" together.

The professor walked over to the armchair where Professor Coote was sitting. Down on the floor, hidden by the shadow of the armchair, lay a large black book. Stooping, the professor picked the book up and carried it out into the center of the room. Johnny, Gramma, and Grampa all leaned forward eagerly to look as the professor flipped the heavy cover back. Inside the book lay the shattered, charred fragments of the blue figurine.

"My gosh!" Johnny exclaimed. "Did you do that to it, Professor?"

The professor shook his head. "Nope. I found the figurine like this when I got back home from our trip. I think it must have happened when you scattered the ashes of our dear old friend Father Baart. The ring got the same treatment. I took it out of my pocket when I paid our bill at the motel, and it looked like this."

He reached into the pocket of his smoking jacket and took out a twisted wad of blackened metal. "The stone was gone," he added as he showed the remains of the ring around. "It vaporized, or exploded, or something. I found little bits of fingernail parings and hair—I think that's what they were. They were clinging to the metal part of the ring, and I imagine they were under the stone. I burned them in my fireplace, which is the proper thing to do with such rubbish, I believe."

"Yes," said Professor Coote, nodding. "I believe you did the right thing." He smiled prissily and added, "You also ought to bury the remains of the *ushabti* and the ring. Bury the pieces under the roots of a yew tree in a cemetery by the light of a new moon. That is the method of disposing of cursed objects that is recommended by the great astrologer Regiomontanus. He says that—"

"You mean Johannes Müller of Königsberg, don't you?" said the professor, interrupting. "That's his real name, you know."

Professor Coote gave his friend a dirty look. "Yes, I *know* what his real name is. But it would be stuffy and pedantic to call him Johannes Müller, wouldn't it? And we wouldn't want to be stuffy and pedantic, would we?" Professor Coote had been looking for some way of getting even for the "shut your trap" remark. Now he sat back in his chair, satisfied.

Johnny spoke up again at this point. There was still a lot about this business that seemed puzzling to him. "How come old Father Baart wanted to kill me?" he asked. "Was it just because he was evil, or what?"

The professor studied the burning tobacco in the bowl of his pipe. "I think," he said slowly, "that it was going to be a case of a life for a life. Baart was dead, you see.

He was an evil sorcerer, and he made some mistake in the middle of his sorcerizing. What he did wrong we'll never ever know, but it got him killed. His body was burnt to ashes, and it was buried up in the mountains by . . . by whom? The wood-carver? The Powers of Darkness? I don't suppose we'll ever know. But to continue: Baart was dead, but his spirit still hung around on the earth. He haunted St. Michael's Church, and he would have gone on haunting it—harmlessly—forever, I suppose. But you took the lid off the cauldron, Johnny. You disregarded the warning and took the figurine out of the church. A church is a sacred place. It can keep the powers of evil in check. But once you removed the figurine from the protection of the church, then—quite literally—all hell broke loose. And what did our old pal Baart want? He wanted to be *alive* again in the world. So he appeared to you as Mr. Beard, and he gave you a ring. And the ring gave you power, power against bullies like Eddie, but that was not its real purpose. No. The ring gave Baart power over *you*. It was part of his plan. With the ring on your finger you were going to die at midnight in Duston Park, and he was going to come back to the world of the living. In what form, I wonder? As young Johnny Dixon? As Father Baart? As Mr. Beard? God only knows."

Johnny shuddered. "He said I would die if I took the ring off my finger. That's why I kept it on."

The professor grimaced. "That was just a lot of threatening folderol, my boy. You could have taken the ring off whenever you wanted to. Actually the situation was just the opposite of what that old devil said it was. You would die if you *did* keep the ring on your finger. So it was really very fortunate that . . . that . . ."

The professor's voice trailed away. He suddenly became very gloomy and bit his lip.

"What's the matter, Professor?" Johnny asked anxiously.

The professor heaved a deep despairing sigh. He walked to the fireplace and knocked his pipe out against one of the andirons. "Oh, nothing," he said sadly. "Nothing much. It just suddenly occurred to me that Dr. Melkonian probably saved your life. He took the ring off, as you know, when you were asleep in his office. If you had still had the ring on when we went to Duston Park at midnight, the old buzzard would've made short work of you—and of me too, perhaps. And was I nice to Dr. Melkonian? Was I grateful? No. I chewed him out over the phone because he was wrong about what was wrong with you. Sometimes I think I'm really not a very nice person." Tears came to the professor's eyes. It looked as if he was going to break down and bawl right there in front of everybody.

Johnny jumped to his feet. There were tears in his eyes too. "No, Professor!" he exclaimed loudly. "You're not a bad guy! Really, you're not! If you hadn't've come up to rescue me, I'd be dead! You stood right up to the ghost, and you're a real brave guy! Honest, I mean it! Don't cry! Please don't!"

The professor blinked and sniffled. He took out a red cotton handkerchief and blew his nose loudly. "You think I'm okay after all?" he asked, looking around uncertainly.

"Of *course* you're okay!" put in Professor Coote. He reached up from where he was sitting and patted the professor reassuringly on the arm. "You have one of the filthiest tempers I've ever seen in my life, but when you're not screaming and raging or throwing the furniture around, you're an extremely kind and thoughtful person. Of course," he added, poking a forefinger at the professor, "it *would* help your reputation if you'd sit down tomorrow and write a nice note to Dr. Melkonian explaining how you really feel now and apologizing to him for your boorish behavior. I mean, it would be the decent thing to do."

The professor took off his glasses and dabbed at his eyes with his soggy handkerchief. Then he put his glasses back on and looked around the room. Everyone was smiling at him. Grampa was grinning and puffing contentedly at his pipe. Even Gramma, whose normal expression was a frown, was smiling now.

The professor harrumphed and rubbed his elbows. He stuck his pipe back in his mouth and tried to act stuffy. "Hmh!" he snorted. "Well now, is . . . is there anything more I can get for anybody? Eh?"

"There certainly is," said Professor Coote in a dry, sarcastic voice. "I believe it is the custom to serve cookies and other edible goodies with sherry. And indeed, when

I was in your kitchen earlier this evening, I saw a plate loaded with such items. It was sitting on the counter by the sink. And that's where it still is."

The professor's face turned red. He slapped his forehead with the flat of his hand. "Phooey!" he roared. "I *knew* I had forgotten something! Just a minute." He turned on his heel and dashed out of the room. A moment later he returned. In his hands was a china platter, and it was loaded with all sorts of tasty things. Peanut-butter cookies and chocolate brownies with chocolate frosting and chocolate candies (creams—the professor hated caramel fillings) and piles of bonbons on paper doilies. Then the professor went back and came in a second time. This time he was carrying a plate with a Sacher torte on it. A Sacher torte is a kind of super chocolate cake. It has lots of layers, and the spaces between the layers are filled with apricot jam. And on the outside is lots of rich, dark chocolate frosting. The professor had made the Sacher torte the night before, and he had hidden it away in a cupboard to bring out as a surprise. But amid the fuss and flurry of getting ready for guests, he had forgotten all about it.

Now that the serious part of the evening was over with, everybody ate and drank and talked and had a good time. Later Professor Coote wandered upstairs and while looking for the bathroom accidentally discovered the fuss closet. The professor had never told him about the closet, so naturally he wondered what it was for. But when he went downstairs and asked, the professor told him that he was thinking of becoming a Buddhist monk in his old age and was practicing meditation. This explanation did not quite fit the sign on the inside of the closet door, but Professor Coote was not one to pry, so he let it go at that. Then the professor sat down at the piano in the living room and played old songs, and everybody joined in, singing along. Gramma insisted that the professor play "Just a Song at Twilight," and he did, and Gramma got very weepy, because that had been her mother's favorite song. And then the professor played "The Star-Spangled Banner" and told everybody that the evening was over and they had to go home.

Out on the front walk under the stars the professor was saying good-bye to Johnny. Professor Coote was upstairs in bed. He was staying overnight at the professor's house and was going back to Durham in the morning. Gramma and Grampa had already gone back to their house. Johnny didn't want to go—not yet. He kept thinking that there were more things that he wanted to ask the professor. But he was so sleepy and stuffed with goodies that he could not think what these things might be.

"Well, John," said the professor amiably, "you've had quite an adventure! Did you think it was as good as the ones you listen to on the radio? Hmm?"

Johnny made a face. He was thinking that adventures were fine as long as you could sit in your living room and listen to or read about them. "You know what I wish?" he said suddenly.

"What? What do you wish?"

"I wish I had a nice safe kind of magic ring that would keep Eddie Tompke off of my back."

The professor shook his head vigorously. "No, you don't! You don't wish that at all! If you had a ring like that, it would be . . . well, it would be like carrying a loaded pistol around all the time. Sooner or later you'd be tempted to use it in some evil way, and then you'd be horribly sorry afterward. People don't know when they're well off. I knew a fellow in college, and he was fun to be around. But he was all weak and wasty—didn't have any muscles. So he worked out with weights and ran for miles, and he turned into a real rough and tough bruiser. He also turned into one of the biggest bores on the face of the earth. All he would ever talk about was how he had turned himself into a muscleman. Stay like you are. You'll be a lot—"

"John-nee! John-nee!"

Johnny turned and looked. It was Gramma. She was standing on the front steps with her hands cupped to her mouth.

"What is it, Gramma?" he yelled. "What's the matter?"

"It's your father! He's on the phone! He's calling all the way from some place I never heard of! Come on! Hurry!"

Johnny was overjoyed. He hadn't heard from his dad in a long time, and he had been wondering what was happening to him. "Oh, my gosh!" he exclaimed excitedly. "Hey, Professor, I gotta go! Thanks for everything! I . . . g'bye! G'bye!"

He started across the street, but at the curb he came to a sudden halt. He turned and gazed forlornly at the professor. He had just realized that his dad would never, ever believe the stuff he had to tell him.

The professor had read Johnny's thoughts. He started to chuckle. "What's the matter, John?" he asked.

Johnny did not see what was so funny. "What'm I gonna tell him, Professor? My dad, I mean. What'll I say?"

The professor thought a second. "Tell him that you got all A's in school, except for the D you got in penmanship. And don't lie about the D. It's always best to tell the truth."

Johnny stared in astonishment. Then he burst out laughing. Still laughing, he turned and ran back across the street toward the lighted doorway of his house.

The Mummy, the Will, and the Crypt

JOHN BELLAIRS

~❧ ❧~

Frontispiece and maps
by Edward Gorey

For Candice, a fellow writer and a good friend

The Mummy, the Will, and the Crypt

CHAPTER ONE

❧ ● ❧

"Professor, can we go home yet? My feet feel like they're gonna fall off."

"No," said the professor firmly. "We can *not* go home yet. We still have two more rooms full of pictures to look at, and then there's Mr. Glomus's office. No doubt there are art treasures in there. And if you are ever going to become a cultivated young man, you are going to have to learn to appreciate great art. So come along. You can rest your tired feet later."

"But, Professor . . ."

"But me no buts, John. If an old coot who's pushing seventy from the wrong side can keep on his feet, so can you. I'd hum a marching song for you, but I'm afraid that guard over there would not be pleased. I'll give you another two minutes to rest, and then we'll have to move on."

Johnny's voice was a despairing wail. "*Two minutes?*"

"Yes, two minutes. And I'll be counting them on my watch. So relax while you can."

Johnny Dixon and Professor Childermass were sitting on a padded bench in a room full of oil paintings by seventeenth-century Dutch masters with names like Rembrandt and Ruysdael and De Hooch. For hours they had been tramping through the rooms in the vast Glomus mansion—rooms full of the paintings, suits of armor, weapons, and art objects that H. Bagwell Glomus had collected during his long life. Mr. Glomus had been able to collect art because he was rich. And he had gotten rich by starting a cereal company.

A real health nut, Mr. Glomus had invented a cereal drink called Glomar. It was black and looked like coffee, but it was made out of wheat. Even though Glomar tasted terrible, people bought it because they wanted to stay healthy. Later Mr. Glomus invented Oaty Crisps, a cereal that was sort of like Kellogg's Corn Flakes. Oaty Crisps really caught on, and soon Mr. Glomus was able to build a large cereal factory in the town of Gildersleeve, Massachusetts. The factory was right across the street from Mr. Glomus's mansion, and Johnny and the professor had toured it earlier in the day.

Johnny sat still and tried to relax while the professor glowered at his pocket watch, mentally ticking off the seconds. They were an odd pair, these two. Johnny was twelve. He was pale, blond, and freckled, wore glasses, and was rather shy. The professor was short, his nose was red and pitted, and he had muttonchop whiskers that sprouted wildly from the sides of his head. The professor looked crabby, and he actually did have a rotten temper. But he was also a very kind man. He lived across the street from Johnny and his grandparents, and as strange as it may seem, he had become the boy's close friend.

Johnny needed friends. He had a bad habit of avoiding other kids his own age, and after a year of living in the town of Duston Heights, Massachusetts, he had only just begun to change. Most of the time—when he was not at home curled up with a book—Johnny preferred being with the professor.

"Well, time's up! On your feet!" The professor barked out this command and stood up. He stuffed his watch into his pants pocket and turned to Johnny.

"Oh, okay!" Johnny groaned. Wincing, he dragged himself up into a standing position.

However, the professor was not in a sympathetic mood. "What's the matter, John?" he said, in a dry, sarcastic tone. "Is it arthritis or tetanus or frostbite?"

Johnny gave the professor a dirty look. "When this is over with, I want a hot fudge sundae," he muttered sullenly. "Can we go get one?"

The professor smiled as he thought of hot fudge. As Johnny well knew, chocolate was one of the professor's obsessions. "Yes, indeed," he answered, nodding agreeably. "I was planning to do that. There is a wonderful ice cream parlor here in Gildersleeve, and they make big gloppy calorie-filled hot fudge sundaes. We will go there —*after* we visit Mr. Glomus's office. So march!"

Mr. Glomus's mansion was built like a castle, and his office was at the top of a tower at the northeast corner. Johnny and Professor Childermass had to walk down a corridor, up a flight of marble steps, down another corridor, and up a curving flight of cast iron steps before they finally got there. The furnishings in the large circular room were heavy and gloomy. There was a grandfather clock and two heavy mahogany cabinets with glass windows. Mr. Glomus's desk was made of paneled oak, and it looked as if it weighed a ton. On top was a clock made of black marble. The chairs were massive, with black leather upholstery, and there was a dark green rug. A row of narrow windows ran all the way around the room, and in the top part of each one was a piece of colored glass. Since it was a sunny day, the light that came in threw circles of red and purple and green and blue light on the floor, the only cheerful things to be seen.

As Johnny and the professor entered the room they suddenly realized that they had walked in on a guided tour. Clustered together near the desk was a small group of elderly men and women. The guide, a rather bored-looking young woman with a portable loudspeaker in her hand, was rattling off a speech that she must have memorized. Her voice had a singsongy rise and fall, and from the expression on her face she might as well have been talking about the price of beef in Argentina.

". . . and so, in the year 1936, although he had acquired great wealth and built up a thriving business, Mr. Glomus became depressed. He worried and stayed awake nights and began acting strangely. His family doctor advised him to try new things to break out of his rut. So Mr. Glomus began to study demonology and witchcraft, reading all the great books that have been written on this rather sinister subject. He took a trip to Europe and came back with some objects that had once been associated with the practice of witchcraft. Some of these may be seen in the small cabinet by the grandfather clock, including the so-called magic mirror that once belonged to Dr. John Dee, the sixteenth-century sorcerer. But, alas, in spite of his newfound hobby Mr. Glomus continued to feel depressed. And on the evening of November 13, 1936, Mr. H. Bagwell Glomus left his office—this very office that you are standing in—and he went home and drank a mixture of strychnine and cognac. The next morning his servants found him dead on the floor of his bedroom."

Several people gasped. The professor smiled knowingly and nudged Johnny in the ribs.

"Pay attention," he whispered. "This next part is really interesting."

"On the morning following Mr. Glomus's death," the guide went on, "a sealed envelope was found on his desk. In the envelope was a note that revealed the startling fact that Mr. Glomus had *not* left a will!"

There were more gasps and cries of "Oh, no!" and "How 'bout that!" One old lady with a raspy, irritating voice spoke up and said, "What happened to all his moolah, then?"

The guide coughed and looked pained. "Mr. Glomus's . . . uh, his money was divided up among his heirs according to the laws of the Commonwealth of Massachusetts. But this is not the end of the story. It seems that soon after Mr. Glomus's death some odd notes were found in his diary. The members of the Glomus family have deduced from them that a will does indeed exist. And they think that Mr. Glomus left behind clues to its whereabouts. The clues are supposedly right here in this very room!"

Immediately everybody in the group began gawking, turning their heads this way and that. But with a smug smile on her face, the guide went on.

"A great effort has been made to keep things in this office *exactly* as they were on the day Mr. Glomus died. And Mrs. Annabelle Glomus, Mr. Glomus's widow, has offered a reward of $10,000 to anyone who can figure out the hiding place of the will." The guide sighed. "Puzzle experts—people who know about cryptograms and codes—have been brought here from all over the world in an attempt to figure out where the mysterious will is hidden. Many have tried, but all have failed. It is generally thought, though, that the clues are to be found among this rather odd collection of objects on the library table over there. If you will all follow me, please."

With a lot of shuffling and whispering, the group followed the guide across the room to a large walnut table. The tourists talked a good deal among themselves about the objects. Some of them snapped pictures. Poor Johnny kept trying to get a good look at the table, but he couldn't see a blessed thing. He was blocked by several people, but most of all by a tall and very fat man who wore a New York Yankees baseball cap.

"Now, then," said the guide, smiling politely, "this concludes our tour. There is another group due to arrive in a very few minutes, so I must ask you to follow me downstairs to the main hall, where souvenirs may be purchased. Thank you."

Muttering and snapping still more pictures, the group filed out of the room. Johnny and the professor stepped aside to let them pass. Now the two of them were alone, with no one blocking their view. Johnny looked around. Although he could peer at the tantalizing objects on the table now, he decided to save that for last. With the professor following close behind, he started on a little tour of the room. There was Mr. Glomus's desk, with its gloomy marble clock and some pens and pencils laid out in a neat row on the dusty green blotter. Johnny's gaze traveled along the curve of the wall, past the grandfather clock. Between two windows was a china closet, and next to it stood the cabinet with the witchcraft collection in it. Farther along the wall were some paintings in heavy gilt frames. One showed a sunset scene in the White Mountains of New Hampshire. Another showed the Hudson River near West Point. Then there were some chairs, a marble bust of Mr. Glomus on a fluted column, and finally the library table with its peculiar assortment of objects. Johnny walked up to the table and stood with arms folded, looking down. At the front of the table was a big sign that said DO NOT TOUCH. Behind the sign in one corner of the table was a very handsome walnut-and-ivory chess set. It stood on a polished wooden board, and the pieces were all lined up the way they are at the start of a game. Next to the chess set lay an old, yellowed Greek newspaper. It was folded neatly in half so that the top part of the front page showed. The large black letters at the top told—Johnny figured—the name of the newspaper:

ΕΘΝΙΚΟΣ ΚΗΡΥΞ

The second word in the title had a circle drawn around it in red ink. The third item on the table was an old, weathered signboard. It was shield-shaped, with a fancy scalloped border at the top. Johnny could see two rusted screw-eyes sticking out of the top of the board, and he figured that the sign had once hung from a crosspiece on a post or on an iron bracket of some kind. The lettering on the sign was faded, but it could be read. It said YE OLDE TEA SHOPPE. That was it—there was nothing else on the table.

The professor stood watching Johnny with amusement. "Well?" he said in a raspy, needling voice. "Have you figured out where Mr. Glomus's will is? You've had oodles of time."

Johnny gave the professor an exasperated glance. "Aw, come on, Professor! You know darned well that nobody could figure this out! Not even if they had a million and a half years to do it!"

The professor grinned and rubbed his chin. "I will admit," he said dryly, "that the puzzle is a tough one. What possible connection can there be between a chess set, a Greek newspaper, and a sign from somebody's tea shop? Of course, there may not be any connection at all. What I mean is, if I were you, I wouldn't beat my brains out over this ridiculous puzzle. As the young lady pointed out, Mr. Glomus was a bit sick in the head at the end of his life. He may have just wanted to irritate his relatives by holding out the possibility that there was a will after all."

Johnny was about to open his mouth to say something when a mean-looking woman with narrow hornrimmed glasses appeared at the door.

"You two will have to leave now," she snapped. "Didn't you hear what the guide said? There's another group due in."

The professor turned to her with a malicious gleam in his eye. He hated bossy, officious people. "Is it your job to be nasty and impolite?" he asked. "Or are you just doing what comes naturally?"

The woman's mouth dropped open, and while she stood there looking astonished, Johnny and the professor walked out past her and down the stairs. As they went, the professor began to chuckle in a self-satisfied way.

A few minutes later Johnny and the professor were sitting in an ice cream parlor that had old-fashioned wooden booths and Tiffany glass lampshades and a marble counter and even a jukebox. The jukebox was playing "Come On-A My House," a song that the professor hated, and he flinched now and then while digging into his hot fudge sundae. Johnny was having a tin roof sundae, which is a hot fudge sundae with peanuts on top. And as he slurped and munched and crunched he felt at peace with the world. But Johnny liked puzzles—chess puzzles and picture puzzles and Chinese puzzles and all the other kinds—and so his mind kept drifting back to Mr. Glomus's office and the mysterious array of objects on the table.

The professor was a shrewd man, and he could tell from the expression on Johnny's face that he was still wrestling with the problem. "Come on, John," he said. "Give it up! It's a puzzle that can't be solved. It's like the Mad Hatter's riddle: *Why is a raven like a writing desk?* There isn't any solution."

Johnny popped a fudge-covered peanut into his mouth. He chewed it slowly and stubbornly. "Professor," he said thoughtfully, "what do you think would *really* happen if somebody found Mr. Glomus's will?"

The professor shrugged. "The law divided up Mr. Glomus's estate among his heirs. His wife and his two worthless sons got some money, and so did his two surviving brothers, and his sister. If a will turned up, there'd be fights in court and yelling and screaming, some reshuffling of the money, and then a lot of hatefulness and ill will. It'd be like setting off a bomb in a fireworks factory."

Johnny laughed at the professor's description. But then he paused. "Hey, wait a minute! If it's gonna cause so much trouble to find the will, how come Mrs. Glomus wants to find it?" he said.

The professor licked his spoon pensively. "Well," he said slowly, "I don't know much about Mrs. Glomus, but I suspect she is one of these fussy, finicky types that think everything in life should come out neatly, with straight edges and all. Rich people are *supposed* to leave wills, and so it may really gripe her to think that her late hubby didn't leave one. Or maybe she's just greedy. She may not be satisfied with the money she got under the present arrangement and may be gambling that she'll get more if a will is found. I don't know. But if I were her, I'd leave things the way they are. If a will is found, she may lose her ten thousand dollars, and more besides."

Suddenly the professor jumped up. "See here, now! I've had enough of chewing over the affairs of the Glomus family. It's time for us to pay up and hit the road, because I have mountains of papers to get through tonight. Term papers! *Arrgh!* Reams and reams of indigestible nonsense! But they have to be done, I suppose. Come on, John. Let's get a move on."

Later, as the car roared on through the twilight toward Duston Heights, Johnny sat slumped in the front seat with his eyes closed. It had been a busy, exciting day, and now the motion of the car, the droning of the motor, and the whiz of passing cars were putting him to sleep.

CHAPTER TWO

✹❂✹

It was a few weeks later, a chilly night in late September. Johnny was walking home from a Monday night Boy Scout meeting at the Methodist church, wearing his new Boy Scout uniform with the red neckerchief and the bright red-and-white numerals *112* sewed on the right shoulder. For months the professor and Johnny's gramma and grandpa had been trying to persuade him to join. They were worried that Johnny was too much of a loner, and they wanted him to break out of his shell and make some friends. And so he had finally signed up with Troop 112. The first meeting had not been much. Before the scoutmaster showed up, the boys spent their time horsing around, playing games of Steal the Bacon (using a knotted towel for the bacon) and throwing the cakes of Ivory soap at each other that they were supposed to be carving into little animals and things like that. But when the meeting started and things quieted down a bit, Johnny decided he liked the scoutmaster and most of the other boys too. He was stubborn about changing his mind, but he was beginning to think that maybe—just maybe—this Boy Scout business was a good idea.

As Johnny walked on, all sorts of thoughts came crowding into his mind. He thought about his mother, who had been in her grave for over a year now. He thought about his dad, who was flying a jet for the Air Force, over in Korea. The year was 1951, and the Korean War was raging. Mr. Dixon didn't have to be over there, because he had already served in the Air Force in World War Two. Besides, he was the only surviving parent of a dependent child. But he had volunteered anyway, because he liked flying. Johnny did not understand why his dad wanted to do such a dangerous thing. He didn't understand why the Americans had to go help the South Koreans fight the North Koreans and the Chinese Communists. But he did know one thing— he knew that he was scared. Sometimes before he went to bed at night Johnny would imagine seeing his dad's jet plane hurtling through the sky. Suddenly it would burst, exploding in flame and smoke, with pieces flying everywhere. Johnny would close his eyes and shudder. He worried about his dad a lot. Sometimes when the mail arrived on Saturday afternoons, Johnny wondered if there was an official U.S. government telegram in the pile, a telegram that began *We regret to inform you.* . . .

Johnny wished that he could stop worrying about his dad and just go along with what the professor had told him: There was one big rule in life—the things you worried about never happened, and the things that happened were never the ones you expected. Not that this bit of advice helped Johnny much. It simply meant that he spent more time guessing at what the unexpected disasters in his life would be.

When Johnny started up the walk toward his front door, he was suddenly hit with the chilling feeling that something was wrong. Quickly he glanced toward the big bay window. The window was dark. This was odd, because usually at this time of night Gramma would be in the living room watching TV. The Dixons were poor, and they hadn't had a television set until recently, when Professor Childermass had bought them one as a present. At first Gramma had been suspicious of this newfangled invention, convinced that the rays it emitted were harmful. But before long she was a regular TV addict, watching the *Kate Smith Hour*, Milton Berle, and soap operas like *Search for Tomorrow*. But no gray aquarium glow hovered about the walls tonight. Johnny wondered what Gramma was doing.

Oh, well. She might be up to any number of things. She might be lying down upstairs with a headache—she had had a lot of headaches lately, for some reason. She might be making fudge or a lemon meringue pie in the kitchen. She might be in the bathroom. So Johnny shrugged and started up the steps. *Slam* went the screen door. He walked across the porch and opened the front door. Now he was in the long, musty-smelling hall that ran from the front to the back of the house. With a strong sense of foreboding, Johnny opened the door to the living room and peered in. It was dark. Johnny could see various shapes: the rounded bulk of the brown armchair, the boxy shape of the television set. And as his eyes got used to the dark, he saw his grandmother sitting, rigid and still, on the couch. Her glasses glimmered faintly, but she was not moving a muscle. Terror clutched at Johnny's heart. *What was the matter with her?*

Johnny swallowed several times. When he finally spoke, his voice was weak. "Gramma?"

"Hullo, John. How're you?" Gramma sounded dull and lifeless, like a recording.

Not knowing what to say, Johnny hovered in the doorway. Then Gramma spoke again, unexpectedly, in the same flat voice.

"You're home from school early, arncha? They letcha out early, did they?"

Early. It was nine o'clock at night. Gramma had gone crazy. Or else she was drunk. But, no, she was death on liquor, wouldn't even stay in the same room with people who were drinking. Johnny felt sick. How had this happened? What could he do? He wanted to run out the door yelling and screaming. But instead he stood rooted to the spot. Suddenly he heard footsteps behind him. Somebody was coming up the walk. The sound broke Johnny's trance, and he dashed down the hall to flip the switch that turned on the porch light. When he stepped out onto the porch, he saw his grampa and Professor Childermass. Even in the pale light he could see that their faces were grim and haggard. And Johnny knew in a flash that they too knew something was wrong with Gramma.

The screen door opened, and the two old men entered. Grampa walked slowly forward and put his hand gently on Johnny's shoulder.

"Johnny, we hafta talk to you," he said quietly.

Johnny followed the professor and Grampa through the house to the kitchen. Grampa switched on the kitchen light, closed the door, and went to the stove to turn on the gas under the teakettle. Johnny could see now that Grampa's eyes were red-rimmed, and there were wet streaks on his loose, leathery cheeks. He had been crying.

The professor stood in the middle of the room with his arms folded. He stared hard at the floor. "John," he said, "there is something the matter with your grandmother. I'm sorry you had to come upon her alone like that, but I was across the street with your grampa. He was . . . well, he was terribly upset, as you might imagine."

Johnny's eyes were wide with fear. And now his voice trembled as he spoke. "Professor, what is it? Why . . . why's she actin' that way?"

The professor looked forlornly at Johnny. He opened his mouth to speak, but all he said was "My cousin . . ." Then he snapped his mouth shut suddenly and turned to stare at the wallpaper. His face became a frozen, secretive mask.

Johnny wondered for a second, but then it hit him. He knew what the professor had been about to say: *My cousin Bea died of a brain tumor.* Many times Johnny had heard the professor talking to Grampa about how Cousin Bea had had a brain tumor, only Doc Schermerhorn diagnosed it as bad teeth, so she died. A brain tumor. It sounded so horrible, so hopeless. Johnny hoped that the professor was wrong.

Grampa gently put his hand on Johnny's shoulder. "We called the . . . the hospital," he said in a broken, tearful voice. "The ambulance is comin' to get her."

Johnny looked dully at Grampa. He waited for Grampa to take his hand away, and then he walked over to a kitchen chair and slumped into it. He felt stunned, as if he had been hit on the head with a baseball bat. He couldn't cry. He couldn't feel anything or think anything except *This isn't really happening. It's not real.* In spite of what the professor had said, the things you are afraid of sometimes really *do* happen. And when they do, it feels worse than any nightmare.

The red electric clock over the stove buzzed, but

there was no other sound in the room. Finally the professor coughed. He turned and took Grampa firmly by the arm.

"Come on, Henry," he said in a low voice. "I know it's not going to be any fun, but we have to get Kate ready to go. The ambulance'll be here any minute. The sooner the doctors examine your wife, the sooner they can start fixing her up. She may not know why we want her to go, but . . . well, I don't expect she'll give us a whole lot of trouble. Are you with me?"

Grampa nodded. Then he opened the kitchen door, and he and the professor went out. Johnny followed them timidly through the dining room and the front room to the parlor. The professor went into the darkness, and a few minutes later he came out with Gramma holding on to his arm. She shuffled along uncertainly, and Johnny noticed that she was wearing her blue cloth slippers, the ones with the little blue felt rosettes. Her stockings were wrinkly and saggy, and her face was blank. She looked as if she did not have the slightest idea of what was happening.

The ambulance arrived. It stood in front of the house with its red light flashing. Two attendants got out and took a wheeled cot out of the back of the vehicle. They helped Gramma down the front steps, gently eased her onto the cot, and wheeled the cot out to the ambulance. Gramma was lifted inside, and the rear doors were closed. The big white vehicle roared away, its siren screaming. The professor watched it go for a second, and then he went across the street to get his car—he was going to drive Grampa to the hospital. As he was about to leave the house, Grampa turned to Johnny and asked him if he wanted to go with them. But Johnny said no, he would stay home. He stood in the doorway watching as the car backed out of the driveway and rolled away down the street.

While Gramma was in the hospital the days passed in a blur for Johnny. During school he had a hard time keeping his mind on his work because he was thinking about her so much. He told Sister Mary Anthony, his eighth grade teacher, about what had happened, and she asked the whole class to pray for Johnny's grandmother. And each day, after school had let out, Johnny went into the gloomy, echoing church next door and lit a candle in front of the Blessed Virgin's altar. Kneeling at the altar rail, he prayed that nothing bad would happen to his gramma.

Finally the news came. Yes, Gramma had a brain tumor. The doctor at the hospital explained to Johnny and Grampa that there were two kinds of tumors, benign and malignant. A benign tumor was just a little lump in the brain. It might grow, but it usually wouldn't do any harm. A malignant tumor would grow and eventually kill the patient. Unfortunately you couldn't tell if a tumor was benign or malignant until you actually operated and took it out. The doctor was an honest sort of person, and he laid it on the line: It was going to be a dangerous operation, especially for someone as old as Gramma was. Something might go wrong, or they might not get all of the tumor out. Everybody would just have to sit tight.

Grampa drove Johnny home after the session with the doctor. Neither of them said a word until the car had stopped in the driveway and Grampa muttered, "Gotta go fix supper." Then he got out of the car, closed the door, and loped off toward the house. Johnny watched him go. Grampa looked utterly defeated. His shoulders sagged, and his head hung. Tears came to Johnny's eyes, but with a snorting sound and a shudder he forced the sobs down. He got out of the car and was starting to walk down the driveway to the garage when he heard someone call.

"John! Over here!"

Johnny turned. It was the professor. He was standing in his front yard with a golf club in his hand. The professor played a perfectly terrible game of golf, but he kept at it anyway. Sometimes he practiced his swing in his backyard with a little plastic practice ball. The practice swings didn't help his game any, but—as he often said, sourly—he had chopped some lovely big holes in his back lawn.

"Johnny! Come here a minute. Can I talk to you?"

Johnny walked back up the driveway and across the street.

"Yeah, Professor? Whaddaya want?" The tone of his voice showed how rotten he felt.

The professor smiled sadly. "Is it as bad as all that?" he asked.

Johnny nodded gloomily. "It sure is. We talked to the doctor and he said—"

"Yes. I know. I called up the doctor earlier and got a full report. It's awful, I know, but . . . well, let's hope everything will turn out okay."

"Fat chance," said Johnny bitterly. He was in such a black mood that he did not want to be cheered up, and he did not want the professor to be painting fake rosy pictures for him.

"John," said the professor gravely, and he walked closer to the boy. He put his arm around him and smiled in a pained way. "I think you need to get away from here. I think you need to go on a vacation."

CHAPTER THREE

Johnny was stunned—stunned, shocked, and angry. It was as if the professor had said, *Come on! Let's throw a party!* When he tried to speak, Johnny found that all he could do was splutter and stammer.

"Professor, I . . . I mean how could you . . . with, with, you know. . . ."

The professor was unmoved. He did not act as if he had said anything outrageous. "I mean it, John. It may sound a bit unlikely to you right now, but . . . well, tell you what. After supper I'm going to be making a cake, and I'd appreciate some kitchen help. Why don't you come over after you've eaten, and I'll explain my immodest proposal, okay?"

Johnny just stared at the professor. He was genuinely puzzled. He knew that the professor was not a hard or unfeeling person. Maybe when he had explained what he had on his mind, it would all make sense. "Okay," he said hesitantly. "I'll . . . I'll come over later." And Johnny turned abruptly and walked back to the house.

Supper that night was really pretty awful. It was another example of grampa's horrible cooking: the hamburgers were not only overdone, they were charred. Instead of mashed potatoes there was a slice of Wonder bread. And the canned peas had been cooked so long that they tasted like mushy green spit wads. After one bite of the hamburger Johnny went out to the kitchen cupboard and brought out all the sauces and condiments he could find: A-1 sauce, ketchup, mustard, and Heinz 57 sauce. And with the aid of these he managed to choke the food down. Grampa never said a word all through the meal. It was painful just to look at him. As soon as he could, Johnny excused himself and went across the street.

When Johnny arrived, the professor was all done up in one of his chef's outfits—a big white apron and a puffy white hat. On the kitchen table were boxes of flour and sugar, a bottle of milk, a can of baking powder, and some tiny bottles of vanilla extract and artificial food coloring. In front of the professor was a big green crockery bowl with some creamy yellow cake mixture in it. When he saw Johnny, the professor looked up quickly and grinned. Using a big wooden spoon, he began to stir the batter.

"Now, then," he said brusquely, "where were we? Ah, yes. I was trying to convince you to go away for a while. Do you want to know why? Well, it's all very simple. You're not doing your gramma any good by being here. You may think that you are, but you're not. If you go to visit her in the hospital, you'll find that she's in a rather strange state. And after the operation she'll be sleeping a lot. When you're at home, you'll see that your grampa is not much fun to be with. The two of you will just sit around making each other moody."

The professor paused. He dipped his finger into the raw batter, came up with a big sticky glob, and put it in his mouth. The professor had a passion for raw cake batter. "So, John," he went on as he stirred, "I think you should go somewhere. As you know, next week is Massachusetts State Physical Fitness Week."

Johnny was dumbfounded. What was the connection between Physical Fitness Week and going on a vacation? Between October 1 and 7 the kids in all the grade schools in the state would go to lectures and slide shows and movies and panel discussions on physical fitness instead of attending classes. In Duston Heights there would be special events like relay races and baseball and tug-of-wars every day out at the athletic field. All this left Johnny cold. He was not a big athlete. He could just barely play softball, but not well enough to please the tough kids who ran things on the St. Michael's

School playground. At all other sports he was a complete washout. And so he was expecting to spend Physical Fitness Week standing on the sidelines and watching other kids have fun.

"Yeah," Johnny said sullenly. "I know all about Physical Whoozis Week. What the heck does that have to do with going someplace on a vacation?"

The professor held up a gooey forefinger. "It has this to do with it, my fine feathered friend! As part of the big whoopy-doo of this wonderful week a group of Boy Scouts from this area is going to take a bus trip up into the White Mountains, to a scout camp near Lake Chocorua. When they get there, they're going to spend a glorious, delightful week hiking along mountain trails and singing around campfires and having a grand time. You'll enjoy it—I know you will. And it'll be a million times better than moping around at home. What do you say, eh? Can I twist your arm?"

Johnny looked doubtful. The whole thing sounded like it would be fun, but, well, he didn't think he ought to be having fun right now. It would be like going to a movie on the afternoon of someone's mother's funeral.

"I don't think Grampa would want me to go," he said.

The professor snorted and added a handful of sugar to the batter. "Oh, yes, he would. He might deny it, but at this point I think he'd be extremely glad to have you somewhere else for a short time."

Johnny picked up the measuring spoons and clacked them together. He was really torn. He liked the Boy

Scouts, and he loved the White Mountains. And hiking was something he could do.

"It'd cost a lot of money, wouldn't it?"

"Oh, I'll pay for it," said the professor, shrugging carelessly. "What's the use of having money in the bank if you can't do something nice with it? Now, come on. Be a good sport and say yes."

Johnny was still uncertain, and since the professor had decided that no more good would come of coaxing and wheedling, they agreed that Johnny would think about the professor's plan until tomorrow.

Johnny stayed and helped the professor with his baking. The cake came out perfectly, and after the professor made Ma Perkins's Own Spice Frosting, the two of them sat down to gobble. Then the professor went back across the street with Johnny and half of the cake on a plate inside an aluminum cake carrier. Johnny went up to his room to read while the professor sat down to talk to his old friend Grampa Dixon. He wanted to visit with Grampa to cheer him up. And of course he also wanted to do a little persuading.

A few days later, on Sunday, October 1, Johnny was riding northward in a school bus full of Boy Scouts. In the metal rack above his seat was a backpack, his cardboard suitcase, and his sleeping bag. Johnny was wearing his Boy Scout uniform, and all around him were other boys in uniform. They had just finished singing "Ninety-eight Bottles of Beer on the Wall," the song that is calculated to drive bus drivers out of their minds. Now, while most of the boys were talking and laughing and pestering each other, Johnny sat quietly, staring at the ring binder filled with notes on his lap. On the seat next to him was an illustrated guidebook from the Glomus mansion. He was working on the Glomus puzzle, trying to make sense out of the objects on the late cereal king's office table. He didn't really expect to solve the mystery; this was just something he had brought along to pass the time. As usual, Johnny was approaching the whole thing logically, trying to list all the qualities of the objects on the table, but oddly enough, logic wasn't helping him much.

CHESS SET

Material: wood and ivory

Arrangement: just the way it is before a game starts.

Design: Staunton

NEWSPAPER

Language: Greek

Material: coarse paper known as newsprint

Lettering of headline: large black letters in Greek alphabet. Word circled in red is ΚΗΡΥΞ. It means "herald." Whole title ΕΘΝΙΚΟΣ ΚΗΡΥΞ means NATIONAL HERALD.

SIGNBOARD

Material: wood. Don't know what kind.

Notes: Wood is pretty beat up. Probably was outdoors for a long time. Blue letters say YE OLDE TEA SHOPPE.

Johnny looked glumly at the orderly list that he had made. No, it was not much help. On the other hand, he was proud of what he had been able to find out about this curious collection of things. The guidebook had helped a lot. It had a close-up color picture of the table with the puzzle on it, and another close-up photo of the Greek newspaper. The professor had told Johnny the meaning of the Greek words. And Johnny himself had added the information about the Staunton design. Johnny was a chess nut, and he knew that the Staunton design was the most common. All this information was fine, just fine, except for one tiny little thing: It didn't bring Johnny any closer to solving the puzzle.

Johnny sighed. He picked up the guidebook that lay beside him and began to leaf absentmindedly through it. He looked again at the picture of the table with its mysterious collection of objects. This was all he had to go on. It would have been nice if he could have popped back to Gildersleeve, where the mansion was, before the bus trip began. But Gildersleeve was forty miles from Duston Heights—the trip would've taken too much time. Still, it would have been nice to have another look at the clues. *Clues, shmooze!* he said to himself as he slammed the book shut and threw it back down on the seat. The professor was probably right. The puzzle was a cruel, pointless joke. It could not be solved and was not meant to be solved. It was just something that Mr. Glomus had whipped up to drive his family crazy. Why was Johnny so interested in this idiotic puzzle, anyway?

Was it just because he liked difficult mental challenges? No, there was something else too: There was the reward. Ten thousand dollars for anyone who could figure out the hiding place of the will. He would use the money to pay for Gramma's operation. Johnny knew that operations were expensive. Gramma and Grampa were poor.

There was one more reason why Johnny was going after the will: Like a lot of people, he was always hoping that someday he would get to do something terribly distinguished and exciting, like finding a lost city buried under the sands of Egypt. The Glomus will was like a lost city to Johnny. If he found it, he would get a reward, he would become famous, and he would be able to do something wonderfully generous and kind for his grandparents. What more could anyone ask?

Johnny gazed dreamily out the window of the bus. The mountains were getting closer. In the distance, on the horizon, he could see long rumpled gray and blue lines. Lazily Johnny leaned back in his seat and wondered what the week at Camp Chocorua would be like.

CHAPTER FOUR

❧•❧

Lake Chocorua looks as if it had been intended by God to be a mirror for noble Mount Chocorua. And Mount Chocorua deserves a mirror, because it is a mountain that has *presence*. It stands out. Most of the White Mountains of New Hampshire have been worn down by millions of years of wind and weather into gently rounded, tree-covered humps. But at the top of Mount Chocorua a sharp horn of rock thrusts up into the sky. When Johnny first saw it, the mountain was at its most beautiful. It was the height of the fall foliage season, and the maple trees that grow on the mountain's sides were lit up with brilliant reds and oranges. Johnny looked up and hoped for a day when the wind wouldn't blow, so that he would see Mount Chocorua perfectly reflected in the still waters of its own special lake.

The bus followed New Hampshire State Route 16 past the mountain and the lake onto a dirt road that branched off from the highway. It crossed a rickety wooden bridge until it came to a wooded area where rich people had their summer homes.

In a clearing in the middle of a big patch of wooded land stood Camp Chocorua, which consisted of four two-story log buildings and a flagpole. Johnny and the other boys were assigned their bunks in these buildings. That night a fire was made in the big brick fireplace in one of the dormitory buildings, and the boys and the counselors gathered around to sing songs and tell ghost stories and eat popcorn and drink cider. The next day the camp routine would begin.

On Tuesday morning, after breakfast, Johnny was hiking up a dusty road with a group of other boys. Everybody was in uniform, and Mr. Brentlinger, the head counselor, led the way. Mr. Brentlinger was a big, hulking, rather kindly man who loved to sing songs. As they tramped along, raising clouds of yellow dust, they sang "We're on the Upward Trail," "The Happy Wanderer," and the ever-popular Army hiking song, "Sound Off!" It was a warm day, and Johnny was happy. Here he was, with kids who talked and joked and played games with him. It felt good, and he didn't want it to end.

Around noon the hikers stopped for lunch. The place

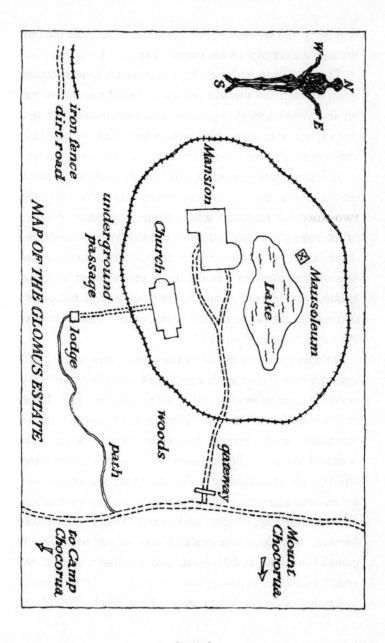

MAP OF THE GLOMUS ESTATE

iron fence
dirt road

underground passage

Mansion

Church

lodge

woods

path

Lake

Mausoleum

gateway

Mount Chocorua

to Camp Chocorua

N

W

S

E

where they stopped was interesting because of the strange collection of buildings that stood nearby. The boys were standing on the rim of a gently sloping ridge. On their left the ground fell away fairly steeply. In the valley below them they could see a small stone church by a quiet lake, a grove of willow trees, and a grim gray stone mansion with clusters of spires, minarets, turrets, and funny bulbous domes. And in the distance Johnny could see the high rusty iron fence that surrounded the grounds of the estate. There were iron gates, chained shut, and a rutted disused road that wound away from the fence right up to the road the boys were standing on. The place where it met the road was marked by a big stone arch. Monster heads and leering human faces were carved on the arch, and there was also a name: STAUN-TON HAROLD.

Johnny stood with his sandwich in his hand as he gazed up at the arch. *Staunton Harold*. The name was familiar, somehow, but he couldn't for the life of him say why. Hmm. Staunton Harold. Had he ever known anybody named Harold Staunton? Nope. Not that he could remember. He shrugged, sat down on the low stone wall that bordered the road, and started eating.

"Looks like Dracula's castle, doesn't it?" said a boy who was sitting on the wall near Johnny. Johnny had noticed him before, because he was so odd-looking. He looked like somebody who had been pulled at from both ends. His face was long and droopy, and his ears stuck out. He had a long, blunt-ended nose and greasy, curly black hair. His gangly arms hung down, and his legs were long too. His feet were enormous. The shoes he was wearing were the kind that kids call gunboats. The boy was eating a huge ham-and-cheese sandwich, and when he stopped chewing, his mouth curled up into a friendly, sarcastic grin.

"What's your name?" he asked.

Johnny smiled shyly. "John Dixon. What's yours?"

The boy grimaced. "Byron Ferguson, believe it or not. But I wish you'd call me Fergie, on account of nobody in their right mind wants to be called Byron." Fergie took another bite of his sandwich. He chewed meditatively and jerked his thumb at the cluster of buildings. "You own this place?"

Johnny stared for a second, but then he realized that the kid was joking. "Oh, sure," he said, grinning. "It's all mine, and I'm Count Dracula. I eat and chew with the lower intestinal tract! I bite the head from the body and suck the blood! Born in Madagascar in 1892! Shot dead and come to life again!" This last part was a sideshow barker's routine that Johnny's dad had memorized and recited so many times that it had worn a groove in Johnny's memory.

Fergie laughed and spat bits of sandwich across the grass. "Where the heck'd you learn *that*?"

Johnny shrugged. "Oh, I know lots of things like that. I know poems and weird facts and all kinds of stuff."

Fergie turned to him suddenly. There was a gleam in his eye. "What happened to the Colossus of Rhodes?" he asked.

Johnny was startled. All he knew was that the Colossus of Rhodes was a huge bronze statue that had been one of the Seven Wonders of the World at one time and that it wasn't around anymore.

"Time's up," snapped Fergie. He grinned triumphantly. "Don't know? Well, it fell down during an earthquake and got sold to a Saracen junk dealer."

Johnny's eyes narrowed. He was not going to take this lying down. "Name the eight guys who killed Julius Caesar," he said.

This one stumped Fergie. He said he didn't know, and Johnny proudly rattled off the eight Roman names. Fergie looked at him with admiration, and Johnny realized that they were going to become friends.

Fergie and Johnny talked a blue streak to each other all during the rest of the hike. Johnny told Fergie about the professor, and about his dad, and Gramma's upcoming operation. At dinnertime that night the two boys met outside the door of the dining hall so they could get a seat together and talk some more. Tonight dinner consisted of hot dogs on buns, potato chips, baked beans, and "bug juice"—otherwise known as Kool-Aid. Soon Fergie and Johnny were seated across from each other at one of the long tables. They talked about baseball. Since Johnny wore glasses, he was naturally an expert on bespectacled players. Dom DiMaggio was a special favorite of his, and he had been to Red Sox games at Fenway Park, where the kids chanted:

> He's better than his brother Joe,
> Do-mi-nic Di-Mag-gi-o!

Next the boys went on to players who had other disabilities. Like Monty Stratton, who pitched with a wooden leg, and Mordecai Brown of the Cubs, who had only three fingers on his pitching hand. But in the midst of all this odd-fact fun, Johnny suddenly grew thoughtful and silent.

Fergie stared. " 'Smatter? Somethin' on your mind?"

"Yeah. I keep thinkin' about that name on that stone arch. It . . . well, it kinda reminds me of somethin'. I dunno what, though."

Fergie shrugged. "Well, it'll come to you in the middle of the night. That's what my mom always says."

Johnny mumbled "Yeah" and went on thinking about Staunton Harold. Later, after dinner, he went to the rec room with Fergie and played a couple of games of chess. Then, around ten, he dragged his weary, aching body up to his room. Johnny had a double room that he shared with a fat, obnoxious kid named Duane Eckelbecker, or "Double-decker" Eckelbecker, as he was known. When Johnny walked in, he found Eckelbecker sprawled on his cot, reading a comic book.

"H'lo, Duane," he said.

Eckelbecker grunted. He flipped a page and went on reading.

Johnny sat down on his cot and picked up the blue binder that had his Glomus puzzle stuff inside. He reached over to the bureau drawer and dug out a sheaf of letter paper and some envelopes. Then, using the blue binder as a desk, Johnny started writing. He wrote a letter to his grandmother in the hospital and another to his grandfather and one to the professor. In his letter to Grampa, he asked if Gramma was okay and when the operation was going to be. Then he folded the letters neatly, put them into the envelopes, and got out the address list that was tucked into a pocket inside the front cover of the binder. But just as he was beginning to address the first letter, he stopped. His pen halted in midstroke.

He had thought of something.

Quickly Johnny flipped open the binder. His eyes traveled down the page. *Chess Set . . . Design: Staunton.* Then, farther down the page, Johnny found the word in the Greek newspaper that was circled in red. The word *KHPYΞ*, which meant "herald."

Staunton. Herald. Staunton Harold.

What did it mean? Was it all a crazy coincidence? Johnny's mind began to race madly. Then suddenly he jumped up. There was something he had to know. Eckelbecker looked at Johnny with sluggish curiosity as he raced for the door, opened it, and slammed it behind him.

With the binder still in his hands, Johnny ran downstairs to the dining room. The huge room was mostly dark, but a fire was crackling in the big brick fireplace, and shadows danced over the trophies and drinking mugs that littered the stone mantelpiece. In a big leather armchair before the fire sat Mr. Brentlinger. His legs were stretched out comfortably in front of him, and he was puffing on a big briar pipe. When Johnny saw Mr. Brentlinger, he paused. He was scared of counselors and teachers and policemen and other grown-ups who had authority over him. On the other hand, he knew that Mr. Brentlinger was a very nice, easygoing guy. And Johnny also knew that he would go out of his mind if he didn't find out the things that he wanted to know.

Cautiously Johnny walked forward until he was standing near the armchair. He coughed, and suddenly Mr. Brentlinger became aware of his presence. He turned his head and spewed out a long, thin stream of pipe smoke.

"Hi, John. It is John, isn't it?"

Johnny nodded tightly. "Yes, sir. That's my name."

"I thought it was. Well, John, what can I do for you?"

He's gonna think this is crazy, thought Johnny. But he plunged ahead. "Uh . . . well . . . Mr. Brentlinger, could . . . could you . . . I mean, would you happen to know the name of the people who own that old mansion that's near the place where we ate our lunch? You know, with the towers on it and the little church next door to it? I was just kinda . . . well, interested in knowing."

Mr. Brentlinger turned and looked at Johnny. He laughed and shook his head. "Well, now! That *is* a strange thing to be asking. Were you hoping that the place was haunted or something?"

Johnny squirmed and clutched the binder tightly against his chest. He began to think that it had been a mistake to bring it with him. What if Mr. Brentlinger wanted to see what was inside? Would he laugh and decide that Johnny was a Grade-A lunatic? "I just wondered if you knew," he mumbled. Johnny could feel his face turning red.

Mr. Brentlinger looked at Johnny sympathetically. "I wasn't trying to make fun of you, John," he said gently. "I just couldn't resist having my little joke. Actually I think I do remember who owns that place. It's the family that owns the cereal company. You know, the people that make Oaty Crisps and all that other gunk. They have a really weird name. It's Glomfield or Glimp or something like that. Anyway, it was the old man, the founder of the business, that built the place. It's falling down now—the mansion, I mean, and I keep wondering what they're gonna *do* with the place. I wish I could remember that name for you. Hmm . . . hmm . . . let me think a bit. . . ."

Mr. Brentlinger went on hmming and puffing at his pipe. Johnny stood there in the darkness, trembling. He felt cold all over, but he also felt wildly triumphant. He had doped out the puzzle—part of it, anyway. Could he be wrong? Johnny didn't think so. The lost Glomus will was out here, out in that old mansion—or somewhere near it maybe. Johnny wanted to do eighteen things at once. He wanted to rush out and find a phone and tell the professor what he had discovered. He wanted to tell his new friend, Fergie, and he wanted to be out at the mansion, prowling around.

Mr. Brentlinger's voice broke in on Johnny's thoughts. "Nope, I just can *not* come up with that name! Anything else I can do for you, John? John? Are you there?"

Mr. Brentlinger turned his head and peered into the darkness behind his chair. Johnny was there, all right. At least his body was there. His mind was out among the crumbling stones of the Staunton Harold estate.

"Huh?" said Johnny, startled. "Uh . . . yes, sir . . . er, I mean, what did you say, Mr. Brentlinger?"

Mr. Brentlinger chuckled. "Never mind. So is there anything else I can do for you?"

"Uh . . . no. No, sir," Johnny said. He felt flustered, and he was looking for an exit line. "You told me what I wanted to know, so . . . so I guess I'll go up to bed now. Thanks a lot."

"Don't mention it. Sleep tight."

Johnny went up to his bedroom, but he did not go to sleep. He felt like a wound-up spring. Mechanically he put on his pajamas and went down the hall to brush his teeth and wash his face. Then he came back and crawled into bed, where he lay tossing and turning all night while Eckelbecker snored like a chain saw. If the human brain were a machine with an on-off button, Johnny would have shut his mind off, and he would have gotten some sleep. But he kept thinking about the objects on the table in Mr. Glomus's office. That signboard—what did it mean? Was the will hidden in a teapot? Johnny tossed and turned and moaned.

Finally the room got lighter, and Johnny heard the bugler blasting away, playing reveille outside his window. It was time to get up.

CHAPTER FIVE

❧•❧

Somehow Johnny stumbled through the early morning routine at Camp Chocorua. He washed up, pulled on his clothes, combed his hair, and staggered out to the flag-raising ceremony that always began the day. The skin of his face felt prickly, and he was nervous. But one thing was perfectly clear to him. Before the morning was over, he had to get to a phone so he could talk to the professor. He was dying to tell him about the discovery he had made, and he also wanted very much to know how Gramma was doing.

After the flag had been raised, the boys were dismissed. The orderly khaki-and-red lines broke up into a mob of boys running madly. Johnny tried to fight his way up to the flagpole so he could catch Mr. Brentlinger before he got away, but it was like trying to go up a staircase when everybody else is going down. Stubbornly battling his way forward, he finally reached it, just as Mr. Brentlinger was leaving.

"Mr. Brentlinger? Sir? Can I talk to you for just a minute?"

The head counselor turned and eyed Johnny curiously. He chuckled and shook his head. "Okay, Dixon, what is it now? I think I oughta charge you a fee for services above and beyond the call of duty."

Johnny was flustered. He paused and pulled himself together so he could ask his question. "Sir . . . I'd . . . I'd like to use a phone, if I may. I need to make a long-distance call, but it'd be a collect call. It wouldn't cost the camp any money."

Mr. Brentlinger looked pained. "Oh, God. You *would* ask for *that*! Dixon, look. There's kind of a problem about phones. This whole deal of having the camp open for this week, it was, well, kind of a spur-of-the-moment idea. The place was all shut down, and we had to turn the lights and the gas and everything back on. And you know how there's always something that doesn't get done? Well, the phone didn't get reconnected. Sooo . . . we're out here without a phone. How about that?"

Johnny's heart sank. He felt helpless and horribly frustrated. What was he going to do now?

"*However*," Mr. Brentlinger added, "there is a solution to this dilemma. In about five minutes I have to make a trip into town to mail some letters and make a few phone calls of my own. I use the public phone at the Squam House, which is the hotel in town. Mrs. Woodley knows me, and she'd be glad to let you make a call. So would you like to ride in with me?"

Johnny nodded happily. His problem was solved.

"Town" turned out to be Kancamagus Center, a small village about two miles down Route 16. It had a few side streets with comfortable-looking white clapboard houses, and a main street with a post office, a couple of stores, a gas station, a movie theater called the Scenic, an Odd Fellows Hall, and a white wooden church with a stubby square steeple. These buildings stood along one side of a grassy village common. On the other side of the common was the Squam House. It was a long, two-story structure with green shutters and a porch that ran across its entire front. There were rocking chairs on the porch, and there was a white sign by the steps. The sign said TOURIST ACCOMMODATIONS. *Reasonable Rates*. B. Woodley, proprietor.

Mr. Brentlinger and Johnny went to the post office first. Then they walked across the common to the Squam House. The lobby was deserted except for a young man who was sitting in an easy chair, reading a newspaper. As Johnny passed the man he stopped short. He had seen the man before. But where? He couldn't for the life of him remember. Even though Johnny had always been taught that staring was impolite, he couldn't stop himself. At first the young man tried to ignore him, but finally he put his paper down and gave Johnny a dirty look. He had pale blond eyebrows and frazzled reddish hair, hooded eyes, and a receding chin. He looked secretive, and he looked mean.

Johnny glanced quickly away and walked across the lobby to join Mr. Brentlinger, who was standing at the desk and talking with the proprietor, a fussy-looking old lady with her white hair pulled back in a bun. As she talked the lady pointed off to her left. There was the phone, a scarred black thing in one corner that stood on an antique table with bowed legs. Next to the phone was a skinny blue glass vase that looked like it would tip over if you breathed on it, and there was a funny little stool to sit on. Johnny almost groaned aloud. He had expected a regular phone booth with folding doors. He had wanted to make this a very private conversation, but that was not going to be possible.

Mr. Brentlinger told Johnny that he could use the phone for a long-distance call, as long as it was collect. Also he had to keep it brief, as Mrs. Woodley did not like to have people tying up the phone for too long. So Johnny went and sat in one of the easy chairs in the middle of the room while Mr. Brentlinger made his calls. He was staring aimlessly around the room, when— quite suddenly—he realized that the unpleasant young man was staring at him over the top of his newspaper. And the stare was not just curious, it was hateful. Johnny was startled. What did this creepy-looking guy have against him? Nervously Johnny snatched up an old copy of *Yankee* magazine from a little table and hid behind it.

Time passed. Finally Mr. Brentlinger was through with the phone, and Johnny got to use it. Soon the phone was ringing down in the professor's house in Duston Heights.

When the professor answered, he was in an exceptionally crabby mood. He had been defrosting his refrigerator, which was something that he absolutely hated to do. For about an hour he had been putting pans of boiling water inside the refrigerator and poking at the ice with his Knights of Columbus sword, while cursing loudly, fervently, and picturesquely. Now waves of crankiness were sweeping over him, and he was trying hard to make himself cheerful again.

"Hello," he snapped. "Who is it?"

The voice at the other end was timid and apologetic. "It's me, Johnny. I . . . I need to talk to you."

"John, why the devil are you whispering? Are you involved in a conspiracy? Is the FBI after you?"

Johnny explained that he was sitting out in the open in a hotel lobby.

"So what?" rasped the professor. "Do you have government secrets to pass on? What the blazes do you have to say that's so private?"

Johnny swallowed hard several times. His face got red, and the palms of his hands were sweaty. When people crabbed at him, he always became very flustered.

"I . . . I j-just wanted to t-talk to you for a m-minute," he stammered. "Is . . . is that okay?"

The professor calmed down. He knew about Johnny's problems, and he was sorry he had been such a bear a moment before. "Go ahead," he said, mildly. "I'm listening. Shoot."

"Well, I . . . first of all I just wanted to know how Gramma is. Have they operated on her yet?"

"Yes, they have. She had her operation on Monday night, and she is doing reasonably well, considering her age and everything. The doctors think that they got the whole tumor out, and it was malignant, I'm sorry to say. I'd be lying if I said that I thought that everything was going to be rosy from now on: there may be problems."

"Problems?" Johnny's heart sank.

"Yes, problems. There's always the possibility that the doctors didn't get the whole tumor out, and if that was the case . . . well, it'd be pretty bad. Also, there's your grampa. He's still fairly depressed, and it may be some time before he's his old bouncy self again. So there! I've given you the news, and it's mostly good. Do you have anything else that you want to discuss with me?"

Once again Johnny was hesitant. He looked around nervously and then said in a loud whisper, "I found out something about Mr. Glomus's will!"

The professor groaned. He clenched his fists and struggled against the urge to chew Johnny out. "John," he said through his teeth, "you are supposed to be *en-*

joying yourself! You are supposed to be tramping about on woodland paths among the autumnal splendors of the White Mountains! What on *earth* are you doing thinking about dear old Mr. Glomus's will?"

Johnny explained. He told the professor about the arch that said Staunton Harold, and he told him why he thought the puzzle on the table fit in with it.

". . . and so I think that will just has to be on that old estate somewhere," Johnny went on breathlessly. "Don't you think I must be right?"

The professor was silent for so long that Johnny was afraid they had been cut off.

"Professor? Hello? Hello? Are you there?"

"Yes, I'm here," said the professor in a strained, testy voice. "But if I were *there*, I'd be driving you into the ground like a tent stake! John, this puzzle solution of yours is terribly ingenious, but it is absolutely cockeyed! *Please* put it out of your mind and go back to hiking and . . . and whatever else you're supposed to be doing! Do you hear me?"

"But the place out here really does belong to the Glomuses!" said Johnny desperately. "It—"

"I don't care if it belongs to Nebuchadnezzar or Czar Nicholas the Second!" roared the professor, cutting him off. "Let us change the subject! Enjoy yourself! Go out and hike till your feet are sore! Collect autumn leaves and put them into albums! Do anything, but please get your mind off that idiotic will! That is an order!"

"Yes, sir," said Johnny, meekly. He wanted to argue,

but he knew it would be no use. So he promised the professor that he would really try to enjoy himself, and then he said good-bye.

After Johnny had hung up, he looked around. First he turned toward the chair where the creepy young man had been sitting. He was delighted to see that the man was gone. Then Johnny noticed that Mrs. Woodley was standing, stock-still, behind the hotel desk. She was glowering at him. Johnny wondered if everybody in this hotel was crazy. First there was the young man, and now this old bat was making ugly faces at him, even though he hadn't done anything. Johnny happened to glance at the skinny blue glass vase that stood next to the phone. *She thinks I'm gonna smash it*, he said to himself. He had half a mind to knock the vase over and then catch it quickly before it broke, just to see what Mrs. Woodley would do. But most of all he wanted to get out of this creepy hotel as quickly as he could.

Johnny hurried across the lobby, down the front steps, and out into the autumn sunshine. As he crossed the common he thought about the phone conversation he had just had. He felt frustrated, but in an odd way he also felt relieved. He was glad to know that Gramma's operation was over, and that it had been a success. As for the puzzle business, it was true that the professor had not taken him seriously, but at least he had said what he wanted to say. And maybe the professor was right after all. Maybe Johnny should just forget about

Staunton Harold and the Glomus will, shove the whole stupid mess out of his mind.

Mr. Brentlinger's station wagon was parked outside the post office, but Mr. Brentlinger was not there. Probably he was still shopping or chewing the fat with some friend of his. Johnny started to get into the car and wait for him, but as soon as he opened the car door, he noticed something lying on the seat. It was a small square of heavy white paper with ragged edges. Carelessly Johnny picked the paper up and turned it over. What he saw was an old-fashioned black-and-white woodcut. It showed some young men drinking in a tavern. Outside the tavern door stood a skeleton. It held a spear up over its head, and it looked like it was getting ready to throw the spear at the young men. Underneath the picture was a little two-line poem, printed in old-fashioned lettering. It read:

> While Youth do chear
> DEATH may be near

CHAPTER SIX

❧●❧

Johnny sat rigid and still. He felt cold creeping over his body, as if he were slowly turning into a block of ice. The square of paper had been left on the car seat by someone who wanted him to find it. The drawing was familiar to him—in a hazy way. He had seen it in a history book somewhere. And its meaning seemed very clear to Johnny: It was a death threat. But who was threatening him? And why?

Suddenly Johnny looked up. Through the windshield he could see Mr. Brentlinger walking down the sidewalk toward the car. Johnny made a very quick decision. He scrunched the drawing up into a ball in his hand and stuffed it into his pants pocket. He really did not want to discuss this with Mr. Brentlinger or to be told that the drawing was just an ad for a Halloween dance or a free gift from somebody's funeral parlor. He had had enough of calm, reasonable advice from the professor. All he wanted was time to think and figure out what to do.

When the station wagon pulled into the parking lot at Camp Chocorua, Johnny thanked Mr. Brentlinger, got out of the car, and ran up to his room to get his baseball glove. Johnny had seen the kids playing softball as he rode back along the road toward the camp. He loved to play, even though he was not very good at it. And he was always hoping that somehow, mysteriously, he would turn into a better fielder and hitter. Now as he raced through the long grass his mind kept coming back to the evil thing that was wadded up in his pocket. He had to tell somebody about it or he would burst. He couldn't call the professor again. So then who . . .

As he jogged nearer to the mob of yelling, gesturing boys Johnny began to grin broadly. He waved excitedly. There was Fergie.

Fergie was sitting in the long grass, looking absolutely nonchalant as he chewed on a tufted weed. He was on the team that was up at bat. It was a chilly day, and so he was wearing an old scruffy gray sweat shirt with CYCLOPS ATHLETIC CLUB printed in white block letters across the front.

"Hi, Fergie," said Johnny, slumping down on the grass. Johnny tried hard to smile, but when he thought of the wadded paper in his pocket, his smile turned to a tense frown.

Fergie looked at Johnny curiously. "Hey, what's the matter with you? Did you bet on the Germans to win the Second World War?"

Normally Johnny would have laughed, but he was not in a very jokey mood. He dug his hand into his pants pocket and pulled out the piece of paper. Carefully he uncrumpled it, smoothed it out on his knee, and handed it to Fergie.

"I found this in the car when I went downtown with Mr. Brentlinger. I think it's a death threat."

Fergie squinted at the crumpled drawing and laughed. "A *death threat*? Are you out of your jug? This is one of those things from that book, whatsitsname, that the Pilgrims made so kids would learn their ABC's. I looked at it in the library once. This one's for the letter Y. What made you think it was a death threat?"

"Somebody left it on the seat where I was sitting in Mr. Brentlinger's car. Doncha see? They're after me on account of I know where the will is, and . . ." Johnny paused and stared at the ground. He bit his lip and felt his cheeks getting red with embarrassment. He had been running on because he was excited and scared, and he had not stopped to think that this would make absolutely no sense to Fergie. And now Fergie would probably decide that Johnny was weird. He would get up and walk away, and that would be the end of their friendship.

But that was not what happened. Fergie was staring at Johnny, but it was an interested stare. There was a gleam in his eyes and a faint curling smile on his lips. "He-ey," he said slowly, "are you mixed up in something? You can tell me, I won't rat on you. Come on."

So Johnny started to tell Fergie about Staunton Harold and the lost Glomus will and the table with the weird collection of objects on it. While they talked there was a lot of yelling and screaming going on behind their backs. Fergie's team was knocking the cover off the ball. Pretty soon the bases were loaded.

"Hey, Fergie!" somebody yelled. "You're up!"

"Oops. 'Scuse me! I'll be right back," said Fergie, and he scrambled to his feet. He picked up a bat and loped toward the plate. As Johnny watched, Fergie got ready to hit. The pitcher barreled the ball in, and Fergie swung. It was an awkward, lunging swing, and he missed. Johnny felt sympathetic and got ready to cheer Fergie up when he struck out. But then the ball came whizzing toward the plate again, and Fergie swung and connected. *Wok!* The ball sailed upward in a high, beautiful arc. It flew out over the head of the center fielder and came down in some bushes at the far end of the field. Fergie raced around the bases as all the boys on his team whooped and cheered. After he crossed home plate, Fergie stumbled back to where he'd been sitting before. He sat down, crossed his legs, and smiled modestly.

"Natural ability," he said, brushing an imaginary

speck of dust off his sweat shirt. "Okay, now. You wanna tell me some more about this trouble you're in?"

So Johnny told Fergie the rest of what he knew and what he guessed. He told him that he thought the lost Glomus will must be out at the estate called Staunton Harold. Fergie listened to all this thoughtfully. He nodded sometimes or shook his head, and now and then he would say something like "Hot dog! How about that!" or "Boy, that old guy must really have been out of his jug!" "Out of his jug" was one of Fergie's favorite expressions.

Finally Johnny was finished. He folded his arms and glanced nervously at Fergie. "Whaddaya think?" he asked.

Fergie was quiet a second before answering. "I think you're the only kid I know who's ever had a death threat handed to him. Honest! I never heard of it happening before!"

Johnny felt confused and kind of angry. First Fergie had said that the picture wasn't a death threat, and now he said that it was. Was he trying to be funny? "It's not like the Congressional Medal of Honor," he snapped back. "I mean, I might get killed."

"Yeah, you might." Fergie said this in an abstracted, dreamy way. It was plain that his mind was elsewhere. As Johnny stared at him anxiously Fergie hummed and gazed off into space. Suddenly a light came into his eyes. He snapped his fingers and turned to Johnny. "Hey!" he said. "You know what we oughta do?"

"What?"

"We oughta sneak out of our rooms tonight and go see if we can find a way to get into that Statler Harrison place. Whaddaya say?"

"It's Staunton Harold," said Johnny severely. He hated to hear people mispronounce names.

"Statler Hilton, Staunton Harold, what's the difference?" said Fergie with an irritated shrug. "Come on, answer the question. Do you wanta go or don't you?"

Johnny hemmed and hawed. He had a holy terror of violating rules and regulations, and camp regulations said that you couldn't leave your dormitory between lights-out and reveille. "We can't go," said Johnny fretfully. "If we get caught, they'll throw us out, and my grampa and gramma'll really feel awful if that happens."

Fergie snorted disgustedly. "Oh, come on, Dixon! Are you gonna spend the rest of your life wrapped up in a blanket in your bedroom? The only way to have any fun is to break the rules sometimes! Come on! I'll meet you at eleven P.M. out by the flagpole. There's a path over there," Fergie said, pointing off toward a mass of bushes near the tennis courts, "and it leads out toward that road. You know, the one we were hikin' on when we saw the old place. We'll just go out an' peek at the old dump an' come right back. Who's to know? You'll be in bed before anybody knows you left. Whaddaya say?"

Johnny still looked hesitant. "Eckelbecker'll turn me in if he finds out I've gone out."

Fergie looked grim. "You tell that lard bucket that

Byron Q. Ferguson told him to keep his trap shut unless he wants to have his ears tied into a bowknot behind his head."

Johnny was torn with indecision. The professor was always telling him that he ought to be more adventurous. Maybe he ought to quit worrying and live a little. "Oh, okay!" he said finally. "I'll be there."

At about five past eleven that night Johnny was standing out by the flagpole, waiting. It was a chilly, raw night with a fine mist in the air, and he was shivering as he peered up at the overcast sky. He was wearing his Notre Dame warm-up jacket over his pajama tops, and he also had on his blue jeans and his heavy socks and tennis shoes. He looked off toward the log buildings. So where was Fergie? Had he chickened out in spite of all his brave talk? But then Johnny saw a shape moving toward him. Fergie was sprinting across the wet grass, carrying something in his hand. Suddenly Johnny realized what it was—a flashlight. And then he felt very stupid: he had a flashlight, but it was in his suitcase. He had been so nervous and flustered about this whole deal that he had forgotten to bring it.

Fergie arrived, panting. "Hi!" he whispered. "Glad you didn't cop out on me. You bring a flashlight?"

"I don't have one," said Johnny untruthfully. "Is . . . is that all right?"

"Naw," said Fergie, grinning. "You get three demerits an' no supper tonight. Sure it's all right! Stop bein' such a fussbudget! This flashlight here is one of those super-duper sealed-beam jobbies. It shines for miles. So don't worry. Let's get started."

Fergie and Johnny jogged off into the drizzly darkness. After a couple of minutes Fergie switched on the wonderful sealed-beam flashlight. The effect was quite dramatic: A long bar of pale light shot out into the gloom. As Johnny watched, Fergie moved the beam back and forth. It lit up the hump of the pitcher's mound on the baseball diamond, and then it moved slowly across the mass of bushes beyond the field. The beam picked out a cleft in the wall of shrubbery.

"Aha!" said Fergie. "Aha, and other expressions of delight! Come on! We've got it knocked!"

The two boys marched on. They reached the edge of the wide grassy field and plunged into the gap in the bushes. It was a narrow path, and they had to go single file. Fergie went first with the light. Wet leaves slapped across Johnny's face, and he put out his arm to fend them off. His head was sopping wet now, and water was running down his neck. He thought about his gramma, and how she believed that if you got wet out in the rain, you might die of pneumonia. Poor Gramma! Johnny hoped that she was really going to get better. Silently he said a Hail Mary and an Our Father for her.

After what seemed like hours of slopping along through wet underbrush, the boys came out onto a road covered with wet gravel. Johnny had a vague idea that they were walking through a forest, but when he looked up, he couldn't tell where the trees ended and the sky began. Fergie's light slashed out through the mist like a sword. Neither boy spoke.

Johnny began to brood about the mysterious place that they had set out to explore. The old mansion was evil-looking, even in bright sunlight. What would it be like at night?

Fergie grabbed Johnny's arm. "Hey! What was that?" he said sharply, and he sounded alarmed.

Both boys halted and stood dead-still, listening. Off to their left they heard noises. *Crunch, crunch, crackle, crunch*. Somebody—or something—was thrashing through the wet underbrush. Johnny wanted to run. But he had his pride; if Fergie was going to stand his ground, then so would he.

"Hey! What the heck d'ya think *that* was?" Fergie was trying to sound brave, but Johnny could hear the trembling in his voice.

"I dunno. Maybe it was a dog."

"Naw. Too much noise for a dog. I'd say it was a hunter, only any hunter who was out here on a lousy night like this would have to be out of his jug. Some old bum maybe."

Johnny didn't think it was a bum. In his mind's eye he saw a Frankensteinish creature dripping green slime from its horny paws. Any minute now it would come charging out of the darkness at them, uttering strange cries and lusting for their blood.

Suddenly the noise in the underbrush died away. Fergie took a deep breath and let it out.

"Hot dog!" he said, grinning. "He must've gone away." Fergie chuckled. His old jaunty, swaggering self was coming back. "Let's move it! It's just a little ways down the road to the old place."

On the boys hiked while the wet gravel went *squrch*, *squrch* under their feet. The mist turned into a steady drizzle. Johnny kept straining to see, but he could not make out much except more road and vague leafy shadows crowding in close on either side. Finally, though, as they started down a hill, the close shadows of trees and bushes fell away. The long beam of Fergie's flashlight swerved to the left and picked out the heavily ornamented stone arch, with its swags and urns and columns. They were there. They had reached Staunton Harold.

And standing under the arch, waiting for them, was a man. He wore a yellow rubber raincoat and a black rubber rain hat with a wide floppy brim. Under his armpit the man held a flashlight, and in his hands was a rifle—pointed straight at Johnny and Fergie.

CHAPTER SEVEN

❖

The drizzling rain kept falling. The still beam of Fergie's flashlight shone straight at the menacing figure's face. Even with the brim of the rain hat partially hiding the face, Johnny knew who it was immediately. It was the young man with the bug eyes and receding chin who had glared at him in the lobby of the Squam House.

Shifting the gun in his hands, the man took a step forward. "Okay, you two," he said nastily. "Just you hold it, right there! Now, would you mind tellin' me what you're supposed to be doin'? Huh?"

Johnny was terrified. He had a sudden vision of himself and Fergie lying by the roadside, shot full of holes and covered with blood.

Fergie, however, was made of sterner stuff. He stepped forward and challenged the man angrily. "Hey, you, what do you mean pointin' that gun at us? This's a public road. We ain't done nothin' wrong!"

The man looked at Fergie thoughtfully for a second. He looked down at the rifle in his hand. And then, amazingly, his whole attitude changed. "*Darnit!*" he yelled disgustedly, and he threw the rifle down on the ground. "Darnit all anyway!" He tore off his rain hat and threw it into a mud puddle. Then he sat down on a piece of carved stone that stood in the grass near the arch. "Go ahead!" he said, wringing his hands and staring gloomily at the ground. "Do what you want! Steal my gun! Break into the house! Make fun of me! See if I care! I try to be tough, but I just can't do it!"

Johnny and Fergie were totally stunned by this dramatic turnaround. They looked at each other, and then Fergie stepped forward.

"We don't want your dumb gun," he said. "And we're not gonna break into anybody's house. We just don't like to have people threatening us." Fergie pointed off into the darkness. "That house over there—is it yours?"

The young man nodded glumly. "Sort of. It belongs to my family. My name is Chadwick Glomus, and my grandfather was good old H. Bagwell Glomus. Or Grampa Herbie, as he was known in the family. I have too much money, and a lot of time on my hands, so every now and then I come up to this old place and look for Grampa Herbie's will."

Johnny was astonished. He had figured that he was the only one in the world who knew that the puzzle in Mr. Glomus's office pointed toward this place. Without pausing to think, he said excitedly, "Hey! How'd you guess that—"

The young man gave him a sour glance. "Oh, I'm clever. Very clever. And I gather you worked out that part of the riddle too. When I saw you at the hotel, I figured that you had come up here to search for the will. You see, I was working in the gift shop the day you visited my dear grandfather's cereal factory. You were babbling a blue streak about the puzzle to that old man you were with, and so I figured you might be on to something."

Johnny gasped. So that was it. He *had* seen the man before!

The young man smiled unpleasantly. "I hope you find the will, and I hope it turns out that everybody in the Glomus family has been cut out of it. I hope that Grampa Herbie left his dough to the Christian Scientists or the Red Sox or a home for retired organ-grinders! I hope nobody in my family gets a red cent!"

Fergie looked at the young man strangely. "Why don't you like your family? What's the matter with them?"

The young man put his hand over his face. "Oh, don't ask! Don't ask! But if you really want to know, the main reason why everybody is such a mess is Grampa Herbie. He was one of the most awful people you'd ever want to meet in your life! Always harping on the importance of a balanced diet. Chew your food thirty-two times before you swallow it! Did you know that a bowl of Oaty Crisps contains ninety-three percent of your recommended daily allowance of iron, riboflavin, and niacin? *Yaargh!* And then, at the end of his life, to start messing around with black magic the way he did! And to top it all off, that insane puzzle about the will!"

The young man shook his head and winced. "Ow! I wish you hadn't gotten me started on my family. I think it's giving me a headache!"

Agin Johnny and Fergie glanced at each other. They both felt sorry for the young man, but right now they wanted to go back to camp. They had decided that their adventure had reached a dead end, and they needed some nice, polite way of saying good-bye.

"Uh, we . . . we better be gettin' back to our camp," said Fergie, with a nervous glance over his shoulder. "If the counselors find out we're not in bed, they'll really blow their tops."

The young man looked very unhappy. At first he had seemed threatening, but now he merely seemed strange, wistful, and more than a little bit lonely.

"Oh, please don't go yet!" he pleaded. "I'm sorry I pointed that gun at you! Look, if you stay just a bit, I'll show you something."

Fergie wrinkled up his nose suspiciously. "Yeah? What?"

"It's a secret passage that runs under the fence and comes up inside the chapel next to the big house. The tunnel is a big Glomus family secret, but I'll let you in on it."

Johnny felt very nervous about this. He had always had it drummed into his head, ever since he was little, that you never went anywhere with strangers. And this was a stranger who was stranger than most.

The young man looked at Fergie and Johnny, and read their thoughts. With a pained expression on his face he got up and fished his rain hat out of the mud puddle. He shook it a few times and jammed it back onto his head. "Please believe me!" he said in a pleading, sad voice. "I'm not a murderer! I can't even shoot squirrels! That gun is empty. See for yourselves!"

Fergie took a few steps forward and picked up the gun. He slid the bolt back and pointed the beam of his flashlight in the chamber. Then he slammed the bolt back into place and handed it to the young man. "Yeah, you're right," he said, nodding. "Okay, look. I'll level with you. We were just gonna peer through the fence at that old dump over there and then hightail it back to camp. But if you wanna show us somethin', we could stay for, oh, maybe about half an hour." Fergie paused and turned to look back at Johnny, who was just standing there fidgeting. "That okay with you, John baby?"

Johnny glanced fretfully over his shoulder. He had mixed emotions. He was afraid of getting caught if he stayed out too late, but the idea of a secret passage really excited him. It was the kind of thing he had always dreamed of finding.

"I guess we could stay for a little while," he said hesitantly.

And so it was settled. The young man turned and walked back toward the stone arch, motioning for the other two to follow him. They headed along a narrow muddy path that ran down a little slope and off into the woods. As they tramped along, Johnny found that he was getting really nervous, but he was also getting really interested. He wondered what the passage would be like.

On they marched, over masses of soggy leaves, while water dripped all around them. Finally they came to a small clearing where Johnny could see the dark shadow of a small building. It seemed to be a funny little cottage of some kind. Fergie swept his flashlight beam upward, and Johnny saw part of a slate roof, a brick wall, and a little window with diamond-shaped panes. A door was set in a fancy stone arch. Over the arch was a stone banner with the inscription *Health Is Wealth*.

"This is one of those cute little outbuildings or lodges that you find around big estates sometimes," said the young man as he fumbled in his pocket for a key. He turned it in the lock and gave the door a good hard shove. Then he disappeared inside. Johnny and Fergie hesitated for a second and then followed him into a musty-smelling room with no furniture in it. Built into one wall was a very fancy marble fireplace. It was covered with stone knobs carved to look like the tiny heads of children. They were smiling and apple-cheeked, and were slurping cereal from bowls. Over the mantel was a mildewed oil painting of good old Mr. Glomus himself, with a box of Oaty Crisps in his hands.

The young man laid his rifle on the mantel. Then he grabbed one of the carved heads and twisted it. Johnny heard the clanking and clattering of hidden weights and chains. And then, as the young man pointed the beam of his flashlight into the dark mouth of the fireplace, Johnny saw the back wall of the hearth slide up. A low opening was revealed, with steps leading down.

The young man folded his arms and stared calmly down into the dark opening, laughing harshly. "Good old Grampa Herbie really thought of everything! If you're out shooting quail and a thunderstorm hits, you duck in here. And then you can scoot right over, zippity-zoo, to the chapel without getting your head wet. And now, if you've got a few minutes more, I'll show you part of the passage."

But before starting out, the young man did a strange thing. He stepped back, reached up onto the mantel, and took down a candle and a book of matches. Then he poked around in the darkness for a few minutes and came up with a long knobby bronze candlestick. Humming tunelessly, he screwed the candle into the holder and lit it.

"Whaddaya need that for?" asked Fergie. "You've got a flashlight, doncha? Or did your batteries run out?"

"The batteries are Everready batteries and will last for centuries," said the young man dryly. "This is for something else." His face suddenly grew grim and hard. In the candlelight it looked like the face of a gaunt and cadaverous ghost. "Have you two heard about the Guardian?"

Johnny stared. This was something new to him, and to Fergie too.

"Don't know, eh?" said the young man tauntingly. "Well, kiddies, the Guardian is something my irresponsible grandfather whipped up when he was fooling around with the black arts. He called it up out of the depths, out of the void, and it's still here, wandering around this old estate. The Guardian can be anything: It might be a pool of moonlight on the floor, or a chair, or smoke drifting in the air. And if it catches you . . . well, one of my great-uncles was caught by it. Afterward they buried him in a hurry." The young man paused and grinned unpleasantly. "Do you know what a mummy looks like after it's been unwrapped? Just a dried brown husk that used to be a human being, with holes for eyes? Well, that's what Great-Uncle Platt looked like after the Guardian got him. And I'll tell you something else you may not know. Three people have disappeared in this area in the last five years. No bodies were ever found, but I'll bet you—dollars to doughnuts—that the Guardian got them too."

Fergie's eyebrows went up. He was pretty suspicious about all this. "So, if there's this monster down there," he said, "why are we goin' on down to meet it? Is it monster-feeding time or what?"

The young man stared stonily at Fergie. "You can make fun all you want, my friend," he said grumpily. "But what I'm telling you happens to be true! And in answer to your question, the Guardian isn't there all the time. But I suspect that it will come for you if you get too close to the will. I have this candle. If an evil presence is near, candle flames burn blue. That's what Shakespeare says, and it happens to be the truth. So come along. . . ."

Fergie and Johnny looked at each other. Neither of them believed a word the young man was saying.

"Yeah, sure, let's go," said Fergie, with a jaunty leer and a devil-may-care shrug of his shoulders. "If you don't mind about monsters, neither do we."

The young man smiled a crooked, mocking smile. With the candlestick in one hand and a flashlight in the other, he bent over and stepped down into the narrow opening. Fergie went next, and Johnny came last. Down a dark, damp-smelling staircase passage they went. Johnny counted twenty-three steps to the bottom. Then the floor leveled off, and the passage grew wider. They were in a stone tunnel where three people could walk abreast. Fergie flashed his light around, and Johnny saw, at the top of an arch they were passing under, a smiling stone cherub and the carved motto *Mens sana in sano corpore*, which means "a sound mind in a sound body." Over by one wall of the tunnel some junk was piled up.

"Charming place, isn't it?" said the young man as they walked along. "I understand Grampa Herbie originally wanted to make this a little subway line, with a pneumatic-powered car and all. But he lost interest when he found out how much it would cost."

They walked on. In places there was a strong smell of earth, and Johnny noticed that pieces of the ceiling had caved in. Sometimes the walls were slick with damp, and here and there Johnny saw streaks of yellowish-green niter oozing down over carved corbels and columns. Every now and then he glanced at the flame of the candle that the young man was carrying. It burned sluggishly, because the air in this underground place was rather stale. But it did not burn blue.

Finally they stopped. Before them was a nail-studded wooden door set in a stone arch with a zigzag molding around it.

"End of the line," said the young man with a little sigh. He turned to face the two boys. "This door leads to the crypt under the chapel next to the big ghastly old house. You two must have seen it from the road. But I don't think we ought to go upstairs. No, I wouldn't want to take the responsibility if anything happened to you two. Let's head back."

Johnny was disappointed. He had not believed any of the young man's warnings about the Guardian and he wanted to see the inside of the spooky old chapel. Also he had a funny idea that was lodged firmly in his head:

If he could only get onto the grounds of the estate, he would be able to figure out the rest of the Glomus puzzle.

Fergie protested and Johnny wheedled, but the young man was quite firm. So, back they went and up the narrow stairs into the dusty little room where the journey had started. The young man blew out his candle and set it on the mantelpiece. He twisted the carved knob, and the stone slab at the back of the hearth came bumping and grumbling back down. Then, taking the rifle again and tucking it under his arm, he led the boys out of the lodge, locked the door, and slid the key into a hole in one of the carved ball-flowers over the door. And now the three of them were tramping back along the muddy path through the trees.

When they reached the gravel road, the young man stopped again. "Gentlemen, I am going to take my leave," he said, bowing stiffly. "My car is parked not far from here, and I gather you two can make it back to camp all right. I'm so glad I had a chance to entertain you. And if you ever think of me, remember that there are things in this world that are better than having lots of money. Like having all your marbles, which I don't seem to. Good day. It's really been, as they say."

And with that the young man wheeled abruptly and marched off down the road.

"Weird," said Fergie, shaking his head. "Weird is the word for that character."

"Yeah, but he was kind of nice, anyway," said Johnny thoughtfully.

"Uh-huh," grunted Fergie, and he screwed his mouth up into a distrustful frown. Then the two explorers turned and began walking quickly back toward camp. For a few minutes the only sound was the pattering of rain and the crunching of gravel under the soles of their shoes. Then suddenly the air was split by long, loud, hideous yells and shrieks.

Johnny and Fergie stopped dead in their tracks. The yelling had come from the stretch of road that the young man had just been heading for. The two boys did not discuss what they ought to do. Instead, they turned around and set off running, pell-mell, in the direction they had come from. Johnny was not a great runner, but he ran hard, determined not to be left behind in the dark. Suddenly the two of them stopped, breathless, in the middle of the road. The jumping, bouncing beam of Fergie's flashlight had picked out something. On the rain-soaked gravel lay two objects: One was a rifle, and the other was a flashlight. The flashlight was still on, and it cast its long, narrow beam out across the gravel of the road. On the handle was a raised oval medallion that bore the gold initials *CG*.

CHAPTER EIGHT

✹ ● ✹

Horrified, Johnny looked at Fergie. Fergie was staring down at the rifle and the flashlight, still breathing hard from the long run. Abruptly he stopped to pick up the flashlight. He flipped it over to Johnny, who was so surprised that he almost dropped it.

"Here," said Fergie. "Now we've each got one. Come on. Let's get headed back to camp."

Johnny was flabbergasted. He stood there opening and shutting his mouth. Finally he managed to speak. "You mean . . . you mean you're gonna just . . . just . . ."

Fergie hesitated. For a second he stared off into the darkness, and there was fear in his eyes. Then he laughed harshly. His lips curled into a cynical and knowing smile. "Yeah," he said, "we're gonna *just*. We're gonna mosey on back and get some sleepy-bye, if we can. Look, John baby, don't you see what happened? He dropped his stuff here in the road. Then he yelled bloody murder for a coupla minutes, an' then he lit out into the woods. He's probably out there right now, laughin' at us. You didn't *believe* all that junk about a monster that turns people into mummies, did you?"

Johnny was silent. Up until now he had not believed the strange young man's stories, but he was beginning to have second thoughts. Johnny looked down at the chrome-plated flashlight he held in his hands. It looked expensive. And there was the rifle lying there too. "Maybe you're right," he said slowly, "but . . . well, would he really have left this stuff just layin' here?"

Fergie shrugged. "Why not? He's rich as Croesus, so he can buy himself more rifles and flashlights, can't he? Besides, he's got a screw loose. Crazy people do crazy things."

Again Johnny was silent. It seemed to him that Fergie was being very reasonable and logical. All the same, he had his doubts. Finally, with a weary shrug, he said "Oh, okay! Let's go on back."

"Right," said Fergie, nodding. Then, on a sudden impulse, he tucked his flashlight under his armpit and cupped his hands to his mouth. "NIGHTY-NIGHT, CHAD BABY!" he yelled. There was no answer. But then, the boys didn't expect one.

Fergie and Johnny did not try to take the rifle back

with them. They left it lying on the rain-soaked road and slogged on back to camp. At the flagpole they parted, and each one ran back to his own building. As he slipped in, closing the door softly behind him, Johnny noticed the clock in the downstairs hall. It said five minutes before two.

Johnny didn't get much sleep that night. He was still terribly keyed up, and he lay tossing and turning for a long time, until—around five A.M.—he dozed off, and had a dream about Mr. Glomus chasing him through an endless tunnel. And then, before he knew it, reveille was blowing again, and Johnny crawled out of bed to face another day.

When he came stumbling into the dining hall for breakfast, Johnny felt like one of the walking dead. For two straight nights he had gone without much sleep, and now it was beginning to get to him. He shuffled along the cafeteria line, sliding his tray over the stainless-steel bars. As he was staring blearily at the bins of scrambled eggs, he heard the women behind the counter talking to each other.

"Hey, Edna!" said one, "didja hear that thing on the radio? About the guy that got lost last night?"

"No, I didn't. So what happened?"

"Well, it was the same like all o' the others. He just disappeared! They found his gun layin' in the road out near that old mansion—you know the one I mean. An' then they found his car parked up the road, with the keys in it. I betcha they never find him! Remember old Mrs. Spofford an' Charley Holmes an' that bum—what was his name, anyway? They never found none of 'em! An' I bet they never will, either!"

Johnny was wide awake now. He stared so hard at the woman who was telling the story that she noticed him and suddenly clammed up. "Milk or Kool-Aid?" she asked in a toneless voice as she shoved a plate of scrambled eggs and bacon at Johnny.

Mechanically Johnny took a glass of milk and moved on down the line with his tray. His brain was racing madly. So it hadn't been just a tall tale. Chad really had disappeared, and there were others who had gone before him. Distractedly Johnny looked this way and that. Ah, there was Fergie waving and motioning for him to come and sit down.

Scuttling sideways, Johnny made his way down the narrow aisle between two rows of tables. He put his tray down, climbed onto a seat, and immediately began talking.

"Guess what!" he said breathlessly, "I just listened to those two women up there at the counter, and they claim that that guy we met really *has* disappeared! And there's others who've been missing too!"

Fergie looked at Johnny scornfully. "Aw, come on, Dixon! Those two old bags'd believe anything they heard."

"You . . . you mean you don't think—"

Fergie laughed and shook his head vigorously. "Naah,

I *don't* think! Really, Dixon, you're one of the most superstitious kids I ever met in my life! Look. That guy was a crazy, right? He was playin' a joke, an' then maybe he screwed up an' he really *did* get lost. An' you wanna know what else I think? I think he's the one that left that weird picture in the car for you. It'd be just like him. He's really out of his jug! So don't worry about him—he'll turn up, one way or the other."

"Uh-huh," said Johnny weakly. He was not convinced by what Fergie had said, but he didn't feel like arguing. He remembered the awful, agonized screams they had heard. Johnny felt sorry for Chad. He really had kind of liked him. And then, suddenly, it occurred to him that they shouldn't be talking about last night's escapade at all. What if some creepy kid like Eckelbecker heard them and turned them in? Anxiously Johnny shot a glance at the kid who was sitting across the table. But he did not seem to be paying any attention to Johnny and Fergie. His eyes were on his plate, and he was busy stuffing scrambled eggs into his mouth.

Fergie elbowed Johnny in the side. "Don't worry about him," he said, snickering. "His ears are fulla strawberry jam."

At this, however, Eckelbecker did look up.

Days passed. Johnny learned Indian lore and made a belt out of little interlocking pieces of leather. With the other boys he hiked for miles and miles, and on Saturday he got to climb Mount Chocorua. It was a long, exhausting climb, and near the top it got scary because the path skirted the edge of a drop-off. But Johnny made it to the top like everyone else, and it gave him a great sense of accomplishment. He had done something courageous and difficult that he wouldn't have been able to do a week or a month ago.

At the last fireside folk sing on Saturday night Johnny stood proudly with the other Scouts as they sang:

> Softly falls the light of day
> As our campfire fades away
> Silently each Scout should ask
> Have I done my daily task?
> Have I kept my honor bright?
> Can I guiltless rest tonight?
> Have I done and have I dared
> Everything to Be Prepared?

Johnny felt the warmth of the fire on his face, and he felt friendly toward the other boys around him. He was sad about leaving, but he would be glad to see Gramma and find out how she was doing. Then he thought about Chad Glomus. He had never been found. For days search parties had been combing the wooded areas around Mount Chocorua, but he had not turned up. Johnny wondered if he should come forward and tell about what he and Fergie had seen. But to do that, Johnny would have had to admit that he had been out in the woods running around after taps. And he was scared of getting into trouble.

And there was something else on Johnny's mind too. It was the whole business of the Glomus will and the baffling collection of clues on the table. Johnny was absolutely convinced that he had figured out the first part of the puzzle, that the will was out at the estate called Staunton Harold. But beyond that point he was stuck. And come Sunday he was going to be even more stuck because he'd be back in Duston Heights and the secret hiding place of the Glomus will would be far, far away from him. Even if he ever solved the riddle of the sign from the tea shop, he would probably never get a chance to test his theories—or collect that lovely ten thousand dollar reward.

Sunday arrived, and Johnny packed up his things, shook hands with Mr. Brentlinger, and said good-bye. Then he climbed aboard the big black-and-yellow bus with all the other Scouts. He was really sorry that he had to go, and as the bus pulled away from camp there were tears in Johnny's eyes.

But on the ride back, he had a good time. He got a seat with Fergie, and the two of them really talked up a storm. For the first time Johnny discovered that Fergie lived in Duston Heights! The two of them had never met because Fergie lived over on the other side of town, and he went to public school. Johnny wondered at first why Fergie had been so closemouthed about where he lived, but it gradually dawned on him that Fergie was poor. He and his family lived on the third floor of a triple-decker apartment house down near the railroad tracks, and Fergie's father sold mail-order shoes and encyclopedias for a living.

Around three o'clock in the afternoon the bus pulled into the parking lot next to the town hall in Duston Heights. When Johnny got out, he had his pack and his sleeping bag strapped on his back and his cardboard suitcase in his hand. He looked this way and that, and then he saw the professor and Grampa standing next to the professor's old mud-spattered Ford. Although Grampa was wearing his usual gray shirt and gray wash pants, the professor was all done up in his blue pinstripe suit, with the vest and the Phi Beta Kappa key that dangled from his gold watch chain. They were both smiling and waving at Johnny, but as he waved back it suddenly struck him that their smiles were forced. There was something in their eyes that said *Johnny, we have bad news for you.* With fear clutching at his heart, Johnny wondered if the bad news had something to do with Gramma.

CHAPTER NINE

Johnny shook hands with the professor and Grampa. He introduced Fergie, who plunged into the milling crowd of relatives and Scouts and came back dragging his dad. Mr. Ferguson turned out to be a mild little man with glasses and thinning hair. He said hello and then headed off with Fergie in the direction of their car. There was an awkward silence until the professor coughed and said brusquely that it was time to be heading back.

Johnny stowed his luggage in the trunk of the car. He climbed into the front with the professor, Grampa climbed into the back, and off they went. Except for the hum of the motor there was absolute silence. To Johnny this was maddening. He wanted to yell, *What is it? What's the matter?*, but his fear and his usual timidity forced him to keep his mouth shut. Finally they arrived at 28 Fillmore Street.

The professor pulled up with a jolt and a sudden screech of the brakes. There, standing on the steps with a big smile on her face, was Gramma! Johnny was amazed, and he felt very relieved. The way Grampa and the professor had been acting, he had expected to find a wreath with a black ribbon on the door and Gramma laid out in a coffin in the living room. But, no, there she was, leaning on a cane with a funny white stocking cap on her head. Her eyes were bright, and she seemed very cheerful. Johnny let out a wild shriek of delight, ran up the walk, and threw his arms around her.

"Gramma!" he yelled. "You're okay! Hooray!"

"Well, I'm sorta okay," said Gramma, frowning. "Your grandfather is gonna scold me for comin' out here. But I didn't wanta be lollin' around in the parlor like some kinda *invalid*."

Soon Grampa and the professor were at Gramma's side. They were clucking like a couple of elderly hens, telling her that she was supposed to be inside lying down. Somehow, with a lot of door-slamming and shuffling around, everybody got back inside the house. Grampa helped Gramma into the parlor and got her seated in the big bristly brown easy chair. Then the professor went out to the kitchen and started fixing Sunday dinner. The professor could cook, which was a good thing—Johnny didn't know if he could take another of Grampa's ghastly meals. Every now and then Johnny would glance at Grampa and see the same secretive look he had noticed before. What were they hiding from him?

Eventually dinner was served in the dining room. With Grampa's help Gramma hobbled out to join them. It was a good meal—shepherd's pie, a dish the professor had learned to make when he was in England, and ice cream sundaes for dessert. But halfway through dinner Gramma got drowsy and started to complain of a headache. So Grampa helped her into the back bedroom, made her comfortable, and came back to finish his meal.

After dinner the professor asked Johnny to join him and Grampa in the parlor. *Uh oh*, thought Johnny, *here comes the bad news.*

The professor sat down on the sofa. He rubbed his hands nervously and looked solemn. "John," he began, in a tight, strained voice, "there is a passage in Shakespeare that goes, *When troubles come, they come not single spies, but in battalions*. And that has certainly been the case lately around here. Your grandmother's trouble is over with—at least, we hope it is. But on Thursday your grandfather got a telegram from the Department of Defense. And it was bad news. Your father's plane was shot down over North Korea, in enemy territory."

There was a heavy silence in the room. Johnny felt a

tightening in his chest. With an effort he forced himself to speak. "Is . . . is he . . ."

The professor sighed wearily. "We don't know. There's no word one way or the other. He was a good pilot, with good reflexes. I think there's reason to believe that he could have parachuted to safety, in which case he is probably a prisoner now, or will be soon. But as bad as that is, it's better, far better than . . . the alternative."

"It sure is," said Grampa, nodding. He patted Johnny on the back and smiled sadly at him. "Don't you worry, John. Your dad'll be okay. I read in the paper the other day about how a pilot who got shot down stole a rowboat an' rowed all the way to Japan an' got rescued. Don't you worry—he'll be back soon."

Yeah, thought Johnny gloomily. *He will if he's still alive*. He thought about Chad Glomus, who either was or was not alive. And then he thought about all the stories he had ever read about missing persons. There was the famous Judge Crater, who had gone out to dinner one evening and had never come back. There was Amelia Earhart, the aviator who had disappeared in her plane. Would his dad become a missing person like that? Would Johnny be waiting twenty or thirty years from now for some news of the great Korean War pilot who had vanished without a trace? Black despair filled his heart. He had been so happy about coming home. He had planned to tell Grampa and the professor about his mysterious midnight meeting with Chad Glomus and about the secret passage and everything. But now he didn't want to talk about anything.

The late-afternoon sunlight fell slanting through the parlor windows. It was a nice day outside—for some people.

Finally the professor spoke. He was not much good at comforting other people because he was such a prickly, snappish person, but he tried. "Well, John," he said, "all we can do is hope and pray. There's no reason to despair until there are definite *reasons* for despair."

The professor was being logical, but logic wasn't going to help Johnny much right now. It took a real effort to shove himself to his feet and go upstairs to work on the Latin homework assignment that Sister Mary Anthony had given the class to do during the week's vacation. He opened his Latin book, heaved a great sigh, and soon he was busy with *fruor* and *ulciscor* and *fungor* and lots of other lovely deponent verbs. But over and over as he turned the pages of his book he saw in his mind's eye his father's jet plane bursting into a bright bloom of fire.

October passed. The loud winds of autumn stripped the leaves from the trees on Fillmore Street. Johnny helped his grandfather rake the leaves into a pile in the driveway, and then they had a bonfire, and Johnny threw chestnuts into the fire to make them pop. Gramma got steadily better every day, and soon she was up and about—against the doctor's advice. On school days Johnny went back and forth between his home and St. Michael's School. Some days after school he would go down to Peter's Sweet Shop, a soda fountain on Merrimack Street, and talk with Fergie, and gobble various gooey concoctions. And often in the evening Fergie would come over to Johnny's house to play chess or have weird-fact contests or just sit around and blab. At six P.M. every day Johnny would turn on the television set and listen to the *CBS Evening News*. He kept hoping that he would hear some news about a jet pilot named Harrison Dixon or see a picture of his dad being turned loose by the North Koreans. But the Korean War raged on, and the newscasters said nothing about any prisoners being released. "No news is good news," said the professor, meaning that at least they hadn't heard that Johnny's dad was dead. But this bit of "comfort" did not help Johnny, and day by day, bit by bit, his gloom and pessimism deepened.

Ever since his mother had died of cancer, Johnny had been gnawed by the fear that he would be abandoned, that he would be left alone. To Johnny this now seemed like more than a possibility—it seemed terribly likely. His mother was dead, and his dad was missing in action; his grandmother had been terribly ill, and her illness might return. And then, if Gramma died, Grampa might get so gloomy that he wouldn't want to go on living. Then he would die, and Johnny would be left alone. There was the professor, of course, but Johnny was sure he wouldn't want to adopt him. Hadn't he heard the professor say, many times, that he enjoyed living alone? No. There would be no help there. If everybody close to him died, Johnny would be alone.

Johnny let this fear of abandonment grow. He worried about his father a lot, and he was always glancing anxiously at his gramma to see if she was all right. And now, strangely enough, Johnny's brooding about his grandmother's health brought him back to the lost Glomus will. His reasoning was that if Gramma got sick again, it would take a great brain surgeon to save her. They'd need money to pay one, but now that they had cashed in their savings bonds to pay for her first operation, they were next door to broke. All they had left was a small nest egg, something in a savings account, and something more in that tin can in their kitchen. Johnny didn't know how much great brain surgeons charged for their services, but he figured that it must be a lot. If only he could get the ten thousand dollar reward for finding the Glomus will, he would hire the best surgeon there was to operate on Gramma if her sickness came back.

This "reasoning" of Johnny's was a daydream, but it helped him handle his deep, dark fears. The Glomus will would save him when all else failed, and soon Johnny became obsessed with it. He thought about it all the time, and he became strangely secretive. He never did tell Grampa or the professor about his strange midnight meeting with Chad Glomus. Nor did he tell Grampa about his "Staunton Harold" theory, his guess about where the will was hidden. He wanted very much to discuss his theory with Fergie, but something made him hold back. He was afraid that Fergie might accidentally tell the professor or Grampa and that the two of them would get worried and try to stop him from going after the will. If he was going to save Gramma, he would have to be allowed to work out the puzzle and then do whatever was necessary after that. Until he was ready to make his move, Johnny figured that he'd better stay clammed up.

Often in the evening Johnny went to the public library to find out what he could about the Glomus family and their estate up in the White Mountains. He didn't find much, except for a little about Chad's disappearance in the back issues of *The Boston Globe*. He also managed to locate an article about the Staunton Harold estate in an old picture book called *Stately Homes of New England*. There were a few murky engravings, and there was the surprising information that Mr. Glomus was buried in a mausoleum on the grounds of the estate. All this was very interesting, but it did not throw any light on what the YE OLDE TEA SHOPPE sign meant. Sadly Johnny had to admit that he was up against a blank wall. He had tracked the will as far as the estate, but unless he were Superman, with X-ray vision, he didn't see how he was ever going to discover where it was hidden.

One cold, dark day early in November Johnny came home from school to find that nobody was there. Under the sugar bowl on the dining room table was a note, and it said,

> *Dear Johnny,*
> *Have gone to take your grandmother to the*
> *hospital. Nothing to worry about. Just a checkup.*
> *We'll be back by dinnertime.*
>
> *Grampa*

As he read this Johnny felt his blood run cold. If he had been in a more reasonable frame of mind, he would have known that there was nothing strange about Gramma's going back to the hospital for a checkup. But now he was convinced that Gramma was dying. What on earth could he do?

Johnny sat very still on one of the dining room chairs. Some people yell and scream when they are upset, but Johnny always got very quiet, cold, and withdrawn. He stared at the picture of the Last Supper that hung over the sideboard. But the picture was just a blur to him. Instead, he saw Mount Chocorua and the crumbling stone arch that said Staunton Harold. He saw a train chugging northward up into the White Mountains. And now, slowly, as the Sessions clock ticked on the sideboard, a plan began to form in Johnny's fevered brain. He would go up to New Hampshire, to the estate called Staunton Harold. He would get a room at the hotel that the fussy old lady ran. What was its name? Oh, well, it didn't matter. He had some stationery with the hotel's name and phone number on it—it had been passed out to the Scouts so they could write letters home. Then he'd go out to the estate, and somehow, by hook or by crook, he would find the lost Glomus will, claim the reward, and use the money to get a brain surgeon for Gramma.

This was a crazy plan, and in one corner of his brain Johnny knew it. It was also dangerous, but, strangely enough, the danger attracted him. Even though Johnny was timid, the kind of kid who always looks six ways before crossing the street, every now and then he got the urge to do wild, untimid things. He was always longing to break free from his nervous, scaredy-cat side. *All right, then. He would go.* He wouldn't tell the professor and he wouldn't tell Fergie, either. Johnny wanted this to be his triumph, his alone. *Okay. Let's get organized.* What did he need?

The quiet, reasonable Sessions clock ticked on. The shadows in the dining room grew longer. Johnny sat like somebody who is under a spell. His eyes shone, and his mind was racing like a runaway steam engine, churning out a plan, a wonderful, improbable plan.

CHAPTER TEN

❧◦❧

Later that same day, when Gramma and Grampa got back from the hospital, they told Johnny that the checkup had gone okay—everything was all right. Johnny did not believe them for a minute. He was convinced they were faking. And so, quietly and secretly, as the November days passed, Johnny got ready to put his plan into action. He went down to the railroad station and asked the station master about trains that ran up into the White Mountains. He found there was a Boston & Maine train that stopped in Kancamagus Center twice a day, early in the morning and then again late at night. The late train, which left Duston Heights at five P.M. was the one Johnny wanted. He could duck out of the house around four thirty, catch the train, and be far away before anyone knew that he was missing.

Then there was the matter of money. He would need to pay for the train ticket and for his hotel room. Although Johnny didn't have any money stashed away, he knew that his grandparents did. They'd lived through the Depression of the 1930's, when the banks had failed, and they'd never gotten over their distrust of banks. So they kept most of their savings on the top kitchen cupboard shelf, inside a red Prince Albert tobacco can. It wasn't much—about a hundred dollars in small bills. Johnny felt very bad about taking it, but he told himself that it was the only way. To keep Grampa from getting suspicious he decided to leave the money where it was until the day came when, suddenly, he would leave.

Johnny also replaced the batteries in his old beat-up flashlight and started picking out the clothes he would need. He'd want all his warm winter things, that was for sure—his parka, his stocking cap, his leather gloves, and his woolen muffler. New Hampshire could turn into a real icebox, and according to the weather reports, there had already been snow up in the northern counties. He wondered what the chapel and the old gloomy mansion would look like in the winter. With a little thrill and a little nervousness, he realized that he would soon be finding out.

And when was he leaving? For a while he himself wasn't sure, but then he decided on November 15 for no special reason. Since it was coming up soon, he stepped up his preparations. And through it all he hugged his secret tightly to him, like a miser with a bag of gold, terribly afraid that somebody would find out what he was up to and try to stop him.

On the morning of November 14 Johnny woke up and found that he had a cold. He felt feverish and achy, and his head was all stuffed up.

Johnny groaned. He wanted to be in top shape for the expedition. Should he postpone it, then? Wouldn't it be better to wait till he was really ready? He wavered and fussed all through breakfast, on his way to school, and during school too. The more he thought, the more convinced he became that he should wait till he was feeling better. But, on the other hand, Gramma could be dying. Time was important. At three thirty, when school let out, he had still not reached a decision.

On his way home Johnny stopped by the library. He wanted to look at that book that contained the article about the Glomus estate. He headed straight into the stacks, took the book down, went to a table, and opened it up. The first time Johnny had read it, the article hadn't really sunk in. But this time it made an unforgettable impression. Once again he read that the mansion was adorned with statues of the Nine Worthies, whoever they were. The chapel was a replica of a seventeenth-century English chapel built by an English nobleman named Sir Robert Shirley. His estate was called Staunton Harold, which was where Glomus got the name from. And then Johnny noticed something new: an inscription over the doorway of Glomus's chapel in honor of Sir Robert Shirley, just as there was over the doorway of the original chapel. At the bottom of the page there was an enlarged version of this inscription so it could be easily read. Johnny had studied it before, but he had only half-understood it. Now he read it again.

Suddenly it was as if a light had gone on in his brain. Another part of the puzzle was, maybe, solved.

"Wow!" Johnny exclaimed. He slammed the book shut and got a loud "Shhh!" from the librarian. Normally he would have been embarrassed, but right now nothing mattered except the lost will. He was closer to it than ever. Well, that settled it. He would go tomorrow evening as he had planned, and he would find it.

That evening went by quickly, with dinner, dishes, and homework. After everybody had gone to bed, Johnny got up and started packing his battered cardboard suitcase. He threw in clothes and the big screwdriver from the tool chest in the basement. Then he went downstairs to the kitchen, climbed up on a chair, took down the Prince Albert can, and counted out the money. Johnny still felt very bad about doing this, but he believed it was the only way he could save Gramma's life. With a heavy heart he went back upstairs to finish his packing.

The next morning when Johnny looked out the window, he saw that it was going to be a bright, sunny day. In the sky was a flock of those little gray clouds that have dark bottoms. They always reminded Johnny of boats and made him think of travel.

Downstairs at breakfast he heard on the radio that the first big snowstorm of the winter was sweeping down out of Canada. It would be snowing hard in the White Mountains area by that night. That might put a crimp in things. . . . But, then, weather reports were often wrong —the professor was always saying that. Johnny went hastily over his plans in his mind: He would have to sneak out of the house with his suitcase about half an hour before the train came. Then he would have to hike across town to the railroad station. Should he leave a note of some kind? He'd better, or Gramma and Grampa would think that he had thrown himself into the Merrimack River.

"So, what's on your mind besides hair? Huh?" This was Gramma, who was sitting across from Johnny, munching toast and drinking coffee.

Johnny looked up, alarmed. "Oh, nothin', Gramma," he said quickly. "I was just . . . worryin' about my Latin test."

Gramma snorted. "You can thank your stars that's all you got to worry about," she grumbled. "I hafta go back to the hospital again for more o' them crazy tests. This time it's that hospital over in Amesbury. What's its name, now, Henry?"

"Bon Sekoors," he said, after thinking a second. "French name—dunno what it means, though. We won't be back till after dinnertime, Johnny. Gramma made some sandwiches and put 'em in the icebox for ya."

Johnny looked at Gramma and Grampa. He felt like crying. They were so nice to him, so kind, and here he was running out on them! And with the money out of the can, on top of everything else! They would feel awful when they found out he was gone. How could he tell them that he was doing it all for Gramma?

Johnny went off to school, and the day passed like some sort of strange dream. He felt that everybody was looking at him, that Sister Mary Anthony and all the kids knew what he was up to. Finally, when he walked down the stone steps and out into the sunlight at a quarter past three, Johnny found that he was getting cold feet. He really didn't want to go. It would be so easy just to head home, unpack his suitcase, and relax. Johnny sighed wearily. Yes, that was what he would do, call the whole stupid thing off.

As he walked home Johnny felt better. A great weight had been lifted from his shoulders. He ran quickly up the steps of his house and across the porch and opened the front door. On the kitchen floor lay the day's mail. It must have arrived after Gramma and Grampa had left. As Johnny bent over to pick up the letters, he stiffened. He could see the return address on the businesslike envelope that was lying at the top of the heap:

DIGBY AND COUGHLAN / UNDERTAKERS

Johnny's heart began to pound. He knew what this meant. Gramma was getting ready for her own funeral. She was a very practical, no-nonsense sort of person. And it was just like her to plan the whole business beforehand. A choking sob rose up in Johnny's throat. He couldn't stand by and let something like this happen! The best brain surgeon in the world would be at her side soon if John Michael Dixon had anything to say about it!

Up the stairs he galloped. He tore open the door of his room and then, panting, forced himself to calm down. It was only twenty minutes to four. He had lots of time. First he opened the top drawer of his bureau. Inside lay the wad of bills from the Prince Albert can with a rubber band around it. Next to it was a brass waterproof matchbox with an enameled inset of an Indian's head against the background of a large white star on the lid. This was the lucky matchbox Professor Childermass had given to Johnny. The professor had carried it all through World War One and had come out with only one small injury. *If I ever needed luck, I need it now*, thought Johnny, and he stuck the matchbox in his pocket. He put thirty dollars in his wallet and stuffed the rest into his suitcase, which he dragged out, all packed, from under his bed. He checked its contents once more, then ran downstairs to the basement and came back with an old rusty iron crowbar. After that was packed too, he ran back downstairs to eat the sandwiches they had left for him. Mmmm—roast beef with mustard and mayonnaise! Normally this would have been a real treat, but Johnny's nose was stuffed up, and everything tasted funny. Oh, well—it was food, and he was hungry. He wolfed them down, drank a glass of milk, and then headed upstairs again. He sat down at his desk and wrote the following note:

> Dear Gramma and Grampa,
> I have to do something very important. It is a life or death matter, and it can't wait. I'll be back in a few days, so don't worry. Don't be angry, please. I'll explain everything later.
>
> > Sincerely yours,
> > John
>
> PS: I'm sorry I can't tell you where I'm going. It must remain a secret.

Sadly Johnny took the note downstairs and left it under the sugar bowl. For the last time he tramped back upstairs to his room. With his suitcase in hand and a lump in his throat he wondered when he would see it again. Then quickly he turned, marched out the door and down the stairs. His suitcase banged against the banister as he went. Though Johnny's face was pale and drawn, he looked incredibly determined. He also looked scared.

Professor Childermass had not seen Johnny for a while. And for a good reason—he had been out in Springfield, in the western part of the state, attending his brother's funeral. Having arrived back in Duston Heights on the evening of the fourteenth, dead tired and in a foul mood, he had not wanted to see anyone. But now, twenty-four hours after his return, he was anxious to play a few tough, hard-fought games of chess with Johnny. After fixing an early dinner, he drove up to a candy shop in New Hampshire, bought a pound of dark chocolate creams (they were for Gramma, who loved them), and roared back down Route 125 toward Duston Heights. He pulled up in front of the Dixons' house at just about the time that Johnny was buying his ticket at the railroad station.

The professor jumped out of the car, whistling a jaunty tune. With the candy box in his hand he trotted up the front walk, mounted the steps, threw open the screen door, and marched quickly across the porch. There was a bell, but he preferred to bang on the door with his fist. No answer. He hammered some more and finally in desperation pushed the bell button. Still no answer. "Bah! Phooey!" he said, and started back across the porch. But just then he heard the sound of a motor, saw the flash of headlights, and turned toward the Dixons' car coming into the driveway.

"Ah!" said the professor, grinning, as he ran down the steps to meet his friends. Grampa rolled down his window and peered out.

"That you, Rod?" he called.

"It is, indeed!" intoned the professor. "Who did you think it'd be, the Grand Master of the Knights of St.

John? And I was just about to give up on you folks and go home. By the way, where's John?"

Grampa looked puzzled. "Huh? You mean he's not in the house?"

The professor scowled. "Well, he may be in the bathroom or hiding in the coal cellar. But I am not in the habit of barging into my friends' houses when no one answers the door. Now, then! As soon as you folks can pry yourselves out of your car, let's go in and see if he's anywhere on the premises."

A few minutes later Gramma, Grampa, and the professor were huddled around the dining room table. Gramma was shaking her head, and she was starting to cry. Grampa looked stunned. The flesh of his face sagged, and he seemed very old. The professor, who was standing across the table from Grampa, was holding the note in his trembling hand. The muscle in the corner of his mouth had begun to twitch. Suddenly he threw the note out onto the middle of the table.

"We ... have ... got ... to ... stay ... *calm*! LET'S STAY CALM, FOR GOD'S SAKE!" he roared. And to show how calm he was, the professor pounded both fists on the table. The sugar bowl jumped and came down on its side, spilling sugar everywhere. "*Where* on *earth* can he have gone? This is not like him—not like him at all. Oh, John, John, I thought you were so levelheaded and reasonable! Judgment, thou art fled to brutish beasts, and men have lost their reason! Oh, God, God, God!"

Ranting and raving in this way, the professor paced up and down the dining room. Grampa kept staring vacantly into space while Gramma cried silently. Finally the professor stopped and planted himself next to Grampa.

"Henry, you must have *some* idea where he has gone!" he cried out in exasperation.

Grampa turned slowly to face the professor, his cheeks wet with tears. As soon as he saw Grampa's face the professor's attitude changed. He winced, sank down into a chair, and put his head in his hands.

"I'm a cranky old man," he said quietly, through his fingers. "Please forgive me. Now, we must keep our heads and try to figure out where he is." He drew a shuddering breath and wiped his hands over his face. "All right, he can't have gone to Korea to look for his dad, so we can eliminate *that* possibility. I assume he hasn't got enough money to go far. Henry, how much allowance do you give him?"

"A dollar a week," said Grampa wearily. "I wish we could give him more'n that, but . . ." His voice trailed away. A thought had just struck him. "Oh, dear!" he exclaimed, clapping his hand to his forehead. "You don't think . . ."

While the professor stood watching, Grampa went out to the kitchen. There was a sound of scuffling and bumping, and then he came back with the Prince Albert can. He dumped it, upside down, on the table; it was empty.

"A hundred dollars!" he gasped. "He took the hull darned thing! I don't believe it!"

Gramma blew her nose loudly and looked up. "I bet I know what happened," she said in a voice thick with crying. "Some burglar probably broke in an' made Johnny give him the money. Then he held a gun to Johnny's head an' made him write that note. An' then he kidnaped Johnny."

The professor gazed skeptically at Gramma. "Madam," he said solemnly, "not to insult you, but your house is not the sort that would be selected by a burglar, unless that burglar was a nitwit." The professor scratched his nose and gazed abstractedly out the window. Then he snatched up the note and read it again.

"Life-or-death matter . . ." he muttered. "What in blue blazes does *that* mean?" He turned to Grampa. "Henry, would you mind terribly if I went up to Johnny's room and poked around a bit? I might find something that would indicate what he was up to. I mean . . ."

Suddenly the professor's mouth grew wide with alarm. "Great Caesar! You don't suppose . . . but no. He wouldn't! But even so. . . . Look, you two must excuse me for a minute."

And with that the professor ran out into the front hall and dashed up the stairs. Gramma and Grampa watched him through the wide arch that separated the front hall from the dining room. And then they turned and looked at each other in utter astonishment.

CHAPTER ELEVEN

❦

The train whistle blew. It was a long, lonely, mournful sound. Johnny heard it and smiled faintly. He was sitting in a seat near a window, and he felt groggy. Because of his cold and fever, he kept drifting in and out of sleep. He wondered what Gramma and Grampa and the professor were doing. Were they ranting and raving and tearing their hair? Had they called the police? Or were they crying? Johnny felt guilty. *But it's the only way*, he said silently. *It'll all work out—I promise. You'll see, you'll see. . . .*

Johnny looked around. There was only one other passenger in the car, an old lady in a brown winter coat and a flowered babushka. Apparently not many people wanted to travel up to the White Mountains at this time of year. Now a frightening thought struck him: What if the Squam House was closed for the winter? Well, then, he would find some other place to stay.

The door at the end of the car slammed open. A fat man in a blue uniform stepped in.

"Kancamagus Center!" he called out. "This way out!"

It was a little after nine o'clock at night. Johnny dragged himself to his feet, pulled his suitcase down from the overhead rack, and moved toward the door. Steam hissed and billowed around him as he walked down the iron steps. Blearily he looked around. A light was on in the little old-fashioned station, and next to it was a car with an illuminated sign on top that said TAXI. Johnny started to walk faster. Now, if only the cab would take him where he wanted to go!

A few minutes later Johnny's cab pulled up in front of the Squam House. The old inn looked pretty much the way it had when he had seen it last, and the downstairs windows were lit up, which was a hopeful sign. Johnny got out, dragging his suitcase out after him. As he was paying the driver, another wave of fear and loneliness swept over him.

"Is . . . is this place open in the winter?" he asked falteringly.

The driver laughed. "Well, if it ain't, kid, you're gonna hafta sleep under them bushes over there!" Then, when he saw Johnny's scared look, he added, "Old Mrs. Woodley keeps this place open all winter for the rich types who come up here to ski." He looked at Johnny. "By the way, you're kinda young to be ridin' the rails alone, aintcha? What're you up here for?"

Johnny thought quickly. "I'm here to meet my grampa," he said, glancing toward the hotel. "He's coming over from Center Sandwich to get me."

The driver peered at Johnny closely. He seemed to be on the verge of saying something. But he changed his mind, and without another word he rolled up his window and drove off.

Again Johnny felt afraid. But with an effort he pulled himself together, grabbed his suitcase, and walked toward the hotel.

At first there was no answer when he rang the bell. Then Johnny saw a shape moving behind the pleated curtain in the window on his right. The door rattled open, and there stood Mrs. Woodley, looking just as grim and forbidding as Johnny had remembered her being back in October. When she saw who was on her porch, she seemed startled. But then her whole attitude changed. The scowl vanished, and Mrs. Woodley smiled a warm, welcoming smile.

"Why, my goodness!" she exclaimed. "It's the young man from the camp who came to use my phone! What on earth are *you* doing up here? Come in, come in! You'll catch your death of cold out there!"

Johnny was startled by the woman's sudden change in attitude. But he was glad that Mrs. Woodley wasn't throwing him out. Incredibly tired, feverish, and sniffly, he lugged his suitcase in and set it down by the reception desk. Mrs. Woodley told him to wait there, that she'd be back in a minute. She disappeared into a back room, and Johnny stood by the desk. He dug his hand into his parka pocket, and it closed over something cold and hard—the lucky matchbox. Johnny pulled the matchbox out and fiddled with it. Rubbing the smooth surface comforted him somehow.

When Mrs. Woodley returned, she was holding a guest book bound in green leather and a fountain pen. She set the book down in front of Johnny and handed him the pen. Johnny paused before signing. Should he use a fake name? No, it was possible that Mrs. Woodley remembered his real name. Bending over the book, he signed *Johnny Dixon* slowly and carefully.

Mrs. Woodley went on chattering while he signed the book. "Well, it certainly is nice to have guests this time of year!" she said cheerfully. "This is the in-between season, you know. The leaves are off the trees, and the snow hasn't fallen yet. What are you up here for, by the way? If you don't mind my asking, that is?"

Johnny laid down the pen and glanced distrustfully at Mrs. Woodley. He did not like this incredible cheeriness. *Was she putting on an act or what?* As for the question about what he was doing, Johnny had figured it was coming, sooner or later. And he had an answer ready—the same one that he had given the taxi driver.

"I uh, I'm gonna meet my grampa. He lives near here, over in Center Sandwich. He's gonna come over and get me tomorrow, soon's he can. He, uh, he might be late on account of his . . . his cow is sick." Rather unnecessarily Johnny added, "He, uh, he lives on a farm."

Johnny paused and waited for Mrs. Woodley's reaction. He had pored over a road map on the way up, and he had picked Center Sandwich because it didn't look like it was on any railway line. Would Mrs. Woodley fall for this little fib?

Apparently she would. Closing the guest book, she gazed placidly at Johnny. "Well, young man, you're welcome to stay here as long as you need to. You're my only guest at present, and I'll show you all the hospitality that I can. Have you had dinner?"

Johnny had eaten before he left home. But that didn't matter—he still felt hungry. "Uh, no, I . . . I haven't," he muttered, looking around stupidly. "Can I get something to eat?"

Once again Mrs. Woodley was all grandmotherly kindness. "Why, of course you can! Good heavens, and you've got a cold too! You're supposed to eat well when you have a cold—it builds up your resistance. Come on, now, let's go out to the kitchen and see what we can find."

And, clucking and crooning like the Queen of All Grandmothers, Mrs. Woodley led Johnny out of the lobby and down a short hall that smelled of wood smoke and into a big, old-fashioned kitchen.

Later, after Johnny had finished his meal, Mrs. Woodley took him upstairs to his room. It was a comfortable room with white woodwork and a high walnut bed. Over the bureau hung a little picture that seemed odd to Johnny. It showed an eye shining out of a pyramid, and on top of the pyramid was a motto:

Thou God seest ME

After Mrs. Woodley had explained to Johnny where the bathroom was and told him to sleep well, she left, closing the door softly behind her. Johnny was alone. He looked around the room. Except for the weird picture, it seemed very homey and friendly. He ought to be worn out and ready for bed, but for some reason he wasn't. Something inside him was humming like a dynamo, keeping him keyed up and wide awake. He threw his suitcase on the bed and started taking things out of it and putting them in the drawers of the bureau. When the suitcase was empty—except for the crowbar, the screwdriver, and the flashlight—Johnny snapped it shut and stood it in a corner. He folded down the bed covers and fluffed up the pillow. Still there was this humming in his ears. Still there was a voice inside him saying, *Watch out. There's something wrong.*

Johnny felt frustrated and puzzled. Unless he got some sleep tonight, he would be a total wreck tomorrow when he was supposed to go out to the estate and hunt for the will. He went to the bureau and got out his pajamas. He laid them on the bed, and he was just starting to unbutton his shirt when he had a silly, ungovernable urge to play with his flashlight. Johnny laughed.

Ever since he was a small kid, he had loved flashlights. He'd owned a wonderful old-fashioned one once, with a long, nickel-plated handle that he would shine out his bedroom window at night for fun. This flashlight had had a blinker button on it, and Johnny had used it to send pretend Morse code messages from imaginary spies or people on sinking ships. Maybe playing with the flashlight now would help him relax. Johnny went to the suitcase and snapped it open. With the flashlight in his hand he moved to the window.

It was a small, slightly crooked sash window, but with some shoving Johnny got it to slide up. Cold air flowed in, and Johnny shivered. He snapped on the flashlight and shone it out into a mass of pine trees in the distance. The circle of light moved over banks of dark green needles. *Flash-flash-flash*. Johnny pushed the button—this flashlight had one too—and imaginary messages leaped out into the night. *Ship sinking. Send Help.* What Johnny was really sending with his flasher was just *dah-dit, dah-dit, dit-dit-dit-dah*. This was Morse for CV, the initials of Champagne Velvet, the champagne of bottled beer. He had gotten it from the radio commercials, and he sent it over and over again. But this little routine soon got boring. Now Johnny wanted to see how far the flashlight's beam would carry. He could just barely make out, in the open space beyond the pines, the side of a white clapboard house. Would the beam reach it? He held his arm out the window, stretching as far as he could. Despite his efforts, the shaft of light died before it could reach the house. Sighing, Johnny snapped the flashlight off and jerked his arm back. But as he did this, the tip of his elbow struck the sill. His arm went numb, his hand opened, and the flashlight fell.

"Darn!" Johnny yelled. Annoyed, he peered down at the ground, where there were several little bushes. Maybe they had broken the fall. If the flashlight was smashed . . . well, Johnny didn't want to think about that. Hastily he ducked his head back inside the window and slid the sash down. He went to the closet, got out his coat, and put it on. Then, moving slowly and cautiously, he opened the door and stepped out into the hall. It was true that he was the only guest in the hotel, but he certainly didn't want Mrs. Woodley to hear him. He tiptoed down the hall and down the narrow back staircase. The steps complained loudly, but there was not much that Johnny could do about that. At the bottom of the stairs there was a door with a bolt on the inside. Johnny drew back the bolt, opened the door, and moved out into the chilly, dark yard. Suddenly he had a thought. He went back, found a brick, and stuck it in the door.

Twigs and gravel crunched under his feet as he picked his way around the corner of the building. Now he was on the side of the inn where his window was. Stooped over, he sidled along, rubbing his rear against the foundation stones. It was pitch black. With his hand Johnny combed the top of a low juniper bush. Nothing there. Well, on to the next one. . . . Ah! There it was, lying on a soft, springy bush, as neat as could be! Johnny reached out and picked the flashlight up. He clicked it on and off. It worked. He heaved a deep sigh of relief and was about to start back toward the door he had come out of when suddenly he froze.

A voice was speaking, somewhere above him. It was Mrs. Woodley's voice, drifting out through a partly opened window. Johnny held his breath and listened. At first it just sounded like a wordless muttering, but as he listened more intently Johnny could make out what the old woman was saying. And the words made the hairs on the back of his neck stand on end.

CHAPTER TWELVE

⊷●⊷

"Chad? Chad? Is that you?" said the cracked, querulous voice. "You've come to stare at me again, have you? Well, my fine young nephew—my *former* nephew, I suppose I should say—I've put up with worse things in my time than your homely face peering down at me. When I learned to control the Guardian, I did some things that you would have run screaming away from when you were alive. Go ahead, shake your head, see if I care! I know, I'm supposed to feel guilty because I put you out of the way. Well, I don't. I have some rights in this life. I've worked hard, and I deserve to have some comforts in my old age. If I had let you find my dear brother's will—and you were just the one who might have done it—what would have happened to me? Answer me that! What if the will had said that dear Herbert had cut me off without a cent? At least, without the will I get *something*! And that, dear boy, is why you had to leave us. I don't know if you were close to finding it. But I wasn't going to take any chances—no sirree!"

Mrs. Woodley had stopped talking. Johnny heard the faint sound of perhaps a bed or chair creaking, a coughing noise, and then the old woman's voice again. "Don't look at me like that, please. I know you feel bad, but there's nothing I can do about it, is there? You were a reckless and irresponsible young man, and well, what's done is done. And I'll tell you something else. There's somebody who's going to be joining you soon. It's that little snot, that boy who was up here last month. You remember—the one I sent that little greeting card to, to try and warn him off? Yes, he's here right now, staying at my hotel!"

Mrs. Woodley laughed, a nasty, sneering laugh. "Yes, and he's after the will. How do I know? Well, when he was here in October, he made a phone call at my hotel, and it so happens that I can read lips. Of course he had no idea that I understood every word he was saying. Yes, he's figured out a great deal, and I'm sure he'd find the will, if I were to let him continue. But just between you and me let me tell you something: He's not going to get anywhere near it, because tomorrow morning he's going to meet with a little accident, and then he'll be where you are. Just think! You'll have some company! Won't that be nice?"

Silence. Johnny crouched under the windowsill. Sweat was pouring down his face, and his body felt goose-pimply all over. So Mrs. Woodley was Mr. Glomus's sister! She knew the will was up there on the estate, and she had killed Chad—or had she? Maybe she was just crazy. She was just talking to herself, or . . .

At that moment Johnny saw something—saw it and felt it too. It was like a gray luminous fog, a hovering cloud shaped like a human being. It drifted out of Mrs. Woodley's bedroom window, and as it moved away Johnny felt icy cold. His scalp tingled, his heart beat faster, and he found it hard to breathe. The shape moved off into the darkness, hovered by the pines, and then faded into nothing.

Johnny closed his eyes and shuddered convulsively. He wished with all his heart that he had never come up here. He wanted to be home safe in his bed. But he wasn't at home. He was up here in New Hampshire, out in the cold and dark, staying in a hotel run by a woman who was planning to kill him. What should he do? He wanted to run off suddenly into the night and hide down by the railroad station till a train came. But his money was up in the dresser drawer in his room. Everything was up there, including the tools he was going to use during his search for the will. Was he going to have to give up on his search, then, to escape from this wicked old woman who seemed to have some kind of super-natural powers?

But Johnny was a pretty strong person, in spite of his timidity. He was panicked, scared half out of his mind, but as he huddled there against the wall he fought it down. Once again his old determination came back.

Johnny thought hard. Many times in chess games he had tried to figure out what his opponent would do next so that he could outwit him. Now he tried to figure out what Mrs. Woodley was going to do. Nothing, probably, for the time being. Tomorrow morning, when he was getting ready to go out to the Glomus estate to poke around—that was when she said she would try to stop him. All right, then, he would mess up her plans. He would escape tonight. He'd just have to go back upstairs and get a few things—the crowbar, the screwdriver, his money, and the map of the roads around Lake Chocorua. Could he summon up enough courage to go back up there? Johnny bit his lip. He closed his eyes, took a deep breath and let it out slowly. Yes, he was ready now. He had to go back.

Cautiously Johnny moved down the wall, scuttling sideways like a crab and gripping the precious flashlight tight in his hand. Around the corner he went and then straightened up to open the door. He set the doorstop aside. Soundlessly he let the door close, and then up the stairs he tiptoed. More creaking—he couldn't stop that. Then down the hall to his room. Johnny slipped inside, closed the door, and let out a deep sigh of relief. Quickly, darting this way and that, he moved about the little room, gathering up the things he needed. Crowbar. Screwdriver. Map. Money. Wallet. Finally he was ready to go again.

It wasn't far to Mount Chocorua and the Glomus estate. Johnny had a fairly good sense of direction, and once he got out onto Route 16, he thought he would remember which way to go. Fearfully he eyed the door of his room. What might be waiting for him outside? With an effort he jerked it open. Nothing but the musty carpeted hallway. Johnny made the sign of the cross, awkwardly, because he was still holding the flashlight, then out into the hall he went.

For hours the professor's car had been speeding along on New Hampshire State Route 16. The professor was behind the wheel, hunched over, gripping it tightly. In his mouth was an unlit Sobranie cigarette, and on his face was a look of crabby determination. A scrubby old deerstalker's cap was on his head, and the fur-lined flaps were tied down over his ears. Sitting next to the professor was Fergie Ferguson. The professor had persuaded him to come along because he was convinced that Fergie could help him find Johnny. After dashing madly from the Dixons' house with some "clues" crammed into his pocket, the professor had driven with lightning speed across town to the Fergusons'. He had barged in on them in the middle of their dinner and, after frightening poor Mrs. Ferguson half to death, had managed to convince the family that he badly needed Fergie's help. The professor was a good guesser. He had found some stationery from the Squam House in Johnny's bureau and was sure that Johnny was after the Glomus will. Then, guessing wildly this time, the professor had decided that maybe Johnny and Fergie knew something about it that they weren't telling him. So after taking Fergie into a back room of the Ferguson home, he gave him the good old-fashioned third degree. At first Fergie had refused to tell him anything. But then, when he realized that Johnny's life might be in danger, he changed his mind and told him about the strange midnight meeting with Chad Glomus and Chad's terrifying disappearance. That was all the professor needed. He persuaded the puzzled Fergusons that their son ought to go with him. They were reluctant to give their permission at first, but the professor pleaded and wheedled. He also added that there was no danger involved—this was not true, but the professor was not above lying to get something he wanted. Finally the Fergusons had insisted that the police be contacted. And the professor had said blandly that of course he intended to do so immediately. This was another lie—for reasons of his own the professor had no intention of bringing the police into this strange and desperate manhunt.

On roared the professor's car. He was a terror on wheels, even when he wasn't on a life-or-death mission. He jammed the accelerator down, and the needle flicked past ninety. Fergie sat rigidly, gripping the edge of the seat with his hands. Once he had ridden with Father Higgins, the parish priest at St. Michael's. He had been bad, but he hadn't been anything like this.

"Professor?" said Fergie in a tight, strained voice. "How . . . how far do we have to go?"

"Oh, not so far now. That town we just passed through is Center Ossipee. It's only about twelve miles to Kancamagus Center. We'll get there soon—don't worry."

Now the tires squeeched loudly as the car rounded a difficult S-curve. Fergie was thrown first against the door, then back the other way.

"Where do you think he'd go?" the professor barked out suddenly without taking his eyes off the road.

Fergie thought hard. "Gee. I dunno. Did you say he bought a ticket at the train station?"

"Yes. I checked there because it was the only possible way for Johnny to get up to that idiotic estate. The ticket was to Kancamagus Center. Could he walk out to the Glomus place from there?"

Fergie thought some more. "Maybe, only I don't think he would want to, unless he's *really* flipped his lid. I bet he'll just sack out somewhere for the night, and then bomb on out to the old estate in the morning."

The professor considered Fergie's suggestion. He grimaced, as he often did when he was thinking, and the cigarette bobbed up and down in his mouth. "Hmm. I think, Byron, that you are most probably right. After all, John doesn't know that anyone is following him, and he can certainly afford to pay for a room. Did I tell you that he swiped about a hundred dollars from his grandparents before he lit out?"

"Yeah, you did. That's not so great."

The professor opened his mouth to sigh, but as he did the cigarette fell out. "Blast!" he snapped. Then he shook his head, and his face tensed up. "I certainly hope he's all right," he said softly, and he pushed the accelerator pedal down harder.

CHAPTER THIRTEEN

❈❖❈

A short time later the professor's car came rolling into Kancamagus Center, where houses, trees, steeples, the wide grassy common, all were still and dreamlike on this frosty November night. The sky was clear, and you would never have guessed that a snowstorm was on its way. But snow was what the weatherman on the radio had said. The professor had heard the report more than once today, and it had filled his mind with fear for Johnny's safety. Now he pulled over to the curb next to the deserted common, turned the motor off, and heaved a small sigh. After some fumbling in the glove compartment, he found his pack of Balkan Sobranie cigarettes and lit one.

"So, Byron," he said, turning to Fergie. "I wonder what our next move ought to be. If we are right, Johnny is holed up somewhere here in town. This Squam House —the one whose letter paper Johnny had—is probably our best bet, don't you agree?"

Fergie nodded. "Yeah, I guess so. We could ask the lady that runs the place if he's there. Only it's really late, an' Johnny told me that she's an unbelievable witch. I think she'd raise hell if we was just to go up an' hammer on her door now."

The professor turned on the dome light in his car. He peered at his watch, which said ten after twelve, and then flipped the light off. "Ye-es," he said slowly, considering, "I imagine she would get into a bit of a snit if we woke her up now. Unfortunately, however, I am a very impatient sort, and I am not going to sit here smoking cigarettes and fidgeting until the dawn's early light. So Mrs. Whosis will just have to get herself into a Grade-A snit. We are going over there *now*!"

And with that the professor turned the ignition kev. The car sprang to life. But then, abruptly, the professor turned the motor off.

"What's wrong?" Fergie asked anxiously.

"Nothing much. I just realized I don't know where that idiotic inn is." Suddenly an idea struck him. He turned the dome light on, again reached over and dug into the glove compartment, and came out with a wrinkled piece of letter paper. He uncrumpled it, and Fergie saw that it was a piece of the Squam House's stationery. At the top was a picture of the inn in green ink, and down below was the motto *The friendly white inn on the common.*

The professor's mouth curled into a sarcastic grin. "Friendly, eh? Well, we shall see."

The professor started up his car again. Slowly the battered old Ford crawled along the dark street, which was getting darker by the minute as black clouds rushed in to cover the moon. The professor peered out the car window owlishly as he examined one blank staring house front, then crept on to the next one and the next one. Finally, with a look of triumph on his face, he put on the brakes. There was the inn, identical to its picture on the letterhead. Although a carriage lamp on a post was shining out in front, the windows were dark.

The professor turned off the motor and sat with arms folded. Looking out at the inn, he shook his head slowly. "She's going to be in a rare mood when we wake her up," he said. "But I'm afraid there's no help for it. Come on, Byron—unless, of course, you'd rather stay in the car."

"Naw, I'll come," said Fergie, grinning maliciously. He thought it might be fun to see a nasty old woman after she had been awakened out of a sound sleep.

Two car doors slammed. Walking side by side, Fergie and the professor strode up the walk, up the steps, and onto the wide porch. The professor harrumphed in a nervous way and jabbed at the bell with his index finger. It was a loud bell, and they could hear it ringing deep inside the inn. At first nothing happened. Fergie rubbed his mittened hands and the professor puffed his cigarette and sang "*Cadet Roussel*," a French nonsense song that he liked. But soon lights began to come on. There was the sound of chains rattling, and then the door swung open. Mrs. Woodley stood before them, wearing a blue quilted dressing gown with a little ruffled collar and holding a small black flashlight. Cold cream covered her face, and she looked very, very angry.

"Well?" she said. Her voice trembled with indignation as she eyed the two of them. "You've gotten me up in the middle of the night—I congratulate you. What do you want?"

Normally the professor was able to hold his own against even the crankiest and most forbidding people. But there was a strange aura about Mrs. Woodley that suggested . . . well, something more than ordinary nastiness. The professor took a step backward, and there was genuine fear in his eyes. But then he pulled himself together and put on his most brusque and businesslike manner.

"Madam," he said crisply, "I deeply apologize for waking you out of a sound sleep on such a cold night and at such a late hour. But the fact is, this is somewhat of an emergency. We are looking for a young man named John Dixon. He's about twelve, and he's pale, blond, and wears glasses. We have reason to believe that he came up here by train and intended to spend the night at your, uh, establishment. Is he here?"

Mrs. Woodley's mind was racing. If she told this man

that the boy was here, then he'd take the boy away, and she'd be rid of him, wouldn't she? But he might come back. No, it would be better to be rid of him once and for all.

"There's nobody staying here tonight but me," she said in her grimmest, most final tone. "I don't get much business at this time of year. Now, if that is all you have to say to me . . ."

Mrs. Woodley stepped back and took hold of the edge of the door, getting ready to shut the two intruders out. But the professor had been watching her like a hawk, and he thought he saw something in her eyes that suggested she might be lying. With a sudden spring he leapt forward and planted both feet on the doorsill.

Mrs. Woodley's mouth dropped open. "I beg your *pardon!*" she began, her voice rising an octave or two.

"Thank you, I accept your invitation," snapped the professor, and with that he shoved rudely past Mrs. Woodley and dashed into the lighted lobby of the inn. This was a desperate gamble on the professor's part. He wanted to get inside to see if he could find something, anything that would prove that Johnny had been there. Wildly the professor looked this way and that. He took in the couches, the easy chairs, the fussy mahogany tables with oil lamps and bric-a-brac on them. But meanwhile Mrs. Woodley was advancing on him, bubbling over with rage.

"*Now, see here, you!*" she yelled. "*What do you think gives you the right to come barging in here and—*"

"Ah-*hah*!" screeched the professor. He leaped toward the reception desk and swept up something in his right hand. He held it up triumphantly between his thumb and index finger. It was Johnny's waterproof matchbox. "So he *was* here after all! And you were lying to me, you foul-tempered old bat! *Lying!*"

The professor waved his accusing finger in Mrs. Woodley's face. But now she had grown dangerously calm. She folded her arms and glowered at him. "That matchbox is mine," she said grimly. "And you are trespassing. I'll thank you to give it back to me, take that ugly little snot over there, and leave *right now*, before I call the police!"

As Fergie watched the professor and Mrs. Woodley facing each other down in the middle of the room, the air between them seemed to shimmer with tension. The professor held the matchbox up and waved it back and forth before Mrs. Woodley's eyes.

"You deny that this is Johnny's?" he shouted, in a voice that was rising in pitch with every instant. "You actually *deny it*?"

Mrs. Woodley glared stonily, saying nothing. A sudden evil inspiration darted into the professor's head. He turned on his heel and strode to the long polished table that stood between the two rows of armchairs. On it was a group of carefully arranged objects: Staffordshire china dogs and cats, glass paperweights, a blue glass medicine bottle, and a Dresden figurine of a minstrel playing a mandolin. The professor remembered now the story Johnny had told him about the fussy old lady who was afraid he would break the vase on her phone table. With a sudden swoop he reached out and picked up a small china dog, wheeled around, and threw it into the fireplace. The dog shattered into thousands of tiny white pieces.

"There!" said the professor with a snort of satisfaction. He turned back to Mrs. Woodley. "Now, then! If you don't want something like that to happen again, you malignant old hag, I suggest that you tell me what you have done with Johnny!"

Mrs. Woodley's face was a mask of cold hatred, and a vein in her neck was throbbing. Suddenly she flicked out her left hand, and as she did this the professor felt a sharp stab of numbing pain. His right hand—which he had used to throw the dog—felt as if an enormous bee had stung it. Clutching the throbbing hand to his chest, the professor reeled back. His eyes were wide with fear.

"That's what you get," crooned the old woman maliciously, "for willfully destroying private property!" Now her tone became harder, angrier. She advanced on the professor, and he retreated, still clutching his wounded hand. "Get out of here!" she snarled. "Get out of here, and don't come back!"

The professor and Fergie did not need any more encouragement. Fergie went first, and the professor dashed after him, slamming the door as he went. Together they stumbled down the stairs, and they were halfway down the walk before Mrs. Woodley emerged on the porch. Her face was purple with rage, and little white flecks of foam appeared at the corners of her mouth.

"*If you ever find him, you may not like what you see!*" she screeched in a voice that was scarcely human. "*And if you try to meddle in things that don't concern you, you'll wish you hadn't!*" With that she stepped back and slammed the door loudly. The thunderous sound seemed to reverberate in the still, frosty night air. Then there was silence, and the lights inside the inn went out.

The professor and Fergie stood by the car, staring in wide-eyed horror at the darkened building. Neither of them said anything for a long while.

Finally the professor spoke. "My God! I never imagined . . . I mean, who could possibly have guessed . . . ?"

Fergie glanced nervously back at the inn. He tugged at the professor's arm. "Come on. Let's get outa here before she comes back and really takes care of us."

The professor nodded. They ran around the car and jumped in.

"I'm going to have to do this one-handed for a bit," said the professor, gasping with pain. "It'll be awkward, but I'll manage." He turned the key and the motor started. Then, bracing his left arm against the wheel and shifting gears with his right, he got the car going. It moved in a wobbly, uncertain way, and he nosed it around to the other side of the common. Then he pulled over to the curb, turned off the motor, and just sat staring blankly at the windshield.

Fergie was worried. Maybe the professor was sick, or dying. "Are . . . are you okay, sir?" he asked falteringly.

"No," intoned the professor. Then he laughed and smiled reassuringly. "In my mind I am blowing up the Squam House with sticks of dynamite. But except for that, I am as well as can be expected, as my sickly aunt Sally always used to say. But what do we do now? *That* is what I want to know!"

Fergie also tried hard to think. "Is she a witch?" he asked at last.

The professor groaned. "Oh, God! Let's not go into that! She's a . . . a *something*, that's for bloody sure!" And with his good hand he pounded on the steering wheel.

"Do you suppose she's holdin' Johnny prisoner?" Fergie asked. "I mean, bound and gagged in a cellar or . . . or somethin' like that?"

The professor shook his head. "No. No, I don't think so. That last thing she shrieked, about 'if you ever find him' . . . that says to me that he's out there in the dark somewhere. No, he must have escaped from her—for now, anyway. That may be why she's so incredibly angry. We can't be sure of anything, of course. But first of all I guess we'd better head out to that awful estate . . . Tooting Stanton, or whatever its name is. If Johnny is anywhere, he's out there. And I hope, I very much hope that we can get in by way of that secret passage that you told me about. Do you think you can direct me to the estate?" Fergie nodded. "I . . . I guess so, Professor Childermass. It's dark, but once we get to the road that goes out to the camp, I think it'll look kinda familiar."

The professor flipped on the headlights and started the motor. "I hope so," he said. Then he put the car in gear and roared away in a cloud of exhaust smoke.

Meanwhile, up in her bedroom, Mrs. Woodley was dragging a strange, bulky object from her closet. It was like a small square chest covered with cracked, goose-pimply leather. Muttering unpleasantly to herself, the old woman folded the top back and part of the front down. Now the box resembled a small stage on which miniature actors might move about. It was dark inside but . . . No! Mrs. Woodley said a word, and it started to glow with a quivering blue light. Strange signs and a picture of a comet with a long flaring tail slowly became visible on the wood. In a row on the tiny stage stood several glass bottles. One was tall and thin, one was pear-shaped, one was very small, and another was all bulbs with a long spout projecting from it. A hissing blue flame shot from the spout, making all the bottles glow. Twisted strands and loops of fire burned inside each one—purple, red, orange, yellow. From a drawer in the front of the box Mrs. Woodley took a small metal holy-water sprinkler. She shook drops over the glowing bottles, and they began to shiver and send up a high-pitched wailing music, like the sound of a glass harmonica. Suddenly a formless patch of golden light appeared on the wall behind the box. In the center of the patch of light was a pyramid with an eye in its center. And over the pyramid were some Hebrew letters glowing with red fire. The mingled colored lights flitted about Mrs. Woodley's face as she stared at them intently. Her lips formed strange phrases, and an incantation rose to mingle with the bottles' eerie wail.

Johnny walked quickly along a dark, gravelly road that cut through great masses of trees. It led from Camp Chocorua to the old estate, and it was a road that he remembered well. Passing through the deserted picnic grounds by dark, still Lake Chocorua had been strange. Although he had not been able to see the mountain itself, he had felt its looming presence. Johnny was surprised to find out what a good hiker he was. Maybe the week in October had done him some good. Whatever the reason, he had covered the three miles in a relatively short time.

His head cold was still a problem, of course. Every now and then he had to set down his crowbar and fish his handkerchief out of his pocket so he could blow his nose. But he wasn't collapsing or anything. He felt strong and brave and purposeful, even though the fear of Mrs. Woodley hovered in the back of his mind.

Johnny slowed down. He played the flashlight's pale beam along the left-hand side of the road as he searched for the little stone that marked the path to the lodge.

Had he come too far? No! There it was, half-buried in leaves. He felt a triumphant surge in his chest. He was doing it! He was on his way!

Johnny turned onto the path and walked on, peering into the darkness as he went. It was easier to see through the trees now that they were bare. In the distance he could make out the quaint steep-gabled cottage with its gothic doodads and carvings. Rushing toward it now, Johnny felt something cold hit his cheek. Snow! Oh, well, it wasn't coming down very hard. As Johnny tramped on, swinging the crowbar jauntily, the lodge drew closer and closer until finally he was standing before it.

Johnny laughed. He felt like Hansel and Gretel at the old witch's cottage. The lodge was like that, a weird fairy-tale house that an old witch might live in. What if he opened the door and found Mrs. Woodley standing there, grinning evilly at him? Johnny shuddered. He really did not like thoughts like that.

After a quick nervous look around, Johnny set the crowbar down next to the doorway. He played the flashlight beam along the row of carved stone ballflowers that ran along the lintel over the door. *Which one had it been?* Ah . . . that one, with the hole in it! Standing on tiptoe, Johnny reached in and pulled out the small, old-fashioned key, fit it into the lock, and heaved open the door. Then he picked up the crowbar and stepped inside.

The room was as musty and dismal and empty as it had been before. Mr. Glomus leered down at him from his frame over the mantel, and for the thousandth time Johnny thought about what a very strange old coot he must have been. However, he had not come here to think about Mr. Glomus. He was here on business.

Johnny examined the front of the fireplace. The smiling children with their cereal bowls gazed blandly down at him. One of those heads was the knob. One, two, three . . . the third one up from the right looked slightly worn. Cautiously Johnny reached up and tried to twist the head. It moved. To his great delight Johnny heard the grumbling of machinery, of hidden chains and counterweights. Slowly, inch by inch, the massive stone slab at the back of the hearth rose up. But then, quite suddenly, the noise stopped. The slab was stuck! By the light of the flashlight Johnny could see a dark opening that was only about a foot high.

Johnny sighed. He knelt down and shuffled on his knees into the mouth of the fireplace to inspect the narrow opening. Could he fit through it? Well, he would have to. First he slid the all-important crowbar into the opening as far as it would go. Then, with his flashlight in his hand, he flattened himself on the floor, wriggled forward over the sooty hearthstone, and squeezed himself through.

On the other side Johnny pulled himself to his feet. For a moment he thought about searching for the lever that would make the slab go back down. But it occurred to him that he might want to come back this way, and if he closed the door, he might—for all he knew—be closing it for good. So Johnny brushed the soot off the front of his parka and picked up the crowbar once more. With the flashlight beam playing before him, he advanced into the dank, foul-smelling tunnel.

Johnny moved forward through the dark. Suddenly, for no reason at all, he remembered his matchbox. He felt in his pockets. Oh, no! It was gone! He had probably left it back at the inn. No time to go back now, though. He pressed on. And now the fear of the Guardian began to creep over him. Inside his head he heard Chad Glomus's horrible screams and remembered what he had said: "The Guardian might be anything: It might be a pool of moonlight on the floor, or a chair, or smoke drifting in the air. It will come for you if you get too close to the will. . . ."

Johnny tried to laugh his fear off. He tried to believe what Fergie believed, and he told himself stubbornly that Chad's disappearance had been faked. He was rich and screwy, and right now he was probably drinking a gin and tonic in a bar in Bermuda. Anything was possible if you were rich, Johnny told himself. But then he thought of the things he had seen and heard when he was crouching under Mrs. Woodley's window, and the fear crept back, chilling him to the bone.

Johnny kept walking. He went up two broad shallow steps to the second level of the tunnel, till he finally saw, far ahead, the stout nail-studded door that led to the crypt beneath the chapel. He stopped, listening for sounds. Nothing. The silence was complete and abso-

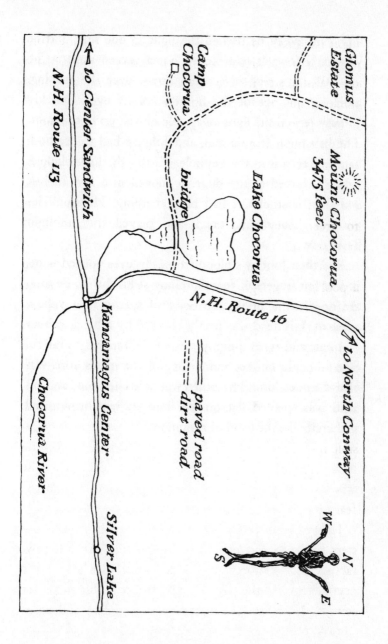

Glomus
Estate

Camp
Chocorua

Mount Chocorua
3475 feet

to Center Sandwich

N.H. Route 113

bridge

Lake Chocorua

N. H. Route 16

to North Conway

Kancamagus Center.

Chocorua River.

Silver Lake

paved road
dirt road

N
W
S
E

lute. Nervously he flashed the light to one side, and he jumped a foot. It had picked out a carved skeleton on the wall. A streak of ice ran down over the carving, blocking out one of the figure's hollow eyes. Quickly Johnny jerked the light away. He moved up to the door. The key hung from a nail, and Johnny had to use both hands to turn it in the keyhole. Finally the lock clicked. Johnny shoved at the door. It moved in a few inches, and then it stuck—it had hit something. He stuck his head in through the crack and played the flashlight beam down.

And then Johnny's blood froze. His eyes opened wide, and he felt fingers of fear clutching at his throat. Beyond the door lay a body, the body of a man in a yellow raincoat. His head was partly covered by a black rubber rain hat, and what Johnny saw made him very grateful that he could not see more. One of the man's arms was folded under him. The other was stretched out, and his hand was splayed flat on the floor. It was brown and withered, like the hand of a mummy.

CHAPTER FOURTEEN

Johnny closed his eyes. A wave of sick terror swept over him. He was afraid that he would faint, or die. But his resolve was strong, and he summoned up all the courage that was in him.

When he opened his eyes, the horrible shape was still there, sprawled on the cold stones. In the midst of his panic Johnny felt terribly sorry for Chad. He had been peculiar, but he had tried to be nice to Johnny and Fergie. He hadn't been particularly likable, but he hadn't been evil. Johnny swallowed hard, and another sick, convulsive shudder ran through his body. This cleared his head, somehow. He had no time to get upset, not now. He had to press on, and if the Guardian caught up with him . . . well, at least he would go down fighting. Johnny got a good tight grip on the crowbar and the flashlight. Then, turning his eyes away, he edged around the slumped body and flashed his light this way and that. The crypt was a low, gloomy chamber, a sort of basement under the chapel. Rows of stone arches stretched away into the distance. *Was there a door that led upstairs?* There had to be. Johnny crept forward cautiously, past heavy round pillars. Ahead, at the top of a low flight of stone steps, he saw what he was looking for. Up the steps he went. The door opened easily, and he found that he was peering into a narrow stairwell. More steps corkscrewed upward. He followed them, and at the top was yet another door. He opened it and found that he was in the chapel.

Because it was dark, Johnny had only a dim idea of what the place looked like. He played the flashlight beam about and saw high wooden pews, a stone altar with a bronze crucifix on it, and a series of gothic arches that marched down the side aisles. Johnny loved strange old buildings, and at another time he might have stopped to explore. But he was in a hurry. So, putting on a look of the grimmest determination, he tramped purposefully down the aisle. At the back of the chapel, under the organ loft, was a big, pointed wooden door with two leaves that were held together by a bolt in the middle. There were spring bolts at the top and the bottom. Johnny slid them back. He pulled the handle and the door swung outward. Cold air rushed in, and snowflakes stung Johnny's face. He was out in the open air again at last.

Johnny felt grateful and extremely relieved. He just stood there a moment, eyes closed, and let the tiny frigid white dots hit his face. He had not been cooped up in the tunnel and the crypt for very long, but it had seemed like ages. Greedily he gulped cold air into his lungs. Johnny wanted to stand there forever, but he knew he couldn't. Doggedly he dragged his mind back to the job that was at hand.

Johnny picked his way down the short flight of steps that led to the open space in front of the chapel. He turned and glanced to his right. Beyond the swirling snow he could just barely see the vast black shadow of the mansion. Before him rose the chapel's tower, a stubby structure with battlements on top. Although the church was gothic, the doorway was classical. It was flanked by fluted pillars with scrolled capitals, and there was a fancy stone cornice over the door. Above the cornice was a triangular stone slab called a pediment. Set in its center was a square tablet made of white marble, and on the tablet was the inscription that had excited Johnny so much when he'd read it for the second time in the book he had found in the library. He had copied the inscription out of the book and had pored over it on the train ride up to New Hampshire. In the dark Johnny could not make out the inscription. Nevertheless he could have recited it by heart:

In the yeare 1653 when
all thinges Sacred were throughout ye nation
Either demolisht or profaned
Sir Robert Shirley, Barronet,
Founded this church;
Whose singular praise it is,
to haue done the best things in ye worst times,
and
hoped them in the most callamitous.
The righteous shall be had
in everlasting remembrance.

Johnny loved the inscription. It sounded grand and thrilling, even though he didn't know anything about Sir Robert Shirley or the calamitous times that he had lived in. He was also filled with smug self-satisfaction, because he had figured out that the *ye* in YE OLDE TEA SHOPPE referred to the two *ye*'s in the inscription. He even knew, thanks to the professor, that *ye* in the old days was sometimes just a funny way of writing *the*. But Johnny didn't have time to pat himself on the back. He had to find some way of getting up to the place where the inscription was so he could examine it more closely.

With a sinking heart Johnny realized that this was not a part of the treasure hunt that he had planned very carefully. Were there any ladders around? He hadn't seen any, and ladders were not the kinds of things that people left lying about on a deserted estate in the wintertime. Then suddenly Johnny grinned. He had been staring at the solution all the time. A mass of ivy vines grew up one side of the carved doorway, twisting about the columns till they spread their hundreds of spidery tendrils across the inscribed stone tablet at the top. And there was even a little ledge under the tablet. If he ever got up that high, Johnny was sure he could stand on it.

Johnny took off his gloves and put them into a pocket of his parka. Then he reached out, took hold of the vines, and started to climb. It turned out to be surprisingly easy. The vines were spread out all across the face of the doorway, and Johnny found handholds and footholds everywhere. And so, before long, Johnny was stepping out onto the narrow ledge that stood atop the doorway. He was still clinging to the vines for dear life, terribly afraid he might slip. But when he finally had a firm footing on the ledge, he let go. Now he was standing over the doorway of the church. It was not a terribly long way down, but even so, if he had taken a step backward, he would have had a pretty nasty fall. Johnny tried not to think about that. Instead he slowly lowered himself to his knees until the inscription was at eye level. From the left-hand pocket of his parka he took out the flashlight. He examined the first *ye*, but there was nothing odd about it. The letters were no more deeply cut than the others around them. Johnny tried the other *ye*, and this time his heart jumped. Around the word was a faint ragged line—a crack in the stonework. It looked as if the crack had been smeared over with plaster at one time, but wind and weather had eaten most of the plaster away. Johnny dug his hand into the pocket on the right side of his parka and pulled out the screwdriver. Holding the flashlight steady with his left hand, he poked at the crack. Immediately more plaster flaked away. The crack got wider, the tip of the screwdriver sank in deeper, and Johnny wiggled it around to widen the crack. All around the wandering circle he went, poking and prying and loosening. Tiny gray flakes fluttered down onto the ledge. Excitedly Johnny pulled back his right hand, and he stabbed as hard as he could. The tip of the screwdriver sank in an inch or more. Johnny pried, and the slab started to move. But the work would take two hands, and so he laid down the flashlight. Now he heaved with all his strength, and the thick slab of stone fell out onto the ledge with a *chunk*. Excited, Johnny snatched up his flashlight and peered into the ragged hole. He expected to see a legal-looking bundle tied with red ribbon, or a metal strongbox with a padlock on it.

But what he saw was neither of these. It was a small square can. The label said Herb-Ox Bouillon Cubes.

Johnny could have cried. Was this it then? Was this what he had come up here for, in the snow, in the dark, in the cold? One last flickering hope remained. Maybe the can contained microfilm, and the will was printed on it. Impatiently Johnny pried the lid off. Inside were little cubes wrapped in gold-colored foil. He unwrapped the first one. And the second and the third and all the rest. Chicken bouillon cubes.

With a violent heave, Johnny hurled the can off the ledge and listened as it clattered on the pavement below. He felt like the biggest fool who ever walked on two legs. By now the professor and his grandparents would be frantic with worry. The police were probably out beating the bushes around Duston Heights. Police dogs were sniffing for him in the woods outside town. And when he came back to them, what could he bring? Bouillon cubes.

Johnny knelt there, facing the wall. He wanted to cry, but the tears would not come. His mind was racing through all the possibilities. If Mrs. Woodley really was a witch, maybe she had changed the will into a can of Herb-Ox Bouillon Cubes. It was an idiotic thought, but right now the idea seemed about as reasonable as anything else that he could come up with. He shook his head and heaved a deep, shuddering sigh. The game was over. He would just have to go home. Glumly Johnny picked up the flashlight, stuffed the screwdriver into his pocket, and carefully pulled himself to his feet. Edging to the right, he reached out in the dark and felt for handholds and footholds among the tangled vines. Now he was making his way down, and he found, strangely enough, that he was thinking of hot cereal. He wanted to be in a nice warm room, in his pajamas and bathrobe, eating a steaming bowl of Gramma's oatmeal, with maple syrup and brown sugar and cream.

But when his foot touched the ground Johnny turned around. It seemed to be snowing harder. He wanted to get away, far from this awful place as quickly as he could. With a sinking heart, he realized that he would probably have to go back down through the crypt. There was a high, spike-topped iron fence around the estate, and he didn't feel up to scaling it. But as he turned back toward the dark doorway of the chapel, he saw something. Someone was coming down the steps toward him with arms outstretched. A figure in a yellow raincoat. A figure with hollow mummy eyes and a withered mummy face and clawlike mummy hands. Moving with an awful, tottering, unsteady gait, it came toward him.

CHAPTER FIFTEEN

✻●✻

Johnny screamed. He dropped the flashlight and ran blindly into the night as the snow swirled around him. Now he saw the vast shadow of the old mansion looming up before him. He could make out its blank, forbidding wall of stone towering up into the night. Madly Johnny raced along the wall, looking for a door. He wished he could see where he was going! It was pitch black out, and if a pit suddenly opened up before his feet, he would fall right in. Now the wall was turning. Johnny turned too. He had seen a couple of tall windows in heavy stone frames. But no doors, none at all. . . .

Then he saw it. A low door, half-sunk in the ground. He could hide till morning, and maybe the awful thing would go away. Johnny was filled with terror. He didn't want to die. He didn't want to end up like Chad. No, not like that. . . .

He was at the door. He shook the knob, but it held tight. Johnny shut his eyes and screeched: *"Let me in!* LET ME IN!" He pounded on the door. Horribly he felt something clawing weakly at his back. Was Chad trying to stop him from entering the building? Was he trying to help him? The thought raced madly through Johnny's brain. *Oh, God, oh, God, please* . . . Johnny gasped, and then, incredibly, the door opened. He did not stop to wonder why but plunged in and slammed it shut behind him.

He had escaped. But what had he escaped into? There had been a little light outside, but there was none at all here. Groping like a blind man, Johnny found a stair railing. Up he went, shuffling, one step at a time. At the top he found another door and opened it. A musty, shut-up smell rushed out to meet him. While Johnny was wondering what kind of room he was in, thunder rumbled overhead, and lightning flashed. For a brief instant he saw a huge kitchen with a long counter running down the middle, and copper kettles hanging from a rack overhead. At the far end of the kitchen was another door. He felt like a rat caught in a maze, or the pinball in a pinball machine. Lightning flashed again, and this time Johnny made a dash for it.

The heavy door boomed behind him. Now he was in the dark again. But as he felt his way along, his hand rubbed the top of something smooth—a table, probably.

Again there was a sudden flash of lightning in the three tall windows, and Johnny had a brief glimpse of an enormous paneled dining room. A table as long as a bowling alley ran down the middle, and rows of high-backed chairs flanked it. He was standing by a low side table, and on the table were . . . candles! Just what he needed! Now, if only he could find some matches! Blindly he groped across the dusty surface of the table. He heard things fall, and something rolled off the table and smashed on the floor. Then his hand closed over a small box. He pushed at the end, and it slid in. A match-box! Johnny's fumbling fingers found small stick matches. He felt the side of the box and *br-rr-rip!* went the match. A pinpoint of sulfurous light flared, and with a trembling hand Johnny lit the candle. Ah, blessed light! Johnny tottered forward across the dusty floor. The candlelight glimmered in a row of tall mirrors to his right. His shadowy reflection made Johnny jump. He stumbled this way and that, holding the candle up and straining his eyes till his head ached. There had to be a way out—a main entrance, or another side entrance . . . something, anything! Johnny gritted his teeth. He would get out if it killed him. Ghosts or no ghosts, mummies or no . . .

A silvery voice began to sing, high-pitched and mock-ing:

> A tisket, a tasket,
> A will in a wicker basket!

and then:

I found it, I found it,
I green and yellow found it!

The voice died away. Then Johnny glanced at his candle. The flame was burning blue! The Guardian was here! For a second he went numb with terror, but he summoned up all his willpower and forced himself to stumble ahead across the dusty floor. He pushed open a set of tall French doors and crossed another room. He paused and looked this way and that in utter bewilderment. And then the walls of the room began to shake. A cobwebbed chandelier trembled overhead, and its thousands of glass pendants set up a loud, alarmed clattering. Panicked, Johnny rushed off to the right. He had seen another set of French doors there. The walls and the floor continued to pitch and heave, like the deck of a ship in a storm. Johnny slipped to his knees. The flame of the candle wavered but did not go out. Staggering to his feet, he made it to the doors, shoved them open, and stepped out onto a curved stone balcony. In the distance, beyond the chapel and the iron fence, he saw headlights. A car! But whose car, and what were they doing? Then he turned and looked up. A row of ornamental stone doodads ran along the top of the mansion —vases, balls, obelisks with carved swags and lions' heads on them. And they were all lit with a ghostly green fire that flickered and made haloes in the air.

A sudden gust of wind blew snow at Johnny, and his candle went out. But then lightning flashed, and Johnny saw that he was standing next to something—a huge statue of a warrior in chain mail. The warrior wore over his suit of mail a surcoat with a Maltese cross on it. The warrior's face was grim, and he had a long drooping mustache. His enormous arm clutched the hilt of his sword, and he seemed to be just about to draw it from the scabbard. On the base of the statue a name was carved. Johnny had seen it only for a tenth of a second, but he had been able to make it out. It was a name he knew from history books: *Godfrey de Bouillon*.

Godfrey de Bouillon
Herb-Ox Bouillon Cubes

Johnny's brain turned somersaults. It spun like a merry-go-round gone crazy. What if? What if he had found the will? Had he thrown away the greatest clue of all? Could he still . . .

As if in answer, the building rocked. It shook as if the walls were made of cardboard, and pieces of stone, roof tiles, and bricks from the chimney stack came raining down. The room that Johnny had just left was already on fire. Huge jagged cracks had opened in the floor, and red flames were shooting up through them. Again the mansion shook. The enormous statue tottered on its base and then went crashing through the railing of the balcony. Johnny clung to a carved pilaster and prayed: *Jesus, Mary, and Joseph, hear our prayers and grant our petitions, Jesus, Mary, and—*

Something hit him in the head, and he blacked out.

CHAPTER SIXTEEN

❧ ● ❧

When Johnny woke up he found that he was lying in a hospital bed. It was daytime, and cold winter light was streaming in through large windows. Next to him, sitting in an armchair by the bed, was the professor. He was wearing an egg-stained brown sweater, and he was smoking one of his eternal black-and-gold cigarettes as he grinned broadly at Johnny.

"So!" he exclaimed in a pretend-gruff voice. "You've decided to favor us with your presence at last! And about time too! How do you feel?"

Johnny was still dazed and uncertain. He didn't know quite how he felt. But now he realized that there was something on his head. He reached up and touched the stiff white cloth of a bandage. Then he remembered being out on the balcony and getting hit on the head.

"Have I been . . . ?" he began, but he found he was having trouble putting words together. He felt vaguely dizzy, and when he moved, a throbbing headache started, just above his left eye.

"Yes, you have been *indeed*!" said the professor, smiling gently. "You have been totally unconscious for about two days. It's a concussion—no, don't worry, it's not fatal. I had one myself once, when I was hit in the head with a shell casing at the Battle of the Argonne Forest. You'll be up and around in a few days. In case you're wondering, you're in a hospital in North Conway, New Hampshire. It's the nearest one we could find. North Conway is a rich little town where people come to ski and drink and sit around and be bored. You should see the overpriced dump that *I'm* staying in. It's a fake Swiss chalet, with cuckoo clocks and everything. Fortunately it isn't the skiing season yet, or the room would cost me half my year's salary at the college. And the bed is lumpy too—would you believe it?"

The professor crabbed on. Johnny grinned and listened appreciatively. He knew that this was cheerful crabbing, a sign the professor was in a good mood. And as the professor talked Johnny found that the cobwebs in his head were clearing away. He remembered why he had come up here—the will, the reward, and everything. He thought about Mrs. Woodley, and Chad, and Godfrey de Bouillon. There were a million questions that he wanted to ask.

"Is . . . is the mansion all burned down?"

The professor nodded. "It is indeed. Burned to a nice crunchy crisp. It's just a heap of rubble now. But it was still going strong when Fergie and I arrived on the scene. We—"

"*Fergie?*" exclaimed Johnny, interrupting. "What was he doing up here?"

The professor eyed Johnny sardonically. "He came up here with me to rescue you. And you will have to admit, my friend, that you needed some rescuing. You were lying in the bushes near the mansion when we found you. The mansion was going like . . . well, it was going like a house afire. Flames shooting out of all the windows, walls crashing down all over the place. Well, Fergie—or Byron, as I prefer to call him—Byron and I fought our way in, and it was hot, let me tell you. But we got to you and pulled you free just before the whole bloody wall came down—blooey, crash, bam!—right where you'd been not a moment before. How about that, eh?"

Johnny was silent. So he had missed death by just that much.

"Mrs. Woodley probably started that fire," the professor went on as he lit another cigarette. "And she started the earthquake and the lightning and all the other fireworks that helped to wreck the mansion. She did it by remote control, with the aid of a very strange witchcraftical box that she found when she was nosing around out at the estate, looking for the will. And how do I know all this? Because of a diary that was found in the bedroom of the dear sweet departed old—"

"*Departed?* You mean she's—"

The professor nodded solemnly. "Yes, I'm afraid so. Kindly old Mrs. Woodley, the proprietor of the friendly Squam House, has gone to glory . . . or she has gone to someplace, at any rate. They found her in her bedroom, slumped over that witch box I told you about. Heart attack, I'm told. If she were alive, she'd have a lot to answer for. According to her diary, she did in Chad Glomus and three other people she found poking around the estate. She was obsessed with her brother's will—terrified somebody would find it and it would turn out that she had been cut off without a nickel. Mrs. Woodley was a clever old bat, I'll give her that. Like you, she figured out the "Staunton Harold" part of the puzzle. But she couldn't get any further. Did you manage to figure it all out? The tea shop sign and everything?"

Johnny frowned. "Sort of. Only I didn't know it. When I got to the last clue, I didn't realize what it was. I thought I'd got rooked. Do you wanta hear about it?"

The professor nodded. And as he smoked, Johnny told him about the inscription over the chapel door. He explained about the two *ye*'s and the can of bouillon cubes and the statue of Godfrey de Bouillon. ". . . and so I think the will has got to be inside of the statue," Johnny concluded. "I mean, it stands to reason that that's where it'd be. Do . . . do you think you could have the police go and find out if it really is there?"

The professor considered this. "Hmm. Well, I guess we'd better have them investigate the matter. The mansion is just a ruin now, as I said before. But the statue is probably there somewhere in the rubble. Godfrey de Bouillon. Huh! Well, you know, while I was waiting for you to recover, I read the little guidebook that you had in your coat pocket. And I did notice the part about the Nine Worthies."

"Yeah," said Johnny. "Who were they, anyway?"

The professor smiled smugly, as he always did when he knew something that somebody else didn't know. "They were sort of a Hit Parade of warriors and heroes of the ancient world," he said. "Let's see, there's Joshua, David, Judas Maccabeus, Hector, Alexander . . . um, don't rush me. . . . Ah, yes! And there's Julius Caesar, and King Arthur, good old Charlemagne, and of course our soupy old friend, Godfrey de Bouillon, the noted knight and leader of the Crusaders. That's nine, isn't it? And in case you're interested, I also know all about the inscription over the chapel door and what it means. But I'll bore you with that some other time. We have more important things to discuss now."

The professor's jaunty, kidding manner disappeared. He grew serious and solemn. "Did you know that Fergie and I were arrested?" he asked.

Johnny was stunned. "You *were*? What for?"

"For arson, trespassing, and attempted burglary . . . those are all the charges, I think, though there may be more. You see, as soon as we had dragged you away from the burning building, we heard this incredible racket. It was the firemen and policemen bashing open the gate in the fence to get in! Yes, indeedy! There must've been about eight fire trucks and I don't know how many police cars, and, luckily, there was also an ambulance. But when the cops found us, they figured we had set the fire. Can you imagine! I mean, what a bunch of ninnies!"

Johnny was worried. "Are . . . are you gonna hafta go to jail?"

The professor chuckled and shook his head. "No, we aren't going to jail. You see, in a case of this sort the owners of the property would have to prefer charges. As you know, the owners are the surviving members of the Glomus family. And when they found out about Mrs. Woodley—Mr. Glomus's sister that was—and the *thing* that was discovered in the ruins of the mansion, and all the other *things* that were scattered all over the grounds of the estate . . . well, they were in no mood to prefer charges against *anybody*!"

Johnny's mouth dropped open. "Things? What things?"

The professor smiled wryly and flicked the ash off the end of his cigarette. "Oh, not much. Just a few hard-to-explain items. First, the police found a mummified body in the ruins of the house. From the clothes, and from the ring and the wallet and the other personal belongings, they have concluded, reluctantly, that it is the body of Chad Glomus. They're going to have to consult dental records to be sure, but for myself I have no doubt that it's the young man who disappeared early in October. Nobody can figure out how the body came to be—"

"I didn't tell you everything," said Johnny, interrupting. "I mean, Fergie and me, we were with Chad just before he died. We . . . we kind of wanted to keep it a secret."

"Yes," said the professor quietly. "I know. Fergie has already spilled the beans. And I must say, it is quite an amazing tale. There's more too. The police decided to do a thorough search of all the buildings on the estate. And what do you suppose they found in Mr. Glomus's mausoleum? The bodies of three other people who disappeared up here during the last few years. They were mummies too, and they were standing up, stiff as boards, against a wall. They were all local characters—two old derelicts and a woman who lived in a tar-paper shack near Mount Chocorua. And they all must've made the mistake of breaking into the estate and nosing around. Mrs. Woodley found out, and that was the end of *them*!"

The professor paused for breath. He heaved a deep sigh and folded his arms. "Well, now, would you like to see what the newspapers have been making of all this?"

Without waiting for an answer, the professor reached

down beside his armchair, picked up a thick sheaf of newspapers, and threw them onto Johnny's bed. They were all copies of the Manchester *Union-Leader*, the most popular paper in New Hampshire. Johnny looked at the headline that was lying on top. HORROR MUMMIES IN CEREAL MAGNATE'S TOMB. He flipped to the next one and read THE WITCH OF KANCAMAGUS CENTER? Another said WAS CHAD MURDERED? MYSTERY DEEPENS.

Johnny flipped quickly through the stack. "Oh, my gosh," he said. It was not much of a comment, but it was the only one he could come up with.

"You see?" said the professor, cocking his head to one side and grinning in that know-it-all way that he had. "This whole shindig has given the Glomus family some very undesirable publicity. And as far as I can tell, they would like to have it all hushed up as quickly as possible. So unless I miss my guess, they're not going to charge the three of us with anything. There will, however, be an inquest. There *has* to be when four bodies are discovered. And you know something? I would *love* to know what those crime-lab clowns are going to say about those mummies! I wonder what sort of silly, trashy, pseudoscientific flummery they will—"

"Hey!" said Johnny, interrupting again. He sat up suddenly, and then, as a sharp searing pain slashed through his head, he sank back onto the pillow. "I . . . we . . . we have to do something! Right now! We have to get the cops to go out to the mansion an' look inside of that statue to see if the will's there! I mean . . . I mean,

Gramma's sick, an' if I don't get the reward money right away, she might *die*! Please, professor! Can you get 'em to do something, right now? Can you?"

The professor put his hand over his face. "For Pete's sake!" he said through his fingers. "Is *that* why you went after the will? John, as Jimmy Durante would say, you been laborin' under a misprehamprehension! Your grandmother isn't dying! The operation was a success, a complete and unqualified success! Of course, she's no spring chicken, but still . . . good grief, why didn't you *ask* somebody?"

A tear trickled down Johnny's cheek. "I was scared. I mean . . . I mean, I got all this bad news, about Dad and all, and I thought the world was comin' to an end! And then I found that letter from the undertakers, so I thought . . ."

The professor nodded somberly. "I see it all now. What a comedy of errors! John, my lad, do you know what that letter was probably about?"

Johnny sniffled. He took a tissue from a box on the table and blew his nose. "Nope. What was it about?"

The professor grinned. "A few years ago your grandfather's brother Willie died. He was next door to being a bum, and after the funeral Willie's wife wrote a check to the funeral parlor, and the check bounced. Well, the undertakers had a fit, and they got after Willie's widow, and she went to your grampa for help. There was a big fight in your grampa's family about who would foot the bill, and, well, your grampa finally persuaded his other brother, Vic, to pay it. Vic is a filthy rich farmer up in Menominee, Wisconsin, and he could afford it. So I suspect—though I'm not absolutely sure—that the letter you saw was just a note from somebody at the funeral parlor thanking your grampa because he had managed to pry the money out of his tight-fisted brother. I'd be willing to bet that that's all there was to that ridiculous letter. And next time if you have any doubts about a letter's contents, steam the bloody thing open and peek inside, for heaven's sake!" With an exasperated "Hmph!" the professor ground out his cigarette in the ashtray. He dug another one out of his pocket and lit it.

Johnny's lower lip began to tremble. Tears were rolling down his cheeks. "I . . . I'm sorry," he stammered. "I didn't know, I . . ."

The professor was shocked—he hadn't meant to make Johnny cry. With an agonized look on his face he jumped out of his chair and rushed over to Johnny's bed. He took the cigarette from his mouth and, after looking about distractedly, he dunked it in a glass of water that stood on the bedside table. When he turned back to Johnny, the professor's eyes were filled with tears.

"Oh, John!" he cried as he seized the bedsheet in his hands and began to twist it. "*Please* don't cry! I'm just a cranky old man, and I can't help sounding grumpy sometimes! It's one of my many faults."

Johnny smiled and dried his eyes with a tissue. "It's okay, Professor," he said, sniffling. "I just feel . . . kinda weird right now, and it's easy to cry. And I'm happy I'm not gonna be alone in the world. That makes me wanta cry too."

"Well, you mustn't!" said the professor, and he smiled a weak, wan, half-joking smile. Still twisting the bedsheet, he stared hard at Johnny. "Look," he said in a grave but gentle voice. "I . . . I think I understand why you did what you did. And in connection with that I have something to tell you. I was going to save this for later, but . . . your dad has been found." Johnny's eyes opened wide and he exclaimed, "When—" But the professor replied quickly, "I'll give you the details later; I just wanted you to know he's all right. But even if he hadn't been found, and even if both your grandfather and your grandmother were to die, I'd still be there to take care of you. I've never had any children of my own, but if they'd let me, I'd adopt you. I'm only seventy, you know. My father made it to a hundred and three, and his father was ninety-eight when the horse he was riding threw him. You don't need to worry about ever being an orphan."

Johnny was going to say something in answer to the professor, but the old man turned away quickly and walked to the window. As he stood glaring out at the snow-covered hillside he harrumphed loudly several times and clicked his false teeth in and out. The professor hated it when he got emotional in front of other people. Then he sat down and talked with Johnny about his father.

Johnny stayed at the hospital in North Conway for a week. During that time the professor went on living at the expensive hotel, and Fergie stayed with him for a day or two. Together they visited Johnny at the hospital every day. Finally Fergie gave a statement to the local police, and then he went home on the train to Duston Heights. After the police got statements from Johnny and the professor, an inquest was held. The coroner's jury decided that Chad and the other three had died "of unexplained causes."

Acting on information from Johnny, the police went out to the Glomus estate, poked around in the ruins, and found the broken, charred statue of Godfrey de Bouillon. By tapping with hammers they discovered that the base of the statue was hollow. A sliding panel of stone could be pulled back, and inside the base of the statue they found . . . a small heap of ashes. The statue had fallen into the basement of the burning building, and the heat there had been so intense that it had been like a brick oven. The will of Mr. H. Bagwell Glomus was gone forever.

Johnny was unhappy when he heard this, but now that he knew his grandmother wasn't dying, the will had become far less important to him. The professor merely repeated what he had said when he heard that Mrs. Woodley had died—*Good riddance to bad rubbish!*

After a week the professor drove Johnny home to Duston Heights. When he arrived, he got lots of hugs and kisses from his grandmother, who was bustling around like her old self now. And Grampa shook the professor's hand so many times that the professor finally had to tell him to stop.

That evening Fergie came to visit Johnny. Despite their chats at the hospital, they had not had a chance to have a really private conversation. So, the first chance Johnny got, he took Fergie up to his room, and they had a long and excited gabfest. Later, while they played chess, it occurred to Johnny that he had at least gotten one good thing out of this whole mess: He had found a new friend.

The next day Johnny went back to school. He tried to pretend that nothing had happened, but everyone had read about Johnny's adventure in the newspapers. They all wanted to ask him questions, and some kids even wanted his autograph. So, by the time he left school at three fifteen, his nerves were thoroughly frazzled. As he turned onto Fillmore Street and started walking toward his house, he found that he had yet another jolt in store for him on this busy, trying day. There was a car parked in front of his house, a sleek black limousine with a chauffeur at the wheel. A wild thought leaped into Johnny's mind: Could it be his dad?

But it wasn't his dad. Johnny's grandmother met him at the door. She was clearly quite upset and nervous as she explained that there was a lady waiting for him in the parlor. Johnny felt let down, but he was still curious. Who could it be? When he walked in, he saw, seated on the couch, a tall, haughty-looking old woman. She wore an expensive flowered silk dress and a pearl necklace. Rings glittered on her fingers, and her iron-gray hair was arranged in a ripply permanent wave. When she saw Johnny, the woman smiled. Surprisingly it was not merely a polite smile but one of genuine warmth and friendliness.

"How are you!" she said, rising and holding out her hand. "My name is Annabelle Glomus. My husband was H. Bagwell Glomus. You've heard of him, I believe?" Mrs. Glomus's eyes gleamed with amusement. And to Johnny's amazement she winked at him!

"I, uh . . . I, uh . . ." Johnny began, but he couldn't get any further than that. He was really tongue-tied.

Still smiling, Mrs. Glomus sat down again. Johnny sank into a seat next to her. What on earth did she want?

Then Mrs. Glomus picked up her large patent-leather purse. She opened it up and took out a checkbook and a gold-plated fountain pen. As Johnny watched she began to write out a check.

"I have heard about your exploits up in New Hampshire," she said with a faint tinge of amusement in her voice. "And I must say that I'm sorry, profoundly sorry, that the famous Glomus puzzle led you on a wild-goose chase and almost turned out very badly indeed. For myself I never thought there was a will at all. I believed the puzzle was merely something dreamed up by my late husband to drive us all mad. But now that it seems there was a will, I must say that I am *extremely* glad it was destroyed. At my age I have no stomach for bickering. It was those greedy sons of mine who advertised in the paper and hounded me into putting up the reward money. They both thought that the will would make them richer—though I could never figure out why. I mean, my dear sweet late husband was capable of doing a lot of strange things. He *might* have left my sons a bundle. On the other hand, he might have left his money to the Ku Klux Klan or to a cat hospital in New South Wales. So, on the whole, I think we're much better off with no will at all. But since you did find the will— that is, you found out where it was hidden—and fair is fair, I want you to have this."

When she had gotten out this last sentence, Mrs. Glomus tore the check out of her checkbook and handed it to Johnny. It was made out to him, for ten thousand dollars.

Johnny was stunned. He tried to say something, but once again words failed him. While he was stammering, Mrs. Glomus stood up and started to leave. At the door she paused and turned back to him once more.

"Good day to you, young man. I hope you do something enjoyable with the money. And I hope you will realize that not all of the members of the Glomus family are like my late husband's sister. Some of us are quite sane and reasonable . . . and nice people too." And with that, Mrs. Glomus turned and swept grandly out of the room, leaving Johnny alone with the check in his hands.

As soon as Johnny had recovered from the shock he ran out into the kitchen to tell his grandmother and grandfather.

"Well, my Lord!" exclaimed Gramma, holding the check up and peering at it in astonishment. "Who woulda thought it? I mean, heavens to Betsy, *who*?" She handed it back to Johnny and shook her head solemnly. "Well, my boy," she said, putting her hand on Johnny's arm, "this has really been a time for s'prises for us all lately! Do you think the s'prises are all over with? For now, I mean?"

Johnny said that he figured they were. But he was wrong. In fact, he had just barely finished speaking when there was a loud squeal of brakes outside. His first thought was that it was Mrs. Glomus coming to take the check back. But when he rushed out to the bay window in the parlor, he saw that the car that had just pulled up was khaki-colored. On its door words were stenciled in white paint: U.S. ARMY. Then Johnny saw the door on the passenger side open. Somebody got out. With a joyful whoop Johnny rushed to the front door and tore it open. He galloped across the porch and down the front steps. Standing next to the car was a man in a gray U.S. Air Force uniform. Battle ribbons and medals covered the left side of the man's uniform jacket, and on his cap and shoulders were the insignia of a captain. His face was craggy, seamed with wrinkles, and deeply tanned. But in spite of the tan, the man's face looked pinched and worn, as if he had just been through a bad time. Nonetheless he was smiling broadly and holding out his arms to Johnny. Rushing forward with happy yells and yips and whoops, Johnny threw himself against the man and hugged him tight. The man hugged him back, and now he was crying. The two of them just stood there, holding each other for a long time.

The Spell of the Sorcerer's Skull

JOHN BELLAIRS

❧

Frontispiece
by Edward Gorey

The Spell of the Sorcerer's Skull

CHAPTER ONE

❧

"Phooey! Phooey on winter and snowy white snow and jingle bells and walking in winter wonderlands! Bah! We should never have come up here in the first place!"

It was a cold February night in the year 1952, and snow swirled around the picturesque white houses and the sprawling old Fitzwilliam Inn in the beautiful little New Hampshire town of Fitzwilliam. It whitened roofs and the grass of the town common, an oblong park that the town was built around, and fell on the heads and shoulders of two people who were trudging slowly around the common. One of these was a short, red-faced elderly man, Professor Roderick Childermass. He had a strawberry nose and wildly sprouting muttonchop whiskers, and he was wearing a battered, shapeless fedora and a threadbare and dirty tweed overcoat. His hands were jammed into the pockets of the coat, and as he stomped along, he kept making bad-tempered comments. Walking next to him was a pale, bespectacled boy named Johnny Dixon in a red stocking cap and a blue parka and galoshes. Johnny was shy and nervous-acting. He kept looking anxiously at the professor, and every now and then he would open his mouth to say something. Suddenly he would change his mind and stay silent.

"Winter paradise indeed!" snorted the professor, glancing fiercely this way and that. "I'd like to give a piece of my mind to the boneheads who settled up in this godforsaken wilderness! *And* to the cheapo types who run the state and don't provide enough money to clear the roads or sand them in the wintertime!"

"Please, professor!" Johnny said in a mild, placating voice. "Don't be angry, please, don't! Everything'll be all right! It really will, you'll see! We've got a room at the inn for tonight, and they're towing your car right now. It's not so bad, really it isn't! And I'm having a good time. The town is wonderful, and I like the inn a lot, and I like going places with you. So don't worry—it'll be all right!"

The professor stopped scowling. He turned and smiled kindly at Johnny, and then he reached out and patted him on the shoulder. "Well, as long as you're not *too* disappointed," he said. "I'm sorry I lost my temper, but I get wrathful every time I think of that slippery road, and us skidding and sliding into that ditch! I wanted to show you New Hampshire in the wintertime, and it really is quite beautiful in the snow. We were having a good time, and then that dratted accident had to happen!" The professor paused. He turned and looked across at the large shadowy inn on the far side of the common. Its windows glowed yellow, and smoke curled from the tall chimneys. All around the common, houses were filled with lamplight. Candles winked in the darkness here and there. Snow swirled everywhere, and was piling up on gateposts and ledges and roofs. It was a lovely, dreamy Christmas-card scene.

"Ah, well," said the professor. "I suppose things *could* be worse!" A gust of wind hit him, and he shivered. "Brrh! But it is getting *cold* out here! How about it? Shall we head back to the inn and have a nice hot drink by the fire before we turn in? I think a hot toddy or a brandy or two would improve my disposition immensely."

Johnny agreed, and they started back. As they drew near to the inn, they heard the grinding sound of an engine, and, turning to their left, they saw a tow truck crawling up out of the dark hollow behind the inn. Hanging from the tow chain was the professor's maroon Pontiac. Its right headlight had been gouged out, and the right front fender was a shapeless mass of dented, squashed metal. The two travelers watched solemnly as the tow truck rolled past. Again Johnny shot a glance at the professor, and he was relieved to see that the old man was taking things calmly.

Johnny liked the professor a lot. He had met the professor a little over a year ago, right after he came to live with his grandparents in the city of Duston Heights, Massachusetts. At the time he had been scared and lonely: his mother had died recently, and his dad had gone off to fly a jet in the Korean War. Later his dad had been discharged from the Air Force, but he had re-enlisted because the Air Force had needed his special skills as a pilot. The professor had befriended Johnny, and his friendship had been like a wonderful gift: he played chess with Johnny, taught him to bake cakes, and went places with him. He argued with him about war and politics, and really listened when Johnny tried to give his opinion about something. For a shy kid who was used to being ignored by grown-ups, this was really something incredible. Johnny was proud to be the professor's friend, and he was willing to forgive him when— every now and then—the professor lost his famous temper.

A little later the two of them were relaxing in one of the parlors on the first floor of the old inn. It was a cozy room, with its cushiony armchairs and sofas, frilly-shaded floor lamps, and faded, tattered red Oriental rug. A fire was roaring in the fireplace, and its light flickered over old dusky paintings and a gilded banjo clock with a brass eagle on top. The professor was sitting in a saggy armchair by the fire with his shoes off and his feet propped up on a low footstool. In his hand was a glass of brandy, and he was smoking one of his black-and-gold Balkan Sobranie cigarettes. His eyes were half-closed, and the look on his face said that he was at peace with the world. Johnny was standing over by a low bookcase in a corner leafing through some of the books. He was trying to find one that would be fun to read in bed.

The professor sipped his brandy and smiled blissfully. "Aaah!" he said. "Sitting around and doing nothing is one of the great underrated pleasures of life! Tomorrow I know that I will have to do something about that wretched car, but right now I wouldn't move a muscle to save it if it was about to fall off a—"

"Hi there!" said a friendly, rumbly voice by the door. "Can I come in and join you guys?"

The professor and Johnny turned and looked. It was the owner of the inn—a man about sixty years old, with grizzled gray hair and a leathery, seamed face. He wore a plaid shirt and a saggy, unbuttoned woolen sweater, old stained work pants, and battered hiking boots. He was smoking a pipe and leaning against the doorpost with his arms folded across his chest, looking very relaxed and at home.

"Of course, of course. Please come in!" said the professor, motioning with his hand. "There's an extra chair here, right by the fire, and it *is* your inn, after all! Have you met my young friend, John Dixon? He's my partner on this ill-fated northern expedition."

Mr. Spofford walked across the room and shook Johnny's hand warmly. Then he went to the armchair that stood near the professor's and sank into it. He leaned back and stared at the fire, puffing his pipe for a minute or two. He looked tired, and was obviously glad to have a chance just to sit and catch his breath for a bit.

After a few more minutes of silent meditation, Mr. Spofford turned and smiled at the professor. "They get your car outa that ditch okay, did they?"

The professor nodded glumly. "Yes, they did. I'm going over to whosis' garage tomorrow morning to see if it will be possible to drive the filthy heap of rust back home. But for now, I'm just glad to be here, safe and sound."

"Glad to have ya, glad to have ya," said Mr. Spofford pleasantly. He leaned back and blew a stream of smoke at the mantelpiece. "I see by the way you signed the guest book that you're a professor, Mr. . . . Mr. . . ." He paused and grinned apologetically at the professor. "I'm sorry. I hate to admit it, but I couldn't read your hand-writin'. Mine's nothin' t'brag about, but yours is worse. Is it Chilmark or Chillingsworth or what?"

The professor glared at Mr. Spofford. His handwriting was awful, and he knew it, but he hated to have people comment on it. "It is Childermass," he said stiffly. "Roderick Childermass, Ph.D."

Mr. Spofford looked shocked. His hand flew to his mouth, and there was an uncomfortable silence in the room. Johnny was bewildered. He glanced from one man to the other. What on earth had happened?

The professor set his brandy glass down on a table by the armchair. He stubbed out his cigarette in an ashtray and folded his hands in his lap. "My dear sir," he began, coldly, "there are a few traitors and renegades in our family history, but on the whole, Childermass is an ancient and honorable name. There was a Childermass at the battle of Agincourt, and another with the barons who forced King John to sign the Magna Carta. So may I ask why my name has given you such a turn?"

Mr. Spofford gave the professor an embarrassed sidelong glance. "Oh, it ain't nothin' against . . . against you personally. Or . . . or your family name. It's only jist that, well, we got this clock here that we show to visitors sometimes, an' it's s'posed to be haunted, an' . . . well, it's called the Childermass clock."

Now it was the professor's turn to be astounded. His mouth dropped open, and he looked positively aghast. "Good Lord!" he said, in a slow, awestruck voice. "So *that's* what became of it!"

At the word *haunted* Johnny's eyes lit up. He had been listening to this conversation with growing interest, and now he was totally fascinated. "Hey!" he exclaimed. "Is it really haunted? And . . . and can we see it? I'd really like to . . ." His voice trailed off. Embarrassment overcame him, and he wondered if maybe he had said something he shouldn't have.

The innkeeper glanced quickly at Johnny, and then he turned back to the professor. "Do . . . do you *know* about this darned thing? I mean, why it was made and what it's for, an' . . . an' everything?"

The professor sighed. He picked up his brandy glass,

swirled the liquid inside, and took a sip. "Alas, yes," he said gloomily. "I know far too much about that clock. And I wouldn't be a bit surprised to hear that it was haunted. Not one bit. So it's here! Good gravy! It was stolen when the old Childermass place—our family home, up in Vermont—got broken into about ten years ago." The professor paused and smiled wryly at Mr. Spofford. "I assume," he went on, "that you wouldn't have told me about the clock if you had been the thief yourself. So would you mind telling me how in blazes it wound up here, at this place?"

Mr. Spofford shrugged. "No. I wouldn't mind tellin' you. It's a weird story, though: y'see, it got left on the front porch here, one night durin' a snowstorm. Next mornin' my wife stuck her head out the front door, an' there 'twas, with a piece o' burlap sackin' pulled over the top of it. No note with it, er nothin'." Mr. Spofford paused and stared at the fire. "Somebody musta wanted t'get rid of it," he added in an odd tone of voice.

There was a brief silence. Johnny could hear the banjo clock ticking and the fire crackling. Suddenly Mr. Spofford leaped to his feet.

"*Well!*" he said a bit too loudly. "Would you two like t'see the darned thing? How about it?"

Johnny said yes, he'd love to see the clock, and the professor agreed. They followed the innkeeper out of the parlor and around a couple of corners, and then down a wide hall that ran from the front to the back of the old building. On their left rose the staircase that led to the second floor. On their right were closed doors. Mr. Spofford opened a door at the far end of the hall, and he flipped a light switch. Johnny and the professor found themselves in a small disorderly room full of broken or unused pieces of furniture. There were cane-bottomed chairs with the seats smashed out, and end tables with broken legs. Against one wall was a stout workbench with a vise clamped to one end, and next to it was a dusty library table. On the table stood the clock.

It was quite large for a shelf clock: two feet wide and about four feet high. The case was made of dark, close-grained wood that shone with varnish. The upper half of the clock was a lot like the shelf and mantel clocks that were made by the Willard Brothers of Massachusetts back in the early 1800s. There was a churchy pointed "roof" on top, and it was flanked by two carved wooden spires. The face of the clock was made of white painted metal with black numerals, and the hands were of curly, fancy cast bronze. Painted neatly on the face were the words *M. Childermass fecit* and the date 1889. In the bottom part of a clock of this sort, you usually saw a pendulum behind a square glass door. But in this case, what you saw was a dollhouse room. It was made to look like the parlor of a well-to-do Victorian house of the 1870s or '80s. Everything was done very carefully in miniature: when Johnny squatted down and peered into the shadow-box room, he saw a red Turkish carpet on the floor and an oval antique table with a green plush cover. On the table were an oil lamp, a pair of glasses, and a Bible.

Next to the table was an old-fashioned easy chair, upholstered in black leather. On the left was a fireplace, with candlesticks and a mantel clock, and against the rear wall was a sideboard with two tiny wine decanters on it. Above the decanters hung an oil painting in a gilt frame. A fussy, curly backed, red velvet sofa stood against the right-hand wall, and near it a door stood ajar, showing a cloak and a top hat hanging on pegs in the hallway. The wall to the left of the fireplace had a built-in bookcase, and before it stood a doll that was made to look like an old man. It had a silky gray beard, a black suit, and a black string tie. The doll appeared to be studying the bookcase, and its hand was stretched out in the act of taking a book from a shelf.

Johnny and the professor squatted down, with their heads close together. They peered into the room, taking in all the odd, intricate details.

"Over there—look at that!" said the professor, pointing a long, tobacco-stained forefinger. "Those things on the shelves on the left side of the fireplace. Aren't they marvelous?"

Johnny looked at the row of built-in shelves. Instead of books, these shelves held objects: teeny baskets of fruit, a set of scales, a wine bottle, and a skull.

"That skull has always kind of fascinated me," said

the professor, reaching farther into the room. "It was brought back from California by my granduncle, and I suppose that it is ivory, or maybe it's bone. At any rate, it's a very curious little doojigger, and cleverly made, but I cannot for the life of me figure out why my father decided to put it into this room. After all, the room is supposed to be an exact replica of the study of our old family home up in Vermont, but there was never any—ah!"

With a sudden indrawn hiss, the professor jerked his hand back. The tip of his finger had accidentally touched the miniature skull.

Johnny was alarmed. "What is it? What's wrong?"

The professor examined his fingertip curiously. "Hmm . . . Well, there's nothing wrong, actually. I just got the oddest sensation from touching that skull. But I suppose it's all my imagination—there seems to be no harm done."

"Cut yourself, did you?" asked Mr. Spofford, stepping forward.

"No, no—nothing of the sort!" said the professor, waving him away. "I'm just an old man, and my nerves are on edge after the trouble we've had today."

Mr. Spofford glanced quickly at the professor, and he seemed to be about to say something. But he changed his mind and turned instead to the clock.

"It's really somethin', ain't it?" he said, patting the side of the heavy wooden case. "By the way, professor.

You said you knew the guy who made this thing. Would you mind tellin' me about this M. Childermass? I'd kinda like t'know."

The professor straightened up and turned to face Mr. Spofford. "Very well," he said dryly. "If you're dying to know, I'll tell you. The clock was made by my father, Marcus Childermass, and it took him five years to do it. He began work on it shortly after my granduncle, Lucius J. Childermass, died. The doll is supposed to represent Uncle Lucius, who died in a very strange manner, and very suddenly, in this room—or rather, in the room of which this is a replica."

Johnny turned and stared in wonder at the professor. "You never told me anything about that," he said in a half-accusing tone.

The professor grimaced. "It's not a thing that I like to think about, or talk about. Uncle Lucius was found dead one snowy evening, on the day after Christmas. He was sitting in that black leather chair there, by the oval table. His head was thrown back and on his face was the most awful look of terror. Also—and this is the strangest part —those who examined the body found bits of foul-smelling earth in his mouth and on the front of his coat. Make something of *that*, if you can!"

"Boy, that is strange!" said Mr. Spofford, scratching his head. "Did they ever find out what the old—er, I mean, your granduncle—died of?"

The professor shook his head. "No, they did not. There was an inquest, and the coroner's verdict was 'Death by unknown causes.' It was what they used to call 'Death by the visitation of God.' And indeed, that is what a lot of people thought—that God had reached out and robbed Uncle Lucius of his life." The professor sighed. "I will add that that explanation was as good as any that people were able to come up with. No one was ever able to find any evidence of foul play."

Mr. Spofford looked thoughtful. He folded his arms on his chest and scowled, and then he threw a quick look at the clock. "And so your dad started to work on that clock there right after your uncle died? Did he mean it to be . . . like a memorial?"

"I suppose you might say that," muttered the professor. "Whatever the clock was supposed to be, it became an obsession with my father. He worked on it every chance he could get—but since he was a busy man, it took him a long time to finish the thing." The professor turned suddenly to Mr. Spofford and stared at him hard. "But tell me," he said, "what's all this business about the clock being haunted?"

Mr. Spofford acted startled, and then he looked a bit frightened. He laughed, but it was an unconvincing laugh—it sounded forced, and a bit hoarse. "Oh, *that*! Well, uh . . . well, that was just a *story*! You know how things get started. My wife, she had a funny dream about the clock an' . . . well, that's where that idea came from. Just one o' my wife's dumb notions, that's all!"

Mr. Spofford *heh-heh*'ed a bit and tried to act nonchalant, but he was not fooling the professor. He hated it when people tried to get evasive with him, and now his stare became fierce and hostile.

"Look!" he said angrily, jabbing his finger at Mr. Spofford. "You told me a few minutes ago that there were rumors of the clock being haunted. You seemed quite serious at the time, but now you're trying to make it all into a big fat joke. Would you mind leveling with me? I'm not three years old, you know, and I'd really like to find out the truth in this matter."

But Mr. Spofford would not say anything more, and so there was nothing left for the professor to do but say good night. Johnny shook Mr. Spofford's hand and thanked him, and then he and his elderly friend went upstairs to their nice warm beds.

Later that night Johnny was awakened from a deep sleep by a rattling sound. He sat up and shook his head groggily. What was making that noise? He glanced to his left and saw a window whitened by frost. Outside, the wind was blowing, and a bare branch was clattering and clawing against the window. The end of the branch was shaped a bit like a hand, and so it was easy for Johnny to imagine that it was some awful creature out there trying to get in. Johnny closed his eyes and shook his head. He tried to get rid of the unpleasant pictures that were forming in his mind. Then he opened his eyes again and stared out into the dark room. The professor was asleep in a bed over against the far wall. Johnny could hear the regular snortling sounds he was making. Noiselessly Johnny slipped out of bed and put on his slippers and bathrobe. He padded to the door, opened it, and stepped out into the hall. The hall was chilly and drafty. A dim night-light burned at the top of the stairs. With an odd, dreamy look on his face, Johnny gripped the railing and started down.

The downstairs hall was dark, and it was even colder than upstairs. Icy air slithered in through the crack at the bottom of the front door, and it stung Johnny's bare ankles. But he moved on, like a sleepwalker, to the door that led to the workroom where the Childermass clock was kept. He paused outside the dark door and put his hands on the wood paneling, listening. He heard sounds, voices. It was as if people were muttering excitedly inside the room. What were they saying? It was impossible to make it out. Johnny's hand moved toward the white china knob. He twisted it and pushed the door inward. Then he gasped.

CHAPTER TWO

Johnny was surrounded by darkness, not the darkness of a small room, but an immense well of blackness. It was as if he were standing in a great hall or a cathedral. Before him, like a window in the night, was a lighted room. It was small and seemed very far away, yet somehow he could see every detail. It was like the dollhouse room in the old clock, but it was a real room in a real house. It was night, and Johnny could see snow falling outside the window at the back of the room. The oil lamp on the table was lit, and a fire burned in the white marble fireplace.

The figure in the room was like the doll, but it was a living man, an old, distinguished-looking gentleman with a gray beard and rimless spectacles. He was pacing back and forth before the fire, and he looked worried. As Johnny watched, he sat down in the leather chair by the table, picked up the Bible, and began to leaf through it. Eventually he found a part that interested him, and he settled down to read. From far away Johnny heard the ghostly ticking of the mantel clock and the crackling of the fire. The old man read for a while and soon grew tired. He took off his glasses and slid them into the case on the table. After stifling a yawn, he rubbed his hands over his face. Then he leaned his head back, folded his hands in his lap, and dozed off. Johnny watched, wide-eyed. Blood roared in his ears, and his fists were clenched, but he stayed rooted to the spot: what would happen next?

He didn't have long to wait. As the old man slept, a subtle change came over the room. The flame of the oil lamp grew dim and dwindled to a blue point. The fire in the fireplace died, as if some unseen force were smothering it. And then a door in the rear wall of the room began to open. The light that fell through the doorway was cold, pale, and wavering. At first Johnny saw only the open door and the watery, shimmering light. Then he saw a tall, gaunt shadow that moved with dragging steps through the doorway and into the room. The light was poor, and so Johnny could not tell much about the shape, except that it was fearfully thin and appeared to be wearing ragged clothes. As he watched, the shape moved toward the sleeping man and hovered over him. The old man opened his eyes and looked up, and Johnny heard him scream. It was a thin wailing sound that seemed to come from far away, and it chilled Johnny to the bone. The old man shrank back in his chair as the gaunt, menacing figure bent over him. It stretched out a long thin hand and covered the old man's face, and then the old man began to struggle and writhe. Frantically he tried to push the hand away, but his struggles got weaker and weaker, and finally he lay still, slumped back in the chair. A pause. Then the figure took its hand away from the old man's face, bent over, and peered horribly close, as if it were trying to make sure that the man was really dead. Finally the shadowy form straightened up, shuffled toward the door, and went out. Immediately the scene went black. And Johnny was left alone in the dark cold workroom, listening to the wind that keened and moaned around the corners of the ancient inn.

For a long time Johnny cowered in the dark, wide-eyed and wondering. He was awed and frightened by what he had seen. But what was it that he had witnessed? It looked like the murder of Professor Childermass's granduncle. If that was it, then who had the murderer been? Was it a ghost who had snuffed out the life of the old man? And finally Johnny asked himself this question: Why had he, John Dixon, been brought down here to see this strange, ghostly drama? Was he supposed to warn the professor about something? And if so, what? Johnny had no answers for any of these questions. As he peered nervously around in the dark, he saw the faint outline of the old clock looming on the table next to the workbench. Shuddering, he turned and felt his way to the door. But the room was very dark, and as Johnny groped along, he caught his toe on the end of a loose floorboard and lurched up against the table that held the Childermass clock. From inside the clock came a jangling of chimes and a rattle of machinery, and then —to his horror—Johnny heard something roll out across the tabletop and drop onto the floor. It sounded like something small, maybe one of the delicate pieces of furniture from the dollhouse room.

Filled with guilt and worry, and already making up apologies in his mind, Johnny dropped to his knees and began scrabbling around on the floor with his hands. His fingers closed over something small and round, like a marble. Pulling himself to his feet, Johnny took a step toward the dark clock. But shouldn't he switch the light on so he could see what he was doing? Turning, Johnny took a few stumbling steps toward the door. Then— strangely—instead of trying to find the light switch, he grasped the doorknob, opened the door, and stepped out into the hall.

With the door closed behind him, Johnny leaned against the wall, breathing heavily, and opened his hand. The light out here in the hall was dim, but he could see what he had—the skull! With an odd, fasci- nated expression on his face, Johnny turned the grotesque little object over in his hand. Then, with a sudden motion, he shoved the skull into his bathrobe pocket and padded on down the hall.

Johnny did not get any more sleep that night. He went back up to bed, but he tossed and turned and kept glancing nervously at the door of his bedroom. If it had suddenly begun to open, he was sure that he would have gone out of his mind with fear. But the door stayed shut, and Johnny lay there fretting and listening to the wind. He thought about what he had seen and about the tiny, toylike skull that he had stolen. It was in the pocket of his corduroy pants now, where he had stuffed it for safe-keeping. Why didn't he want to give it back? Johnny couldn't say, but he did know one thing: when dawn came, he was very glad to see it.

Later that morning Johnny and the professor were down in the dining room of the inn having a wonderful wintertime breakfast, pancakes and sausage and hot coffee, but Johnny was not eating much of it. He felt totally socked. There were dark circles around his eyes, and his face felt prickly.

"John," the professor said anxiously, "you really look *terrible* this morning! What on earth is the matter? Did my snoring keep you awake?"

Johnny put down the piece of sausage that he was toying with and glanced warily at the professor. He realized that he ought to tell his friend what had happened last night. It was a strange and unlikely tale, but he was sure the professor would believe him. And it would get an incredible load off his chest. Nervously Johnny stuck his right hand into his pants pocket. His fingers twiddled with the ivory skull, and he opened his mouth to speak—but something unexpected happened. He found that he couldn't talk! His jaw shuddered, and he struggled, but nothing came out. There was a pain in his chest, as if a band of steel were wrapped around his body, and someone were twisting it tighter. Finally Johnny stopped trying. He slumped back in his chair, exhausted. Sweat was streaming down his face, and he was scared half out of his mind.

The professor was stunned. "My Lord, John!" he exclaimed. "What in heaven's name is the matter? I've never seen you like this before! Do you want me to call a doctor? What should I do?"

Johnny didn't know what to say—he didn't even know if he *could* say anything. But the pain in his chest had gone, and he was breathing more easily. He was feeling better because he had stopped trying to tell the professor about the vision he had seen. Frightened, Johnny knew that he had to yield to this spell—or whatever it was—that had been cast on him.

"I . . . I guess it was just heart-heartburn or something like that," he muttered faintly. He closed his eyes, took out his handkerchief, and mopped his forehead. "I . . . I'm sorry I scared you," he added.

The professor was still quite concerned. He had seen cases of food poisoning when he was in the army, and he knew it could be fatal. He was ready to go out to the kitchen and give the cook a severe talking-to, but Johnny insisted that he was okay. And so the two of them went back to eating.

After an uncomfortable silence Johnny spoke up again. "How's your car doing?" he asked. "Is . . . is it wrecked, or can we go home in it?"

The professor made a sour face. "Ah, yes, my car! Well, I went over to Finsterwald's Garage before break-fast, and they told me that I could stagger on home with it. They said I might get picked up for having only one headlight, but considering all the one-eyed cars I've seen driving around in the last year, I will be *very* put out if the cops stop me. Yes, it's driveable . . . but the bill for the towing and the etcetera is not pretty, it's not pretty at all! However, I suppose it must be paid. . . ." The professor's voice trailed off. He leaned forward and stared hard at Johnny. "Are you *sure* you're okay? You're in my care while we're on this trip, and I'd feel awful if something happened to you. Please be honest with me. If you're feeling ill, I'll take you to a doctor and have you checked up."

Johnny really got flustered this time. He did not want to be taken anywhere for a checkup. So he gritted his teeth, smiled in what he hoped was a reassuring way, and forced himself to eat two mouthfuls of pancakes and syrup. "Yeah, I'm all right," he mumbled, as he chewed. "Let's not talk about it anymore, okay?"

After they had finished their meal, the professor went out to the front desk to settle the bill and Johnny went upstairs to the bedroom to get the suitcases. Then the two of them got ready to stump off through the snow to Finsterwald's Garage to fetch the poor battered Pontiac so they could drive home.

A month passed. The snow melted, and the ice on the Merrimack River broke up and washed out to sea. As the March winds boomed in the trees, kids started playing softball on muddy vacant lots. Johnny Dixon went on with his usual life. He did homework, watched television, and went places with his best friend, Fergie. He helped his grandfather carry out the ashes from the furnace and raked up some soggy leaves that were left from last fall. He visited with the professor and ate pieces of his delicious cakes and played chess and backgammon with him. But all the while, in the back of his mind, he carried around the memory of the eerie scene that had been played before his eyes in that dark back room in the Fitzwilliam Inn. Several times he got his courage up and decided that he would try to tell the professor about what had happened. But each time he felt that awful tightening pain in the chest and a deep nameless fear that was enough to stop him. Of course, he could have tried to tell somebody else about his experience, but in his mind the whole incident was surrounded with fear. It was as if he had done something horrible that he didn't dare talk about. So Johnny just kept quiet about that cold windy February night. He didn't tell Grampa or Gramma or Fergie or anybody.

He also kept clammed up about the skull. It was funny how he felt about it: He wanted to protect the thing, to preserve it from harm. For a while he carried it in his pocket, but he got worried that it would drop out through a hole in his pants or get scarred up by coins or his house keys. So he put the skull in an old blue watch-case with a snap lid, and he kept it hidden under the shirts in his top bureau drawer. Now and then his conscience would prick him, and he would feel guilty about keeping the skull. Shouldn't he wrap it up and send it back to the Fitzwilliam Inn? He could do it anonymously and stay out of trouble that way. But then he told himself that skulls were lucky. He remembered the story the professor had told him about Mexican village festivals, where they made candy skulls and ate them for good luck. And now that he thought about it, it was possible that the skull had saved him from an awful fate. He remembered the shadowy evil shape he had seen in the vision. What if it had decided to go after him? It might have done just that if the skull had not fallen out of the dollhouse room and landed at his feet. Perhaps there was some kindly force at work in the haunted clock, a force that had said, *Here, take this talisman—it will protect you from harm.* This was the way Johnny reasoned, and his reasoning always led him to one conclusion—he'd better hang on to the skull and keep it safe.

On a Thursday night late in the month of March, Johnny and his friend Fergie were doing their homework in the parlor of the Dixon house. They went to different schools, in different parts of the city, but they both were taking Latin, and right now they were helping each other memorize the demonstrative pronoun *hic, haec, hoc. Hic, haec, hoc* just means *this*, but it has lots of forms, and you have to memorize them if you are going to pass beginning Latin. Fergie was a gangly, skinny kid with dark skin, black, greasy, curly hair, a long, blunt-ended nose, enormous ears, and droopy features. At this moment he was trying to get through *hic, haec, hoc* without a mistake.

"*Hic, haec, hoc,*" Fergie began, "*hujus, hupus, hujus; huic, huic, huic; hunc, hanc, hoc . . .*" Fergie's voice began to waver—he was getting the giggles, as he always did when he said these silly words too many times. He fought the laughter down and struggled on: "*Hoc, hac, hoc. Hi, hae, haec; horum, harum . . .*" But it was no use—he couldn't go on. He was giggling helplessly now.

Usually when this kind of thing happened, Johnny would break into laughter too. But this time he got angry. His face turned red, and he slammed the book shut. "Oh, come *on*, Fergie!" he yelled. "Will you cut that out! We've got *work* to do!"

Fergie was so startled by Johnny's outburst that he stopped giggling. He stared, open-mouthed. What on earth was the matter with his friend?

"Hey," he said in a soft, wondering tone, "what's got into you, John baby? I mean, it's not all *that* important, to lose your temper about! It's just a crummy Latin test, and you'll probably cream it anyway—you always do. So why're you in such an uproar, huh?"

Johnny put down the book he was holding. He wiped his hand across his face and shook his head. Sometimes you can be in a rotten mood and not know it until you pop off at somebody. That was the way it was with Johnny today. And it wasn't just bad temper all by itself. He had had a deep sense of foreboding all day. In his belly he felt that something bad was going to happen to somebody that he knew. He had brooded and worried, and that was why he was so edgy right now. He felt like somebody who is waiting for a thunderstorm to break loose on the world.

"I . . . I'm sorry, Fergie, honest I am," he stammered. "I dunno what's the matter with me. I've been worried all day about . . . about something. I keep thinking that a really awful thing is gonna happen."

"You mean, like you might step on a nail and get tetanus?" said Fergie, grinning. He knew about Johnny's fear of tetanus, and it amused him no end.

Johnny shook his head. "Nope," he said miserably. "It's not something that's gonna happen to me. It's gonna happen to somebody I know, like you or Gramma or Grampa or the professor. I don't know why I have this darned feeling. I just do, that's all."

Fergie frowned skeptically. He was a real no-nonsense type—at least he tried to be. In some ways he was just as superstitious as Johnny, but he put up a good front. He was always saying that he believed in science and cold, hard facts. "You're probably just comin' down with a cold," he said, shrugging. "My uncle Harvey always used to think that he was gonna die durin' the night, while he was sleepin'. But he didn't—he got killed in a car crash. You can't believe in these funny feelings that you get."

"Maybe not," said Johnny. He grimaced and bit his lip. "All the same," he went on, "I wish I knew why I felt this . . ."

Johnny's voice died. He had been looking around while he talked, and he had happened to peer out the big bay window. Across the street was the professor's house, an enormous two-story barn of a place. There were lights on downstairs, but the upstairs windows were dark. Except for one. In it an orange jack-o'-lantern face glowed.

Johnny was utterly astonished. "Hey!" he exclaimed, poking Fergie in the arm. "Look at that, would you!"

Fergie looked, and he did a double take. Then he let out a long, low whistle. "Wow!" he said, shaking his head in awe. "Your pal the professor has finally gone out of his jug! I mean, he's only about seven months early for Halloween! My gosh! Whaddaya think of that?"

Johnny didn't know what to think. But his sense of foreboding came back, stronger than ever. It was true that the professor had a weird sense of humor, but making a jack-o'-lantern in March . . . well, it just didn't seem like the kind of thing he would do. For a long time Johnny just stood there, watching, while the grinning orange mask hovered in the darkness. Then—reluctantly —he went back to working on his Latin with Fergie.

Johnny thought a lot about the jack-o'-lantern that evening. After Fergie had gone home, he wondered if maybe he ought to call the professor up and see if everything was all right. Which—as Johnny told himself— was a silly, worrywart kind of thought. Why *shouldn't* everything be all right? If the professor wanted to make jack-o'-lanterns in March, that was his business. And it probably didn't mean that he had gone out of his mind, or was going to hang himself from the chandelier in the dining room. The professor was an oddball, and oddballs did peculiar, unpredictable things. And yet . . . there were still a lot of *and yet*'s in Johnny's anxious mind when he went to bed that night.

The next morning, as Johnny was leaving the house to go to school, he saw the professor backing his car out of his driveway. Probably he was heading for Haggstrum College, where he taught history. Suddenly a thought seized Johnny: He ought to go over and make some mention of the jack-o'-lantern to the professor, just to see what his reaction would be. Quickly he ran down the steps and out into the street. He was waiting as the professor's car slid slowly past, spewing clouds of exhaust smoke. Johnny reached out and rapped on the car window with his knuckles, so the professor would know he was there. The car halted, and the window rolled down. As soon as the professor saw that it was Johnny, he grinned.

"Good morning, John!" he said, smiling wearily. "As you see, I'm on my way to that wonderful temple of learning where I try to beat ideas into the heads of dullards. Would you care for a ride to school?"

Johnny said that yes, he'd like a ride. But there was something he wanted to ask the professor about first.

"Oh, really?" said the professor dryly. "Would you like to know about torture methods in sixteenth-century England? Or how many blows of the axe it took to chop off the Duke of Monmouth's head? Something like that?"

Johnny laughed. "Nope. I just wanta know how come you made a jack-o'-lantern when it's only March."

The professor's mouth dropped open. He was utterly dumbfounded. "You want to know how come I made a *what?*"

Now it was Johnny's turn to be astonished. This was not a reply that he had expected. Of course, the professor might be kidding—but he didn't act it. "I . . . I mean the j-jack-o'-lantern that w-was in your up-upstairs window last n-night," said Johnny. He often stammered when he was flustered or upset.

The professor continued to stare at Johnny. "My dear friend," he said slowly and gravely, "either this is some kind of bizarre joke that you're trying out on me, or you need to get a new pair of glasses! I don't make jack-o'-lanterns even when it *is* Halloween! They attract trick-or-treaters, and I cannot stand that kind of silly, greedy rigmarole! John, honestly, I have no idea of what you're talking about. Are you sure you didn't see the reflection of the moon? Or maybe it was my bedside lamp. It has a reddish shade. Well, if you don't mind, I think we'd better be getting on, or we'll both be late for school. Hop in, won't you?"

Johnny opened and shut his mouth a couple of times, but he couldn't think of anything to say. He sighed weakly, walked around the car, and climbed in. As they drove down the street he sat staring numbly at the dashboard. He felt dazed. Was he going out of his mind? No, that couldn't be, because Fergie had seen the jack-o'-lantern too. With a sick feeling he realized that there was another possible explanation: The professor might be losing *his* mind. Johnny had heard that sometimes old people got very scatty and did peculiar things, and even forgot the names and faces of people they had known all their lives. But the professor did not act like someone who had lost his marbles—he was behaving just like his usual cranky but likeable self. It was all very strange. Again Johnny had the urge to tell the professor about the vision—or dream, or whatever it was—that he had seen at the Fitzwilliam Inn. He opened his mouth to speak, but suddenly he felt that shortness of breath, that tightening in the chest. And he decided that he had better think of other things until it was time to get out of the car.

That evening, after school, Johnny and Fergie went to the movies together. This was a Friday-night habit of theirs, and they went in good weather or bad, to lousy movies or to good ones. On this particular Friday, they happened to land a really rousing, slam-bang pirate movie. They always sat way down in front and munched popcorn and made smart remarks, until the usher came down and threatened to throw them out if they didn't shut up. After the show, as they walked the dark, windy streets, Fergie and Johnny talked about the professor and the problem of the jack-o'-lantern that was—or was not—there.

". . . and he claimed that he never made one, and he got really huffy and acted insulted when I said he did," Johnny was saying as they stood at a corner, waiting for the light to change. "But you saw it, didn't you?"

"Yeah . . . I guess so," said Fergie uncertainly. He wrinkled up his nose, as if he were smelling something unpleasant. Fergie liked mysteries, but he always felt they ought to have nice, reasonable explanations. "Sure —there was a jack-o'-lantern," he added as the light changed and they started across the street. "An' I'll tell you how come the old so-and-so made it: He got a little schnockered an' he carved it out, jist fer fun, an' then when you asked him about it, he got embarrassed an' tried to lie his way out. How's that for an answer to your great big fat mystery? Huh?"

Johnny gave Fergie a dirty look. He liked the professor a lot, and he didn't enjoy hearing anybody call him an "old so-and-so." Also, to tell the truth, he did not think much of Fergie's wonderful explanation.

"The professor doesn't ever get drunk," said Johnny, frowning stubbornly. "And besides, when I asked him about the jack-o'-lantern, he didn't act embarrassed—he really didn't! He just looked at me like I was from outer space. Like he'd never heard anything so unbelievable in his life."

Fergie stooped and picked up a rock that lay on the sidewalk. He threw it across the street, and it pinged loudly as it bounced off a fire hydrant. "Maybe he's a real good actor," said Fergie, who could be just as stubborn as Johnny when he thought he was right.

"He's not *that* good an actor," muttered Johnny, digging his hands deep into the pockets of his jacket.

"Well, then, what the heck *was* the darned thing?" exclaimed Fergie impatiently. "Was it a mirage, like the kind they have out in the desert? It had to be real—it just *had* to be! And don't tell me it was a ghost. That's the next thing you'll be tryin' to say!"

Silence fell. The two boys trudged moodily along, staring at the sidewalk. Two blocks passed, and then they reached the Main Street Bridge. Fergie lived over in Cranbrook, on the other side of the bridge.

Fergie threw a shamefaced glance at Johnny. He wanted to stay friends, and he was beginning to be afraid that he had hurt Johnny's feelings by telling him that his ideas were dumb.

"Look," said Fergie hurriedly, "I gotta go. But we can talk about this later. Maybe we can figure out what really happened."

"Yeah, maybe," muttered Johnny. He wanted to be alone, so he could think things out. "See ya around."

Fergie turned and walked off into the darkness. Johnny trotted across Main Street and started climbing the steep hill toward home. The wind had let up, and the night was still. Up ahead, off to the right, loomed the dark shadow of the professor's house. Johnny glanced up, and his jaw dropped. There, leering down at him from a second-story window, was the jack-o'-lantern.

Fear clutched at Johnny's heart. He told himself that he was being silly, that this was the professor's idea of a joke. For a long time Johnny just stood there, gazing like a hypnotized person at the sinister, grinning mask. Then, abruptly, he made a decision: he had to find out what was going on. Johnny raced across the street and cut through a gap in the spirea hedge that bordered the professor's front yard. Nervously he scanned the front of the house. Overhead the lantern burned, but the downstairs windows were dark. He could see that the window over the porch was lit—that was the professor's study, where he often was at this time of night.

Warily Johnny crept forward. Acorns and twigs crunched under his feet, and he stumbled over a dead limb. But he righted himself and moved steadily on. He could see that the back porch light was on, and there was a lamp lit in the kitchen too. Johnny paused. *Why was he so tense?* Blood was pounding in his temples, and he kept expecting to see horrible things come rushing at him out of nowhere. But nothing happened, and he edged closer to the back porch. He tried the screen door.

It was unlocked. So was the inside door. The professor's kitchen was in its usual messy state, with unwashed dishes piled in the sink. A saucepan with something black burned inside it was sitting on the stove, and the kitchen table was covered with flour. An old-fashioned Waterbury clock ticked quietly on a shelf above the spice rack.

"Hello!" Johnny called, cupping his hands to his mouth. "Professor? Are you home?"

No answer. Johnny felt embarrassed. He shouldn't be barging in on his old friend this way. But he just *had* to find out about that lantern. Also, for no reason that he could put his finger on, there was a growing fear that something bad might have happened to Professor Childermass.

Johnny walked through the first floor of the house, peering into empty rooms and calling the professor's name. At the bottom of the stairs he paused again. Should he go up? Maybe the professor was just out for an evening stroll. He might come back at any minute. Or he might be upstairs in his study, correcting papers or reading. Johnny gritted his teeth.

One more try first. Cupping his hands, Johnny bellowed up the stairs: *"Hey, professor! Are you home?"*

Again no answer. Clenching his fists resolutely, Johnny strode up the steps. At the top he paused a second longer and then headed for the professor's study. The door was ajar, and the desk lamp was on. Everything looked perfectly normal. The professor's desk was littered with blue examination books, and the stuffed owl on the pillar in the corner glowered indignantly at Johnny. But the desk chair was empty. As Johnny moved farther into the room, he saw some things that astonished and disturbed him. On the desk pad, next to the pile of exam books, was a cup of coffee. Steam curled up from it—it was still hot! And, perched on the lip of the glass ashtray, was one of the professor's black-and-gold Balkan Sobranie cigarettes. It was half-smoked and still lit. The pungent aroma of the cigarette tickled Johnny's nostrils. Had the professor been called out of the room a second or two ago? If so, where was he?

Johnny went out into the hall. He glanced toward the bathroom. But the door was open, and from where he was standing he could see that the room was dark. He was really panicky now—he could feel his palms sweating. He crept to the entrance of the professor's bedroom and, with a sudden motion, flung the door inward. It banged loudly against the wall, and the violent noise almost made Johnny scream. But he got control of himself and flipped on the overhead light: nobody there. Johnny braced himself for the next step. He had to go down to the room where the jack-o'-lantern was. Nervously he clenched and unclenched his fists and tried to calm himself. *Why was he so scared to do this?* With a grim frown on his face, he strode boldly down the hall and stopped outside the massive paneled oak door. With a loud exclamation he seized the knob and twisted it. The door flew open, and Johnny's hand fumbled for the light switch. A harsh glare flooded the room. In it was a gloomy mahogany bed, a marble-topped bureau, and a chair with a caned seat. White lace curtains hung on the room's only window. There was no jack-o'-lantern. There wasn't even a table or stand on which one could have been standing. Nor was there the smell of hot pumpkin and candle wax that hung in the air where a jack-o'-lantern had been burning. The only smell in the room was the wonderful aroma of balsam-fir needles that rose from a pillow-shaped white packet that lay on top of the bureau. A canoeing scene was picked out in green thread on the surface of the cloth packet, along with the words WELCOME TO NEW HAMPSHIRE.

Johnny fought down the shapeless fear that was in his mind. At the far end of the narrow room, next to the window, was a closet door. Could there be a jack-o'-lantern in there? Maybe one of those new plastic ones, with a light bulb in it. That would explain why . . .

Halfway to the window Johnny froze. He had seen something out of the corner of his eye, a sudden image in the small rectangular mirror that hung over the bureau. He turned and looked. In the mirror he saw the professor's face, looking haggard and disheveled. His eyes pleaded and, as Johnny watched, his lips formed silent words. *"Help me."*

CHAPTER THREE

Johnny gazed, horror-struck. As he watched, the picture in the mirror dissolved into writhing curls of steam. The steam evaporated, and Johnny was looking at his own frightened face. Somehow, he got out of the room. He galloped down the hall, down the stairs, and out the back door, slamming it hard behind him. Outside, under the cold stars again, he halted. His face was streaming with sweat, and he was breathing hard. *"What can I do, what can I do, what . . ."* Johnny babbled hysterically. Then he pulled himself together. There was nothing he could do—not right away. Something awful, something supernatural, had happened to the professor. But at least he was alive. If he weren't, he would not have been able to speak to Johnny from the mirror. But where was he? In outer space? In another dimension? Buried deep under the earth? Where? And what did his disappearance have to do with the ghostly scene that Johnny had seen in the Fitzwilliam Inn? Johnny had no answer to any of these questions. He was totally, thoroughly stumped.

Suddenly Johnny realized that he was supposed to be home. His grandmother always worried about him when he was out at night. By now she would be phoning all the—

A sound interrupted Johnny's thoughts. It was a phone ringing inside the professor's house. He knew who that was. Throwing a quick glance at the silent, empty house, he set out for home on the run.

Gramma was waiting for him on the front steps. The porch light was on, and he could see plainly that she was not in a good mood. Gramma was frowning darkly, and her arms were folded across the front of her apron.

"John Dixon," she said angrily, "what on *earth* do you mean by stayin' out so late? I've been worried sick about you! I called the movie theater, an'—"

"Gramma," said Johnny, cutting in on her excitedly, "there . . . there's something wrong across the street. The professor's gone! He's disappeared!"

Gramma snorted skeptically. "Huh! I'll just bet he has! Young man, is that the best excuse you c'n come up with? Eh?"

Johnny's heart sank. He felt utterly helpless. How was he ever going to explain to his grandmother what he had seen? Gramma was superstitious, but she would hardly believe what he had to tell her. What would she say if he started talking about phantom jack-o'-lanterns and ghostly faces in mirrors?

Johnny hung his head and looked ashamed. "I . . . I'm sorry I stayed out late," he said in a low, hesitant voice. "I forgot what time it was and . . . and I had a question about my schoolwork that I wanted to ask the professor. I won't do it again. Please don't be angry."

Gramma's harsh look softened, and she smiled and opened the screen door for Johnny. "All right, young man," she said, trying hard to sound stern and forbidding, "but don't let this kind of behavior turn into a habit. You run on upstairs 'n' brush your teeth 'n' wash your face 'n' get off to bed! It's gonna be rise 'n' shine early tomorrow mornin', so you better catch some shut-eye."

"He really is gone, Gramma," said Johnny, glancing quickly at the old woman. "The professor, I mean—he's not there!"

Gramma shrugged. "Old bachelors like him keep funny kinds of hours," she said as she hooked the screen. "If you're all by yourself you c'n stay up all night 'n' nobody'll mind. But don't you worry. He'll be comin' outa that front door in the early A.M., just like he always does."

Johnny shook his head gloomily. After what he had seen, he knew very well that the professor was not going to be there tomorrow. Or the next day, or the day after that. Johnny felt horribly frustrated. He wanted to yell that she was wrong. He wanted to tell her that witchcraft and dark mysterious forces were involved in the professor's disappearance. But with a mighty effort, he forced his feelings back down inside. Grimly he plodded up the stairs. He went to his room and put on his pajamas. After brushing his teeth he flung himself into bed and lay there, wide-eyed, waiting for the sleep that he knew was not going to come.

All that night Johnny tossed and turned. Again and again the professor's tormented face appeared before him. *Help me. Help me.* And Johnny wanted to scream back at him, *How? How'm I gonna help you, I don't even know where you are!* Twice he jumped out of bed and ran to the window to stare wildly at the professor's house. He kept hoping that he would see his old friend come ambling up the walk. But the street lamp threw its cold light on the empty sidewalk, and the professor's house stayed dark. Back in bed again, Johnny tried a new angle: Had he been hallucinating? The mind could play tricks—he knew that. But he was so utterly sure that he had seen the face in the mirror. And then there was the jack-o'-lantern—Fergie had seen it too. And on top of everything else, Johnny still had the nagging feeling that the vision he had seen in the Fitzwilliam Inn— the vision that he couldn't tell the professor about—had something to do with this mystery. Some evil force had kept him from telling the professor about the ghostly scene he had witnessed. Why? If the professor had known about the vision, would he have guessed about what was going to happen to him? Nothing made any sense to Johnny at this point. In his mind he feverishly chased old clocks and inns and grinning jack-o'-lanterns around and around and around. When dawn came, he felt exhausted, as if he had been running for miles. He also felt heartsick: He knew his dear old friend was gone, and he wondered if he would ever see him again.

In the morning Johnny was so socked that he hardly knew what he was doing. He clumped down the front staircase slowly, as if there were weights on his feet. When he reached the bottom, he saw the front door was open. Grampa was standing out on the porch, taking in the morning air. He was a tall, stooped, friendly old man in his midseventies, and he wore gray work shirts and gray wash pants all the time. Instead of heading out to the kitchen for breakfast, Johnny decided that he would go out and talk to Grampa for a minute. And he was desperately hoping that he would see the professor come out of his house as usual, get into his car, and drive off to the college to teach his Saturday-morning World History class.

Grampa turned as he heard the porch boards creak behind him. "Oh, hi, Johnny!" he said with a little wave of his hand. "Nice mornin', huh?"

"Uh huh," said Johnny, and he forced himself to smile. He stepped out onto the front stoop and stood next to Grampa. Putting his hands in his pockets, he tried to act casual. But he wasn't really nonchalant—he was terribly interested in seeing signs of life across the street. Straining his eyes, he tried to see through the dingy windows of the professor's garage door. But it was impossible for him to tell if the old beat-up Pontiac was in or out.

"Has the professor left yet?" he asked in a tense voice.

Grampa frowned and shook his head. "Nope. He might be sick t'day, er else maybe he finally got rid o' that Saturday class of his. Funny though . . . most o' the time he's up an' out by now."

Again Johnny experienced that sick feeling rising inside him. He felt totally helpless. He wanted to drag Grampa across the street and make him search the professor's house. But what good would that do? Johnny felt uncontrollable tears welling up inside him. Abruptly he turned and ran inside, and Grampa watched him go with a wondering frown on his face.

Somehow Johnny got through breakfast. Then an idea hit him. He would call up Fergie and get him to meet him. Skeptic or no skeptic, Fergie was his best friend. He was going to have to listen to his story.

"Hello? Ferguson residence. Byron speaking." Fergie sounded grumpy, but then he always did in the morning. Johnny had been to Boy Scout camp with Fergie, and he knew he was the slowest waker-upper in the world.

"Hi. It's me, John. Can I talk to you a minute?"

"Yeah, I guess so. I was just on my way out the door. So what's up?"

"I want you to meet me down at Peter's Sweet Shop right away. I've got something I have to talk to you about."

Fergie snickered. "What is it? You gettin' married? You want my advice about your love life?"

Now Johnny felt irritated. Fergie knew that he was shy with girls, and he liked to kid him about it. "No, it isn't that, lover boy. So can you meet me or not?"

"Yeah, sure, I'll meet you," said Fergie amiably. "See ya later." And he hung up.

Peter's Sweet Shop was an old-fashioned soda fountain with a marble counter and high stools and deep wooden booths with curly sides. There were colored glass lamps, and a jukebox, plus a display case up in front with boxes of candy in it. The kids of Duston Heights came to Peter's all the time after school and on weekends to eat hot fudge sundaes and slurp sodas and other gooey treats. As soon as he could get away from the house, Johnny headed straight down there. When he arrived, he found Fergie perched on a stool, drinking a cherry Coke.

"Hi, Dixon!" he said, smiling sarcastically. "So what's the big deal? Government secrets? Are you a Commie, and you wanta confess to me?"

Johnny frowned. He was not in a mood for kidding. "C'mon," he muttered, motioning toward the back of the store. "Let's get a booth, an' then I'll tell you the whole deal."

Fergie followed Johnny to the back of the shop. They

slid into one of the booths, and a waitress came over and asked for their order. Fergie ordered a dish of fudge ripple ice cream to go with his Coke, and Johnny asked for a chocolate frappe. The waitress went away, and Johnny eyed Fergie nervously. How was he going to manage to tell him this strange, unlikely tale?

"Well?" said Fergie, grinning expectantly.

Johnny squirmed in his seat. He folded and unfolded his hands and stared hard at the Formica tabletop. "Look," he began slowly, "you . . . you remember that jack-o'-lantern we were talkin' about?"

Fergie groaned and covered his face with his hand. "Oh, *no*! Dixon, come *off* it! Not that jack-o'-lantern business again! Can't you just—"

"No, I can't! This is serious business, Fergie, so just be quiet and listen, or else leave!" Color had flooded into Johnny's face, and he looked wild.

Fergie was startled. Most of the time Johnny was a mild-mannered, timid kid. This outburst caught Fergie off guard—now he was the one who felt shy and nervous.

"Okay, okay!" said Fergie softly. "Don't have a fit! Just tell me what it is you wanta tell me!"

So Johnny told about seeing the jack-o'-lantern again and about what he had found when he entered the professor's dark, silent house. He didn't leave anything out, and as he plunged headlong through this tale, he kept thinking: *I don't care if he thinks I'm crazy! I've GOTTA tell him!* Finally he was done. He sat back, tense and expectant. What would Fergie say?

At first Fergie was silent. Though he never would have admitted it, tales of the supernatural fascinated him. On the other hand he wasn't going to swallow every wild tale that his friend threw at him. He wanted some kind of proof before he accepted anything.

Fergie folded his hands and cracked his knuckles. He gazed out the window and tried to act skeptical and calm.

"Look, Dixon," he said quietly, "you don't wanta go flyin' off the handle. I mean, you might've seen somethin', but on the other hand you might've got panicky and *imagined* that you saw somethin'. No offense meant, but I think that's possible."

Johnny glared at Fergie. "I didn't imagine anything, and I saw what I saw! Now, are you gonna help me, or not?"

Fergie threw Johnny a quick, frightened glance. He had never seen Johnny act quite so forceful and downright certain before. This helped to convince Fergie that Johnny's tale might possibly be true.

"Oh, *okay*!" said Fergie, slamming his hand down hard on the table. "I feel like a dope, but I guess I hafta help you. Whaddaya think we oughta do?"

This question took Johnny by surprise. He really didn't have a plan of any kind. "I dunno," he said sheepishly. "I thought you might have some kind of an idea."

Fergie grinned. "Whaddaya think, I look like Sherlock Holmes er somethin'?" Seeing that Johnny was not amused, Fergie grew serious again. He drummed his fingers on the tabletop and stared hard at the melting ice cream in front of him. "Okay," he said wearily, "here's what I think: If the prof's really gone off into Dimension X or out to Mars, we aren't gonna get him back in a hurry. I mean, are we?"

Johnny shook his head glumly. "Nope," he said.

"*But!*" said Fergie, stabbing a forefinger at Johnny. "But still, and even if, he might be somewheres right on this earth, mightn't he?"

Johnny nodded.

"Right!" said Fergie. His eyes shone, and he acted agitated, as he always did when he was putting a logical train of thought together. "Okay then. We hafta find out where he is. And even if he's off with the mullygrubs on another planet, maybe we can figure out some way to bring him back. I mean, it's possible—*anything's* possible! But we need some clues. We hafta have something to go on! I think we oughta go back to his house an' snoop around. An' we better do it in a hurry. Pretty soon they're gonna know that the old guy really *is* missin'! I mean, your grampa and gramma and Mrs. Kovacs and the cops are gonna know, and they're all gonna be in the house pokin' around an' knockin' things over an' takin' things an' labelin' 'em Exhibit A an' so on. So we better get ourselves in gear an' hike on back to his place. Sound like a good idea to you?"

Johnny agreed. He took a few more slurps of his frappe, and Fergie gobbled some ice cream quickly. Then they paid their bill and headed out the door. Just as they were turning onto Fillmore Street they saw a police car parked out in front of the professor's house. Apparently the professor had missed his morning class, and someone from the college had driven out to his place to check up on him. The front door of the gray stucco mansion was open, and a small crowd of people had gathered on the sidewalk that led to the front porch. Johnny recognized Gramma and Grampa and Mr. Swartout and a few of the other neighbors. A short burly policeman with bushy gray hair was asking questions and jotting things down on a notepad. Another one was standing in front of the house with his arms folded, as if he were guarding the place.

Johnny's hand flew to his mouth, and his heart sank. "Oh, no!" he groaned. "How are we ever gonna get inside *now*?"

Fergie was not upset, however. "Come on, Dixon!" he snapped. "Use your old bean! We can just double back an' go down the alley that runs behind the garages an' then zip in the back door an' have ourselves a look around. Simple, eh?"

Johnny thought a second. He knew the alley, of course. He had used it many times to get to the other end of Fillmore Street without his grandmother seeing him. "Yeah, but wait a minute!" he said. "What if there's cops inside the house? What d'we do then?"

Fergie smiled cynically. "We just say 'Oops, sorry!' an' then skedaddle! You an' the prof are old friends. You can just say you left one o' your schoolbooks in his house.

It's not anything to get all that worked up about."

So Johnny and Fergie turned around and went back through the narrow alley that ran behind the houses on Fillmore Street. The yard gate next to the professor's garage was open. When they tried the back door, they found that it was locked, but Johnny knew that the spare key was kept under a flowerpot on the ledge of the kitchen window. Soon they were inside.

The kitchen was exactly as Johnny had seen it last night—nothing had been touched. Silently Fergie and Johnny crept through the big old house. Johnny led the way, telling Fergie that he wanted to check out the professor's study again. Last night he had been in such a panic that he hadn't really had a chance to observe much. And he was convinced that if the professor had left a farewell note or anything of that sort, it would be in the study.

The study door creaked as Johnny pushed it open. Everything looked just as it had last night: there on the desk were the scattered exam books, the cup of coffee (now cold), and the half-smoked cigarette in the ashtray.

"Wow! This place's a mess, isn't it?" whispered Fergie.

"Yeah, it usually is!" Johnny whispered back. He looked around. Yes, the professor's study was in its usual slovenly condition. Books were stuck any-which-way into the sagging bricks-and-boards bookcases. A dune of papers and looseleaf notebooks was heaped against the front of the big kneehole desk. Rollers of dust moved across the bare wooden floor, stirred by the breeze from the open window.

"Well, where should we look?" asked Fergie hoarsely. He was still whispering, and with good reason: The study was at the front of the house, and through the open window they could hear the policemen and the others talking down on the front walk.

"How should I know?" Johnny shot back. "Why don't you check out that table by the door? There're some papers on it, and they might be important. I'll have a look at the desk."

Cautiously, with many nervous glances toward the window, Johnny edged around behind the desk. He scanned the things on the desktop, and he noticed, with amusement, that the professor had written a crabby comment on the exam book that lay at the top of the heap. He had given the exam a grade of C minus, and he had scrawled a few words in red ink on the blue cover: *If you could possibly learn to write decent English, you might be able to unscramble your mixed-up . . .* But this was as far as the professor had gotten. His last word had ended with a sharp downstroke of the pen, and at the end of the stroke was a hole, as if the professor had jammed the pen down hard into the book. Near the book lay the professor's green Estabrook fountain pen. The pen point was badly bent.

Johnny pondered this clue, wondering what it might mean. While he was thinking, his gaze wandered. Was there anything more that would help them in any way?

Part of the desktop was covered by a green blotter, on which the professor had doodled his usual geometric patterns and flowers and funny faces. To the left of the blotter stood a small bronze bowl with rubber bands and paper clips and a large green rubber eraser in it. And there was a glass paperweight full of sand from the Great Desert of Maine, a rack of pipes, a gray Balkan Sobranie tobacco can, and a large, tasteless cigarette lighter shaped like a knight in armor. Johnny felt confused and disheartened. There weren't any big fat clues staring him in the face, were there? But then detective work was not supposed to be easy. He pursed his lips and glanced to his left. He noticed something that he hadn't noticed before.

Over in the corner, behind the floor lamp, was a dictionary stand. It looked like a lectern, with a screw mechanism that allowed you to raise or lower it. Propped up on the slanted top was a lined yellow notepad, and the top sheet was entirely covered by a large drawing. It looked like this:

Johnny stared at the drawing. It was done in pencil, and the drawing style was definitely the professor's. But what made the whole thing so odd was this: The professor never did huge drawings. His doodles were always small, like the ones on the desk blotter. So why had he done this sketch, which looked like a capital letter *L* wreathed about with a vine? Was he trying to say something? And if so, what?

Fergie's voice cut in on Johnny's thoughts. "Hey, Dixon!" he hissed. "We better get outa here! I mean, those cops might decide to come back in and have another look around. Didja find anything?"

Johnny sighed. "Nope. Not much. I'm gonna take this drawing back with us. It might be a clue. You're right, though—we better make ourselves scarce. C'mon!"

CHAPTER FOUR

❧

That afternoon Fergie and Johnny got together down at the public library. They were supposed to be doing their homework, but they were actually there to compare notes about their visit to the professor's study. Naturally they couldn't sit in the main reading room and babble at each other. So they went to the upper level of the stacks, where they could stand behind the rows of iron bookshelves and talk in a fairly normal tone of voice. Unfortunately, they soon found that they really did not have a lot to discuss. Fergie had found absolutely nothing, and Johnny had only come up with two things that he thought were of any importance: the pen and the drawing. Fergie was not impressed by either of these "clues."

"So what if he did mash up the point of his pen?" he asked in a bored tone. "Everybody knows he's got a rotten temper. You told me he throws dishes sometimes when he gets mad."

"Yeah, but the dishes are from the ten-cent store," Johnny replied. "He never breaks anything that he really likes. And he was crazy about that pen. He used to keep it in a special case in his desk. It's wrecked now—didja see the way the point looked?" Johnny crossed the index finger and the middle finger of his right hand to show how the two parts of the gold-plated nib had gotten crossed. "He would *never* have done that on purpose!" Johnny added insistently.

"So how do you think the pen got busted?" Fergie asked.

Johnny shrugged. "I dunno."

There was an awkward pause, and then Johnny spoke up again.

"I think that drawing I showed you might be the only real clue we have. But I can't figure out what it means."

Fergie shrugged. "Oh, what the heck, let's see it, Dixon. Didja bring it with you?"

"Uh huh." Johnny took his Latin book out from under his arm. He opened it and pulled out a folded square of lined yellow paper. Unfolding it carefully, he handed the drawing to Fergie.

Fergie examined the picture, humming all the while. Suddenly he snapped his fingers. "Hey! I bet I know what this is! It's a *rebus*! You know what a rebus is?"

Johnny felt insulted. He was proud of all the obscure facts that he knew, and he knew about rebuses. A rebus was when you used objects and letters to represent somebody's name. Rebuses appeared in coats of arms, like the two gates (two-door) that were used as a symbol for the royal house of Tudor.

"Yeah, I know about rebuses, an' I probably know more about 'em than you do!" said Johnny irritably. "So what does this represent? Huh?"

Fergie smiled smugly. "Well, there's an *L* and there's a vine. Put 'em together and you get L-vine. *Levine!* Smart, eh?"

Johnny thought about this for a bit. "Ye-ah, it *might* be . . ." he said slowly. "But where does that get us? I don't think I ever heard the professor mention anybody named Levine. I would've remembered it if he had."

Fergie looked disappointed. But he persisted. "Okay, so you never heard of anybody he knew that was named Levine. So what does that prove? Maybe some guy outa his deep dark past, some gangster named Itchy Thumb Levine, came an' kidnapped him, because the prof owed him some dough. Makes sense, doesn't it?"

Johnny turned to Fergie wearily. The look on his face showed total despair. "You still don't believe I saw his face in that mirror, do you?" he asked. "You just can't admit that it could've been a ghost or a wizard that took the professor away. You've gotta have some kind of one hundred percent proof, or you won't believe *anything*!"

Fergie stared at the floor. "I think we oughta go down

an' finish our homework," he muttered. "We're not gettin' anywhere on this thing!"

"No, I guess we're not," said Johnny gloomily. He was up against a stone wall, and he knew it. He felt angry at Fergie for being so skeptical. Johnny was utterly convinced that he had seen the professor's anguished face in that bedroom mirror. It hadn't been a panicky hallucination or the result of bad nerves or anything like that. But even if Fergie had accepted Johnny's version of the story, where would that leave them? Nowhere. Absolutely nowhere.

Days passed. Weeks passed. The professor became a Missing Person. His picture was shown on TV and printed in the newspapers. His description was read aloud on the radio several times a day. Ponds and rivers were dragged, and forests were searched. But no leads turned up. He hadn't taken his car—it was still parked in his garage. Most of his clothes were still hanging in his bedroom closet. His suitcases gathered dust in his attic. Wherever he had gone to, he had taken the clothes on his back and not much more.

As time went by Johnny began to miss the professor a lot. It was as if a big piece of his life had been swept away. He missed the professor's cranky comments on everything under the sun. He missed the chocolate cakes and the chess games and the long discussions about history and war and politics and life in general. He missed this strange, eccentric, good-hearted old man who had been such a wonderful friend to him. Every day as he walked home from school Johnny would stop and stare at the professor's house. It looked shut up, abandoned. The blinds were drawn, and already some kid in the neighborhood had taken good aim with a rock and had broken an attic window. Sometimes Johnny would stare up at the ridiculous, ramshackle radio aerial on the roof of the cupola. The professor had built it so he could pick up the Red Sox broadcasts better. Whenever he saw the aerial, tears sprang to Johnny's eyes. And then he felt angry and frustrated and wished he were able to wave a magic wand and summon the professor back from wherever he was. But he couldn't do that, and more and more, as the days passed, he began to feel that the old man was probably gone for good.

One Tuesday early in May Johnny was called out of school to help serve at a funeral. Johnny went to a Catholic school, and for him, going to church was very much a part of school life. The church stood right next to the school, and Johnny had been trained as an altar boy. Altar boys help the priest when he says Mass: they light candles and bring him books and cruets of water and wine. To serve at an ordinary daily Mass only two boys are needed. But at a funeral Mass you need at least five: two to carry candles, one to carry the tall gilded cross that is mounted on a pole, and two to carry the censer and the incense bowl as the priest walks around the coffin and offers incense smoke to it. After the service one of the boys rides out to the cemetery with the priest and hands him the holy water sprinkler and the prayer book when the priest says the final prayers at the edge of the grave.

On this particular day Johnny rode out to the cemetery in a big black Cadillac that belonged to the Digby and Coughlan Funeral Home. The driver was a solemn-looking young man in a black suit. Johnny sat in back with Father Higgins, the pastor of St. Michael's church, who was a tall, glowering man with grizzled gray hair and a squarish jaw. He was an old friend of the professor's—Johnny had seen them playing pinochle and arguing many, many times. During the Second World War, Father Higgins had been an army chaplain, and he had been wounded in a battle on the small Pacific island of Guam, which he always pronounced *Goo*-ahm. The war had given Father Higgins a permanent case of bad nerves and a violent temper, and half the kids at St. Michael's school were scared to death of him. Johnny had always gotten along with him, however; partly it was because he was mild-mannered and never gave Father Higgins a hard time. And partly it was because Johnny really knew his Latin and could rattle it off at a furious pace during the church services, without stopping or stumbling over words. As he sat next to the priest in the car an odd notion came floating into Johnny's mind: Maybe he could get Father Higgins to help him find the professor.

At first this thought seemed so ridiculous to Johnny

that he almost laughed out loud. But the more he thought, the more logical the idea seemed: after all, priests were involved in magic. The rituals they performed in church were sort of like magic rituals, and they recited long incantations in Latin that were almost like spells. And Johnny knew that Father Higgins believed in ghosts, witches, vampires, and things of that sort—he was always telling stories about weird and uncanny things that had happened to friends or relatives of his. Unlike Fergie, he would not insist on having everything proved beyond a shadow of a doubt. Anyway, it was worth a try—*anything* was worth a try at this stage of the game. So later, as they were driving back to the church, he decided to take the plunge.

"Uh . . . Father?" he said hesitantly.

Father Higgins was reading his breviary, which is a small black book full of prayers. He looked up, startled. "Hm? Oh! Yes, John? What is it?"

Johnny screwed his face up into several funny expressions. He was just too afraid to tackle this question head-on. Instead he approached it in a roundabout way.

"Father? Er . . . what would you do if you had lost something really valuable and you wanted to get it back?"

Father Higgins closed his book and smiled thoughtfully. "Well," he said, "I know it's just a superstition, but I would pray to Saint Anthony. I lost my keys in the rectory one day, and I prayed to Saint Anthony, and I found 'em right away. You're not *really* supposed to believe in stuff like that, but all the same . . . well, I'd give it a try if I were you. I really would."

Johnny was startled. He really hadn't expected a suggestion of this kind. Of course, he knew about Saint Anthony: He was the patron saint of lost objects. Johnny's grandma was always praying to the saint to help her find pins, needles, and lost money. But could Saint Anthony help you find a lost *person*?

There was silence in the car for a while. Father Higgins laid the book down on the seat and dug his hand into the pocket of his black overcoat. He pulled out a stubby briar pipe with a silver band on the stem. With an odd smile on his face, he turned the pipe over in his hands. Then he glanced suddenly at Johnny—it was a keen, piercing, unnerving glance.

"Of course," he said in an insinuating tone, "if you're looking for lost *people*—lost professors, for instance—there is a ritual that folks use. It's full of hocus-pocus and it's totally unreliable, but it might just be worth a try."

Johnny looked at the priest and blushed. Father Higgins had read his thoughts. The priest was laughing, and Johnny did too. It was a relief to laugh—he had been pretty tense about this whole business.

"I ought to've known that I couldn't put one over on you, Father," said Johnny shyly.

"Darned right you can't," said the priest, still chuckling. "And anyway, the professor is my friend too. I miss him a lot." He paused and added sadly, "I think he was probably one of the few real friends I had in the whole wide world."

Johnny was only half-listening to what Father Higgins was saying. He was all worked up about the "ritual" that Father Higgins had mentioned, and he wanted to quiz him about it. "Father?" he said hesitantly. "What about . . . I mean, you mentioned a ritual of some kind. I wondered if maybe—"

"Ah, yes!" said the priest, cheering up suddenly. He began to study the bowl of his pipe as if there were dark secrets hidden there. "I did mention something of that sort, didn't I? Well, I know I'm going to sound like a superstitious old Irishman, but I think I would leave a petition under the base of the statue of Saint Anthony in our church. You know the statue I mean, don't you?"

Johnny nodded. He knew it well. It was a large painted plaster figure that stood on a pedestal in front of one of the pillars in St. Michael's church.

"Well, then," the priest went on in a conspiratorial tone, "how about if you and I meet in the church this coming Wednesday night, after the service? This was something that I was going to try myself, but I kept thinking that it was an idiotic notion. However, now that you've put the flea in my ear, I'm a bit more eager to try. I have a few little extra—hrrumph!—things to throw in, just to make the ritual more, uh, *effective*. Not that I think we'll get any results worth writing home about, but—as they say—it can't hurt."

Johnny believed in superstitious practices and magic

more than the average kid did. And it seemed logical to him to think that maybe the professor could be located and saved by a magical rite. After all, his disappearance had been surrounded by strange supernatural omens and signs. If magic had snatched him away, maybe magic could bring him back.

And so, when Wednesday evening came around, Johnny went off to St. Michael's church. Every Wednesday night during the month of May special services were held in the church in honor of Mary, the mother of Christ. Normally Johnny did not go to these services, so Gramma and Grampa Dixon were quite surprised when he told them he was attending. Gramma would have gone with him, but she had a cold, and she was afraid the night air would make it worse. Johnny was immensely relieved that she wasn't going: he felt nervous and embarrassed about what he was doing, and he wanted as few spectators as possible when he and Father Higgins did their mumbo jumbo. All through the service his mind was elsewhere. He kept thinking, *Will it work?* Well, he'd know fairly soon.

The service ended, and the people filed out of the church. When Johnny was sure that he was alone, he got up and walked to the front of the church and stood before the statue of Saint Anthony. It was about six feet high, and since it stood on a tall pedestal, it towered over him. The statue showed Saint Anthony as a monk in a brown robe. He was holding a book in one hand; the other hand was raised in a blessing. There was a gilt halo behind his head, and on his face was a blank, wide-eyed stare. Before the statue stood an iron rack with flickering candles in it. People had lit them in honor of the saint, so that he would answer their petitions.

Johnny fidgeted and glanced around. He felt silly, but he reminded himself that Father Higgins was in on this too. But where was he? Probably he was in the sacristy, which was the room where the priest got dressed for Mass and other services. Maybe he had decided that the whole thing was a bad idea and had therefore gone home. Johnny hoped that this was not the case. He fidgeted some more. He drummed his fingers on his legs and walked back and forth, humming softly under his breath. At last he heard the sound of the sacristy door opening and closing. He looked up and saw Father Higgins walking toward him. He was wearing a long white gown called an alb, and around his neck was a kind of embroidered purple scarf called a stole. In one hand he carried a tarnished silver holy water sprinkler. In the other he carried a small pad of paper and a pencil. Johnny was surprised to see that the priest was just as nervous as he was—he kept glancing toward the back of the church to see if anyone was watching.

"Here," said Father Higgins gruffly, and he shoved the pad and pencil at Johnny. He turned toward Saint Anthony and bowed and then walked closer to the statue, raised his hands in a gesture of supplication, and rattled off a prayer in Latin. Johnny did not understand much of it, but he heard the words *Sanctus Antonius* several times, and he figured that the priest was calling on Saint Anthony to hear their prayers. Raising the sprinkler, Father Higgins shook drops of holy water over the base of the statue. Some water fell on the burning candles, which hissed loudly. Again the priest bowed, and once more he turned to Johnny.

"All right, here's what you do," he said brusquely, tapping the pad with his finger. "Write down your petition, fold the paper over twice, and hand it to me."

Johnny raised the pencil and wrote:

> *Dear Saint Anthony:*
> *Please help us to find Professor*
> *Childermass. Please hear us, and do*
> *not fail us. Amen.*
>> *Yours truly,*
>> *John Dixon*

Johnny tore the sheet from the pad and folded it twice. He handed the note to Father Higgins, who asked him to hold the holy water sprinkler for a minute. While Johnny watched, the priest edged in between the candle rack and the statue's pedestal. Reaching up, he placed a brawny hand on the front of the statue and tilted it slightly back. With his other hand he stuffed the note in under the base of the statue. Then, gently, he lowered the statue back down. Johnny heard a soft *chink* as the statue came to rest on its pedestal again. Grunting a little, Father Higgins squeezed himself out from behind the candle rack and walked back to where Johnny was standing. He took the sprinkler from Johnny, showered the statue with more water, and then said another Latin prayer.

"*There!*" he said wearily, folding his arms and stepping back to watch the play of candle shadows on the statue's pallid face. "I didn't think I could remember all that razzmatazz, but I did! And if you *ever* tell anyone in the parish that we did this, I'll have your hide! I think Bishop Monohan would go through the roof if he knew I was such a slave to mummery and flummery!"

Johnny was genuinely grateful for what Father Higgins had done tonight. Whether or not the ritual worked, at least they had tried. However, there were still some lingering questions in his mind.

"What do we do now, Father?" he asked. "I mean, how do we know if what we did worked or not?"

Father Higgins sighed. "I might have known you'd ask that! Well, we're supposed to wait three days and then come back and see what—if anything—is written on the paper. If the saint answers us, he will answer us in that way."

Johnny looked at the priest doubtfully. "Has . . . has this ever worked before? Did anyone ever—"

"No," said the priest with a mournful shake of his head. "Not that I ever heard of, anyway. But as I told you the other day, there's no harm in—"

Suddenly there was a loud sound, like a pistol shot. A door at the back of the church blew open, and it banged loudly against the wall. A cold wind blew in, and the candle flames flickered. Johnny jumped. With a wild look on his face, he peered into the darkness, and then he turned and gaped at Father Higgins. The expression on the priest's face was absolutely unreadable, but his eyes were gleaming. And Johnny wondered: *Was this a sign? Would their prayer really be answered?*

CHAPTER FIVE

❧

For the time being Johnny was not getting any answers. "Stupid door blew open again," muttered Father Higgins, and he stamped on down the aisle to close it.

Three days they had to wait. For Johnny, three days had seldom passed so slowly. Thursday dragged by, and so did Friday. On Friday evening, to make himself feel better, Johnny called up Father Higgins and had a long conversation with him. He had not wanted to talk about the ghostly jack-o'-lantern before for fear that the priest might laugh at him. But now he decided to lay the whole thing out on the table. He told Father Higgins what he had seen, and he described the night when he burst into the professor's house and found that he had vanished. And he added that he was afraid that evil supernatural powers had had something to do with the professor's disappearance. He also mentioned the Childermass clock and told Father Higgins a little about its strange history. But he did not mention the ghostly midnight vision he had had or the skull—these were things that he still wanted to keep secret. Father Higgins listened gravely to what Johnny had to say, and he did not scoff or laugh. He said that Johnny was probably right, that deviltry was almost certainly involved, and he added encouragingly that the powers of light might come to their aid. They'd know on Saturday night.

Finally Saturday evening arrived. There was no church service scheduled for that night, so Johnny said that he was going to light a candle in memory of his mother. When he got to St. Michael's church, he immediately scooted around the block to the rectory, which was where Father Higgins lived. He pushed the door bell, and soon the priest came, holding in his hand a bunch of keys to all the various doors and locked cupboards of St. Michael's church. Father Higgins looked tense and crabby.

"Well," he said, scowling, "I suppose we might as well go see what we can see. I warn you, though: There may be nothing written on the sheet at all—nothing, that is, but the message you wrote the other night."

Johnny had already prepared himself for disappointment. This was a silly, crazy thing they were doing, and he knew it. He told himself not to expect too much.

Father Higgins and Johnny entered the church by a

side door. The old building smelled of wax and incense, and the air was clammy, as it always was, even in the middle of the summer. All around them the dark, empty church loomed. Half a dozen candles burned in the slanted, wax-encrusted iron rack in front of Saint Anthony. As Father Higgins walked toward the statue, Johnny could feel himself growing tense. The priest slid between the candle rack and the pedestal and placed one large, hairy hand on the front of the statue. Johnny heard him mutter something as he tilted the heavy statue back. His fingers were on the folded paper now, and he was yanking it out. Down came the statue again, gently clunking into place. Father Higgins squeezed himself out from behind the rack; he walked toward Johnny with the paper in his hand. The suspense was unbearable. Johnny clenched his fists and felt his nails digging into the palms of his hands. With maddening slowness Father Higgins unfolded the paper. He looked at it, and then he let out a loud exclamation.

"Good God! Come and look at this, would you!"

Johnny edged closer and peered over the priest's arm. Across the note that he had neatly printed was writing. It was large, scrawly, and loopy script, and it reminded Johnny of the marks he had made once when he'd tried to write while holding a pencil in his teeth. At first the writing looked like total nonsense, but Johnny soon realized that there were words and phrases. With a little effort he was able to make out what they said:

Father Higgins's jaw sagged. "Lord!" he whispered. "I would never in my wildest dreams have believed—" Suddenly he stopped speaking. His eyes narrowed, and he turned around and peered into the gloom.

"What's the matter, Father?" asked Johnny, frightened.

"Oh, it was just a thought that occurred to me," muttered the priest. "I wondered if maybe somebody had been hiding in the church and watching when we put this note under the statue. If they had been, they might've taken the note out and written this."

Johnny's heart sank. He knew that this might be the real, true explanation behind the mysterious writing. But he did not want to believe it. "Gee, Father," he said hopefully, "I think the church was empty that night, wasn't it? I mean, didn't we check it out?"

The priest shook his head. "No, John. That's just the trouble—we did *not* check it out. There could've been somebody up in the choir loft or squatting down behind the pews. You know Raymond—that feeble-minded guy that works at the gas station across the street? Well, he could've been in here. He ducks into the church sometimes and does funny things, like movin' the candles around on the altar. And now that I think about it, that might explain the front door bangin' open the other night. I wonder . . ."

Johnny was beginning to feel desperate. If Father Higgins didn't believe this was real supernatural writing, then who would help him find the professor? "I . . . I don't think R-Raymond could've . . . m-moved the statue. . . ." said Johnny in a voice that was beginning to tremble. Tears sprang to his eyes, and he could feel his lower lip quivering. He didn't want to break down and cry, but he was afraid he was going to.

Father Higgins turned to Johnny, and his harsh scowl softened into a sympathetic, sad smile. He really was a kind-hearted man, and he realized how much Johnny wanted to believe that the writing had been done by supernatural powers.

"Look, John," said the priest softly, putting his arm around him. "I'm not tryin' to be mean to you. I'm just tryin' to test out this thing and see if maybe there's an ordinary, everyday explanation to it. I believe in miracles, but they sure don't happen all the time. We've got to keep our heads if we're going to get anywhere."

Johnny was crying now—he couldn't help it. The tears flowed freely, and he dabbed at his eyes with his handkerchief. "Does . . . does that mean you're not gonna help me anymore?" he sobbed.

"Of *course* not!" said the priest loudly and firmly. "Whatever gave you *that* idea? I want to find the professor just as much as you do!" He paused and rubbed his chin, and then he looked at the scrawling on the paper again. Suddenly he grinned. He laughed aloud, and the sound echoed in the vaulted ceiling of the old church.

Johnny took his handkerchief away from his face and blinked. "What . . . what is it?" he asked in a voice that was thick from crying.

"Oh, nothing much," said the priest, still chuckling. "Only I realized all of a sudden that I'd have to be out of my mind to think that Raymond did this! That second sentence there, about the great reckoning in the little room. It's from a play by Shakespeare. Old Raymond might be able to read and write, but he sure didn't write *this*! I ought to've seen that right away!"

Johnny's heart leaped. He was feeling hopeful again. "Does that mean the writing is really from . . . from . . ."

Father Higgins cut him off with a shake of his head. "No. It doesn't mean anything. Somebody else could've done this for all we know. But I don't think we ought to throw this paper away. No, indeed! We ought to study it and think about it and take it very, very seriously. Because you never know! It just might be a miracle from Saint Anthony! And if it is, it could help us find the professor. Anyway, we've got to take the help that's given to us. Like they say, beggars can't be choosers!"

Johnny went home that night thinking that maybe—just maybe—there was some reason to hope. It was possible that Saint Anthony or some higher power had spoken. But whoever it was, he or she had not spoken very clearly. *Where the bays run together*—what could that mean? It seemed to refer to a place, but where? There were lots of bays on the surface of the globe. Johnny knew the names of some of them: Hudson Bay, the Bay of Fundy, Corpus Christi Bay. Was there some place where two bays of water ran into one? He could start combing through an atlas, but it would be like looking for a needle in a haystack. Then Johnny thought some more: He had heard horses referred to as *bays*. They were horses that were reddish-brown in color. Did the clue mean that they should look for some field full of reddish-brown horses? Then there was the other clue: *a great reckoning in a little room*. The "little room" had to be the dollhouse room in the Childermass clock. But except for this little glimmer of meaning, the phrase meant absolutely nothing to Johnny. He turned it over and over in his mind, but the more he thought, the more meaningless the phrase became.

By the time he got to his front door, Johnny's hopeful mood had evaporated. He remembered the things he had read about the Greek oracles, which had given people mysterious messages just to drive them bats. Maybe the messages had been sent by the devil and not by Saint Anthony. Maybe they were stuck up against a dead-end wall.

The next day was Sunday, and Johnny went to church with his gramma and grampa as usual. After Mass everybody filed out of the church. Some went home right away, but others stood around outside and talked with their friends. Gramma and Grampa got into a conversation with Mrs. McGinnis, a silly old lady who was the head of the Catholic Daughters. Johnny couldn't stand Mrs. McGinnis, and so he just stood by, fidgeting nervously and waiting for his grandparents to finish talking. But as he was glancing aimlessly this way and that, Johnny saw Willie Prine elbowing his way through the crowd. Willie was a tall, dopey-looking kid with thick glasses, and he had been one of the altar boys at today's Mass. He was still wearing his long red cassock, and he was grinning from ear to ear. Johnny wondered what he was so pleased about.

"Hey, Dixon!" yelled Willie. "Father Higgins wants ta see ya!" Willie chortled. He was bubbling over with malicious amusement. Obviously Willie thought that Johnny was in trouble, and that pleased him no end. He didn't have anything in particular against Johnny—he just liked seeing other kids get bawled out.

When they heard what Willie was saying, Gramma and Grampa both looked upset. Mrs. McGinnis clucked and acted prissy, as she always did when bad things happened to other people. Johnny, however, was calm. He turned and smiled smugly at Willie.

"Okay," he said quietly. "I'll be with you in a minute." Then he turned back to Gramma and Grampa. "I have to go see Father Higgins about something," he said quickly. "It's . . . it's not very important, it's just about the altar boy schedule. You go ahead—I'll walk home afterward."

Before his grandparents had a chance to say anything, Johnny was plunging off into the crowd behind Willie. The expression on Willie's face showed that he was perplexed. Why was Dixon so eager to go and get chewed out? When they got to the door of the sacristy, there was Father Higgins. The iron doors of the big Mosler walk-in safe were open, and he was putting away the sacred vessels—the chalice, the ciborium, and the gold-plated paten. As the two boys watched, he swung the squealing doors shut and locked them.

"Good morning, John!" said the priest, turning to face him. His eyes were gleaming, and there was a secretive smile on his face. "How goes it with you today, eh?"

"Uh . . . okay, I guess, Father." Johnny's mouth twitched into a nervous smile. Even though the priest was his friend, he often felt nervous around him. Anybody who was in authority gave Johnny the jitters. "Did . . . did you want to talk to me about something?"

"I did indeed!" the priest replied, and his voice sounded ominous. At this Willie smirked expectantly. Now Dixon was going to get it! But to his great surprise, Willie suddenly found the priest glaring at him.

"Well, Mr. Prine," he growled, "I don't think I need you any longer. You had better put out the candles, change into your clothes, and go home."

Willie's face fell. "Uh . . . yeah, sure, Father. See ya later." And with that, he turned and went out, closing the door behind him.

Now Johnny and Father Higgins were alone in the sacristy. At first the priest said nothing. He walked over to the tall walnut dresser where the Mass vestments were kept. On top of the dresser was a heavy iron crucifix. Next to it lay a neatly folded road map. As Johnny watched, Father Higgins picked up the map. He held it up so that Johnny could see the title on the front. It was a road map of the state of Maine.

"I've been doing some thinking about those two little messages that Saint Anthony scrawled down for us," he said, tapping the map against the edge of the dresser. "And you know, all of a sudden, last night at dinner, it came to me! I should've thought of it before, because I have hundreds and hundreds of folk songs rattling around in my head. Here, hold this!"

To Johnny's surprise, Father Higgins handed him the map. Then he turned and strode quickly to the coat closet in the far corner of the room. Opening the door, he reached in and pulled out—a guitar!

Johnny's mouth dropped open. He was completely dumbfounded and also very amused. So Father Higgins played the guitar! He normally looked so stern and forbidding that . . . well, it was like finding out that the mayor loved to roller-skate! As Johnny watched, the priest put the strap of the guitar around his neck, played a few opening chords, and then launched into a loud, lusty chorus:

> Haul down your sails where the bays run together,
> While away your days in the hills of Isle au Haut!

Father Higgins clamped his hand over the strings, and they were silent. "There!" he said triumphantly. "That's it! You get it, don't you?"

Johnny was still mystified. It was clear that one of the lines they had found was from a song. But Johnny did not have the faintest idea of where the hills of Isle au Haut were.

Father Higgins looked at Johnny askance. His lips curled up into a sarcastic grin. "Oh, come on, now! You don't know where Isle au Haut is? You really don't know?"

Johnny shrugged helplessly. "I'm from Long Island, Father! I . . . I don't know very much about New England. Is Isle au Haut someplace in Maine? I mean, there are islands along the coast of Maine, aren't there?"

Father Higgins laughed. "Is it someplace in Maine? Are there islands along the coast? Is the Pope a Catholic? Holy Saint Patrick! You outlanders don't know *anything* about New England, do you?"

Johnny felt sheepish. "Nope, I guess not," he muttered.

"Well, here! I'll show you!" said the priest, and he took off the guitar and leaned it against the dresser. Taking the map from Johnny's hands, he unfolded it and held it up. Father Higgins's large hairy forefinger moved along the coast of Maine, which even on a map looked as if it had had big chunks chewed or ripped out of it. Far up the coast, Johnny saw the two long bays that had been scooped out of the shoreline millions of years ago: Penobscot Bay and Blue Hill Bay. Both bays were full of islands large and small. But at the place where the two bays met was a cluster of islands and islets. Even though the priest was holding the map at a slight distance, Johnny's nearsighted eyes could pick out the names of the larger ones. On the left were two together —the one above was North Haven, and below it was Vinalhaven. Then, slightly to the east of these two, was another fair-sized island called Isle au Haut.

Johnny looked up wonderingly at Father Higgins. "You mean . . . you think the professor is out here somewhere?"

Father Higgins nodded. "That is indeed what I think. But whereabouts in this ungodly wilderness of islands he is, God only knows."

Johnny gazed at the map, and then he shook his head sadly. "But why, Father? I mean, I don't understand why anybody would kidnap the professor and take him out to one of these islands."

Father Higgins looked grave. He folded the map back up and laid it on the dresser. "Neither do I, Johnny. Neither do I. It may not even be a some*body* that's done it—from all that you've told me, it is more likely to be a some*thing* that did it. One of the powers of darkness, in other words. We'll know more when we get to the islands, I suppose, and by that time we may wish that we knew less. Of course, there's always the possibility that he's *not* out on these blasted islands, but the more I think, the more sure I am that we're on the right track. You see, I've doped out the other clue too. And it leads us right to Vinalhaven Island!"

Johnny's mouth dropped open. "Huh?"

Father Higgins scratched his nose and grinned. "Well

you may say, 'huh'! I'll admit it isn't terribly apparent at first, but I'll tell you what I did. You see, I figured that *a great reckoning in a little room* had to refer to that blasted dollhouse you told me about. And I'm sure you reached the same conclusion. Anyway, I called up the owner of the Fitzwilliam Inn to see if we could . . . you know, kind of make an appointment to examine that clock and see what we could find out. And do you know what he told me? He told me that he had sold the clock to a guy who runs a clock museum. The guy's name is Herman Finnick, and his museum is out on Vinalhaven Island! Now, doesn't that just beat everything?"

Johnny nodded. He felt stunned by all the information that had suddenly been dumped on him. And then it was as if a light had come on inside his brain. He snapped his fingers. "Hey, Father!" he exclaimed. "It all fits!"

Father Higgins blinked. "Huh? What fits?"

Johnny grinned. "When a friend of mine and I were pokin' around in the professor's study after he disappeared, we found this drawing that showed a letter *L* with a vine wrapped around it. My friend thought that it stood for *L* plus vine—the name Levine, I mean. But we should've read it the other way around: it's Vine-L, for Vinalhaven!"

"Very good!" said Father Higgins, nodding approvingly. "And that also settles a question that has been banging around in my skull: I was wondering whether we ought to go to Isle au Haut, since it gets mentioned in that little ditty I sang for you. But all the signs seem to point to Vinalhaven, don't they?" Father Higgins paused. "Hmmm!" he said, grimly pounding his fist on the edge of the dresser. "What does that Finnick character have to do with it all? He *must* be in on this plot to do something to the professor. Is this Finnick a sorcerer? Is he in league with the devil? Did he create the jack-o'-lantern vision that you saw? And why on earth does he want the professor? What awful, ghastly, unnameable thing is going to happen to the poor man? As far as I'm concerned, there are about six hundred and fifty unanswered questions in this whole nutty business!" The priest turned suddenly to Johnny and pointed a knobby, hairy finger at him. His face had turned beet-red, and he looked very threatening and sinister. Johnny cringed. He was afraid that Father Higgins was going to yell at him or grab him by the shoulders and shake him.

"What I want to know now, John, is *this*!" roared the priest. "Are you going with me to Vinalhaven to help rescue the prof? What d'ye say?"

CHAPTER SIX

Johnny was overjoyed. He wanted to yell and whoop and throw things around the room. Father Higgins had told him the thing that he wanted most in the world to hear. He was saying that they had a chance to find the professor and rescue him, and what was more, he was saying that he wanted him, John Dixon, to be his right-hand man in this search. If he hadn't been such a polite and well-behaved kid, Johnny would have thrown his arms around the tall, grizzly faced priest. As it was, he just stood there looking grateful, tears streaming down his face.

"Th-thanks, F-Father," he stammered in a voice thick with emotion. "I . . . I'll help you if I can."

Father Higgins smiled happily. He was a pretty

shrewd judge of character, and he had guessed that—underneath his timid exterior—Johnny was a courageous and resourceful kid. However, he didn't want Johnny to think that this expedition of theirs was going to be all fun and games. So he forced himself to frown and be gruff again.

"You may not thank me when this little jaunt is over with," he rumbled. "We may find that we're up against something that we can't handle, or we may not even be able to locate the professor at all. But if people tried to do only those things that they were sure of succeeding at, this country would still be a howling wilderness. Anyway, I'm going to need help—lots of help—and I'm very glad you want to go along. Unfortunately, next weekend is the soonest I can get away. I'll have to phone the bishop's office and ask them to send out a substitute. Do you think your gramma and grampa will let you go on this trip with me?"

"I . . . I guess they'll let me go," he said uncertainly.

"I'll call up your folks and tell them that I'm taking you on a little pleasure jaunt," the priest said, and smiled wryly. "And I'm sure," he added, "that God will forgive me for fibbing a bit, if it's all in a good cause. Now, if you'll excuse me, I have to be getting on over to the Tip Top restaurant for lunch. Father Frisbie of St. Luke's Episcopal is meeting me, and we're going to stuff ourselves with corned beef and cabbage and argue about religion."

Johnny went home in a daze. It took him a day or two

to get used to the idea that he was going on a rescue mission with the rector of St. Michael's church. At times the whole thing seemed unreal to him, and when he thought that they were going because of mysterious words scribbled on a piece of paper that had been left under a statue in a church . . . well, he didn't know whether to laugh or cry. But the trip was actually going to happen. Father Higgins called up the Dixons and discussed the matter with them, and they seemed perfectly willing to let Johnny go. As far as they were concerned, Father Higgins was a reliable, upstanding member of the community, and they were both quite proud that he had chosen Johnny to go with him on a short trip to the islands off the coast of Maine. Gramma and Grampa knew that Johnny was feeling bad because of the professor's disappearance, and they hoped this jaunt would help him get his mind off that sad loss.

So Johnny got out his small, squarish plaid suitcase and started putting things in it: pajamas, toiletries, extra socks, and his best warm woolen sweaters and flannel shirts—it was still pretty chilly in May on those islands, as Gramma kept pointing out. Johnny threw in other odd but useful things, like his waterproof matchbox, his three-bladed jackknife, his Boy Scout compass, and an old battered pair of opera glasses that could be used as a set of binoculars. After some hesitation he decided to put in the "lucky" skull from the Childermass clock.

Johnny didn't quite know what to think about the skull. He had begun to have bad feelings about it lately, for no reason that he could really put his finger on. And he found that he was still being extremely close-mouthed about the skull. He hadn't told Fergie or Father Higgins or any of his friends about it. His mind kept making up reasons why it would be better to keep the skull a secret, at least for a little while longer. If he told Fergie, he might want to steal it. As for Father Higgins, well, Johnny told himself that it would not be a great idea to let your parish priest know that you had swiped something. But then what *should* he do about the skull? Leave it to gather dust forever in his bureau drawer? Arguing back and forth with himself, Johnny finally came back to the notion that the skull might just possibly be lucky. And so he dug the watchcase that held the grotesque object out from under the shirts in his bureau drawer and stuffed it in under the other things in his suitcase. *There!* he said quietly to himself. *I hope you're a good-luck charm, skully baby. Because if I ever needed some good luck, I'm gonna need it now!*

On the Tuesday after his conversation with Father Higgins, Johnny made a big mistake—at least, it seemed like a mistake to him at the time. He spilled the beans to Fergie about the trip that he and the priest were going to take. At first Johnny had kept his mouth shut about the whole enterprise. He hadn't even told Fergie about the mysterious messages that he and Father Higgins had found under Saint Anthony's statue. He hadn't told him because he had been kind of ticked off at him. Fergie had been smart-alecky and sneery about the weird magical happenings that had surrounded the professor's disappearance, and he had demanded proof positive before believing. So Johnny had simply cut him out of the professor-finding project. He had not asked Fergie's advice on this matter lately, and he really had not seen much of him since the night they discussed clues together in the public library. They had met at Peter's Sweet Shop a couple of times since then, but mostly they had just talked about girls, the Red Sox, and homework. Johnny did not feel good about shutting Fergie out. Smart aleck or not, Fergie was his friend. As the Vinalhaven trip got closer, Johnny felt an overpowering urge to let him in on what was going on, regardless of what the result might be.

And so, on Tuesday evening after school, Johnny decided to tell all. They were facing each other across ice cream sundaes at Peter's, and Fergie was going on about how Wanda Sue Geiger was the prettiest girl in the eighth grade. Suddenly Johnny cut in.

"Hey, look, Fergie!" he said, jamming his spoon into the ice cream. "I . . . I've got something to tell you."

Fergie stopped talking and stared levelly across at Johnny. "Yeah," he said. "I know you have!"

Johnny was startled. "You *do*?"

"Yes, I do! Good God, Dixon! You must think I have whipped cream where my brain is supposed to be! You've been givin' me these funny looks, an' peerin' at me squinty-eyed for a coupla weeks now! I thought maybe you were gettin' ready to enlist in the French

Foreign Legion or somethin'! An' I don't mind tellin' you, I got pretty mad at you. After all, I'm supposed to be your best friend, aren't I? Well, aren't I?"

Johnny blushed a deep crimson. He felt stupid and guilty, both at the same time. So Fergie had known all along that he was hiding something from him. Well, in a way this would make things easier. When he had recovered from his embarrassment, Johnny launched into a full explanation: He told about the "Saint Anthony" messages—Fergie giggled during this part—and then explained about the mysterious Mr. Finnick and his clock museum. Finally he explained how Father Higgins had figured out the meaning of one of the messages.

". . . and so we're gonna go out to Vinalhaven this Friday to see what we can find out," said Johnny, finishing up. He stared stubbornly and defiantly at Fergie. "Well, there's your big wonderful explanation," he added. "And if you think it's all so funny, you can stay home and wait to see if we bring the professor back with us. Okay?"

Fergie met Johnny's gaze. "I didn't think the whole thing was funny," he said with a straight face. "Just the part about leavin' notes under statues in churches in the middle of the night—I think that's a riot!"

Johnny was getting more irritated by the minute. "All right, all right, so it's a big fat laugh!" he snapped angrily. "I *knew* you'd make fun of the whole thing! That's why I never told you in the first place! You don't think we have a chance, do you?"

Fergie shrugged. "I dunno. Maybe you do, and maybe you don't. But all the same, I'd like to go along."

Johnny's mouth dropped open. He could hardly believe what he was hearing. Was Fergie kidding? "You wanta *what*?"

"I said, I wanta go along," replied Fergie calmly.

"Why? To make fun of us?"

Fergie shook his head. "Nope. I like trips, an' . . . an' I like goin' places with you. It'll be fun, like it was out at Scout camp. C'mon—let me go along. I promise I won't make fun of you guys. Cross my heart an' hope to die!"

Johnny was flabbergasted and confused as well. He really didn't know what to say. He was infuriated by Fergie's nerviness, and by his strange, confusing attitude toward the trip. But he really did want Fergie to go along. He enjoyed his company most of the time, and he had a hunch that he and Father Higgins might need an extra pair of hands. Fergie was a strong, sinewy, rugged kid. He looked gangly and awkward, but he could beat you at baseball or football or tug-of-war, and he could outrun a lot of the kids that Johnny knew. Johnny had no idea what they would be getting into out among those islands. They could use someone who could row a boat, or climb cliffs, or walk for hours without getting tired.

While Johnny mulled things over in his mind, he sat absolutely silent, staring at a point on the wall above Fergie's head. Fergie's eager grin quickly faded to a hurt frown. He wondered if maybe Johnny was thinking up some nice way of telling him to get lost.

"If you don't want me to come along, just say so!" muttered Fergie. He stabbed at the ice cream with his spoon and shoveled some into his mouth.

"Huh?" Johnny was jolted out of his trance, and in a flash he realized what Fergie was thinking. And he was genuinely touched. Fergie would feel crushed if he was left out. He wanted to be included because he liked trips. But he also wanted to be included because he was Johnny's best friend.

"I . . . I wasn't gonna tell you you couldn't come," said Johnny hastily. "It wasn't that, it was just that . . . well, Father Higgins is the one who's takin' me. He's runnin' the whole show. I was tryin' to figure out if maybe we could get him to take you too."

Fergie beamed, and Johnny felt glad. He really did want Fergie's company on this dangerous trip. But the question still remained: Could he persuade Father Higgins to include him?

"Oh, I think he'll take me along," said Fergie nonchalantly. He stared off into space and smiled secretively. "I mean, if it's up to him, I'm in like Flynn!"

Johnny blinked. "Why? Fergie, what in heck are you talkin' about?"

Fergie's grin got broader. "Oh, didn't I tell ya? I was the cleanup hitter on Father Higgins's City League softball team two years ago. That was before I knew you.

Higgy coaches kids' teams every summer. Well, that was the year that I broke up a no-hitter that some creep was throwin'. I got a triple in the ninth inning, an' Beaky Phelps brought me in with a single, an' we won the game. Didn't I ever tell you about any of that? Me'n Higgy're old buddies from way back!"

After Johnny had gotten over the shock of discovering that Fergie knew Father Higgins, he realized that this was going to be a much better trip than he had thought. Having two reliable friends along was a lot better than just having one. So Fergie and Johnny talked some more and tried to make plans, and then Johnny went home and called up Father Higgins. He knew right away from the way Father Higgins reacted that Fergie hadn't been kidding: the priest knew him and thought that he was a real character. In short, he liked him, and he'd be glad to take him along. First, though, he'd have to get the Fergusons' permission, and that would take a quick phone call and some sweet-talking. So Johnny hung up and paced around the living room.

Finally Father Higgins called back and said that Mrs. Ferguson had given them the go-ahead. Everything was set now. The three of them would be leaving on their journey around three P.M. on Friday. Father Higgins had been on a vacation trip to the Maine islands last year, and he figured that it would take them about three and a half hours of driving to get to Rockland, where they would catch the ferryboat that would take them to Vinalhaven.

The last ferry left at 7:32, so they would have an hour's leeway in case they got delayed. Since the ferryboat ride would take about an hour and a half, the three of them would arrive at the door of the Lobster Pot Inn on Vinalhaven at a little after nine.

It was a cloudy afternoon on Friday when Father Higgins's black Oldsmobile pulled up in front of the Dixon house on Fillmore Street. The horn beeped loudly, but there really was no need for this: Johnny was out on the front porch waiting, his suitcase in hand. Gramma and Grampa were with him. As Johnny watched, Father Higgins got out of the car, slammed the door, and waved at the three of them. He was wearing an open-necked plaid cotton shirt, baggy army fatigue trousers, combat boots, and an old army fatigue jacket. Stitched to the right shoulder of the jacket was a white cross, with a curved patch that said *Chaplain* above it. Johnny had never seen Father Higgins in his old sloppy weekend clothes before, but it was reassuring somehow —it made him seem more human and less stern and priestly and forbidding.

"Hi, there, John!" Father Higgins boomed as he walked toward them waving cheerily. "Are you ready for a voyage to the stern and rockbound coast of Maine and beyond?"

Johnny said yes, but his voice was weak and uncertain. Father Higgins was making it sound as if they were going to the moon. Also, he kept remembering the real purpose of this trip. In his stomach was a tight knot of fear.

Father Higgins saw how pale and tense Johnny looked, and he tried to cheer him up. "Oh, come on, John!" he said loudly as he took Johnny's suitcase from him. "You look like you were going to have your appendix out! This trip is going to be a lot of fun!"

Johnny tried to smile reassuringly. "It's . . . it's okay, Father," he said. "I . . . I always get nervous before I go on trips."

The priest smiled grimly, and in his eyes was a faraway look. "You do, eh? Well, you should try a trip where you're wading in a river with a lot of other soldiers in battle gear and helmets, while people on shore are firing mortar shells and machine-gun bullets at you. Now *there* would be something to be nervous about!"

Again Johnny was reminded that Father Higgins had been in some of the bloodiest battles of World War Two. He had been in the fighting on the Philippine Islands. He hardly ever talked about what had happened to him there, but Johnny got the feeling that he had seen some pretty awful things. And he also got the feeling that Father Higgins was a very courageous man. Johnny wanted to be courageous and bold, but he was having a tough time doing that right now. He told himself that this was a perfectly safe trip, that nothing bad could possibly happen to him. He was silly to be such a nervous nit.

So Johnny gave his grampa a hearty handshake, and he gave Gramma a big hug and a kiss.

"G'bye, John!" said Grampa. "Have a good time, an' bring us back a coupla shells off of the beaches!"

"God love ya, John!" said Gramma as her grandson hugged her tight. "Don't forget to wear your sweater when you go out at night. You don't wanta get strep throat or nothin' like that!"

Johnny turned and waved twice as he went down the walk with Father Higgins. Then the priest opened the trunk, threw in the suitcase, and slammed the lid. They both got into the car, the motor roared to life, and off they went. Their next stop was on Joy Street in Cranbrook, where Fergie lived. Father Higgins beeped his horn, and Fergie came racing out to the car to meet them, his suitcase in his hand. The outfit he was wearing was really something: he was all done up like a motorcycle thug. He had on skintight jeans and motorcycle boots and an amazing leather jacket that was all covered with spiky metal studs and colored glass reflectors. On the back was a picture of a big white skull with red glass reflectors for eyes. Over the skull were ragged white letters that spelled *Snake Eyes*.

Slam. That was the sound of Fergie's suitcase being pitched into the trunk of Father Higgins's car.

"Hi ho, Big John!" said Fergie jauntily as he slid into the wide front seat and slammed the car door. "How goes it, eh?"

Johnny said nothing. He was sitting stiff as a board, staring sightlessly at the windshield. All over his body he felt a ghastly, clammy, soul-numbing chill, a chill he could not explain. It had come over him when he saw the grinning red-eyed skull on the back of Fergie's jacket. Now, in his mind's eye, he saw a strange vision: It was as if he had X-ray eyes and was looking through the walls of his suitcase, which lay zipped and locked in the trunk of Father Higgins's car. Grinning up at him out of the dark, tiny and menacing, was the ivory skull.

CHAPTER SEVEN

Johnny clung to the rail of the gently pitching ferryboat as it plowed forward through the waters of Penobscot Bay. It was getting dark fast, and in the distance he saw the long white sweeping arm of a lighthouse beam. Even so, he could barely make out the vague shapes of islands, and out of the salt-smelling blackness came the dull *clank-clank* of a bell buoy as it rocked on the waves. In his ears throbbed the sound of the ferryboat's motor. It was a stubby little ship, with room for about four cars placed end to end. There were just two cars on this trip: Father Higgins's Oldsmobile and a station wagon that belonged to a lady who lived on the island. The cars stood end to end on the deck, with chocks under their wheels to keep them from moving. On the starboard and port sides of the little ship were small passenger cabins. Inside them were metal seats like the seats on buses, drinking fountains, and toilets. As far as Johnny knew, there was no one in the starboard-side cabin. Except for him all the passengers were in the other one. Johnny had been in there until a few minutes ago. He had been listening to Father Higgins play his guitar and sing Irish folk songs.

This trip had been a real eye-opener for Johnny: He had never realized that Father Higgins could be such a relaxed, life-of-the-party type. He had in his head an incredible collection of songs, mostly songs of the various Irish rebellions against the British crown. The songs were very stirring to Johnny, and when Father Higgins sang and played, he could almost see the lines of ill-clad pikemen marching up hills to do battle with the redcoats. Johnny had been in there with the rest for about an hour, but the fumes of Father Higgins's pipe had started making him dizzy, so he had finally gone out to get some air.

But he had also gone out for another reason. He had decided to do something about the tiny skull that he had stolen from the Childermass clock. All during the car trip Johnny had been haunted by the weird feeling that he had gotten when he saw the skull on Fergie's jacket. And he had finally decided that the skull was an evil thing, and that he'd better get rid of it. Earlier, he had made up a reason to borrow Father Higgins's car keys. He had opened the trunk of the Olds and dug out the watchcase with the skull inside it. Now the case was in the pocket of Johnny's raincoat. He could feel it pressing against his leg. But the time for action had come. After a quick look around, Johnny plunged his hand into the pocket. He pulled out the case and flipped it over the side. The boat's motor was roaring so loud that he did not even hear the splash.

Johnny heaved a sigh of relief. *That* was over with, anyway! It was possible, of course, that he had thrown away a good-luck charm, but ...

A sound interrupted Johnny's thoughts—a clashing, banging noise. Johnny peered around through the gathering darkness, and then he saw it: The door on the empty cabin had come open, and it was hitting against the cabin's metal wall as the ship rolled, making a nerve-racking noise. Quickly he padded across the deck and grabbed the steel door handle. He was about to slam the door shut when he peered into the lighted cabin.

There was somebody . . . no, rather, it seemed to be some*thing* . . . sitting in one of the seats. It looked like a scarecrow. Its back was to Johnny, so he couldn't tell if it had a face, but it was wearing an odd sort of carroty red wig, and it was dressed in some sort of white coarse shirt. Johnny was puzzled. Why on earth would anyone bring a scarecrow onto a ferryboat? And just then, while he stood there wondering, the ship rolled gently, and the scarecrow lurched to one side. Johnny looked down, and he saw the scarecrow's foot sticking out into the aisle.

It was a skeleton foot. A cluster of white bones.

Johnny let out a bloodcurdling shriek. The door slipped from his hand and banged loudly as he reeled backward, spun around, took a few stumbling steps across the slippery steel deck, and clawed at the door of the other cabin. Somehow he found the handle and jerked the door open. Inside, he saw Father Higgins, Fergie, and the lady with the station wagon. They were all on their feet, staring, with their mouths open.

"Good God, John!" Father Higgins exclaimed. "What is it? Why did you yell like that?"

Johnny began a stammering explanation. He was having trouble putting words together, and he babbled something about a scarecrow with a skeleton inside it. "Come quick, please! Please, come and look!"

Father Higgins and Fergie glanced quickly at each other. Then the priest slipped the guitar strap over his head and laid the instrument down on the seat. With Fergie right behind him, he headed for the door.

"What is it?" gasped the woman, who had sunk back down into her seat. "What happened?"

"I don't know," muttered the priest grimly. "But I'm going to find out. You stay here, ma'am. We'll be right back."

Father Higgins and the two boys left the cabin and made their way across the deck to the cabin on the other side. The ferryboat was pitching and rolling more now, and the loose door clattered violently. Propping the door open with one brawny arm, Father Higgins stuck his head in through the doorway. Then he jerked his head back and peered questioningly at Johnny, who was standing behind him on the deck.

"Well?" rumbled Father Higgins. "Where is it? What did you do with it?"

Johnny was stunned. The priest was standing in the doorway of the cabin, and his large body blocked Johnny's view, and Fergie's as well. Johnny rushed forward and squeezed himself in beside Father Higgins to look. The cabin was empty. There was no sign of anyone, or anything on the seats.

Father Higgins turned slowly around and stared down at Johnny. He knew Johnny pretty well by this time, and he did not think Johnny was the kind of kid who would send people on a wild-goose chase just to get a laugh. Besides, Johnny did not look amused—he was ghostly pale. Clearly he had seen something. But what was it?

After a long, tense pause, Father Higgins cleared his throat. "Well! Gentlemen, let us be getting back to our seats."

Fergie and Johnny followed Father Higgins back to the other cabin. They went in and sat down and did not say a word, much to the annoyance of the lady passenger, who was expecting to hear that a murder victim had been found.

"Well? What is it? What did you find?" Her voice was high-pitched, almost hysterical.

"Nothing," said Father Higgins. There was an awful finality in his tone, and he glowered so threateningly that she was afraid to ask any more questions.

The four people in the cabin just sat there silently throughout the rest of the trip. Finally the ferryboat slowed, and Johnny could feel the boat backing into the dock. Putting his hand on the porthole rim, Johnny pulled himself up to look out. But it was so dark that he could hardly see anything at all.

"Come on, you two," said Father Higgins as he picked up his guitar and began to scoot sideways out of the seat. "We'd better be getting into the car. They'll be letting us drive off in a few minutes."

Johnny and Fergie followed Father Higgins out of the cabin, and they all climbed back into the big black Olds. With a shuddering, grinding sound the ferryboat eased itself into its berth between two rows of pilings. Ropes were passed around posts, and then the iron tailgate came clattering down. Father Higgins's car rolled onto the dock and down the winding two-lane road that led into the village of Vinalhaven. They drove down the main street of the picturesque little fishing town, took a sharp right onto a narrow dirt road, and before long they were pulling into the driveway of a small clapboard house that was next to a canal. The side porch of the house was built over the canal and stood on slime-coated pilings. A weathered signboard on the roof of the front porch said Lobster Pot Inn. In front of the sign, on the weathered shingles, lay a real lobster pot, which is a humped cage made of slats with a fishnet lining inside.

Johnny, Fergie, and Father Higgins lugged their suitcases inside, and the owner showed them to their rooms. After they had gotten washed up, they all sat down to a late supper of lobster rolls and cole slaw. The boys had cream soda to drink, and Father Higgins had a Budweiser. Johnny ate silently. His thoughts were on the scarecrow—or whatever it was—that he had seen and on the tiny skull that he had pitched overboard. He had seen the scarecrow right after he got rid of the skull—had he seen the scarecrow *because* he threw the skull away? *Oh well,* he thought wearily, *at least I got rid of the disgusting thing! If it's evil, it can go on being evil down on the bottom of the ocean. It won't bother me anymore.*

The next morning, at breakfast, Father Higgins talked with the boys about the second part of the Saint Anthony clue and his reasons for wanting to get inside Mr. Finnick's clock museum.

"As I told John here," Father Higgins said between sips of coffee, "the quotation 'a great reckoning in a little room' comes from Shakespeare's *As You Like It*. A 'reckoning,' in Shakespeare's time, meant a bill, like a restaurant bill, and the whole quote refers to a murder case that must've been the talk of London back in those days. The playwright Christopher Marlowe got stabbed to death in a drunken argument about a bill in a little bitty back room in a tavern. And now you're going to ask, 'What does this have to do with the professor's disappearance?' I don't know—not yet, anyway. But the 'little room' just *has* to be the little dollhouse room in that weird clock the professor's father made. The reckoning might be a miniature bill, and maybe on the back of it there's a map that'll lead us to where the professor's being held prisoner. All I know is, we've got to take our leads where we find them, so when you fellas finish stuffing your faces, we'll be off. Okay?"

Soon the three travelers had finished eating, so they hiked on over to Mr. Herman Finnick's clock museum. The museum turned out to be a large purple Victorian house covered with lacy iron trimmings and fancy wooden doodads. The house had just been freshly painted, and the lawn was carefully trimmed. A neat border of whitewashed rocks followed the sidewalk up to the ornate front door. Father Higgins stepped forward and pushed the door bell. After a short pause the heavy door rattled open, and there stood Mr. Fennick—short, sixtyish, and prissy-looking, with a pencil-thin gray mustache and a disapproving frown on his face. He was wearing a blue denim apron, and in one hand he held a small can of all-purpose machine oil.

Mr. Finnick glanced at the boys and Father Higgins. He seemed a bit frightened, as if he expected them to leap at him and start pummeling him with their fists.

"Yes? What is it?" he snapped nervously.

Father Higgins stepped forward. "Hem! We've come to tour your clock museum, Mr. Finnick. We're especially interested in seeing . . ."

Mr. Finnick gave Father Higgins his sourest grimace. "Museum's not open till Memorial Day," he snapped. "Come back then, and I'll give you the complete tour." And he started to close the door.

But Father Higgins was not going to be shut out that easily. He put his large meaty hand on the door to keep it from closing. "I'm afraid there's been a misunderstanding," he said with a threatening hint in his voice and a glower on his face. "I'm the Father Thomas Higgins who wrote you from Duston Heights, Massachusetts, and asked if you'd give us a special tour. You said it'd be okay, don't you remember?"

A light dawned in Mr. Finnick's eyes, and a wintry thin smile creased his face. "Ah, yes. I remember now. You weren't wearing your clericals, so naturally I didn't —hrumph!—well, you understand. Please come this way. The tour fee is fifty cents apiece, by the way, payable in advance."

Mr. Finnick held out his thin, well-washed hand, and Father Higgins put a dollar and fifty cents into it. Then the three travelers followed the museum's owner into a vast entry hall that smelled of varnish, Roman Cleanser, and Murphy Oil Soap. The place was immaculate. The woodwork glistened, and the rugs had been freshly shampooed. Everywhere, on shelves and tables and hanging on the walls, were clocks. Tall ones, short ones, spring wound or weight driven. Seth Thomases and Waterbury eight-days and clocks made by all three of the Willard Brothers of Grafton, Massachusetts. Four grandfather clocks stood in a row by the foot of the main staircase—they looked like an overdignified and gloomy welcoming committee. The air was filled with a loud, chaotic storm of ticking, and as he ambled along through the rooms, Johnny couldn't help wondering if Mr. Finnick was annoyed by the fact that the clocks didn't all go *tick* and then *tock* at the same time. This thought made Johnny laugh suddenly, and Mr. Finnick turned and glanced at him unpleasantly.

"What's so funny, young man?" he rasped.

Johnny blushed. "It's, uh . . . it's nothing, sir. I . . . I just thought of a joke."

"Did you indeed?" said Mr. Finnick coldly. "Tell us, and then we all can laugh."

Father Higgins glowered down at Mr. Finnick. He was getting to like this fussy little man less and less. "Uh, Mr. Finnick?" he rumbled. "I wonder if we might see the Childermass clock. That's what we came here to see, after all. We're not especially, uh, clock fanciers, but my young friend John here has a friend who's a member of the Childermass family, and so this particular clock has sort of a . . . a sentimental meaning for him. You know what I mean?"

Mr. Finnick clasped his hands in front of him and cocked his head to one side. "Ah! A senti*mental* meaning!" he said in a nasty, mocking tone. "How nice! Well, now! The Childermass clock is a recent acquisition of mine, and I must say it is intriguing. Fine workmanship, and a real one-of-a-kind item. Very well. If you're bored with the rest of my clocks, I'll take you to see it without further delay. Please follow me."

Johnny, Fergie, and Father Higgins followed Mr. Finnick up a narrow back staircase. They came out on the second floor and walked down a long hall to the door of a room that had probably once been a bedroom. Inside were two large mahogany dining-room tables. One held a display case full of buttons, buttonhooks, pipe tampers, and glass paperweights. The other held the Childermass clock. It looked pretty much the way it had when Johnny saw it at the Fitzwilliam Inn, except that the woodwork was polished to a blinding luster, and the glass door over the face was spotlessly clean. Also, Mr. Finnick had set up a moveable glass-and-wood screen in front of the dollhouse-room part of the clock. Behind the screen the room's furniture was arranged as it had been when Johnny first saw the clock. But, amazingly, the oil lamp on the little oval table was lit! A pinpoint of flame flickered in the delicate glass chimney, and the lamp's yellowish light cast odd shadows over the rug, the bookshelves, and the tastefully papered walls. Quickly Johnny glanced at the row of shelves to the left of the fireplace. There, next to a bowl of tiny apples, was a gap—the space where the skull had been. There was even a tiny glue blob to mark the spot.

Mr. Finnick launched into a long, dull lecture that he must have memorized. Fergie and Father Higgins stood patiently listening with their arms folded, but Johnny kept darting suspicious glances at the little man. Just why had Mr. Finnick bought the clock, anyway? Was he mixed up in Professor Childermass's disappearance? Father Higgins thought that he was—at least, that was what he had said. But now that he had seen Mr. Finnick, Johnny found it hard to believe that this persnickety, irritable man had spirited the professor away by magic. Mr. Finnick did not look much like a wizard. On the other hand, the man might be concealing his true nature behind a mask. All right then, what if he *had* spirited the professor away? Why had he done it?

On droned Mr. Finnick. He was talking about double-foliot escapements and brass balance wheels. Suddenly Father Higgins tapped him on the shoulder—he had a request to make.

"Mr. Finnick? If you don't mind terribly, we'd like to see the inside of this little room up close. I wonder if you could move the screen and give us a little, you know, guided tour."

Mr. Finnick looked genuinely terrified. He seemed to be imagining the awful things that Fergie and Johnny might do with their big clumsy hands if he were to move the screen aside. But then he calmed down. He loved to lecture, and if the three visitors were willing to listen a bit more, he might make the supreme sacrifice.

"If you folks will just move back a teensy bit," said Mr. Finnick, waving them away with his hand. "Ah! Very good! Now, then!"

Johnny, Fergie, and Father Higgins stepped back a few paces. Then, carefully, Mr. Finnick set the screen aside. Taking a long, thin, spindly pair of tweezers from a pocket in his apron, he reached into the miniature room. Daintily he twisted a knob on the gas bracket on the wall. He showed how the drawer in the oval table could be made to slide out and in. He pulled a book out of the bookcase and laid it on the floor of the room. With the tweezer tips, he flipped a page or two to show that this was a real printed book. Mr. Finnick was a mine of information about furniture styles and fabrics and what ormolu really was. But as he rattled on, Johnny got more and more disappointed. He had hoped that a tiny replica of a bill would appear, stuck into a book. Or maybe it would be in the drawer of the oval table, or on the sideboard, or framed on the wall like a painting. But there wasn't anything that looked remotely like a bill. As Mr. Finnick lifted tiny umbrellas from the thimble-size umbrella stand and tweaked the frames of postage-stamp paintings with his tweezers, Johnny felt frustration and anger welling up inside him. They really were not finding out a thing.

Father Higgins scowled. He threw Johnny a sidelong glance, as if to say, *Looks like we lose, eh?* Johnny gave a little shrug. Father Higgins appeared to be fumbling about in his mind for some way to say good-bye. Finally, in the middle of one of Mr. Finnick's long sentences, the priest coughed loudly.

"Mr. Finnick," he said, glancing at his watch, "I am afraid we are going to have to be running along. We've got some other things that we have to do."

Mr. Finnick appeared to be deeply offended. He pulled the tweezers back, turned, and glared icily at the priest. "Am I to understand that you've had enough of my lecture?"

"I didn't say that," Father Higgins replied, with a smile. "I merely said that we'd have to be running along. Now do you suppose that you could show us the way out?"

Without another word, Mr. Finnick slid the glass screen back into place. Curtly, he motioned for the three visitors to follow him, and he led the way to the front door. In silence the glum little procession moved on down the hall and finally out to the front door. When they got there, Mr. Finnick jerked the door inward and stood stiffly at attention, like a dwarfish sentry.

"Good day to you all!" he mumbled, his lips barely moving. "Thank you for visiting the Finnick Clock Museum. Hmph. Hmph."

Father Higgins grinned and made a mock-courteous bow. At this, Mr. Finnick stepped back and slammed the door violently, making the glass pane rattle. Father Higgins shrugged and turned away. Then he and the two boys trotted on down the long walk and out onto a dirt road that wound past a weed-grown granite quarry. For a long while no one said anything. They just trudged along, eyes down. They had used one of the few leads that they had, and it had run them up against a blank wall. A wild idea went flitting through Johnny's head: Maybe they should break into the museum and *really* go over the dollhouse room, turn it inside out, and find the miniature bill or "reckoning" that the message had spoken of. And then Johnny wondered—not for the first time—if Mr. Finnick had been holding out on them. Had he been hiding the "great reckoning" on purpose? He sure didn't act like it. He had been stuffy, finicky, boring, and rude, but he hadn't acted secretive—not really. So where did that leave them all?

Father Higgins sighed loudly and discontentedly. He stooped, picked up a rock, and heaved it into the wilderness of granite blocks off to their right. "Well, boys!" he said. "We are not doing very well in the detection racket, are we?"

"Nope," said Fergie gloomily.

"I guess not," said Johnny, shoving his hands into his pockets. "What're we s'posed to do now? We're never gonna find the professor." Johnny's voice began to crack. He was fighting back the tears now. He had not felt so hopeless since this crazy business began.

Father Higgins stopped in the middle of the road. A few paces away, lying in a ditch, was a rough-hewn pillar of stone. It was covered with moss and lichens, but its top was flat, and so the priest walked over and sat down on it. Johnny and Fergie plumped themselves on the pillar too, and there was total silence for about three minutes.

"Well, gentlemen," said Father Higgins wearily, "it looks as if we have run up against a nice big solid stone wall. We didn't find out anything, did we? Not one single solitary useful fact or clue. However, we shouldn't despair, because—"

At this point Fergie interrupted him. "Whyn't we wait till dark an' then break in an' then turn that crazy clock upside down till we find some clues? I bet there's *somethin'* there—there has to be!"

Father Higgins shook his head. "I thought about breaking in, but it may be easier said than done. Finnick probably has the whole place wired with burglar alarms and electric eyes. But I do think we need to find out a bit more about our friend Finnick. Why don't we pay a trip to the Vinalhaven Public Library?"

Johnny was puzzled by this suggestion. "The library? How come?"

Father Higgins glanced at Johnny skeptically. "Oh, come on, John! For a scholarly kid you can be a bit thick sometimes! Finnick runs a museum, and so there will be articles about him in tourist guides and in books about the state of Maine and in back issues of newspapers. There may even be entries about him in reference books like *Who's Who in the East.* What we need to do is find something, anything, that will tie him in with magic or sorcery or Professor Childermass. After that we can decide whether or not it would be a good idea to do something drastic, like burglarizing his museum. So, off your duffs, me hearties! First we're going to go back to the inn so I can change into my clerical outfit—it may give me more authority, if I have to try to pry favors out of some nice sweet librarian. Then we're off to the library.

As I recall, it's not terribly far from the Main Street section of town. So, let's go! Time's a-wastin'!"

Fergie and Johnny did not think much of Father Higgins's plan, but they did not have a better one to offer, so they got up and followed him to the Lobster Pot Inn. When they got there, the boys waited around on the lawn outside while Father Higgins went to his room to change. In a short time he came back, and this time he was all done up in his black coat, black pants, glossy black shirtfront, and stiff white Roman collar. Down the road they hiked, till they came to the little cluster of shops and stores that was the business district of the island. At one end of the tiny Main Street was a stone watering trough, and a rutty cart track wound away from it up to the top of a grassy knoll. There, sitting all by itself, was a boxy gray one-story stone building.

"That's the library, boys," said Father Higgins, pointing. "It's probably not much, but it may have the answers we're looking for. Come on!"

Along the cart track they marched, single file, like a tiny army advancing against the enemy. On the steps of the library they halted, while Father Higgins brushed lint off his coat—he wanted to make himself as presentable as possible. Then, with Father Higgins in the lead, they trotted up the steps. Just inside the front door the little group stopped again. A few yards away, planted between two varnished golden oak pillars, was a desk. And behind it sat a small, elderly gray-haired woman. Her hair was done up into a bun, and a pencil was stuck into it. She had been reading a book, but now she looked up.

"Yes? What can I do for you?"

Father Higgins stepped forward with his hands folded in front of him. He said that he was writing a book about the Maine seacoast, and he would be grateful if the librarian could supply him with pamphlets and guidebooks on the subject, and paper and pencil to take notes with.

The librarian led Father Higgins and the boys to the tiny reference room, which was not much more than a closet with bookshelves and a window. At a scarred wooden table the three of them sat down, and soon the librarian came in with a stack of books and pamphlets. All the rest of the morning they worked. They leafed busily through the material on the table. Every now and then someone would find a reference to Mr. Finnick's clock museum, and they would all stop and examine it. But they never found anything that seemed to be helpful.

At noon the weary researchers took a break for lunch, but an hour later they were back at their posts. As they ploughed through book after book, Johnny's spirits sank lower and lower. This was a crazy search. So far they had turned up absolutely nothing. Fergie was optimistic by nature, but even he was getting gloomy. Nevertheless, Father Higgins struggled grimly on, his pipe clenched tightly in his teeth. All through the long afternoon they worked, taking occasional brief rest breaks to go outside and stretch their legs. The librarian popped in now and then to bring more books and to ask if she could help in any way.

Soon it was late afternoon. The sun was setting, and its long red slanting rays colored a patch on the wall behind Johnny's head. He was really going stir-crazy. He wanted to find the professor, but . . . well, he didn't care if he never saw another book as long as he lived.

"Father?" he said, breaking the busy silence. "Father? Can . . . can Fergie 'n' me go out for a little bit? I can't see straight anymore!"

Father Higgins smiled kindly. "Sure. You two go on out and walk around for a while. I'm gonna stay at this till dinnertime."

"Have . . . have you found anything?" asked Johnny falteringly.

Father Higgins's grim level gaze met Johnny's. "No," he said quietly. "But that doesn't mean I'm gonna give up. So run along, you two. I'll meet you at the inn for dinner."

Johnny and Fergie left the library and went out into the chilly evening air. The sun had just set, and the western sky was fringed with pale light. Down below, darkness was gathering.

"You know what?" said Fergie bitterly. "I feel like I've been pushin' a peanut up the road with my nose."

"So do I," muttered Johnny. "I just don't see what Father thinks he's gonna find. If old Finnick is a wizard . . . well, it wouldn't be in any guidebook, would it?"

Fergie put a stick of gum in his mouth and chewed it thoughtfully. "Higgy's a smart cookie, though," he said after a brief pause. "We wouldn't be doing all this work if he didn't have *some* kind of bright idea in the back of his head." Fergie scratched his nose. "John baby, I hate to mention this, but I need a bathroom. Wouldja mind waitin' here while I go back inside an' ask Mrs. Whatserface where the little boys' room is?"

Johnny shook his head. It was a lovely evening. Venus was a glistening star hanging high in the west, and the damp, salt-tinged night air tasted good in Johnny's mouth. Whistling softly, he walked a few paces to the left on the dirt road that ran past the library steps. Behind the library, the road sank down into a shadowy hollow full of bushes and trees. Johnny decided that he would walk to the bottom of the hill and back again while he was waiting for Fergie. Down the hill he loped, still whistling. In the growing gloom Johnny could hardly see a thing, and he stumbled a few times over half-buried rocks. He was at the bottom now, and it was really pitch black. The trees and bushes seemed to crowd in around him. Twisting his head, he looked up at the library, a dark outline against the twilit sky. Not much to see down here, was there? Nothing but dark and weeds. Time to be getting back up to . . .

Johnny paused. Now that his eyes had gotten used to the dark, he saw something that he hadn't noticed before: a little house, an abandoned shanty, by the side of the road. The poor place had certainly seen better days: Its windows were broken, and the roof was half caved in. A crooked tree leaned against the side of the house, trailing its snaky branches over the bent chimney. *Gee*, thought Johnny, vaguely, *I wonder who lived in—*

And then two things happened with lightning suddenness. First Johnny felt a stinging cold spot against his thigh—it was as if a lump of ice had suddenly materialized in his pants pocket. Then a light appeared, a flickering orange glow that hovered over the dead leaves and matted grass outside the deserted house. In one window, behind the broken pane, a grinning jack-o'-lantern was burning.

CHAPTER EIGHT

Numb nightmare descended on Johnny. His scalp tingled, and he found it hard to breathe. In a flash he knew what the freezing lump in his pocket was—it was the skull, come back from a watery grave. Ahead of him the evil orange mask seemed to burn a hole in the night. It pulsated, sending out waves of power. Against his will, Johnny shuffled closer. Moving woodenly, like a robot, he clumped up the sagging steps and walked in through the dark doorway. A cobweb brushed his face, and he found that he could not raise his hand to brush it aside. He was in a shadowy room with a rotting plank floor. And he had barely time to wonder why there was no pumpkin in the room when a violent blow brought him to his knees. A ghastly, impossibly huge jack-o'-lantern face appeared spread across one wall of the room. It was throbbing, and the air around Johnny heaved to an insane, feverish rhythm. His chest felt tight, and his eyesight was clouded by an icy mist that wrapped itself around him. Johnny struggled for breath—the life was being pumped out of him. He was going to die. Suddenly a voice burst in on his brain, a harsh, grating, stony voice that told him he would never again meddle in things beyond his understanding. *Death is an eternal sleep*, said the voice, and it said this over and over like a cracked record. Desperately Johnny fought to stay alive, but he knew that he was losing—he was starting to black out. Just before he lost consciousness, he heard something—a commotion in the room. A door slammed, and somebody shouted strange words, words that sounded like *Lumps and crust!* The voice rang out two or three times. And then Johnny was gone.

When he woke up, he was lying on the damp grass outside the old shack. Fergie was kneeling beside him, and Father Higgins was standing over him, looking very huge and forbidding in spite of the friendly smile on his face. In his large hairy hand the priest was holding a small silver crucifix on a chain.

"Wha . . . wha . . ." muttered Johnny thickly. He felt limp and woozy, as if he had just recovered from the flu. With an effort he raised his head and glanced toward the old shack. It was dark, lost in the evening shadows.

Then a sudden stab of terror hit him, and he fumbled at his thigh. It was gone—the skull, the thing that had suddenly appeared in his pocket—it had vanished.

Johnny turned his head and looked at Fergie. "Did . . . did you take it?" he asked in a quavering voice.

Fergie looked puzzled. "Take what, John baby? I dunno what you're talkin' about."

With an effort Johnny forced himself to sit up. As he did this, Father Higgins sank to his knees beside him. He still clutched the crucifix, and he held it up as if he were using it to ward off an attacker. With his other hand he tried to gently force Johnny to lie back down on the ground.

"Easy, John, easy!" said the priest softly. "You've been through something awful, and you're probably still weak. The powers of darkness were here, and they were after you. You need some rest."

But Johnny shook off the priest's hand. He was feeling better by the minute. "Father," he said, pointing toward the dark house, "did . . . did you see it?"

Father Higgins looked grim. "If you mean that Halloween face, yes, I saw it. I saw it from way up at the top o' the hill, where I was talkin' with young Byron here. He was tryin' to figure out where you had gone to, and then all of a sudden I saw that face, and I remembered what you had told me. So I charged on down the hill and busted into that house over there, and all of a sudden I was face to face with that horrible thing on the wall, and I felt the presence of evil all over my body. I don't mind tellin' you, I nearly turned and ran. But I pulled myself together, and then I gave the rotten, miserable thing a good dose of *this*!" He held up the crucifix and shook it menacingly. "This's a blessed crucifix, and there's this glass bubble on it, and underneath are two splinters from the True Cross, the cross Jesus was crucified on. And I said *lumen Christi*, which means *light of Christ*. It's a powerful charm and part of the Holy Saturday service. Y'see . . ."

Johnny laid his hand on the priest's arm. "Father," he said nervously, "I . . . I have to tell you something."

Father Higgins grinned. "I'll just bet you do. Well, go ahead. I'm listening."

Johnny began slowly, with lots of little stops and starts. As clearly as he could, he explained about the skull. He told how he had found it, how he had felt when he owned it, and why he had finally decided to get rid of it. He also described the strange vision that he had had in the workroom of the Fitzwilliam Inn at midnight. This was the first time that Johnny had been able to tell anyone about these things, and it felt wonderful to just get everything off his chest.

"How . . . how come I couldn't talk about this before?" he asked, staring hard at the priest. "I couldn't tell the professor. Every time I tried I got this awful pain in my chest, and I felt like I couldn't breathe. Why couldn't I tell him?"

"John," said Father Higgins slowly and gravely, "it is becoming more and more clear to me that we are dealing with some kind of incredibly evil intelligence, a disembodied spirit that has decided to attack you and the professor for some reason. The skull and the jack-o'-lantern face and the scarecrow you saw on the ferryboat —they are all manifestations of that evil mind. Well, the mind did not want you to tip off the prof that something bad was going to happen to him. It also did not want you to do anything that might clear up the mystery of the prof's disappearance. And do you want to know why you can tell us now? The evil influence was driven off by the power of the True Cross. You feel better now, don't you—getting the thing out in the open, I mean."

Johnny nodded. "Yeah, I do. Do you think that vision I saw at the Fitzwilliam Inn has anything to do with the second clue, the one about the great reckoning in the little room? I should've thought of this before, but it just wasn't clear to me. What I'm tryin' to say is, the room in the vision is the little room, the dollhouse room—only full size."

Father Higgins patted Johnny on the shoulder. "Very good, my friend! Very *good*! And a reckoning is the settling of an account—that is one meaning of the word, anyway—and it certainly looks like you saw a reenactment of the way the professor's granduncle got *his* account settled! Hmmm. Things are getting clearer. Not a whole lot clearer, but somewhat clearer. I wish we knew more about the skull that you took from the dollhouse room. If we knew why the prof's father chose to put it in the—"

"Will it come back?" Johnny blurted suddenly. He sounded very anxious. "That is, it . . . it came back once, so it must be able to come back whenever it wants to. How . . . how'm I gonna get rid of it?"

"I don't know, John," said Father Higgins. He bit his lip and glared into the night. "I wish I knew more about what's goin' on, but I don't. However, I do know this. My crucifix saved you, and so you better keep it for the time being. Here."

Father Higgins pressed the crucifix into Johnny's hand. "There's a chain on it," he went on. "Put it around your neck, and don't take it off for *any* reason! You understand?"

Johnny nodded and smiled gratefully. He looped the chain around his neck and slid the crucifix in under his shirt, but just as he had finished doing this, he turned his head and noticed something. Fergie was gone!

"Hey, Father!" he exclaimed, looking about wildly. "What happened to Fergie?"

With a loud exclamation Father Higgins sprang to his feet. He turned just in time to see Fergie appear out of the darkness. He was coming from the direction of the shack, and he was holding something in his hands.

Father Higgins's jaw sagged. Then he got angry. "Byron!" he roared. "What the devil do you think you're doing?"

Fergie smiled sheepishly and shrugged. "I . . . uh, I just thought I'd like to go an' see what the old place was like. Just to see, y'know."

) 121 (

Father Higgins was stunned. "Good grief, man! Do you realize what that house *is*? It's a den of Satan! Don't you have any sense at all? And what, in the name of heaven, is that thing you've got in your hands?"

Fergie held the thing out, and now Johnny saw that he had in his hands an old leather-bound book with dog-eared covers. It looked very dirty, and a long piece of cobweb trailed from one end of it. With a look of awe and fear on his face, Father Higgins reached into the inner pocket of his jacket and took out a Pen-Lite. He snapped it on and played the narrow beam over the cover of the book. In a gingerly way he took hold of the cover and folded it back. Curious, Johnny scrambled to his feet and joined the other two, who were huddled over the book, peering at the flyleaf. Now Johnny saw that there was old-fashioned writing with lots of odd loops and flowing swirls on the moldy, liver-spotted sheet. But it was not hard to read. It said:

> *Warren Windrow*
> *A great reckoning in a little room—*
> *this I dreamt, April 30, 1842.*

"Well, I'll be darned!" exclaimed Father Higgins. With an odd expression on his face, he reached out and carefully peeled back the flyleaf. Now they were looking at the title page. At the top, large black letters said *La Clavicule de Salomon*. Under this title was a crude engraving of a leering demon's face inside a circle, and around the outside of the circle the word *Azoth* was repeated over and over. Father Higgins wrinkled up his nose, as if he were smelling something unpleasant. As Fergie held the book steady for him, the priest riffled quickly through several pages.

"This is a book of black magic," he said, looking up at last. "It's printed in French, and my French isn't terribly good, but I can make out enough to tell what's being said. Now . . ."

Then something happened. Johnny reached out and—for the first time—actually touched the book, which began to steam and smoke. With a loud yell, Fergie dropped it, and the other two leaped back. The pages of the book began to writhe and twist, and more whitish smoke curled upward. It was burning—being consumed by a fire that could not be seen. In a few minutes there was nothing left on the ground but a heap of gray ashes.

"Angels and ministers of grace defend us!" breathed Father Higgins as he crossed himself.

"What . . . I mean, how come . . ." stammered Johnny in confusion.

"You were wearing the silver cross," said Father Higgins solemnly. "And you touched the cursed thing, and so it was destroyed." He heaved a deep sigh and turned to Fergie. "Byron, I don't know what crazy—or blessed—force it was that drove you to go into that house and bring that book out, but you have given us our first good lead. Warren Windrow . . . hmm. I wonder who he was, and why he dreamed the same phrase that was given to us by the mysterious writing that we found under the statue. Well, come on, gentlemen. We're going back up to the library. John? Are you able to navigate okay?"

Johnny nodded. Most of the queasiness and dizziness had worn off, and he felt more like himself again. With Fergie on one side of him and Father Higgins on the other, he climbed the hill once more. Above them the windows of the library glowed yellow, and all around the trees rustled in the night breeze that had suddenly sprung up. When they reached the front steps of the library, Father Higgins told the boys to wait outside. He said that he had a pretty good idea of the kind of book he wanted to look for, and he wouldn't be long. So Fergie and Johnny sat down on the granite steps and waited. They watched the stars and listened to the shrill piping of May frogs in some nearby pool. Finally Father Higgins returned. And from the way he was grinning and rubbing his hands together, they knew he had found something.

"Hey, Father, what is it?" asked Fergie as he scrambled to his feet. "Didja find out who that guy was?"

"I did indeed!" exclaimed the priest, who was practically bubbling over with self-satisfaction and triumphant glee. "Yes, I most certainly did! Come along, gentlemen, and I'll tell you everything."

Father Higgins started walking toward a clump of dark shadowy trees that rose on the horizon.

"Hey, Father!" exclaimed Johnny, running after him. "The inn's back that way!"

"Yes, I know it is," said Father Higgins as he strode

along. "But we aren't going to the inn. We're going down to the beach, to a boathouse run by a guy named Hank Dodge. When I was out here last year, I rented a boat from him, and I think I'm gonna do it again. He also sells camping supplies and canned food to dumb landlubbers like us who come out here without being prepared to go on an expedition."

Johnny's mouth dropped open. "Expedition? Father, where are we going?"

"Yeah, come on, Father!" added Fergie, who was walking on the other side of him. "Give us the whole story!"

For a few minutes Father Higgins walked on in silence. The boys found that they were on a winding blacktop road, and the tarred surface felt hard now after the spongy earth they had been treading on. At last Father Higgins was ready to talk. He took a deep breath and began to explain that he had had to leaf through three books of old New England legends before he found the story he was looking for. It was in a book called *Weird Tales of the Maine Seacoast* and told the saga of a man named Warren Windrow, whose ghost supposedly had been seen quite a few times on Vinalhaven and on some of the nearby islands. Back in the 1840s he had lived on Cemetery Island, which was just a dot on the map out in Hurricane Sound, not far from Vinalhaven. Windrow had come from a large family that once lived in the Penobscot Bay area, and the family had a sinister reputation, though the book didn't say why.

Well, one day Warren Windrow caught the California gold fever that was sweeping the eastern half of the country in those days, and he went out to California to see if he could strike it rich. Windrow didn't find any gold, but he did get into a saloon fight with another Easterner—a man from Vermont, a man named Lucius J. Childermass. Windrow got beaten up, and apparently he decided to get even, because one night—some time after the fight—he jumped Lucius in a dark alley and tried to kill him with a Bowie knife. Lucius got cut up a bit, but some people who were passing in the street nearby broke up the fight and rescued Lucius. Windrow was taken to San Francisco, where he was tried for attempted murder, convicted, and hanged.

". . . and that's the whole story, as far as I can get it from the book I read," said Father Higgins, finishing up. "So we have the ghostly Warren Windrow, and a book of black magic that he once owned, and a tale that connects him with the professor's granduncle. This is all beginning to make sense, in a weird way. Our next step will be to go and have a little look at Cemetery Island. It's not far, only about half an hour's ride. I know Byron here is rarin' to go, but I thought I'd better ask you if you wanted to stay behind, John. You can wait for us, and no one will think you're cowardly or anything like that. And for all I know, we may not find anything but sand and seashells. We ought to be back pretty quick, in any case. What d'ye say, John?"

Johnny squared his jaw and looked as determined as

he possibly could. He was still feeling a bit shaky because of the ghastly experience he had just had, but he wasn't going to be cheated out of an adventure. Besides, the professor was more his friend than he was anybody else's—or so he felt, anyway.

"I wanta go, Father," he said defiantly. "You'll hafta tie me up an' chain me to a tree if you want me to stay here."

The road they took petered out into a sandy track that wound over some grassy hummocks and past a long narrow pond that glimmered in the starlight. Before long they arrived at a little cove with a few houses clustered around its edges. At the end of a row of white clapboard shanties stood the Old Harbor Boathouse, a big sprawling building with cedar shingles and a slate roof. Next to the boathouse was a little poky building with a sagging roof and a metal stove chimney. A sign that leaned against the house gave the name of the establishment and listed the rental rates and the name of the owner in straggling white letters: *Hank Dodge, prop*.

Father Higgins knocked loudly on the door of the house, and Hank Dodge came out. He wore saggy blue work pants, a red-and-white hunting jacket, and a fishing hat stuck full of fishing flies. His face was red-veined and jowly, and his breath smelled of whiskey. Father Higgins told him what he wanted and pressed a wad of bills into his hand. While waiting for Hank to return, Father Higgins made up a list in his head and rattled it off to Fergie: a couple of cans of beans, a mess kit, a can of Sterno, matches, a tarpaulin, three flashlights, and a bottle of brandy. Fergie recited this list again, took some money from Father Higgins, and raced off down the beach toward a lighted store that he saw in the distance. Hank Dodge returned with the keys to the boat and an oil lantern and led Johnny and Father Higgins around to the back door of the boathouse.

A few minutes later, Fergie, Johnny, and Father Higgins were skimming along over a body of water known as Hurricane Sound. Off to their left, in the distance, rose the low, humped shape of Hurricane Island. Overhead a few stars could be seen through a filmy, overcast sky, and from out in the direction of the open sea came ominous rumbles and occasional lightning flashes—a storm was moving into the mouth of the bay. Johnny sat in the bow seat. He clung tightly to the sides of the boat and felt absolutely petrified—motorboat rides had always scared the dickens out of him. Fergie sat in the middle seat, arms folded and a calm expression on his face, and in the stern sat Father Higgins. He chewed at his empty pipe and maneuvered the steering handle of the motor. Out toward the entrance of the Sound they shot, a long white wake spewing behind them and a loud engine drone filling the air. They were on their way—toward what?

Johnny could not for the life of him imagine how all this was going to end. But as he sat there with the motorboat hurtling along under him, he knew that he was getting more nervous by the minute. Part of this was because of his fear of riding in a speeding boat, but there was more to it than that. Johnny kept thinking of the skull—he couldn't keep his mind off it. The grinning evil, little object was gone again—it had vanished back into the void, where dark things wait, until witchcraft calls them forth. Without a doubt the silver crucifix had driven the skull away—but could it *keep* the skull away? What if the skull reappeared at some time, when he least expected it? Johnny brooded about the skull. He closed his eyes and wished fervently that he had never heard of the Childermass clock, or Cemetery Island, or Penobscot Bay.

"There it is!" Fergie yelled, pointing into the darkness ahead.

Johnny forced his eyes open and twisted his head around. Looming closer and closer was a dark shadowy mass. He couldn't make out any details—it was pitch black out here in the middle of the bay. The drone of the motor grew softer as Father Higgins aimed the boat in toward the shore. Then the engine noise died altogether, and they coasted in. Johnny felt a rough shudder and heard a grumbling of sand under his feet. They had landed.

Awkwardly the tall priest stood up and swung himself out of the boat. He was calf-deep in water, but he didn't seem to mind. Fergie leaped nimbly out and began tugging at the gunwales of the boat. But then he noticed that Johnny was still sitting there, rigidly staring at nothing.

For a second Fergie looked worried, but then he grinned, reached up, and slapped Johnny hard on the knee. "Hey, Dixon!" he said loudly. "Off your duff and on your feet! How're we gonna drag the boat in if you sit there weighin' it down? Come on! Afraid to get your feet wet? Your gramma tell you you'd catch cold if your toesies got damp?"

Fergie was being nasty and sarcastic on purpose. He was a bit scared of the way Johnny was acting, and he figured that it might be best to jolt him into action.

"Huh? Oh . . . oh, yeah," muttered Johnny in a dazed, thick voice. He lurched to his feet and clambered over the side of the rowboat. The icy cold of the water gripped his legs, and he winced. But he bit his lip to keep from yelling—he wanted to prove that he was just as tough as the other two. Moving to the front of the boat, he gripped the iron ring that hung from the prow, and he tugged. The others were shoving too, and the boat slid up onto the gravelly beach.

They walked a few steps over the wet sand and then stopped to stare at the island. Pine trees grew close to the shore, and beyond rose shelves of granite. The wind was picking up now, and the pines waved to and fro, making an eerie keening noise. Then lightning flashed again in the distance, and Father Higgins swore under his breath.

"We're gonna get rained on, gentlemen!" he growled. "I'm kinda glad I thought of that tarpaulin—we might just possibly be in need of it." He turned, put his hands on his hips, and peered into the murky shadows of the island. "Well, prof," he said loudly, "I sure hope you're here! Comin', ready or not, like us kids used to say!"

After this little speech Father Higgins turned abruptly, went back to the boat, and fumbled under the tarpaulin. He came up with the three flashlights, and with a jaunty flick of his wrist, he sent one flying into Fergie's outstretched hands. Johnny caught the other one.

"I wonder if we ought to've brought our raincoats," said Johnny fretfully as he switched on his light. He had a fear of dampness, and he was always fussing about it. Fergie snickered, and Johnny bit his lip ruefully. Why did he say things like that? Like most timid people, Johnny wanted to be brave and resourceful and cunning. Why couldn't he just shrug off fears the way other people did? Then he reminded himself that he was here on the island, after all, with the other two. So maybe he wasn't quite as cowardly as he thought he was.

With flashlights shining, Fergie, Johnny, and Father Higgins tramped up the beach and plunged into the scrubby little clump of pines. They found a narrow winding path that was covered with dead pine needles and decided to follow it. On the other side of the pine grove, the rugged uneven ground of the island opened out before them. It was too dark to see much, but here and there were dark blotches that might be bushes. And there were rocks—Johnny kept tripping over them as he picked his way along. The three of them marched on in silence for some time while the wind whistled around them, and big splatting raindrops started to fall. Suddenly Father Higgins let out an exclamation.

"Hey! Wouldja look at that? Up there!"

Johnny and Fergie looked. Far ahead, in the darkness, was a tiny yellow blot of light. A lamp in a window, maybe.

"Come on, boys!" yelled Father Higgins, waving them ahead excitedly. "This miserable little hunk of real estate isn't supposed to have anybody living on it. But where there's light, there's life, or so they say. Let's go see!"

The three of them walked faster now. Fergie and Father Higgins swung right along—they did not seem to be having any trouble with the uneven stony field. But it was another story for Johnny: He banged his shin on a tree stump, and a little later he stepped into a hole that gave his ankle a vicious twist.

"*Ow!*" yelled Johnny as his foot sank into the hole. "That hurts, it *hurts*!"

Father Higgins and Fergie were a few paces ahead of him. They stopped and turned their flashlight beams on their friend.

"Hey, John!" Fergie called. "Are you okay?"

Johnny did not reply immediately. He yanked his foot out of the hole. Then he took a careful, gingerly step— and sucked in his breath with a sharp, painful hiss. It was agony to walk. Gritting his teeth, he forced himself to take another step. The second step felt just as miserable as the first had, but at least he could move. Hobbling, he made it up to where the other two were standing.

Father Higgins laid his hand on Johnny's arm. "How are you, John? What does it feel like?"

Johnny forced himself to stare straight into the priest's eyes. "It's . . . it's okay," he said in a strained voice. This, of course, was a lie. His ankle felt as if somebody were toasting it over a bonfire. But he wasn't going to be left out of the search. A long time ago somebody had told him that your ankle wasn't broken if you could still walk. Well, he could walk. That was all that mattered, for now.

"You sure you're all right?" asked Father Higgins. He sounded worried.

"I'm fine, Father. It . . . it hurts a little, but not much."

Father Higgins gave Johnny a friendly pat on the back. "Okay, then—we're off! Forward at the gallop, as they say in the cavalry movies!"

The three of them tramped on. The long white beams of their flashlights picked out a low fieldstone wall, and behind it long rows of pale white slabs that marched up a hillside—the graveyard for which Cemetery Island was named. Beyond the wall the ground rose steadily. Johnny could see a rutty little road rising into the darkness. At the top was the shadow of a building—a chapel maybe. And there was the lighted window. As Johnny watched, a shadow passed before the light. Somebody was in there, moving around!

"Holy Saint Patrick!" whispered Father Higgins in an

awestruck voice. "I wonder if . . . Well, come on! What're we waiting for?"

At the entrance to the cemetery was a rusting iron turnstile. It creaked and squealed loudly as the three of them shoved through it. Hobbling badly now, feeling agony in every step and sweat streaming down his face, Johnny struggled to keep up with his friends. Up the road they ran. As they got nearer to the top, they could see that the building was indeed a chapel, a tiny brick church with quatrefoil decorations on the front and a pointed door with a cross over it. One of the long, narrow windows was boarded up, but the other was open, and light was streaming out of it. Father Higgins got to the door first. He jerked it open, and a bar of light fell across the road. Then the priest took a step backward and just stood there, dead still. Johnny and Fergie crowded in next to him to look.

The inside of the little chapel was a mess. Wooden pews were stacked in a corner, and everything seemed to be covered with gritty dust and dirt. The altar at the rear had been used as a dinner table: a checkered tablecloth was thrown over it, and on it lay a dirty plate with a half-eaten piece of bread and a battered tin cup. Near the cup and plate stood an oil lamp that cast a yellowish smoky light. A few paces from the altar stood an old-fashioned iron cookstove, and in one corner was a dirty striped mattress with an old threadbare blanket wadded up on it and a rust-stained pillow with no pillowcase. Pulled up near the stove was a rickety, cane-bottomed rocking chair, and in it sat a little old man. He wore a very soiled and wrinkly white shirt and a scubby brown sweater with egg stains on it. His pants were coated with floury patches of white dust, and the upper parts of his shoes were starting to separate from the soles. You could see his toes through the holes—he wasn't wearing socks. On the old man's head was a wild mess of white hair with bits of twigs in it. His sideburns needed trimming, and his face was smudged with dirt. Perched askew on the man's reddish nose was a pair of rimless spectacles. His fingernails were broken and dirty, and he was clutching a tattered newspaper. Professor Childermass looked up at the priest and the two boys who were standing in the doorway.

"Well?" he snapped crankily, leaning forward to squint at the three intruders. "Who are you, and what do you want? I don't like people bursting into my house without knocking. I asked you a question, and I expect an answer! *What the devil do you want?*"

CHAPTER NINE

❧

The professor leaned forward, waiting for a reply. But his visitors were too astonished to answer. Johnny and Fergie looked at each other, and they both glanced helplessly at Father Higgins, who was just standing there with his mouth open. After an awkward silence Father Higgins spoke. He sounded wary and uncertain, as if he really didn't know what would be best to say.

"Rod? Rod, don't you recognize us? It's me, Father Higgins, from St. Michael's church. And here's your old pal, Johnny, and his friend Fergie. We've been turning the countryside upside down looking for you, and we're so glad we've found you! Come on! Do ... do you *really* not know who we are?"

The professor went on glaring suspiciously at his

visitors. "I can see that you're a priest," he said sullenly. "Or rather, I see that you're wearing a clerical outfit. But I can honestly say that I've never met you before in my life. And the same goes for those two disreputable-looking kids you've got with you. Now, if you don't mind, I'd like you to go away and leave me in peace. Today's my birthday, and tonight—if I'm good—something especially nice is going to happen to me. I wouldn't want to miss out on *that* now, would I? So please make yourselves scarce, the lot of you!"

Again Johnny was stunned. Stunned and horrified. Not only had the professor lost his memory, but he also seemed to be slightly insane. Johnny knew very well when the professor's birthday was: December 8. And what was this "something special" that was going to happen to him?

Father Higgins took a short step forward. He clenched and unclenched his fists, and he looked grim and threatening. But when he spoke, his voice was gentle and kindly.

"Sir? Is it possible that you're really not good old Rod Childermass? I mean, we may have come to the wrong house by mistake, in which case I beg your pardon. But you looked so much like Rod Childermass that . . . Well, would you mind telling us your name?"

The professor seemed a bit taken aback by this question. He put his fingers to his lips and pondered for a bit. "You know," he said in a sincere, matter-of-fact tone, "I can't honestly say *who* I am! But names aren't important, are they? They're like the labels on jars, and they may be misleading. On the other hand, I can tell you a great deal about history. I can tell you about the War of the Spanish Succession, and the Zimmermann Telegram, and the Ostend Manifesto. Would you care to hear a few words about these subjects? Ask me anything, anything at all!"

Tears sprang to Johnny's eyes. He felt utterly helpless and panicky too. If they had found the professor chained to a wall, they could have broken the chains and led him away to safety. But in the state he was in, it would be hard to get him to go away with them peacefully. Johnny threw a quick glance at Father Higgins, who loomed up in the doorway, big and strong. Every muscle in the priest's body seemed tense, and a wild thought leaped into Johnny's head: Would Father Higgins try to take the professor away by force? In his mind's eye Johnny saw the priest swooping down on the little old man and throwing him over his shoulder like a sack of potatoes. Johnny waited, and it seemed as if Father Higgins were gathering himself for a leap. But then he relaxed, stepped back, and turned to the boys.

"Come on, kids," he said softly, turning and putting his hand on Johnny's shoulder. "It's clear that this gentleman wants to be left alone. Let's clear out."

Reluctantly Johnny and Fergie let Father Higgins push them out the chapel door in front of him. When they were all outside, the priest gripped the iron ring on the door and pulled it shut. He squinted grouchily at the falling rain, and then he turned to the boys.

"Gentlemen," he said in a quiet, confidential tone, "we have got a problem on our hands. Something has clearly happened to the prof. Maybe he hit his head, or maybe some kind of evil sorcery is at work. At any rate, he won't budge. What the dickens do you think we ought to do?"

Fergie said what Johnny was thinking. "I think you oughta go in there and put a half nelson on him and drag him away. I mean, he's outa his jug, and that is just about the only way you're gonna get him to come, Father. Anyways, you're bigger'n he is, an' I don't think he'd give you too much of a fight."

Father Higgins rubbed his chin and pondered. "Hmm . . . you may be right, Byron. On the other hand, the prof is tougher than he looks. He works out with dumbbells, and he walks several miles a day. I could pin him down, but it'd be a real job draggin' him away. He told me once he learned to fight dirty in his college wrestling classes, and if he remembers any of his nasty little tricks . . . well, you might have a crippled priest on your hands, and no professor. And anyway, I don't feel right about hitting him—he's my friend, out of his mind or not."

"So what're we gonna do?" asked Fergie irritably. "Do we just stand around out here an' twiddle our thumbs while we wait for the prof to get his marbles back? That seems kinda dumb to me."

"Yes, dumb it would be," muttered Father Higgins. "However, I have a plan in mind: Do you remember that bottle of brandy I had you buy? Well, why don't you two wait here and make sure that our friend doesn't wander away, and I'll scoot back to the boat and get the brandy. It's Hennessy Five Star, and if he still has any of his old taste buds left, he'll *love* it! And once I've managed to pour enough of the old sauce into him, it ought to be a fairly simple matter to get our old pal into the boat and out of this miserable place. Whaddaya say, guys? Sound like a good plan?"

Fergie and Johnny nodded in agreement. Quickly the priest went barreling down the little cemetery road and vaulted over the turnstile with surprising agility. Then his bulky form was swallowed up by the dark, rainy night.

Fergie stood solemnly watching him go, his arms folded. "Boy, I sure hope he'll be all right!" he said with feeling.

Johnny turned to him, alarmed. "Why'd you say that, Fergie? I mean, what . . . whaddaya think could happen?"

Fergie shrugged gloomily. "I dunno. But this is all gettin' to be a pretty weird business, and I keep thinkin' that *anything* is liable to happen! There's that run-in you had down behind the library, for instance. And here's the prof, sittin' in there not knowin' who he is. And there's that skull that you said came back and showed up in your pocket after you threw it away. So like I said, I get the feelin' that the mullygrubs might come and get us any second now." Fergie laughed nervously. He shivered in the drizzle and buttoned the top button of his leather jacket. "By the way," he went on, "what was all that about it bein' the prof's birthday? It isn't, is it?"

Johnny shook his head. "Nope, it sure isn't! I dunno *what* he said that for! But what worries me is, he acts like he's waitin' for somethin' to happen. Whatever it is, I sure hope it doesn't happen till we get him away from here!"

Fergie glanced at the closed chapel door. "I hope we can get him away. Period!" he said, and he bit his lip nervously.

The wind began to blow harder. An old bent elm tree grew in the field that lay beyond the graveyard wall, and they could see it waving its spindly, loopy arms. As the rain poured down, the boys squeezed themselves in against the chapel wall. There was no porch, but the edge of the roof hung out a little over the front of the building, and this kept them a bit drier than they would have been otherwise. Time passed. Every now and then Johnny would glance to his right, at the pool of lamplight that lay on the gravel outside the open window. There was no glass in the window, so he could hear the professor stirring around inside. He heard him sniffle and cough and get up and shuffle around. Then the professor went back and sat in the rocker, which creaked noisily as he moved to and fro. Johnny wanted very much to hammer on the door and demand that the professor let them in. But somehow it seemed wiser to stay outside, even though the rain was giving him and Fergie a good soaking. If the professor's mind was unbalanced, Johnny didn't want to do anything that would push him over the edge into total, screaming madness. Better to wait for Father Higgins to show up with his bottle of Hennessy Five Star. But the minutes ticked on, and Father Higgins did not come back. Johnny switched on his flashlight and peered at his watch, which said five after nine. He wasn't sure when the priest had left, but it seemed like it was an hour ago. Johnny was soaked to the skin, and his sprained ankle burned like fury. And on top of everything else, the chill had gotten into his bones. When he opened his mouth to speak, he found that his teeth were chattering.

"F-Fergie," he stammered, "wh-where do you think F-Father H-Higgins has go-gone to?"

"You got me. He's had enough time to go back to Duston Heights by now. I'm worried, John baby. I think one of us oughta go down to the boat and check up. You wanta do it?"

Johnny grimaced and shook his head. "I better not. I sprained my ankle real bad while we were runnin' across that field out there, an' it's all swelled up now. I think I might faint if I tried to run."

Fergie looked at him in astonishment. "Oh, great! Just great! I thought you said you were okay after you stepped in that hole! Why didn't you tell us about this before, for God's sake?"

"I didn't want you guys to make me go back," said Johnny miserably. "And anyway, I thought it might get better. But it hasn't—it feels awful!"

Fergie groaned. He stared helplessly up at the rain. "Well, then, I guess I better go!" he said, heaving a disgusted sigh. "You stay here 'n' make sure the prof doesn't turn into a bat an' fly away! See you later, John baby!"

And with that, Fergie took off, running. Imitating Father Higgins, he vaulted the turnstile and went galloping off into the gloom. Johnny watched him go. Now both of his friends had vanished into the night. Johnny felt the sick taste of fear rising in his throat. What if they were gone for good? What if something was swallowing up the people on this island, one by one? No, no—that couldn't possibly be! He was allowing his imagination to run away with him. Fidgeting and peering anxiously around, he limped back and forth in front of the chapel door. With each step he took, it felt as if somebody were shooting red-hot needles into his ankle.

Oh well, thought Johnny, *it'll take my mind off of the other stuff I'm worried about.* But he couldn't get rid of his worries that easily—as soon as he stopped walking, they came flooding back. Feverishly he went over in his mind things that could possibly have happened to Father Higgins. What if he had wandered into the ocean accidentally and had gotten drowned? Johnny was a very good worrier. He could dream up dozens of ghastly things that might have happened to Father Higgins. Minutes dragged past. The wind blew, and more rain pelted down. Johnny thought of the song the professor always sang when it was raining:

> When and that I was a little tiny boy
> With hey ho, the wind and the rain,
> A foolish thing was but a toy
> For the rain it raineth every day!
> With hey ho, the wind and the . . .

"Oh, come on, somebody!" Johnny yelled into the wind. *"Please, come back!"* No answer came. Johnny was in an agony of indecision. What should he do? If Fergie and Father Higgins were in trouble, shouldn't he go and rescue them? Around his neck he wore the silver crucifix with the fragments of the True Cross imbedded in it. This was what had saved him from a horrible death just a few short hours ago. It was hard to believe that Father Higgins had come out to this island with his pockets crammed full of sacred things that would ward off evil forces and demonic shapes. So maybe he, John Dixon, was the only one who could save the day. Maybe he ought to dash back to the boat. It wouldn't take long . . . or would it? He remembered his bad ankle. What if it was not just sprained but broken? What if he collapsed from the pain on the way to the boat? Hundreds of *what if*'s came leaping into Johnny's mind—he was so

nervous and frustrated and frightened that he wanted to scream. Unzipping his jacket, he reached inside and closed his hand around the lump of cloth that held the silver crucifix. . . .

And at that moment Johnny heard a sound behind him, a strange unearthly sound that was like the hinges of a hundred doors creaking and men and women and children groaning in agony. Johnny's hand relaxed its grip on the crucifix. Slowly he turned around. And what he saw gave him the shock of his life.

CHAPTER TEN

The chapel was gone. In its place stood a dignified old Victorian mansion with a mansard roof and deep-set attic windows. The ground-floor windows were long and had heavy drapes on the inside. The drapes reached all the way to the floor, and they had been pulled tight so that no glimmer of light could be seen. Over the front door was a fanlight, and flanking the stout oak portal were two flat pilasters with scrolled capitals on top. At Johnny's feet lay a semicircular slab of stone that served as a front stoop for the house. And on the stone lay little wandering white trails of *snow*. Johnny gasped. He staggered back, awestruck. And he saw, off to the left, a light shining. In a dreamlike trance, trembling and holding his breath, he moved around the corner of the house toward the lighted window—and then he got his second shock.

He found that he was peering in at a horribly familiar room. It was the dollhouse room, the one he had seen in his midnight vision at the Fitzwilliam Inn. There was the fireplace, the red Oriental rug, the built-in bookshelves, the table with the oil lamp and the Bible on it—everything. And in the black leather chair sat Professor Childermass. He was still dressed in his ragged shabby clothes, and he appeared to be asleep. His hands were folded in his lap, and Johnny could see his chest moving in and out as he breathed. Icy terror gripped Johnny's heart. This was the death room. Without being told, he somehow knew that a dark shape would soon appear in the doorway off to the right. The unearthly thing that had snuffed out Lucius Childermass's life would be returning, and it would put its hand over the professor's face, and . . .

"*No! No!*" yelled Johnny, and he rushed at the window. With all his might he banged and slammed on the glass. He pounded with his fists till his hands stung. But he might as well have been pounding on sheet metal, for all the good it did. The professor slept on, and the firelight flickered over the red carpet, and the pendulum on the mantel clock wagged. Johnny stumbled back, eyes goggling. Then blind panic seized him, and he turned and ran. He was at the bottom of the hill before he knew it, shoving his way through the creaking turnstile. On over the dark, rainy field he ran, limping badly. He never knew, afterward, how he managed to make it down to the shore. But he did, and only when he had stopped running did he gasp, because of the unbelievably fiery stinging. Madly Johnny looked around. There was the boat. Rain pelted down on the tarpaulin that had been thrown over the food and the other things. Nearby, under a tree that grew close to the shore, lay Father Higgins. As Johnny moved nearer, flashlight dangling from his limp hand, he saw a heavy tree limb that lay near the priest's inert body. Father Higgins didn't move a muscle. Was he dead?

Johnny stumbled closer and dropped to his knees. He played the beam of his flashlight on Father Higgins's head, and he saw a clotted sticky mass of blood in his hair. *Oh, please no!* Johnny prayed desperately. *Please no, not this, not this. . . .*

Father Higgins groaned. He opened his eyes and stared blearily up at Johnny. "We're surrounded," he mumbled thickly. "Pinned down . . . rifle fire . . . can't get out. Gotta take out those mortars! Got any grenades left? Here . . . lemme try."

If Johnny had been able to break down and cry, he would have. But as it was, he just felt numb. Father Higgins's mind was wandering back to the island of Guam, during the Second World War. Johnny put his hands over his face. *"What do I do now?"* he muttered through his fingers. They were all going to be killed, here on this little hunk of rock and sand. People would find their bodies weeks from now and wonder what had happened. Johnny wanted to give up. He wanted to throw his body down on the sand beside Father Higgins and just wait for the end. But with a violent effort he shook off despair. He was still alive, and he was *not* going to give up! Johnny dragged himself to his feet. He tried to force his weary brain to think calmly. Where was Fergie? He had come down to find Father Higgins, but apparently he had never made it. What could . . .

A twig snapped. Bushes rustled. Turning suddenly, Johnny peered off into the dark mass of bushes that loomed nearby, right at the edge of the beach. By straining his eyes he could just make out a shadowy human shape.

"Fergie?" Johnny called in a faltering voice. "Hey, Fergie, is . . . is that you?"

More crackling and snapping. The shape shuffled closer. Johnny felt a deathly chill, and the hairs on the back of his neck stood up. He had a sudden vision of the scarecrow thing that he had seen on the ferryboat. In a flash Johnny plunged his hand in under his shirt and gripped the silver crucifix. The shape halted. It hovered menacingly for a second or two, and then it melted back into the dark bushes. The chill passed away, and Johnny somehow knew that the thing was gone . . . for the time being.

And now what was he going to do? Johnny didn't know. He lifted the crucifix's chain off his neck and played the flashlight's pallid beam over this odd, magical object. At the place where the arms of the crucifix crossed was a tiny dome of glass, and under it were the two holy splinters. This blessed talisman could ward off evil, but it couldn't help him to rescue the professor. No, something else was needed for that. But what? Johnny wished that he was a sorcerer, with reams of powerful curses and incantations rolling around in his head. A great wizard like Albertus Magnus or Count Cagliostro would be able to fight magic with magic. But he was just John Michael Dixon, of 23 Fillmore Street, in Duston Heights, Massachusetts. What could . . .

And then a very odd, unlikely thought came floating into his mind. Father Higgins had told him once that some of the Latin phrases in the Mass were thought to have magical powers. Johnny was an altar boy, and he knew a lot of church Latin by heart. But there was a better source than his poor befogged brain—he would use Father Higgins's breviary, the little prayer book that he carried in his coat pocket. The breviary was full of prayers—some in English and some in Latin—and one of them just might do the trick for him. Once again Johnny knelt down. He took off his rain-soaked jacket and folded it up to make a pillow for Father Higgins's head. Then he fumbled in the right-hand pocket of the priest's clerical jacket. Nothing there but loose change. With a sinking heart Johnny tried the other pocket . . . and his hand closed over a small book. This was it! He had found it!

Johnny stood up and—limping badly—he began to make his way back toward the graveyard. But he had only taken a few steps when he stopped. An awful thought had come to him. What if the scarecrow thing —or whatever it was that had been hovering nearby— what if it came to get Father Higgins? Maybe it had been about to pounce on him when Johnny arrived. What if the blessed book, the breviary, had been the only thing that kept Father Higgins safe? He couldn't just leave him here with no protection at all. Reluctantly Johnny turned back. He reached into his pocket and pulled out the crucifix and chain. Kneeling, he gently slid the chain over the priest's neck. Once again Johnny shone his flashlight beam at Father Higgins's face. His eyes were closed, and he was mumbling something that Johnny couldn't make out. Johnny didn't want to leave him, but he had to. Muttering a prayer, he pulled himself to his feet and set out again.

The rain was stopping, and the clouds, driven by a strong wind, were breaking up. Johnny saw a vague silvery glow overhead, which meant the moon was trying to break through. It was easier to see now, and he forced himself to plod on over the bumpy field and up the little hill to the cemetery. He felt very jittery without the crucifix hanging around his neck. It was true that the breviary had been blessed—at least, Johnny hoped that it had. Father Higgins had told him once that all the sacred implements used by a priest—his Mass vestments, the chalice, and so on—had been blessed by a bishop. But would a blessed book save him? Johnny was in tears now. He was feeling sorry for the professor, for

Father Higgins, for Fergie, for himself. Through the creaking turnstile and up the cemetery road he stomped. Wearily he looked up and he saw the dark, unreal house still looming against the sky. Sniffling, Johnny came to a halt and put the flashlight under his armpit. Holding the book rigidly in both hands, he began to chant loudly:

Judica me, Deus et discerne causam·meam de gente non sancta; ab homo iniquo et doloso erue me.

If he expected the house to disappear, he was disappointed—it was still there. *This is crazy,* thought Johnny, *absolutely crazy!* He flipped a page and read more:

Suscipiat Dominus sacrificium de manibus suis, ad laudam et gloriam nominis tuae . . .

Johnny stopped reading. He stopped because a small cold glowing object had appeared on the page that he held before him. The skull. Grinning with malice, eyes lit by tiny red dots of fire, it hovered in the flashlight's pale beam. And a harsh, pitiless voice burst inside Johnny's brain: *No one will cheat me of my vengeance, which will be visited upon all, even the seventh son of the seventh son! Come, foolish child, and see what I have prepared, for the way of the transgressor is hard, and the lamp of the iniquitous shall be put out!*

Johnny's arms dropped to his sides. The book fell into the mud at his feet, and the flashlight rolled away down the hill. Jerked forward by an irresistible force, Johnny tottered up toward the phantom mansion. He was being led to the lighted window, and he was forced to stop. Invisible hands seized his shoulders and shoved him rudely forward until his face was almost touching the glass. He wanted to close his eyes, but he couldn't—he had to watch. The professor slept on, sunk into the deep leather armchair. And—as Johnny had feared—the scene that now began to unfold was just like the one he had seen in the dark, cold room in the Fitzwilliam Inn. The yellow flame in the oil lamp's chimney dwindled to a sputtering blue point. The flames in the fireplace wavered, shrank, died out. And as the door at the back of the room began to open, the shadowy form moved into the room. *No! No!* Johnny screamed, but the scream burst in his head. He couldn't yell or twitch his nose or move a muscle of his body. The thing was hovering over the professor, bending horribly close to him. The shadowy hand was creeping toward the professor's face. . . .

"*Aaaaaaaah!*"

The air was split by a loud, violent, bull-like bellowing. Up the road charged Father Higgins. In his hand he gripped the silver crucifix. He held it high over his head like a banner, and the chain clinked and shimmered in the air. The big priest's arm was around Johnny's shoulder now, and he felt the cold metal being pressed to his forehead. Suddenly he could move. Reeling backward, he turned and watched as Father Higgins dashed madly to the front door of the mansion, dropped to his knees, and laid the crucifix down on the stone doorstep. In a loud, angry, challenging voice he started chanting:

I bind unto myself today
The strong name of the Trinity
With invocations of the same
The Three in One, and One in Three!
The bursting from the spicéd tomb
The riding up the heavenly way
The coming at the Day of Doom
I bind unto myself today!

As soon as the last word of this incantation was out of Father Higgins's mouth, the solid-looking mansion began to waver and shimmer. It looked like something seen through the windshield of a car in the rain. And then it was gone, and in its place stood the dumpy boarded-up chapel. Silence. The moon slid out from behind a cloud, and a pale ray lit the front door of the chapel. Father Higgins knelt motionless, the silver cross clenched tight in his hand. Johnny could hear his heavy, labored breathing. There came a scuttering, crunching sound, and the chapel door was yanked inward. Professor Childermass stepped out over the doorsill. He looked dazed, and he glanced this way and that. Suddenly he saw Father Higgins kneeling in the mud in front of him, and he let out a joyful croaking yell.

"*Higgy!*" he screeched, rushing forward and throwing his arms around his friend. "*Higgy!* What on earth are *you* doing here? For that matter, what am *I* doing here? Eh? What's going on? And is that John over there? It is! John, you're all wet! Your grandmother will have a fit!"

The professor paused and looked down at the priest, who still knelt motionless before him. Father Higgins was crying now. Tears were streaming down his grizzly cheeks. But the professor was not feeling weepy—he was looking more and more annoyed by the second.

"For the love of Pete!" he roared. "Will *somebody please* tell me what the devil is going on?"

CHAPTER ELEVEN

☙

Somehow the three of them made it back down to the shore. Johnny limped on his sprained ankle, and the professor helped Father Higgins, who was still feeling dizzy from the blow that he had taken on the head. When they got to the boat, they found Fergie sitting on the bow, looking dejected and confused. When he saw his three friends coming toward him, he really went wild— he gave football cheers and jumped and danced around. And finally, when he had calmed down a bit, he explained that he had been led into a thicket by somebody who looked like Father Higgins. Then whoever-it-was had disappeared, and Fergie had gotten totally lost. He had wandered out to the other end of the island, and by the time he got back to the boat, there was no one there at all. At this point, he'd felt so completely mixed up that he just sat down and decided to wait till somebody came to *him* for a change.

When he had finished his little tale, Fergie turned to Father Higgins with a puzzled frown on his face. "So, if it wasn't you, Father . . . then who the heck was I following?"

"Who indeed?" muttered the priest, smiling grimly. "I'll tell you this, though, Byron: *Divide and conquer* is an ancient maxim for those who want to grind others into the dust. But as for all the rest of the whys and whats and wherefores of this affair . . . well, I think we'll have to wait a bit before we can say anything." He put his hand to his head and winced. "Right now," he added with a painful grimace, "I think I could do with about six dozen aspirin. Or a slug or two of that brandy that I was going to use to get the professor hammered."

"Hammered?" said the professor, blinking in astonishment. "Higgy, what in *blazes* are you talking about?"

"I'll tell you later," said Father Higgins, chuckling. "In the meantime, let's get ourselves off of this rotten, cursed sand spit. And don't call me Higgy, Rod. You know I can't stand that!"

The four weary adventurers climbed into the motorboat. Father Higgins pulled the starter cord, and they were off at top speed, heading back toward Vinalhaven. When they got to the island, Father Higgins and the boys took the professor to the Lobster Pot Inn, where he had a hot bath and a much-needed shave. After he had gotten freshened up, the professor found—to his great surprise—that there were clean clothes and freshly shined shoes laid out for him. Father Higgins had taken them from the professor's house, using the key that the professor had left across the street with Grampa Dixon. There were clean pajamas too, and the professor undressed, put on the pajamas, and threw himself into the extra bed in Father Higgins's room. He was asleep in half a minute.

The next morning, while they were all waiting down at the dock for the ferryboat, Father Higgins told the professor all that he knew about the weird incidents that had led all of them on an expedition out to Cemetery Island. He explained about the Saint Anthony "messages," the skull, Johnny's midnight vision, and everything. The professor listened to all this calmly, and when Father Higgins was through, he snorted indignantly.

"Huh!" he muttered. "So some evil spirit decided that he was going to make mincemeat of me. And if this Warren Windrow hadn't scrawled one of his dream-thoughts down on the flyleaf of a book, I might not be standing here right now. The 'great reckoning,' the settling of accounts, would have happened to me! But there's still a lot in this business that is pretty murky. When I get home I'll have to see what I can do to clear things up."

"I think you oughta rest when you get home," suggested Johnny gently. He was afraid the professor would get sick if he exerted himself too much, after all he had been through.

"Rest, ha!" said the professor, glaring arrogantly around. "I never felt better or fitter in my life!"

When Professor Childermass got back to his gray stucco house on Fillmore Street, he found that things were in pretty much of a mess: several windows were broken, the aerial on the cupola was in danger of falling down, and the house was full of grime and dust. But with the help of Grampa Dixon, Johnny, Fergie, and some neighbors, he managed to get the old place fixed up in next to no time at all. And he found that his job at Haggstrum College was still waiting for him. Still, he kept wondering why he had gotten kidnapped in the first place. What forces of demonic magic had been at work? These and some other puzzling questions still remained, and so the professor decided to take a quick car trip up to his ancestral family home in Vermont. He rooted around in the attic, and since he belonged to a family that never threw anything away, he was able to find what he wanted. Not long after he got back, he announced to his friends that he was going to have a party to celebrate his return. A backyard cookout, no less.

And so, on a warm evening early in June, all of the professor's friends were gathered on the lawn behind his house. There were Gramma and Grampa Dixon, Father Higgins, Fergie and Johnny, and Professor Charles Coote of the University of New Hampshire, who was an expert on black magic. Professor Childermass had had some long-distance phone conversations with his old friend, and now he was planning to consult with him further so that some of the loose ends in this crazy business could be resolved.

The professor got all done up in one of his tasteless summer outfits: grass-stained khaki wash pants, a magenta short-sleeved shirt covered with yellow monkeys and guitars, a big apron with witty sayings all over it, and a puffy chef's hat. Then, with tight-jawed determination, he grilled hamburgers and hot dogs on the brick backyard stove that he had not used in at least fourteen years. He felt rather inept and clumsy, and he dropped more than one burger into the fire, but with the aid of lighter fluid and Father Higgins's expert advice about handling charcoal, he managed it all without once losing his temper.

Late in the evening the party goers were all sitting in lawn chairs talking quietly and sipping drinks.

"Now, then," the professor began in his best brusque, no-nonsense manner, "I suppose you'll all be wanting to know what I found out when I went up to Vermont to poke around in my ancestral attic."

"You had bloody well *better* tell us," said Professor Coote dryly, "or we'll roast you over what's left of the fire."

The professor harrumphed a bit and paced nervously back and forth puffing at his cigarette and blowing out little thin streams of smoke. Suddenly his face relaxed, and he smiled. "I suppose," he began, "that Higgy here has spilled the beans to those who weren't in on the hunt for me, and that therefore *everybody* knows that what happened had something to do with Warren Windrow, the man from Cemetery Island who was hanged because he tried to kill my dear old Granduncle Lucius. Are you all with me thus far?"

Everybody nodded, and some murmured *yeah*'s and *uh huh*'s.

"Good!" said the professor, and he began to pace again. "In order to fill in the missing pieces of this rather insane jigsaw puzzle, I took a little jaunt up to my ancestral home, where I rooted about in the attic. There had always been a story in the family that Uncle Lucius had kept a diary, but no one had ever seen it. So I poked about in his steamer trunk—the same one that had gone with him when he took a clipper ship to California and back—and I found the diary sewed up in the lining of the trunk. And imagine my surprise when I discovered that the secretive old cuss had written the diary in *classical Greek!*" The professor smiled in a self-satisfied way. "Little did Lucius know that his grandnephew would become a scholar and learn to read—"

"Oh, cut out the bragging, Roderick!" said Professor Coote, interrupting. "We all know you can read Greek! So *tell* us what you found out!"

The professor was somewhat taken aback, but he

recovered his composure and went on. "Hm . . . what I found out . . . yes, yes, of course! Hem! Well, to begin with, I discovered that Lucius was an even more unpleasant man than I had ever imagined he was. You see, after Windrow was hanged, Lucius bribed some officials so that he could have the body turned over to a small medical school in San Francisco. Medical students can always use fresh cadavers, which they dissect and dismember in various ghoulish ways. Well! Good old Lucius extracted from the doctors the promise that they would turn Windrow's skull over to him when they were finished with the body."

Gramma made an awful face. "His *skull*!" she exclaimed. "What kind of a man was your uncle, to do a thing like that?"

The professor wrinkled his nose. "He was a very vengeful and nasty man. Also possibly unbalanced. And he had read a lot of ancient history, and he was planning to do what the Scythians did with their enemies— namely, to make a drinking cup out of poor Windrow's skull. It would be the final humiliation of the man who had dared to lay murderous hands on him. But, alas, Lucius had bitten off more than he could chew. He didn't know anything about Warren Windrow's background. I didn't, either, until I started digging, but I discovered that the Windrows were a family of witches and warlocks. They lived all over the Penobscot Bay area, on Matinicus and Vinalhaven and in Thomaston and in Camden. And the reason why they kept moving around was this: They kept getting pitched out of wherever they were living because of their nefarious and diabolical practices.

"Ah, but good old Lucius knew nothing of this, so he put Windrow's skull in a hatbox and took it back with him. He went to live at our old place in Vermont, and the hatbox wound up on a shelf in his bedroom closet. Years passed, and oddly enough, Lucius never got around to making his Scythian drinking cup. However—as he records in his diary—he found that the skull obsessed him. He would take it out of its box every now and then, in the privacy of his room, and he would rub and caress it. He never seems to have understood why he did this. Weird, eh?"

"Hey, professor?" said Fergie, speaking up suddenly.

"Yes, Byron? What is it?"

"Didn't . . . well, I mean, didn't your uncle's family think it was kind of batty for him to keep somebody's skull in a hatbox in his room? Did any of them say anything about it to him?"

The professor shook his head. "No. They didn't know the skull was there. When Lucius showed up at the old homestead back in the mid–eighteen-fifties, everyone must've assumed that a hat was in the hatbox. And the old boy never let out a peep about his sordid little secret. Of course, they went through his belongings after his death, but . . . Well, I'm getting ahead of my story."

The professor paused to pull his burned-out cigarette butt from the jade holder. He stuck a new one in and lit it. "To continue," he went on, spewing clouds of smoke as he talked, "the years passed, and things did not go well with Lucius—I got this part of the tale from my father, since I was just a wee little kid when Lucius died. Everything he tried to do flopped, and in the end he became a gloomy hermit who spent a lot of time in his bedroom. On the evening of the day after Christmas, in 1883, Lucius died mysteriously. A few days later, when the members of the family opened his bedroom closet, and took the lid off the hatbox, guess what they found!"

"An empty hatbox?" suggested Johnny.

The professor shook his head solemnly. "No. Guess again!"

"I give up," said Johnny.

Fergie shrugged. "Okay, okay! It's a trick question. They found the skull, right?"

The professor's eyebrows rose, and he made a puckery face. "Well . . . yes and no. That is, they found the skull, but they didn't know they had found the skull."

"*Huh?*" said Fergie, gaping.

In a flash, Johnny guessed. "Oh, my God!" he exclaimed, and he clapped his hand over his mouth.

The professor turned to Johnny, and he made a little mock-courteous bow. "Go to the head of the class, young man! Yes, indeedy! What they found was a teeny-tiny skull, the same one that wound up on the shelf by the fireplace in the dollhouse room that some of us here have seen. You ask, how could this be? Well, remember,

Warren Windrow was a young warlock. And after he had gotten his revenge on Lucius, his evil, disembodied mind had thought up a way to pass on the curse. *Aaaand*, since no one in the Childermass family knew that a full-size skull had been in the hatbox, nobody guessed that the lovely delicate miniature was a real skull!"

Johnny turned very pale. Cold beads of sweat formed on his forehead, and he realized that everyone was looking at him. He felt ashamed and hung his head. "I . . . I should've got rid of it right away," he mumbled. "I mean, I shouldn't've picked it up in the first place."

The professor smiled and patted Johnny on the shoulder sympathetically. "Don't be too hard on yourself, John," he said softly. "The evil spirit of Warren Windrow probably intended for you to pick up the skull. And as you discovered later, it's not an easy matter to throw a thing like that away. But to continue with the story: Marcus Childermass—my father—took the skull away and kept it in his room, and, under its evil influence, he went to work on the Childermass clock. He'd had some experience in carpentry, so the idea wasn't totally—"

"Wait! Wait!" exclaimed Professor Coote, waving his hand in the air like a student who knows the answer. "I think I've discovered a hole in this story!"

The professor folded his arms and pretended to look annoyed. Then he unexpectedly burst out laughing. "Yes, I *know* you think you've found a hole, you insufferable pedant! But I'll plug it for you while you wait. You want to know how come my father didn't get blitzed by the power of Windrow's skull. And the answer is this—he never touched it. I mean, his fingers never actually came in contact with the filthy thing. I don't know for sure that this is the answer—I'm just guessing. But Dad was a meticulous, fussy man—a lot like this Mr. Finnick you folks have told me about, though I will hasten to add that my father was a good deal more warmhearted! Anyway, I think Dad must've handled the skull with tweezers, and that was what saved him. I, on the other hand, was not so lucky. My finger grazed the skull that night in the Fitzwilliam Inn, and it nearly got me killed. I'm just lucky I have such good, kind . . ." The professor's voice trailed off, and he turned away. He was crying now, and he tried to cover it up with a fit of coughing and harrumphing.

Professor Coote jumped up and ran to offer the professor his handkerchief. He took it and blew his nose several times, and he muttered something about Russian cigarettes. Then everybody got up and went to the card table that stood by the brick stove and poured themselves more drinks. For a while after that, the party goers just milled around and talked quietly.

At a little after ten o'clock, Gramma and Grampa announced that it was bedtime for them. They thanked the professor for the party and ambled on home, arm in arm. Johnny and Fergie discussed their narrow escape for a while, and then Fergie went into the house to use the bathroom, and Johnny drifted over to join the professor, Father Higgins, and Professor Coote. The three men had wandered down to the far end of the backyard to look at the sad remains of the professor's vegetable garden. He had been away during the spring planting season, and the plot of ground was just a weed-grown mess.

"By the way, Charley," said the professor, "are you *sure* Finnick didn't have anything to do with this business? I mean, it's a bit hard for me to believe that he and his museum just happened to be out on Vinalhaven, near the place where Warren Windrow lived. Isn't it possible that he's a member of the Windrow clan?"

Professor Coote shook his head. "No, I don't think it's likely. Finnick is a pretty detestable person, I gather, but that doesn't make him a sorcerer. As unlikely as it may seem, his being out on Vinalhaven is exactly what it seems to be—a ridiculous, insane coincidence."

The professor rubbed his chin and looked doubtful. "Well, Charley," he said slowly, "I know you're an expert on hocus-pocus and abracadabra, but still..."

"Professor Coote?" said Johnny, interrupting. "Could ... could I ask you something?"

Professor Coote turned and smiled at Johnny. "Yes, John? You look upset. What is it?"

Johnny wrinkled up his forehead and bit his lip. "Well, I was just wondering ... that is, do you think the curse of the skull and the dollhouse and Warren Windrow is over for good?"

Professor Coote sloshed the brandy in the snifter he was holding. Then he reached out and flicked some fluff off the top of a tall, stalky weed that was growing in the professor's garden. "I was afraid someone would ask me about that," he said in a grave, troubled voice. "And the answer is, I don't know for sure. I'm an expert on magic, but there is a lot I don't understand about it. However, I will say this: The curse was interrupted at the precise moment when it was supposed to have ripened. That is, Roderick here was to have been killed on the anniversary of the day and the hour when Warren Windrow met his end on the gallows. But at that point our friend Father Higgins here came charging in like a Notre Dame fullback, and he dispelled the curse by using the power of the True Cross, and one of the oldest, most potent incantations in the world. By the way, Tom, where on earth did you dig that piece of wizardry up? I know it in Celtic, and in Old Icelandic, but I wasn't aware that it had been translated into English."

Father Higgins sipped his whiskey and smiled. "It's part of an old hymn called 'Saint Patrick's Breastplate.' I've known it since I was a kid, but it never occurred to me that the thing might have magical properties until a couple of years ago. I was playing it over on the organ one night when nobody was in the church, and then it hit me, and I said to myself, *This isn't a hymn, this is a charm*! And darned if I wasn't right!"

Johnny swallowed hard. "You mean . . . you mean you didn't know it would work when you came chargin' up the hill to save us?"

Father Higgins shook his head. "I most certainly did *not*! I felt like it was two out in the ninth, and I was comin' to bat with a toothpick in my hands. But we must never underestimate the power of invocations to the Blessed Trinity."

"Or the power of ancient Irish superstitions," Professor Coote added, chuckling. "You see, John, magic is a rather uncertain science—or as some would have it, a pseudoscience. So to finish what I was saying earlier, if you and Roderick here will just manage to stay away from Cemetery Island for the rest of your lives, I don't think there'll be any problem."

"Don't worry," muttered the professor as he sipped his sherry. "I'll give the place a wide berth! As for this summer, I plan to hang around Duston Heights and work on my golf game and listen to all the Red Sox broadcasts. In fact, I'll probably spend so much time with my ear glued to the radio that I'll never get my new book written."

"Book?" said Johnny innocently. "I didn't know you were writing a book, professor."

The professor glared. "Of *course* I'm writing a book— or rather, I was, until I got whisked off to that island paradise off the coast of Maine. You remember the book, Charley. The one on the causes of the Napoleonic Wars."

"Ah, yes!" said Professor Coote, grinning mischievously. "*That* book! Well, Roderick, if you don't get it finished, it'll be a small loss. After all, who would ever want to read it?"

"*Whaaaaat?*" roared the professor, waving his burning cigarette. "Do you *dare* to insinuate that I, Roderick Childermass, Ph.D., could ever write a dull . . ."

And, still crabbing and cranking good-naturedly, the professor began walking slowly up toward the house in the company of his friends.

Discover the Terrifying World of
John Bellairs!

Johnny Dixon Mysteries
The Bell, the Book, and the Spellbinder
The Chessmen of Doom
The Curse of the Blue Figurine
The Drum, the Doll, and the Zombie
The Eyes of the Killer Robot
The Hand of the Necromancer
The Mummy, the Will, and the Crypt
The Revenge of the Wizard's Ghost
The Secret of the Underground Room
The Spell of the Sorcerer's Skull
The Trolley to Yesterday
The Wrath of the Grinning Ghost

Lewis Barnavelt Mysteries

The Beast Under the Wizard's Bridge
The Doom of the Haunted Opera
The Figure in the Shadows
The Ghost in the Mirror
The House With a Clock in Its Walls
The Letter, the Witch, and the Ring
The Specter from the Magician's Museum
The Tower at the End of the World
The Vengeance of the Witch-Finder
The Whistle, the Grave, and the Ghost

Anthony Monday Mysteries

The Dark Secret of Weatherend
The Lamp from the Warlock's Tomb
The Mansion in the Mist
The Treasure of Alpheus Winterborn